DAVID GIBBINS

"What do you get if you cross Indiana Jones with Dan Brown?
Answer: David Gibbins."*

D0058955

PHARAOH

Don't miss any of these adventures from bestselling author David Gibbins

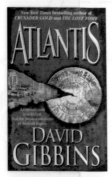

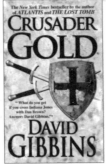

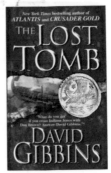

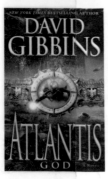

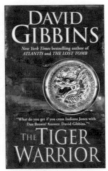

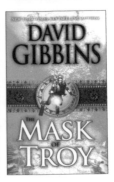

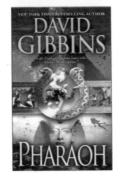

And
coming
soon

PYRAMID

ISBN 978-0-345-53470-5

U.S.A. $9.99

Jack tipped over and floated on his back, smelling the Nile, enjoying the sun on his face. He thought of the site of the Abbas, upstream beyond the great gates, into the forbidding land that had terrified the Egyptians in the time of the pharaohs, and thousands of years later when a new force had risen to confront them in the desert. He thought of the men of the river column, of the unknown man with the rifle in the sangar who had so intrigued him, and how he and Costas now seemed to be dogging the footsteps of the relief expedition. Travelling to a site upstream, they would reach the place where the column had fought its first bloody battles with the Mahdi. And he thought of the lure of something else that had brought Akhenaten here, and perhaps Gordon too.

He thought of the sarcophagus and the plaque, and now the Sobek temple and the golden scepter: they were extraordinary discoveries that had made pursuing this trail more than worthwhile. He could end the season on a high, and look forward to returning to both places next year, if nothing else got in the way. But right now, knowing that there might be more to be found, a potentially greater prize, put him on tenterhooks. He was on a roll, and he could not stop it.

He lifted his head and stared at Hiebermeyer. "Okay. I'll go with it. Let's get Ibrahim to load up the gear. We can leave this evening. It could be the only chance we'll ever have to find out what General Gordon might have hidden in that boat."

"DID YOU FIND
ANYTHING DOWN THERE?"

BY DAVID GIBBINS

Atlantis
Crusader Gold
The Lost Tomb
The Tiger Warrior
The Mask of Troy
Atlantis God
Pharaoh

Books published by The Random House Publishing Group are
available at quantity discounts on bulk purchases for premium,
educational, fund-raising, and special sales use. For details,
please call 1-800-733-3000.

PHARAOH

A Novel

DAVID GIBBINS

DELL • NEW YORK

Pharaoh is a work of fiction. Names, characters, places, and incidents are the products of the author's imagination or are used fictitiously. Any resemblance to actual events, locales, or persons, living or dead, is entirely coincidental.

A Dell Mass Market Original

Copyright © 2013 by David John Lawrance Gibbins

Published in the United States by Dell, an imprint of The Random House Publishing Group, a division of Random House, Inc., New York.

DELL and the HOUSE colophon are registered trademarks of Random House, Inc.

ISBN 978-0-345-53470-5
eBook ISBN 978-0-345-53471-2

Cover design: Carlos Beltran
Cover illustration: Mike Bryan

Printed in the United States of America

www.bantamdell.com

9 8 7 6 5 4 3 2 1

Dell mass market edition: October 2013

Behold now Behemoth, which I made with thee.
He moveth his tail like a cedar; the sinews of his
*   thighs are knit together.*
He is chief of the ways of God.
Who can open the doors of his face?
Round about his teeth is terror.
His strong scales are his pride, shut up together as
*   with a close seal.*
His neesings flash forth light, and his eyes are like
*   the eyelids of the morning;*
Out of his mouth go burning torches, and sparks
*   of fire leap forth.*
In his neck abideth strength, and terror danceth
*   before him.*
When he raiseth himself up, the mighty are afraid;
He maketh the deep to boil like a pot.

On the Leviathan, Job 41

Now MARK THIS, if the Expeditionary Force, and I ask for no more than two hundred men, does not come in ten days, *the town may fall*; and I have done my best for the honour of our country. Good bye.

Final journal entry of Major General Charles Gordon
at Khartoum, 14 December 1884

For this shall everyone that is godly pray unto thee
*   in a time that thou shalt be found;*
In the flood of many waters they shall not come
*   nigh unto him.*

Psalms 32:6

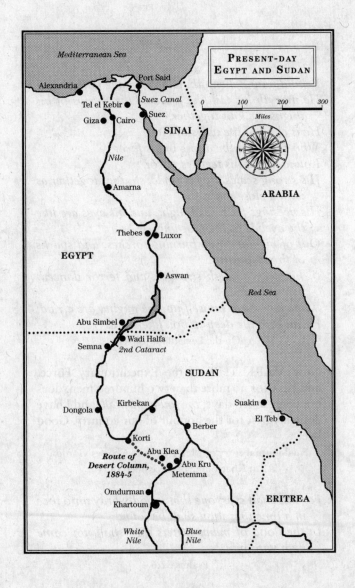

Mediterranean Sea

Alexandria

Port Said

Tel el Kebir

Suez Canal

Giza Cairo

Suez

SINAI

Nile

ARABIA

Amarna

Thebes Luxor

EGYPT

Aswan

Red Sea

Abu Simbel

Wadi Halfa

Semna 2nd Cataract

SUDAN

Kirbekan

Dongola

Suakin

Berber

El Teb

Korti

Abu Klea

Route of
Desert Column,
1884-5

Abu Kru

Metemma

Omdurman

ERITREA

Khartoum

White
Nile

Blue
Nile

0   100   200   300

Miles

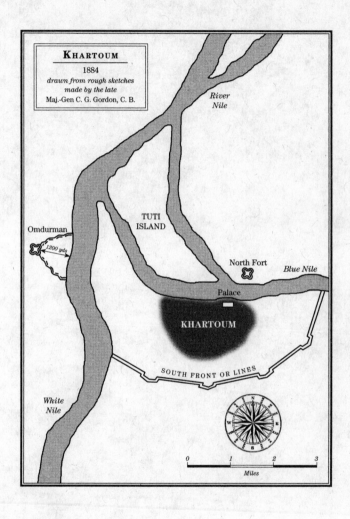

KHARTOUM

1884
*drawn from rough sketches
made by the late*
Maj.-Gen C. G. Gordon, C. B.

*River
Nile*

Omdurman

TUTI
ISLAND

1200 yds

North Fort

Blue Nile

Palace

KHARTOUM

SOUTH FRONT OR LINES

*White
Nile*

0   1   2   3

Miles

PHARAOH

PROLOGUE

THE DESERT OF NUBIA,
IN THE SECOND YEAR OF THE REIGN
OF THE PHARAOH AMENHOTEP IV,
IN THE EIGHTEENTH DYNASTY OF THE NEW KINGDOM,
1351 BC

THE MAN CARRYING THE STAFF OF A HIGH priest and the *ankh* symbol of a pharaoh stood at the entrance to the temple, watching the shaft of light from the setting sun rise up the body of the statue that loomed out of the far wall. Ahead in the gloom the others stood aside to let him pass forward, sprinkling incense and mouthing incantations as they did so. They were all present, the priests of this cult and also the priests of the god Amun from Thebes: those who had grown fat on the wealth that was rightfully his, and had doubted his allegiance to the gods. They had come here, a thousand miles to the south of the pyramids, to the edge of the known world, believing that he had chosen this place to prostrate himself before them, to recant his heresy and purify himself before the gods, to arise once again with the trappings of priesthood that had weighed down his father and generations of pharaohs before that. He passed them now, men with shaven heads and pious expressions who wore the gold-hemmed robes and upturned sandals that showed wealth, and he felt nothing but contempt. Soon they would know the truth.

As his eyes adjusted to the gloom, he began to make out stacks of mummies in the recesses behind the statue, mummies with faces that seemed to snarl out at him from where they had been left as offerings by the priests who had officiated here since the temple was first hacked out of the rock thirty generations before, at the time of the pharaoh Amenenat and his sons. Then, Egyptian armies had fought their way far into the Nubian Desert, hoping to extend the kingdom of the pharaohs over the source of the Nile at the vast lake beyond the horizon, to gain control of the very source of life. But they had been repelled by an enemy so terrifying that they had never again come beyond this point on the Nile, instead building this temple to appease the one who ruled over the river, into whose dark realm they had transgressed; never again would an Egyptian army pass through the veil of dust to the south into the land where the warriors held sway. They had depicted them on the very wall of this temple, a battle scene in which naked men with spears were shown hacking Egyptian soldiers to death; the pharaoh had turned back and left the bodies to the vultures and the scavengers of the deep, the ones they had found lurking in the pool at this place that seemed so like their image of the primeval fount of darkness.

But then the priests who had returned with the pharaoh to Egypt had taken the cult of the beast as their own, in Thebes, in the Faiyum, reducing the beast to a mere cipher, to another manifestation in the cult of Amun that gave the priests control over the people and the pharaoh. They had caught the beasts and kept them in pools and tamed them and offered their mummies to the god. But out here, on the edge of darkness, the truth remained: harsh, visceral, a truth of fear and appeasement, of the sacrifice needed to harness the strength and power of the beast to protect the pharaoh and the army. Here, in a place so far into the desert that the gods of the north hardly held sway, a place where a man could look into the souls of his distant ancestors, here the words that the lector-priest would soon read had true meaning.

Here, to dip your foot into the Nile was to dip it not into a river controlled by men but into primeval darkness. Today the man with the staff would draw all the power back into this place, and he would cleanse Egypt of the falsehoods and artifice created by the priests. He had seen the light in the desert; today would be a new beginning, the start of a time of brilliance that he would spread to the world.

He could see the statue more clearly now; the shaft of light that came through an opening high on the chamber wall continued to rise up the body as the sun set in the west. The lower part was the body of a man, one foot forward, wearing a skirt and naked from the waist up, bearing a sceptre in one hand and the ankh symbol of life in the other. The statue towered over the man, at least twice his height, the massive musculature of the upper torso and arms making the head seem almost natural, as if such a creature could have been born that way. But it was the head of a crocodile, jutting out far into the chamber, fierce and terrifying. The head was still in shadow, a dark silhouette, but above it he could make out the plumed headdress of Amun and the horned sun disk of Ra, with the sacred serpent spiralling around it. As the light rose higher, the snout came into view, mottled green marble with teeth of cloudy quartz, jagged and shimmering. The eyes were just visible, limpid pools of black, and he could see the nostrils, flaring and filled with cut crystals of red agate; they seemed to reveal an inner fire, as if the beast were burning within.

The lector-priest stood before the statue and unravelled his scroll. The man could see the hieroglyphic symbols on it, picked out in gold and red and green. The lector-priest began to recite, his voice high-pitched and shrill in the chamber:

Hail to you, who arose from the dark waters,
Lord of the lowlands, ruler of the desert edge,
Who rules the river, who crosses backwaters;
Mighty god, whose seizing cannot be seen,

Who lives on plunder,
Who goes upstream searching for his own perfec-
    tion,
Who goes downstream after hunting a multitude;
A great number you will devour:
Creator of the Nile,
Sobek, the Raging One.

The man stared at the head of the statue, waiting. He too would go upstream, searching for perfection. And then it happened: the shaft of sunlight reached the snout and the nostrils. A beam of red seemed to shoot out from the crystals, illuminating the smoke from the incense that rose from the priests, a swirling cloud that wreathed the head of the god as if it were rising from fire. The sunbeam seemed to engorge it with light, to ignite the eyes and the teeth, and at the same time to suck the light energy from it, as if it were awakening the beast and then drawing its essence back into the sun.

The man whispered under his breath: "You are no longer Sobek. Now you are Sobek-Re, the pathway of light towards the Aten. And soon you will no longer be Sobek-Re, and the Aten will rule supreme."

He had completed the ritual of purification, and he turned to go. Through the open doorway he could see the orb of the sun setting into the western horizon, orange and glowing. On the wall to the left, in front of the battle scene, was the cartouche of his own name surmounted by the crocodile symbol of a pharaoh, signifying strength and power. Ahead of that was an image he had ordered his masons to carve when he was last here, when he had left Egypt while his father was still pharaoh, fleeing south with his slave friend to escape the suffocating routine of the palace and the cloying control of the priests, the life that he had known would one day be his. The likeness of himself that he had ordered to be carved on the temple wall he now defiantly put everywhere, in Thebes and at Giza and in his new capital of Amarna; it showed the protuberant belly and jutting chin that the priests had so mocked when he was a boy that were suddenly marks of divine favor when he became pharaoh and married the most beautiful woman in Egypt. The carving depicted him in front of the Aten, its rays enveloping him like arms, the image that had so disturbed the priests. He was portrayed without the symbols of priestly office but instead was barefoot and naked except for a skirt; the priests may have imagined that he would now order his masons to add the embellishments, but they would have been wrong.

He looked back one last time. The priests were continuing their incantations, turned away from him. The beam of sunlight had risen above the statue and the shaft of red light had vanished, leaving only a dying glow as the reflection faded; soon it would be extinguished entirely. He looked at the ankh symbol again, and then at the jagged row of teeth. *Giver of life, taker of life.*

He took off his crown and dropped it with his staff on the floor, then cast off his robe; beneath it he was wearing only a loincloth, like the slaves. He opened his arms, face to the sun, feeling it bathe him in warmth, no longer self-conscious about his body. Under the Aten, all were created equal, and all were made beautiful. He passed through the entrance and along the edge of the rock-cut channel that led from the Nile to the temple. The channel was dry now but was caked with desiccated mud from the river that gave off a putrid smell, reptilian. He walked towards a woman, sensuous in her white robe, her jet-black hair curly and long and her eyes surrounded by kohl; the shape of her breasts and thighs pleased him, aroused him, as he thought of the days and nights ahead when they would at last be man and woman, not pharaoh and high priestess. He took her hand and held it high. "Nefertiti-na-Aten," he said, smiling at her, using her new name for the first time. "May the Aten shine on us, and our children."

"It already shines on you, Akhen-Aten. Our son Tutankhamun will be Tutank-Aten, and will forever be known as that, for he shall embrace the light too and his reign shall be long."

He breathed in deeply, savouring it. Akhenaten; no longer Amenhotep, high priest of Amun, but Akhenaten, he on whom the light of the Aten shines, he who would soon return north to lift the veil of ignorance from his people and reveal the presence of the one God. He smiled again and began to walk with her, looking up and seeing his soldiers lining the surrounding cliff tops, the attendants and guards of the priests along the banks of the river below. They came to a cluster of shackled slaves and stopped in front of their leader, a young man with fire in his eyes wearing the beard of the Canaanites. He had been held between a pair of priestly guards, but two soldiers came and released him, and he walked forward to greet them.

"Hail, Akhenaten," he said, embracing him. "Hail, Nefertiti-na-Aten, my sister," he said, kissing her hand.

She held him by the shoulders, kissing him on both cheeks. "Hail, Moses, my brother," she said.

Akhenaten embraced him again. "It is as we planned, my brother, when you came as a slave to my palace and we first sat watching the sun set over the pyramids, and then came here with me. Now I am pharaoh, and our vision has become my quest. I will go into the desert to the land of my forefathers to seek the place where the Aten rises, and then I will bring back the light and it will shine over all Egypt. Where will you go?"

Moses gestured at the slaves. "I will take my people north and return to the land of our fathers, where we will live under the light of the one God. I will await word from your new city that the Aten shines on all Egypt, and then we shall go forth together and spread the word to the world."

"May the Aten reach out and embrace you with his arms like the rays of the sun," Nefertiti said. "May you and your people find your way north in peace."

Akhenaten shut his eyes. He would do something else too. Soon he would release all the knowledge from the temples, knowledge from past ages that the priests had locked away and kept for themselves. The priests who had mocked his appearance as a boy had said that they had the knowledge to cure the illness that caused it, but that Amun and his consorts had instructed them not to, had told them to keep it concealed. For that he would bring down his own judgement on the priests and on the gods; he would extinguish them all. He would take the knowledge from the temple libraries and bring it together in one place, in the one temple to the one God, and he would preside within, the light of the Aten shining through him on those who came for divine dispensation, which he would give freely: the knowledge of the ancients would be laid open for all. He had already begun to depict his vision of this temple of light, this city of knowledge; he had instructed his masons to show it within the image of himself on the temple wall, and soon, when he reached the birthplace of the Aten, he would inscribe it all on stone, when the light gave him the vision to plan his temple and send word for the masons and carvers and quarrymen to begin their work.

He opened his eyes, and Moses gestured towards the slaves, and then at the temple. "But they cannot go. The priests will demand the sacrifice."

Akhenaten smiled again, feeling serene. He looked at the shadow rising up the face of the temple, seeing that the sun would be shining through the aperture at the top for only another few minutes; it was the sign for the ceremony of propitiation to end and the priests to leave, and for the final act of appeasement to take place. He raised one arm, and two teams of soldiers swung shut the stone doors and placed transverse wooden beams across to seal them. He looked towards the juncture of the channel with the river, and raised his hand again. The priestly guards had been pushed aside by his own soldiers, who now began to pull on the ropes on either side of a wooden frame above the channel, slowly raising the sluice gate. The first trickles of water became a torrent, driving down the channel towards the place where it disappeared under the rock face into the temple. The water would fill the chamber with the priests only to the height of a man, but that would be enough.

Suddenly there was a commotion at the sluice gate. The men jumped back, turning away and hiding their faces in their hands, terrified of laying eyes on the one who shall not be seen. A wave ran down the channel, pushed forward by something in the water: the leviathan, five times the length of a man, its great hoary tail slapping the sides of the channel as it surged forward, invisible below the muddy surface of the water. And then it was gone, as if it had clawed its way under the rock into the temple, a great wave sucking and spraying behind it, drenching the soldiers who cowered on either side of the entrance, making sure the doors remained shut.

It had been starving, ravenous. For days now the priests had kept it without food in the pool, and when the procession of shackled slaves had arrived, it had begun crashing its head against the sluice gate, knowing what lay in store. Only this time the feast would be far greater than before: not slaves who had been wasted down to skin and bone, but instead those who had over-indulged their own appetites for excess, and whose flesh would now provide one last gluttonous feast for the god.

For a few moments the rushing sound as the water entered the temple drowned out the cries of the men inside. Then a terrible shriek rose above it, and another, the noise magnified by the hollow space within. The sun dropped below the level of the cliff, and the aperture became a slit of darkness, the noise like a death rattle.

The god had supped its last sacrifice. The beast now ruled the temple, unshackled from the will of the priests, free to return to its pool in the river and prey on any men foolish enough to come this way and linger here again. But the beast would rule to its own measure, no longer as a god.

Akhenaten raised his arm one final time, signalling to

the foreman of the team on the slope beside the temple. They began to heave on a rope attached to a rectangular slab on one side of the aperture that had let in the light high up on the temple wall, drawing it across to close the opening. The final scraping sounds of the rock ended, and the noise inside was gone. All that could be heard was the faint rustling of wind in their clothes, and the distant sound of the river over the rapids to the south. Everyone remained still: his own retinue, his soldiers on the cliff tops, the slaves and their priestly guards. Then one of the guards dropped his whip and ran, and the others followed. The soldiers swooped down on them, spears raised. The guards would not be food for the temple, but carrion for the vultures.

The water that had flowed into the temple had found its level and was now surging back, a wave that lapped the edges of the channel as it rebounded into the river. Akhenaten looked down at the water that had splashed up around his feet, and saw that the muddy brown was sluiced through with blood.

It was done.

He turned towards the setting sun. The soldiers on the cliff top above the temple raised their elephant-tusk horns and blew one blast, the noise booming and echoing down the Nile and then fading away, like the last bellowing of some great beast. He opened his arms, staring into the orange orb, feeling the rays burn into him, letting his soul flow out through his eyes and become as one with the Aten.

The old religion was dead.

Let the new one begin.

PART 1

Chapter 1

Jack Howard eased forward in the con-
fined space of the submersible, raising himself on his
elbows so that he could see through the forward porthole into the azure shimmer of the Mediterranean. The
thick cone of Perspex was designed to withstand the enormous pressures of abyssal depth, and distorted the view
around the edge so that the research vessel *Seaquest II*
some twenty meters above appeared as a strange play of
white superstructure and dark hull. But the view in the
center was undistorted, a tunnel of clarity that seemed
to match the single-minded determination that had
brought Jack this far. As he made out the slope of rock
and sand on the seabed below, his heart began to pound
with excitement. Somewhere out there lay one of the
greatest lost treasures of antiquity. For a moment Jack
saw the image he had seen in his dreams for days now: a
black basalt sarcophagus rising starkly from the seabed
like the toppled statue of a pharaoh half buried in the
desert sand. Only this was not a dream. *This was real*.

"Jack. Shift over. I need space." There was a grunt
and a muttered curse in Greek, and a figure pushed himself forward on his back alongside him so he could see
the tangle of wires that hung from the open control
panel above them. Costas Kazantzakis moved with a
deftness that seemed to belie his barrel chest and thick

forearms, and his shorter frame was more suited than Jack's to fit inside the submersible. Jack knew better than to break his concentration, and he watched as Costas moved his hands swiftly over the panel, pulling out and plugging in cables. In the distorted reflection of the Perspex, Jack saw his face superimposed on Costas's, his thick dark hair appearing above the other man's grizzled chin, and for a moment it seemed as if they were conjoined, two bodies become one. They had been doing this together for almost twenty years now, and it sometimes seemed like that. Jack pushed himself forward to give Costas more space, watching his eyes dart over the panel. Seeing Costas at work quickened Jack's sense of excitement over the discovery that might lie ahead. Costas had been his main dive buddy from before he had founded the International Maritime University, and together they had logged thousands of dives on IMU projects around the world. This one promised to be up there with the best, providing Costas could work out a way of releasing the tethering line that held the submersible suspended below *Seaquest II* like a lure on a fishing line.

Costas turned to him. "You okay in here?"

Jack shifted again. "I'd be happier diving free outside. Six foot five is about a foot too long for this space."

"Once I get this thing running, it'll seem like an extension of your body. You'll forget the cramped space, I promise."

"How much longer?"

Costas gazed back up at the wiring. "I once stared at a control panel for eighteen hours. Then bingo, I got it."

"I thought a PhD from MIT in submersibles engineering would have eased you through a glitch like this."

Costas narrowed his eyes. "And I thought a PhD from Cambridge in archaeology would make you an instant expert in everything. I'm trying to remember the number of times I've watched my air gauge drop to zero while waiting for you to fathom some ancient inscription."

Jack grinned. "Okay. Touché."

"Have patience," Costas muttered, staring up. "It'll come to me."

There was movement from the hatch to the rear compartment beyond Jack's feet, and the third person in the submersible appeared, a short woman with dark curly hair and glasses and wearing an IMU jumpsuit. Sofia Fernandez, a former Spanish navy medic who was now an archaeologist with the local Cartagena museum, had come on board as the official representative of the Spanish antiquities authority. She had arrived on *Seaquest II* only an hour before; Jack had never met her previously, but both men had immediately liked her. At the moment, all that concerned Jack was that she was small enough not to reduce his comfort in the sphere below a tolerable level.

She pulled herself in and sat in the driver's seat. "What gives?" she said.

"Apologies for the glitch," Costas replied, looking at her ruefully. "This is a new submersible fresh out of the engineering department at IMU, and today is its first open-water test. I haven't even given her a name yet. *Seaquest II* can be here for only a day or two, as she's due back for a winter refit in England, and this was the only window I had to get this thing in the water to see how she behaves on a real operation." He paused. "I've been meaning to ask. Where did you get that accent? The sassy attitude. And don't get me wrong. I like it."

Sofia smiled. "From dealing with men like you. I was brought up in Puerto Rico by my American mother."

"But you ended up in the Spanish navy."

"I was a Spanish citizen because of my father, and the navy offered to pay my way through medical school in Seville."

"And now you're an archaeologist."

"After my pre-med year, the call came for medical personnel to join the Spanish contingent in Afghanistan, and I volunteered to go as a combat medic. After that, I decided I'd done my bit for medicine and it was time to move on. At med school I'd developed an interest in operation theater tools for remote surgery, so I did a masters in robotics engineering."

"No way," Costas exclaimed. "Right up my alley. We use the same basic technology for remote excavation from submersibles. We *have* got something to talk about during the long hours while I stare at this panel."

"Not long hours," Jack said firmly. "Short minutes."

"Well, my other fascination was archaeology," Sofia continued, "so I started over again and did a degree in anthropology and got the job at the Cartagena museum. My mother was a dive instructor in Puerto Rico and I'd dived almost before I could walk, so when I heard that you were planning to come to search for the wreck of the *Beatrice* off Cartagena, I couldn't believe my luck."

"Combat medic, robotics engineer, archaeologist, diver," Costas said. "Sounds like a pretty good skill-set to me."

"Anyway, speaking of accents, what's a Greek from the Kazantzakis shipping family doing with a New York accent? And best friends with a Brit?"

"I went to school in Manhattan," Costas said. "And Jack's really a Brit only in his ancestry. He was brought up in New Zealand and Canada before going to boarding school in England. So we're international, really. The International Maritime University. An international team of oddballs."

"That reminds me: a strange guy with long lank hair and a lab coat collared me topside before I got into the submersible. I forgot to tell you."

"Oh God," Costas murmured, staring back at the panel. "Lanowski. What does he want?"

"He said that although Kazantzakis *thinks* he knows everything about submersibles, he's really a concepts man and is pretty useless on computer systems and circuitry. He said that because you agreed to be his best man, it showed that you were his friend now and would have no problem acknowledging his superior mental agility. I think those were his exact words."

Costas grimaced. "He's got it in for me because when

he and his glamour-model wife got married in our top-end submersible, the trim was wrong."

"Correction," Jack said. "You sabotaged the trim so that they would get married at the bottom of the Marianas Trench instead of just below the surface."

"It was a great opportunity to test the new pressure hull," Costas said defensively. "It was the only reason I agreed to be his best man."

"This gets better," Sofia said. "Lanowski has a glamour-model wife and they got married underwater. Let me guess, they met online and it was love at first sight?"

"You bet. Love of submersibles at first sight. She loves really big submarines."

"Uh-huh. And don't tell me, she has a PhD too?"

"Submersibles nanotechnology. Flying tiny drone submersibles into the abyss. Lanowski loves her for it."

"I'm sure he does."

Costas put out his hand resignedly. "Okay, what did he give you?"

Sofia passed over a crumpled piece of paper. "He said it's a circuit diagram. He scribbled it down while I kitted up."

Costas flattened the paper and stared at it. "Why oh why didn't he show me this earlier?" he groaned.

"He said he was giving you the time to work it through yourself and realize you were never going to get there."

Costas reached up, pulled out one cable, and plugged in another. A red light began to flash on the panel. "Okay. We've got maybe half an hour while the system reboots." He leaned back against the Perspex dome and looked at Jack. "Which gives you just enough time to fill me in on exactly what we're doing here. I missed your briefing topside because I was down here apparently failing to spot what Lanowski knew all along. So what do we know about our target?"

Jack did not relish the idea of a further half hour swaying in the submersible under *Seaquest II*, and he welcomed Costas's request. He reached over and clicked on his laptop, then lifted it and turned the screen towards the other two. "It's a fantastic story," he said. "Of all the artifacts looted by European travellers to ancient lands, this one is probably the most extraordinary. In 1837, a British army officer named Richard Vyse and an engineer named John Perring used gunpowder to blow their way into the main burial chamber of the pyramid of Menkaure at Giza. Inside it they found a great basalt sarcophagus and a wooden coffin. After an incredible effort inching the sarcophagus along the entrance shaft, Vyse and his Egyptian workers managed to get it out of the pyramid and down to Alexandria, where it was loaded on to the *Beatrice*. She set sail, and was recorded leaving Malta on the thirteenth of October 1838. That was the last anyone ever heard of her."

"Do we know what the sarcophagus looked like?"

"There's an illustration in Vyse's book." Jack clicked on the laptop and an image came up. "Basalt, two and a half meters long, almost a meter high and a meter wide. There were no hieroglyphs, but you can see it had carved decoration in the style of an ancient Egyptian palace facade. It's one of the most important pieces of Old Kingdom sculpture."

"So what do we know about the *Beatrice*?" Costas asked.

Jack clicked, and another image came up. "This is a facsimile page from Lloyd's *Register* of 1838. The owner and captain was a man called Wichelo, and the ship was built in 1827 at Quebec in Lower Canada. You can see she's described as a snow—a type of brig—and was bound from Liverpool for Alexandria in Egypt on the outward leg of her last ever voyage."

He tapped the keyboard again. The image changed to an old painting of a ship anchored close to shore, its sails furled but the British Red Ensign flying from its stern.

"This is by Raffaello Corsini, a painter based in Ottoman Turkey, and shows *Beatrice* in 1832 in the Bay of Smyrna—modern Izmir in Turkey. At this point she's a brig, meaning two square-rigged masts, fore and main, with a big fore-and-aft sail at the stern hanging from a boom stepped to the mainmast. Sometime between that date and 1838 she was converted to a snow, which meant that a small mast was stepped into the deck immediately abaft the mainmast as a more secure way of flying the fore-and-aft sail."

"She must have been a pretty good runner to merit the upgrade," Costas said.

Jack nodded. "Those were the days when merchant ships were designed to outrun pirates and privateers. People look at an image like this painting and are surprised to be told it wasn't a warship."

"Any guns?"

"Good question. You can see the single row of eight gun ports along the side. They could be painted on, of course, but I think they're real."

"Guns mean a greater chance of seeing the wreck on the seabed, right?" Sofia asked.

"Right," agreed Jack. "In the Mediterranean, any exposed hull timbers would have been eaten by the *Teredo navalis* shipworm, and without big metal artifacts like guns we might not see anything."

"What was her condition recorded in the 1838 *Register*?" Costas asked.

Jack reduced the image so they could see the *Register* again. "First grade, second condition. The little asterisk means that she'd undergone repairs, in this case replacement of the wooden knees holding up her deck timbers with iron girders."

Costas pursed his lips. "Even large iron girders are unlikely to survive after almost two hundred years in seawater. Sofia's right. We're looking for guns."

"Not forgetting eight tons of sarcophagus," Jack said.

"What about the wrecking?" Sofia said. "How did you pin it down to this place?"

Jack paused. This was the revelation that had brought them here, that had preoccupied him for weeks now. He looked at Sofia keenly. "I said that the departure of *Beatrice* from Malta was the last anyone ever heard of her. Well, we now know that's no longer quite true. There have

always been rumors that the ship went down off Cartagena, but they've never been substantiated. Then a couple
of months ago, IMU was contacted by a collector of anti-
quarian books on Egyptology who thought I might be interested in his copy of Vyse's *Operations Carried on at the
Pyramids of Gizeh in 1837*. Here's what Vyse says about
the loss of the sarcophagus: 'It was embarked at Alexandria in the autumn of 1838, on board a merchant ship,
which was supposed to have been lost off Cartagena, as
she was never heard of after her departure from Leghorn
on the twelfth of October that year, and as some parts of
the wreck were picked up near the former port.'

"But that's not all," he continued. "And that's not
why the man contacted me. It was because in his copy,
on the page where Vyse mentions the loss of the *Beatrice*, was an interleaved sheet containing handwritten
latitude and longitude coordinates and a couple of transit bearings from precisely the position we're at now.
They were taken by someone who knew what they were
doing, a trained seafarer, from a boat over the spot. The
sheet was unsigned, but the giveaway was the ex libris
plate at the front of the book, with the name Wichelo."

"No kidding!" Costas exclaimed. "The ship's master,
the one named in the Lloyd's *Register*? So he survived
the wrecking?"

"So it seems. He must have come to this spot again to
take transits, in a local boat. That's perhaps where the
rumors of the wreck originate. But there's no record
anywhere else of his survival. He seems to have disappeared from history."

"Maybe he knew there'd be an insurance claim, and
he'd be found liable," Costas said.

"How can we know that?" Sofia asked.

"Well, let's think of what we've got here. *Beatrice* was
a cargo ship, but not a specialized stone carrier. Looking
at the details in the *Register*, we see she's got a fourteen-
foot beam, fully laden. Where does the captain put the
sarcophagus? On the deck, confident that those new
iron knees will hold the weight."

Jack nodded. "So confident that he fails to calculate the instability of a ship of that size with an eight-ton stone sarcophagus laden so high above the keel."

"She's a good runner, but not as maneuverable against the wind as other ships," Costas said thoughtfully. "She leaves Malta in mid-October, the beginning of the winter season, a time when storms and squalls become more common. That was the captain's first mistake. Add to that the uncharted reefs of a shoreline like this one, and a ship blown northwest off its intended route towards the Strait of Gibraltar is heading for disaster."

"Especially if she was so poorly laden," Jack said, tapping a key again. "Lanowski's done a simulation. Take a look at this. You can see the ship sailing west from Malta, and all is well. The prevailing wind is from the northeast, and the captain decides to sail with the wind on his starboard beam, west-northwest, in order to avoid being blown into the North African shore. He turns with the wind towards Gibraltar when the Spanish coast hoves into view, but he's come too close to the shore and has forgotten how sluggish the cargo makes the ship. He realizes his mistake and tries to veer south back into the open sea with the wind now on his port aft quarter, but it's too late. A sudden squall, a big inshore wave, and the sarcophagus slips, then the ship heels over and is gone, probably so fast that the crew would hardly have known what was happening."

Costas nodded. "So she sinks close to shore but in deep water, here where the bottom shelves off rapidly to abyssal depth. If she'd been in shallow water, there would have been some attempt at salvage, and perhaps more survivors. But if she sank like a stone, at least we should have a fairly well-contained wreck site."

"Trickier to find, though, without a wide debris field."

"We've got the magnetic anomalies from *Seaquest II*'s run over the sector this morning," Costas said. "One of them will come up trumps."

"Fingers crossed," Jack said.

"Lucky Jack," Costas replied, smiling at Sofia. "Jack's luck is better than any science."

Jack closed the computer. "I keep thinking of the captain, Wichelo, perhaps the only survivor, a man afraid of creditors and claimants or overcome with shame, knowing he'd never be trusted again with a cargo, deciding to disappear and change his name and start a new life."

"But not too ashamed to record the location and put it in this book, perhaps many years later when he could use his original name again," Costas said. "Maybe an old man wanting to tie up loose ends, recording the location for someone to find."

Sofia turned and eyed Jack shrewdly. "Let me get this right. The idea that the *Beatrice* was wrecked somewhere off Spain has been floating around for years, but nobody's ever been allowed to search for it inside Spanish territorial waters. Even the Egyptian Antiquities Service with all its wealthy international backers fails to get permission. But then Jack Howard finds some clue to the whereabouts of the wreck, picks up the phone, and, hey, presto, green light."

Jack shrugged. "Our record speaks for itself."

"We're archaeologists, not salvors," Costas said, still eyeing the control panel. "Everything we find in territorial waters goes to a local museum, and everything in international waters to our museum at Carthage or to the IMU campus in England. We fund the entire process of conservation and display. Our commercial wing makes a healthy income from our films and from sales of equipment developed in our engineering facility, but we operate on an endowment, which means there's no need to make a profit. We've got a hell of a benefactor."

"I read about him on the website," Sofia said. "Efram Jacobovich, the software tycoon."

"He's also why we're test-driving this submersible," Costas said. "One of his companies does deepwater mineral extraction, small quantities of rare minerals around hot-air vents, and they use the same robotic manipulator arms that we've developed for excavation. Their success makes Efram richer and he increases our endowment. So you see, everything's linked." He stared again above him, a puzzled look on his face, his voice trailing off as he spoke. "A bit like the wiring in this control panel. All linked somehow. I *wish* I could work out how Lanowski got that right."

Jack smiled at Sofia. "That clear it up for you?"

Costas coughed. "And in this case, there was the small matter of Jack's girlfriend."

Jack narrowed his eyes at Costas. "Not *girlfriend*. Colleague."

"Right." Costas grinned at Sofia. "Her name's Dr. Maria de Montijo. She's head of the Oxford Institute of Epigraphy and an adjunct professor of IMU. She's been with us on a number of expeditions. Her mother also happens to be the Spanish minister of culture."

"Of course," Sofia said. "My boss. So, the old boys' network."

"The old *girls'* network."

"Problem is, Maria always comes up with the goods, but Jack never commits in return. Too busy diving with his buddy Costas."

"Speaking of which," Jack said, "how are we coming along?"

Costas peered at Sofia. "Now that I know you're an engineer too, can I ask you to help?"

"Fire away."

"We've got to manually disengage the cable tethering us to *Seaquest II*. The lever's the red one labelled 'tether' in the ceiling of the double-lock chamber. I need to be here with my hands on about four switches to allow it to unlock. You'll need to shut the chamber door behind you to get at the lever. A red light will fire up beside it when I'm ready. It'll be no more than a couple of minutes. Can you do it?"

"Sure. No problem." She slid off the chair and disappeared back through the hatch, and they heard the clang of the chamber door shutting behind her. Costas quickly turned to Jack. "Okay. Spill it."

Jack stared at him. "What do you mean?"

"Come on, Jack. I know that look. What's going on?"

Jack cleared his throat. "We're searching for one of the greatest archaeological treasures of all time. We're doing our job."

"That's just it. *Doing our job*. It's not enough, is it? Okay, an Egyptian stone sarcophagus, covered with carvings. And not just any old sarcophagus. The sarcophagus of a pharaoh, from one of the pyramids at Giza. That's big-time. I mean, *really* big-time. But to get you this fired up, there just has to be more."

"The sarcophagus would be one of the greatest Egyptian finds since King Tut's tomb. Even including all of Maurice's discoveries."

"That's it, isn't it?" Costas exclaimed. "Maurice Hiebermeyer. He's the missing link. Last year at Troy he found that Egyptian sculpture with the strange hieroglyphic inscriptions and the sculptor's name he recognized. Before you could say golden mummy, he'd shot down to Akhenaten's city at Amarna beside the Nile, digging around for something he'd seen before. And then quick as a flash he was in the Nubian Desert, and then back in Egypt up to his neck in a pyramid. It's not like Hiebermeyer to flit around like that. Once he's got his nose stuck in a site, he stays there until it's done. And not just any old pyramid. The pyramid of Menkaure at Giza, precisely the place where Vyse found the sarcophagus. You're on a trail, aren't you, Jack? What we're doing today, whatever we find, this isn't just about that sarcophagus. There's a bigger prize."

Jack was silent for a moment, then he turned to Costas, his face an image of suppressed excitement. "Right at the moment it could all be a house of cards. We need one more crucial clue. And I don't want to upset your plans for some R and R on the beach tomorrow at Cartagena."

"I knew that was never going to happen," Costas said resignedly. He shook his head, then jerked his thumb towards the porthole. "The clue you need. Is it out there? In the wreck?"

Jack gave him a steely look. "Maybe. Just maybe."

Costas turned back to the panel and flipped the switches. A few seconds later there was a shudder and the submersible seemed to drop in the water, then it pitched and yawed like a boat bobbing in the waves. Costas quickly got up and sat in the pilot's seat, one hand over the control stick and the other on the throttle. Sofia reemerged and slid down in front of the Perspex screen beside Jack. They heard the whine of the electric motor, and then felt the submersible steadying itself in the water. Jack stared again into the blue. There might be nothing down there but bare rock and sand, but Costas was right about one thing. He had always been lucky when it came to archaeology, and he felt it now. He just knew there was something there that would change history forever.

Costas followed Jack's gaze through the porthole. *"Look on my works, ye mighty, and despair,"* he murmured.

Jack glanced at him. "I was just thinking that. About the ancient statue of a pharaoh broken and half buried, just like that sarcophagus somewhere down there." He turned to Sofia. "It's from Shelley's poem 'Ozymandias.'"

She was quiet for a moment, and then recited: " *'Round the decay of that colossal wreck, boundless and bare, the lone and level sands stretch far away."*

Costas turned to her. "You read poetry?"

"Always been a passion."

Costas looked back at the porthole. "Me too."

"There's a lot more to you than meets the eye, Costas Kazantzakis."

Jack grinned, staring back at Costas's dishevelled hair and unshaven face. "There's a lot that *meets* the eye."

There was a final jolt, and then they were as one with the sea. Jack could sense it as if he himself had been released into the depths where he belonged, free at last from the sense of confinement. Costas looked at him, his hands on the controls. "We're good to go."

Jack pointed into the abyss. "Go for it."

CHAPTER 2

ALMOST AN HOUR AFTER THE SUBMERSIBLE had separated from the tethering cable, Costas feathered the controls and brought it down with a soft bump on the sandy seabed some eighty meters below the surface of the Mediterranean. Sofia had moved back from the porthole to the copilot's seat and had been sharing the controls with Costas as they followed the programmed course between the magnetic anomalies located by *Seaquest II* during her survey run a few hours earlier. Jack had remained prone, glued to the porthole the entire time, his excitement rising and falling each time they had approached a rusty pile of metal and then been disappointed; one had been modern building debris dumped in the sea, another a small coastal freighter with a deck gun of First World War vintage, perhaps the victim of a U-boat attack. The fourth anomaly had seemed the most promising, with right-angled features in the magnetometer readout that could have been the iron knees added during the repairs to the *Beatrice* in the 1830s, but as they approached, they had seen that it was the remains of a ditched aircraft, a German Heinkel 111 perhaps downed during the Spanish Civil War. Jack stared out at it now as the silt settled around their landing site, and felt his heart sink. The decay in the metal showed how little might survive of the iron elements of a ship sunk a century earlier, and the deep sand that had covered half the plane could have completely swallowed up the *Beatrice*'s guns and the sarcophagus, leaving nothing to see above the desolate seabed that stretched out around them and sloped down into the abyss.

"What do you think, Jack? Is that the end of the road?" Costas said.

Jack got up on all fours, crawled around, and sat back in the narrow space between the two seats, staring up at the computer screen above the porthole that displayed the bathymetry around them. He pointed to an area in the outer part of the bay, beyond the line of the coast. "I think it's out there," he said. "I think that's where *Beatrice* was more likely to have been exposed to a sudden squall from the northeast. I think we've been looking too close inshore."

Costas magnified the image. "That's more than eight hundred meters deep," he exclaimed.

"Is that a problem for the submersible?"

"It's stretching the envelope for her first sea trials."

"But it could be done."

"Sure. The real problem is the inky blackness at that depth. *Seaquest II* hasn't yet done a magnetometer sweep or a sonar survey of the sector. We'd be blundering around in the dark."

Jack clicked on the intercom and spoke to the submersible control room on *Seaquest II,* where the crew had been monitoring their progress. "Patch me through to Captain Macalister, please."

A voice with a strong east-coast Canadian accent crackled through the speaker. "Macalister here. What's your status?"

"We're waiting on you. There's that final deepwater sector at the head of the bay. If you can do a magnetometer run over it, at least we can cross it off the list."

"We discussed that, Jack. You were going to check out the anomalies we'd found and leave the rest for next year."

"I agreed with you then, but down here, now that

we've got the submersible fine-tuned and running, I feel differently. You know what happens when we leave things for next year. Something else always comes up, another project, other priorities. And it's been a couple of years since IMU hit it big-time. We could do with a major discovery, and this one would be front-page news. I'd love to see that happening now."

"All that concerns me is the safety of the ship and the submersible. You remember the weather prediction? Since you went underwater the southeasterly's really picked up, and my meteorology officer thinks it's going to reach at least force six overnight. It is the beginning of November, after all, the start of the bad time in the Mediterranean. I'm beginning to understand how the master of the *Beatrice* must have felt at this time of year. It's a pretty jagged shoreline, and we're less than a kilometer away."

"Understood," Jack said. "It's your call."

"Give me a moment. Over."

Jack held the handset, waiting. Suddenly everything seemed precarious. What had seemed a dead certainty when he had seen Captain Wichelo's wreck coordinates and then the apparent magnetometer matches had now become a mathematical improbability. He had always told students working with IMU that a square-kilometer search area on the surface should be regarded as the equivalent of at least ten square kilometers underwater; distortions of perspective, variegated seabed topography, and the difficulties of interpreting visual and remote survey data all made the apparently straightforward task of crisscrossing a given area that much more difficult when confronting the realities of the seabed. Perhaps he had been too cocky, too confident of his luck, and was having a dose of his own medicine. He found himself holding his breath, waiting for Macalister's reply, and remembered what he had said to Costas about how it was all a house of cards. If they failed to come up with the goods here, then the entire trail that he and Hieber-meyer had been on, a trail still so elusive that it seemed to come in and out of focus like the anomalies on the seabed, might collapse and disappear. What had seemed like links in a chain of evidence would become isolated fragments of archaeological data, destined to be shelved or slotted into some other story.

He realized that he was drumming his fingers against the console, and stopped himself. He desperately wanted this to work out. He had promised Maurice that he would search every square inch of seabed within Wichelo's co-ordinates for the *Beatrice,* and a promise like that between the two men was a matter of honor: they had never let each other down in all the years since they had first shared their passion for archaeology as boys.

The audio crackled. It was Macalister. "Okay, Jack. I've conferred with my officers and we can do it."

Jack bunched his free hand into a fist. *Yes.* He clicked on the receiver. "We'll hold our position here until you've finished."

"We'll be over a kilometer away from your position, which means you will no longer have the safety net of the tethering line to fall back on, or the support divers. If you have any problem, you'll have to blow the ballast tanks and make an emergency ascent. You'll be able to get away in the inflatable, but the submersible might be a write-off, tossed inshore to the rocks. That has to be your call."

Jack glanced at Sofia and at Costas, who both nodded. He clicked on the handset again. "We're good with that. The submersible's my responsibility."

"Okay. Without the tethering cable, we can't stream our magnetometer and sonar data to you, so you'll be in the dark until we've finished. We should be done within an hour."

"Roger that."

"Hold fast. Over and out."

A red light flashed beside the main computer screen. Costas clicked on the mouse and grunted. "An email reached us before the tether was released, but has only just popped up. It's from Maurice Hiebermeyer."

Jack looked up. "I told him he could be with us live while we searched the seabed. Can you get him on Skype?"

"Apparently not. The message was sent via Aysha, from somewhere in the Nubian Desert just south of the Egyptian border."

"They've been excavating there," Jack said. "I haven't visited the site yet, but it sounds amazing. Pharaonic-period forts as well as material from the British campaigns of the Victorian period. Last year the Egyptians dropped the water level behind the Aswan Dam enough to reveal the upper levels of the forts, so it was a chance for the first excavation since they were inundated in the 1960s. There's still a lot underwater, though."

"Sounds like an IMU project," Sofia said.

"Watch this space," Jack replied.

Costas had been reading the message. "Oh God. The reason Aysha sent it was that Maurice is back in the pyramid of Menkaure again. Apparently some string-pulling and returned favors have resulted in the Egyptian Antiquities Authority appointing him official inspector for the restoration work at the site, a rare honor for a foreigner."

"Excellent," Jack murmured. *"Excellent."*

"Care to share the excitement?" Costas inquired, peering at him.

"I'll let Maurice do it when he's ready. If he finds what I hope he'll find."

"Anyway, why 'Oh God'?" asked Sofia.

Costas sounded anguished. "Because he's got Little Joey, my special robot, with him. To keep Maurice happy, I agreed to have Joey flown out to Alexandria, but I never expected him to get permission to take it into the pyramid. Now he wants the activation code."

"And you're going to give it to him," Jack said firmly. "He needs the robot to explore the narrow shafts in the pyramid. You spent hours showing him how it works. You can't be there every time someone wants to use one of your creations."

"My favorite robot," Costas said sadly, slowly tapping out a sequence of letters and numbers and then clicking the send icon, ensuring that it would be delivered when they were re-tethered to the ship. "I'll never see it again."

Sofia looked at him. "Wasn't Little Joey the robot who made the ultimate sacrifice at Atlantis last year, when the volcano erupted? There's a full obituary by you on the IMU website."

"Ultimate sacrifice," Costas repeated, looking at her appreciatively. "I like that. At least *you* are on my wavelength."

Jack spoke with gravity in his voice. "This one's Little *Josephine*. Little Joey's sister."

"Ah," she said. "Got you."

"That pyramid's a long way from the Nubian Desert, where he was yesterday," Costas said.

Jack nodded. "I always worry about him when he goes south of Egypt. He's like a Victorian explorer on the Nile, with absolutely no sense of his own vulnerability and more than a few strongly voiced opinions. If he doesn't stumble into a holy war, he's likely to start one. That whole region's becoming a powder keg again."

Sofia shook her head. "For me, that's someone else's war. I've had enough of jihad for one lifetime."

"I can appreciate that," Costas said. "I've got the greatest respect for navy medics, whatever country they serve."

"Thanks. That means a lot." She looked at Jack. "I read your bio on the IMU website. Royal Navy commander?"

Jack shrugged. "Just in the reserves, before starting my doctorate. I wanted all the diving experience they could offer, so I started in mine warfare and clearance before moving on to the Special Boat Service."

"You go anywhere interesting?"

"A few hot spots, but Kazantzakis here is the real navy guy."

Costas snorted. "No way. Not like you two. You've

both been in at the sharp end. I'm just a submersibles geek. I needed a job after MIT."

"You mean the U.S. Navy headhunted you. Engineer lieutenant commander. And what about that Navy Cross?"

"I was just in the wrong place at the wrong time."

Jack looked at Sofia. "USS *Madison*. You remember the suicide bomb attack?"

Sofia regarded Costas with amazement. "You were there?"

"All I did was pull a few guys out. I could free-dive deeper than anyone else on the ship that day, so I could reach them. I hate the fact that I couldn't get them all; that's why it's not in my bio."

"He may look like a beach bum whose only fitness activity is to raise a cocktail glass, but Costas comes from generations of Greek sponge divers. He drops like a stone and can hold his breath for two minutes. I've never seen anything like it."

"Ah," Costas said, lying back and closing his eyes. "The beach. Gin and tonics."

"When this is all over."

"That's what you always say."

Sofia turned to Jack. "The German, Hiebermeyer. I've seen a couple of your TV specials. He's the substantial guy with the baggy shorts and the little round glasses? Always with that younger woman, the Egyptian. Was she the one who sent the email?"

"That's Aysha, his wife," Jack said. "Used to be a student of his. She does hieroglyphics and inscriptions; he does the digging. They're a great team."

"Never did understand what she saw in him," Costas said, a glint in his eye.

"You're talking about my oldest friend."

Costas gave him an exaggerated crestfallen look. "What about me?"

"Maurice and I bonded at boarding school. You and I were thrown together ten years later inside a very small recompression chamber. For eight long hours."

Sofia grinned. "Let's hear it."

"I'd just come out of the navy and was about to return to Cambridge to finish my doctorate. Costas was working as a submersibles engineer at the U.S. naval base at Izmir in between graduate studies at MIT. I'd heard about a possible Bronze Age wreck to the northwest of Izmir, so I got my gear, hired a fisherman and his boat, and went to check it out."

"Alone," Costas said. "To seventy-five meters. On compressed air."

"I found the wreck: rows of ox-hide-shaped copper ingots in the blue haze below. The doctor at the base said it was wishful thinking, a hallucination brought on by nitrogen narcosis. But I know what I saw. Of course nowadays I'd use mixed gas or an oxygen rebreather. I'd never take that kind of risk again."

Costas's jaw dropped. "Did I just hear that? How many times have I stopped you going too deep since then?"

Jack looked serious. "Not since I became a father."

"I saw the photos on the bridge," Sofia said. "She looks like a chip off the old block. She must be what, eighteen?"

"Next month," Jack said. "But I've known her for only five years. Her mother and I split before she was born and she kept Rebecca secret from me—for Rebecca's safety, and probably mine too. She was from a Mafia family and there was a vendetta. It's a long story, but Rebecca has come out of it strong, and I can't imagine life without her now. When she's not at school, she's a full member of our team."

"I look forward to meeting her," said Sofia. "So what about Costas? The recompression chamber?"

"Well," said Jack, "I ran out of air and had to come up a little quickly. It was only a niggle in my elbow and a bit of dizziness, but I knew it was the bends and could get a lot worse. Luckily the fisherman had a decent radio, and there was a U.S. Navy helicopter on search-and-rescue exercises only a few miles away.

"Anyway, they got me into the chamber, and there was this slightly overweight sweaty guy surrounded by a jumble of electronics and tools he'd insisted on taking inside to play with. I spent the next eight hours holding bits of wire for him."

"Yeah," Costas said. "But we cooked up the idea of the International Maritime University, and here we are today."

"So what were *you* doing there? In the chamber?"

Jack coughed. "He'd spent too long monitoring the effect of pressure on some submersible component he was developing. Only instead of watching it from the outside, he'd gone into the chamber to cuddle it during its ordeal."

"I had to hold it together with my hands. It was too complex for clamps."

"What was it?" Sofia said.

Costas looked at her shrewdly. "A coupling joint for an external manipulator arm. Later I developed it at IMU and it's now standard on all our equipment."

"What's the pressure rating?"

"Two thousand meters ocean depth. It could be more except for the internal gyro, which is a little sensitive. But that's what allows us to use the arm as a virtual excavator with the finesse of a human hand."

Sofia gestured at the porthole, where the submersible's external arm array was visible. "I know how you could use it down to five thousand meters."

Costas looked astonished. "No way. *No way*. What's the gyro?"

"A Universal Electrics SPC-100, with some modifications. You remember I said I had a flirtation with robotics engineering? It was my master's project."

"You're kidding me. Can I see it?"

"I can talk you through it now."

Jack gave an exaggerated groan. "How long am I stuck here with you two?"

A red light flickered on the console. "I think you're in luck, Jack. It's Macalister."

The familiar voice came crackling over the intercom. "Okay, Jack. We've done two half-kilometer sweeps across the head of the bay, and we've got a result. The magnetometer revealed a scatter of small linear anomalies over an area of flat sandy seabed the size of a tennis court, and the sonar showed a hump in the sediment that might be rectilinear. It's at eight hundred and sixty-two meters depth, about a kilometer and a half from you at compass bearing oh-three-four degrees. We're holding position offshore above the anomaly so we can tether up to you and watch what you find on the video screen. Acknowledge."

"Roger that." Jack clicked the intercom to continuous so that the control room on *Seaquest II* could hear everything that went on. He turned to Costas, his throat dry with excitement. "I think we're in business."

Forty minutes later, they had reached a depth of seven hundred meters, having dropped down the slope at an angle of more than forty-five degrees. On the way they had passed huge outcrops of rock and dramatic slopes of sediment that had tumbled down the edges of the rocks like scree on a mountainside, until the dwindling light made it impossible to make out more than the twenty meters or so of seabed revealed in the cone of light from the submersible's external strobe array ahead of them. Costas had been letting the computer steer the submersible towards a locator beacon at the bottom of the tethering line hanging below *Seaquest II,* and suddenly they saw it, a flashing red light in the inky blackness ahead. As they came to within a few meters, he activated the manipulator arm and extended the pincers at the end of it around the cable, and then let the automated program articulate the arm backwards and slot the cable into its aperture above the double-lock chamber. The blank monitor beside the navigational screen above the console suddenly came to life, an image crowded with the faces of the crew, who were staring down at them. The crew moved aside and the white-bearded Macalister appeared, the gold braid of a captain visible on the epaulettes of his naval sweater. Jack did a thumbs-up, and Macalister nodded curtly. "Let's hope this is it," he said. "The weather's worsening up here by the min-ute, and it's going to be hard enough hauling the sub-mersible into the ship's docking bay as it is. We can't afford more than a few minutes at the target, just enough for a positive identification."

"Roger that," Costas said.

"Who's operating the external video camera?" Jack said.

A girl's face appeared, her long dark hair tied back; she was wearing a new pair of glasses that made her look uncharacteristically studious, Jack thought. She waved and blew him a kiss. "Hi, Dad. Maria sends her love. She met me at Madrid airport on the way here. As you know, we're all supposed to be going climbing in the Pyrenees next week. She'd really like to hear from you."

"Good," Jack said, slightly discomfited. "Great. Later. What I need you to do now is concentrate completely on that console. The camera's mounted on the end of the manipulator arm, and your job is to control it so that Costas and Sofia and I can focus on what we actually see outside. You got that?"

"Roger that, Dad. Good to go."

Sofia grinned. "Like a chip off the old block, as I said."

Costas flipped a switch. "Rebecca, you have control of that arm."

They watched out of the porthole as the end of the arm rose up from the equipment array below the strobes. It turned the camera towards them, the lens staring into the porthole like the outsized eye of some abyssal fish, and then it waved from side to side and turned forward.

Jack looked at the monitor and saw that Rebecca had been replaced by another figure, a man with long lank hair and wearing a lab coat. He lifted a small portable blackboard into view and tapped it, his face flushed with enthusiasm. "Hey, Costas. Glad to see we got the submersible going. You and I. When you're back topside, I've made some time to give you the lowdown on submersible circuitry. I've tailored it specially for you. A kind of idiot's guide."

"Thanks, Jacob," Costas said between gritted teeth. "Really appreciate it."

"Anytime," Lanowski replied cheerily, and disappeared.

Costas shook his head. "What a guy."

"But you love him really," Sofia said.

"We all love him," Costas said, gripping the controls. "Okay. All eyes on the prize. I'm going in."

Jack slid back to his original position lying on his front with his face to the porthole. Costas gunned the submersible forward, and Jack watched the digital depth gauge beside the porthole drop below eight hundred meters. Ahead of him the seabed began to level out, but still there was nothing to see except empty sand and the occasional flash of a reflected eye as some creature strayed into the cone of visibility in front of the submersible, into light of an intensity that nothing down there would ever have experienced before. Costas slowed the submersible right down, and Jack watched the manipulator arm arch some five meters ahead with the camera roving from side to side like some giant insect searching the seafloor. "We should be there now," Costas said.

Jack peered ahead. Still there was nothing. And then a huge hollering and whooping erupted from the crew crowded around the video screen on *Seaquest II*. Jack quickly glanced back at the screen, and saw that Rebecca had positioned the camera directly above the shape of a cannon lying half buried in the sediment. She had spotted it at the farthest swing to port of the manipulator arm, and Costas quickly brought the submersible about to aim in that direction. Then they saw another gun, and another. Had Rebecca not seen the first one, they would probably have missed the site entirely and gone off into the abyss, realizing their mistake too late for another search. Jack felt a surge of pride: she might well have saved the day. "Good work, Rebecca," he said. "Now let's gently hose down that first gun and have a look at it."

They watched as the water jet located about two-thirds of the way up the manipulator arm uncurled itself and looped down like a snake to blow a gentle jet over the gun, dispersing the sediment over the breech and revealing corroded metal. Macalister was the resident naval ordnance expert, and he immediately piped up. "No doubt about it, it's a nine-pounder, a so-called long nine," he said, his voice edged with excitement. "Typical of the guns you'd have found arming merchant ships in the Mediterranean in the early nineteenth century."

There was another noise from the crew, more of a gasp, and Sofia joined in. "Look, Jack. There it is. It's *fantastic*."

She and the crew were watching video from the camera, but Jack was looking at the real scene through the porthole, a few meters behind them. He stared into the gloom, seeing more guns but nothing else. And then he spotted it. Directly ahead, the sediment had formed a hump in the seabed. In the center, almost completely buried, was a rectilinear stone sarcophagus, its lid shifted and much of the sculpted sides buried, but still unmistakable. It was just like the image in Jack's dreams. They had found the sarcophagus of Menkaure.

"Congratulations, Jack," said Macalister, the sound of whistling and clapping coming from the crew behind him. "A marvellous end to the season."

"Congratulations to everyone," Jack said, his voice hoarse with excitement. "A team effort, as always."

Costas drove the submersible a few meters forward and then rose above the sarcophagus so that it was clearly visible. The ten to twelve guns that poked out of the sand around it formed the ghostly outline of a ship. There was nothing else to be seen, just the stone and the guns, and for a moment Jack thought how the sediments of the seabed were like the sands of the desert, how they seemed to reduce the evidence of human endeavor to its bare essentials, to its boldest statements and nothing else. The seafloor was a place that made the efforts to tame it seem minuscule and arrogant, a place whose elemental clarity attracted certain men on a quest for revelation, from the time when the world was beginning to rediscover ancient Egypt, and from deepest antiquity almost five thousand years before, the time of the first pharaohs and the pyramids.

Macalister's voice crackled again. "Okay, Costas. We've got a two-meter swell on the surface. I've asked Rebecca to relinquish control of the manipulator arm and shut it down. We've got all the imagery we need. You need to ascend."

"Roger that," Costas said. "Blowing tanks now."

Jack slid back to the console, flipped off the audio feed to the ship to keep their conversation to themselves, and looked at Costas. "Can you override the system so that I can control the arm?"

"You heard Macalister," Costas said. "Remember your end of the bargain."

"It'd be for only a few minutes. If you shut off the video stream to the ship, they wouldn't know we were still using it. As far as Macalister is concerned, we'd be ascending."

Costas paused and then shook his head. "Okay, Jack. You have the con."

Jack jumped back to the space between the seats and grasped the handle that controlled the manipulator arm. He arched the arm over the lid of the sarcophagus, to the gap where the lid had slid sideways and the interior of the coffin was revealed, and dropped the camera down towards the triangular hole. He had guessed that it might be just large enough, and he had been right. The camera disappeared inside. He activated the powerful miniature light array surrounding the camera, but all he could see on the video screen was sand, a close-up view of the sediment that evidently filled the sarcophagus. He moved the camera from side to side, but still there was nothing. "Come on, Jack," Costas said. "One more minute, max."

He took hold of the handle that controlled the water jet, and aimed the nozzle through the hole, switching the jet to its most powerful setting. There was nothing to lose, and nothing inside the sarcophagus after all this time that would be delicate enough to be damaged. For a second or two the camera would be in the eye of the dust storm created by the water jet, and he might just see something before the silt clouded the image.

He pressed the trigger. The image exploded into a maelstrom of sand, obscuring everything.

And then he saw it.

For a second it was there, the image of a pharaoh, wearing a crown and a skirt but with an oddly shaped physiognomy: a protruding belly and a jutting chin. Beside him was his consort, a queen with shapely breasts and hips, her hair over her shoulders. The pharaoh was leaning over something as if he were creating it, lines forming a matrix like a labyrinth or a maze, a pyramid in the center, and over it all the rays of the sun, shining from a disk above. And then the image was gone, lost in the swirl of sediment. *"Yes!"* exclaimed Jack.

"What the hell was that?" Costas said.

"Do you remember Captain Wichelo's interleaved sheet in his copy of Vyse's book? You wondered whether there was something else I wasn't telling you. Well, that was it. Wichelo mentioned a stone plaque that Vyse had packed in the sarcophagus, something he'd found inside the pyramid. That pharaoh's not Menkaure; it's Akhenaten, and his wife, Nefertiti. Wichelo said that Vyse called the carving 'the City of Light.' "

"Did you get photos?"

"At least one. I need to email it to Maurice. This will astonish him."

"Then the sooner we leave here, the better." Costas pulled a lever to blow air into the ballast tanks, and they began to ascend. Jack kept peering down, watching the sarcophagus as it disappeared into the inky blackness, and then settled back to study the images he had taken.

"That's a hell of a manipulator arm," Sofia said.

"Thanks," Costas replied. "You should come to the IMU engineering lab. Really. I can show you a lot more like that."

"Come and have dinner with me in Cartagena tonight. After I call the minister of culture and tell her about this."

"Tonight. Sure. Cool." Costas looked slightly flummoxed, and then smiled at her. "Yeah. I'd really like to. That'd be great."

Jack tore his eyes away from the screen and turned around. "I hate to throw a spanner in the works, but we might just have to go somewhere else this evening."

"Uh-oh," Costas said. "I should have seen this coming. Sorry, Sofia. I think it'll have to wait."

"No problem. I'm going to have my hands full anyway documenting this and filing my report for the Ministry. They're going to want a press release, pronto. I think they're really going to make a major deal out of this, and it'll be my big break. It'll be great for news of an underwater discovery off Spain to be about archaeology rather than some rip-off treasure hunters who think they can hoodwink us into believing that they're archaeologists. This could lead to a lot more IMU involvement in Spain, and I'd love to push for that. But I'll be waiting for you. And I won't take no for an answer."

"Roger that, Sofia. I'll be back. Meanwhile we'll liaise with the Spanish Civil Guard and have round-the-clock protection over the site."

"You've got it. They're on standby already."

Jack tapped on the intercom. "Is Captain Macalister there?"

"I hear you, Jack."

"Is the Lynx helicopter ready?"

"As you requested. And the IMU Embraer jet is at Cartagena airport. The crews aren't yet on standby, as you weren't sure whether you'd need them."

"Well, I need them now. We're leaving this evening."

"Where to, Jack?" Costas asked. "Sun, sand, and martinis?"

"Lots of sun, lots of sand, not so sure about the martinis. We're going to a place impossibly far removed from here but linked to it by that." He pointed at the image of the figure from the plaque, frozen in blurry outline on the video screen. "By Akhenaten."

"About my guess earlier that there was more there than meets the eye. Game on?"

Jack pursed his lips. "I don't know. There's a lot more to fathom. A lot of threads to follow. But I think if we stick with it, this could be the greatest adventure yet. The biggest prize."

"Well?"

Jack grinned at him. "Okay. *Yes*. Game on."

"Where?"

"You ever ridden a camel before?"

"Oh no. Not camels."

"We're going to the Nubian Desert. To the Sudan."

CHAPTER 3

JACK HELD ON TO THE DOOR HANDLE ON THE passenger side of the Toyota four-wheel drive as it hurtled at breakneck speed down the highway through the desert of northern Sudan, passing a convoy of army trucks that honked at them in unison, the moaning sound trailing off quickly as they sped by. Costas was in the backseat, leaning over and holding the keffiyeh scarf that he had been attempting to wrap around his head in Arab fashion, which was being blown off by the hot wind coming through the open windows. The car was being driven by Ibrahim al-Khalil, a former Sudanese naval officer who was now IMU's representative in Sudan. Ibrahim normally led an ongoing project searching for ancient wrecks along the Red Sea coast of Sudan, but he had been called in at short notice to liaise with Jack for the Nile dive they had planned for today. He was one of IMU's best divers, and Jack would trust him with his life underwater; that, and the stress for Ibrahim of working in the pirate-infested waters off eastern Sudan, allowed Jack to forgive him the adrenaline burst that clearly took over when he got behind the wheel of a car, even though they had no deadline and less than twenty kilometers to go. Not for the first time in over thirty years as a marine archaeologist, Jack felt less safe travelling to the dive site than he ever did underwater.

He forced himself to forget the road and review the journey so far. He and Costas had left *Seaquest II* in the harbor at Alexandria and flown in the ship's Lynx helicopter to Cairo, where IMU's Embraer 190 jet had been waiting to fly them to the Sudanese border town of Wadi Halfa in the Nubian Desert. Some eight hundred kilometers south of Cairo they had flown over the Aswan High Dam and Lake Nasser, the vast reservoir more than five hundred kilometers long that had begun to fill up after the first stage of the dam was completed in 1964. As a small boy, Jack had been riveted by a *National Geographic* article that showed the huge engineering project to relocate the ancient Abu Simbel temples above the rising waters of the lake, and he had asked the captain to fly over the artificial hill where the four colossal statues of Ramses the Great sitting side by side were just visible from twenty thousand feet. He had dreamed of diving deep below the waters of the lake to the original temple site, and imagined swimming through the cavernous chambers that lay behind the facade; in the aircraft he found himself running swiftly through the logistics of an IMU project to take a film crew to the site. He had sensed something else, gazing down at the temple for the first time from the air, so high that he could see the curvature of the Earth through the dust haze on the horizon. The temple was among the most impressive monuments of ancient Egypt, built by Ramses the Great in the thirteenth century BC to intimidate the people of Nubia, yet from Jack's vantage point the statues seemed merely to emphasize the impossibility of controlling this place and the puny efforts of any army to conquer the desert.

At Wadi Halfa they had been met by Ibrahim, who had cleared them through the formalities necessary to bring diving equipment across the Egyptian border. Jack had never before worked in Sudan, and his only personal contact other than Ibrahim was an old Sudanese friend from the Royal Naval College who was now deputy commander of the Sudanese air force and who had

generously agreed to loan them the use of an air force
Mil Mi-8 transport helicopter to take their gear from
Wadi Halfa to Maurice Hiebermeyer's excavation site
near Semna on the Nile, some thirty kilometers to the
south. All that Hiebermeyer had told him was that they
would be looking for structures of pharaonic date submerged since the 1960s, and he had imagined a straightforward dive requiring little more than standard IMU
scuba equipment; if they needed more sophisticated gear,
they could always request it from *Seaquest II*. While
they were waiting at the airport for the paperwork to be
finished, Costas had fired up the compact diesel air compressor and filled their four twelve-liter air tanks so that
they would be good to go on arrival at the site.

They had loaded everything on board the helicopter
and then set off in the Toyota towards the modern highway that ran the length of the Nile towards Khartoum.
The helicopter would not be able to depart from Wadi
Halfa for another few hours, and Jack had wanted to see
the desert from the perspective of the soldiers and adventurers who had come this way when the only transport was on the ground, by foot or camel. He had been
fascinated to drive through Wadi Halfa itself, a staging
post for generations of British soldiers who had campaigned in the desert: the relief expedition sent to rescue
General Gordon from Khartoum in 1884; the army led
by Lord Kitchener to exact revenge against the Mahdist
forces fourteen years later; the soldiers who had garri-
soned Egypt and the Sudan against the Ottoman Turkish enemy during the First World War; and then another
generation who had been here during the Second World
War. Jack knew that this modern history lay over another history of successive campaigns, beginning almost
four thousand years earlier, when the pharaohs of ancient Egypt had attempted to bring the Nubian Desert
and the fabled kingdoms that lay to the south under
their control, and had started to search for the gold ore
deposits that were the source of their wealth. As the
Toyota sped south, he had begun to sense the reasons

why those campaigns seemed always to have been re-buffed, and why the Egyptians had never brought this land under their heel. The Nile to the north was surrounded by fertile floodplains of verdant green, but here it was a ribbon of silver through a wasteland of red, the gorge too deep and the cliffs too high for the adjacent desert ever to be irrigated during the annual flood that was the lifeblood of Egypt to the north. People had always lived here—fishermen, boatmen, farmers on the few patches of lowland where the river water could be hauled out with *shaduf* water-lifting devices, and nomads of the desert wadis and oases—but the Nubian Desert could never sustain the concentrated population of the Nile valley in Egypt, and the people here would be as difficult to control as the sand and dust of the desert itself.

The Toyota slowed down, mercifully, and Ibrahim swung the wheel and engaged the four-wheel drive as they began to wend their way along a bumpy track towards the Nile a kilometer or so to the west. Costas leaned forward from the backseat and tapped his shoulder. "I've been thinking of our dive. How much deeper do you think Lake Nasser made the Nile at this point?"

"We call our end of it Lake Nubia," Ibrahim replied. "A small but mostly amicable dispute with Egypt."

"Okay. Lake Nubia. How deep?"

Ibrahim pulled the Toyota around a pothole and then took one hand off the wheel, fumbling in the glove compartment in front of Jack and pulling out a small folder, which he passed back to Costas. "Take a look at the first paper. It's an offprint from the *Quarterly Journal of the Geological Society* of 1903. The author was a British geologist who studied the narrowest point of the Semna cataract at low water when the rocks on either side were exposed, at the place we're going to now. He dropped a plumb line into the torrent and got twenty-three meters. He then looked at marks on the cliff made by the ancient Egyptians to show maximum high water when the Nile was in flood, and they were some twelve meters *above* the level of the river at maximum spate in the late nineteenth century, showing the amount of riverbed erosion that had occurred over three thousand years. All I know for sure is that those marks are now submerged, and the present level of the river caused by the Aswan Dam is well above that, perhaps ten to fifteen meters."

Costas whistled. "That makes at least fifty meters depth to the base of that channel, maybe sixty. It's a good thing we brought our mixed-gas gear." He flipped the pages and unfolded a plan showing the cataract. "What about this pool below the channel?"

"As far as I know, nobody's ever sounded it. In pharaonic times and during the British expedition in 1884, it was a kind of a harbor, where the boats coming up from Egypt off-loaded their goods for the trek across the desert. When I came here to do a recce for your visit, Maurice and I talked to some fishermen from the local village of Kumna. They confirmed the British army engineer reports that the pool is incredibly calm in the center and on the west side, so the torrent must drop in an underwater current that sweeps around the east side, below where we're heading now. They say that whereas the riverbed elsewhere through the cataract is scoured clear of sediment by the current, in the center of the pool it's covered by meters and meters of mud. Apparently the current does strange things, whirling around, and animals that fall into the pool are sucked down into the mud, never to be seen again. They all know the story of the leviathan of the Old Testament, the terrifying river monster, and they think that this was its birthplace, the place that the ancient Egyptians believed was the dark pool that wells up from the underworld, from which evil sprang. The locals never swim or fish there. One old man told us that a giant immortal crocodile lurks deep in the mud, ravenous and unrequited ever since the ancient Egyptians stopped feeding it slaves."

"Oh no," Costas moaned, shutting the folder. "I'd forgotten. They have crocodiles in the Nile, don't they? Jack, why didn't you remind me?"

"*Crocodylus niloticus,*" Jack said. "It's in the name. Pretty obvious."

"I don't always think in Latin."

"Okay. We're here." Ibrahim pulled the Toyota to a halt and left the engine running. "I'm going back to the road to wait for the helicopter. We chose a landing spot about a kilometer to the south so the dust from the downdraft doesn't mess up the archaeological site. Once Maurice has shown you around, you could walk out to meet me."

Jack felt the shaking in his bones beginning to subside. "Walking would be good," he said.

There was a bump against the back window, pushing the Toyota sideways. "Or take the camel," Ibrahim said.

"What camel?" Costas asked.

"That one." He turned around and pointed to the window. Costas sprang sideways, staring at it. A large face was looming beside him, its huge hooded eyes staring, its jaw moving from side to side. "Are camels another favorite of yours?"

"Childhood trauma," Costas said. "My parents took me on a trip to Jerusalem, and a camel giving tourist rides on the Mount of Olives spat on me."

"Actually, it's not spit. It's regurgitated food." Ibrahim craned his neck around, grinning at Costas. "Anyway, you've got a keffiyeh. It'll take to you like a native."

Costas and Jack opened their doors and got out. Ibrahim quickly drove off in a cloud of dust, leaving them beside the camel, which stood chewing its cud and staring into the middle distance as if nothing had happened. Jack breathed in, tasting the tang of the desert, and then shaded his eyes and looked towards the river, just visible beyond a ridge of sandstone about a hundred meters away. He could see a cluster of large tents and several parked vehicles a few hundred meters farther away to the south, and guessed that the main area of excavations must lie between where they stood and the tents, behind another low ridge ahead. Maurice had warned him that the site might appear deserted; most of the team would be at the other excavation on the far side of the river, having cleaned up the trenches on this side in preparation for an inspection by the Sudanese antiquities people scheduled for later on today.

A figure suddenly appeared over the ridge and barrelled towards them. He was wearing a wide-brimmed cowboy hat with desert goggles pushed up his brow, the tattered remains of an IMU T-shirt, ancient desert boots, and a pair of outsized khaki shorts that Jack had given him years ago, a relic of the German Afrika Korps that he had found in a backstreet market in Tunis. The shorts had a dangerous tendency to fly at half-mast, especially when Maurice was squatting down with a trowel, lost in enthusiasm. Jack looked hard, and heaved a sigh of relief. Maurice was wearing a garishly colored pair of lederhosen braces, which were holding up the shorts. Aysha had sworn that she would marry him only if he did something about them, and Maurice had responded in flamboyant Austrian fashion. But Jack knew that the image of the reformed married man went only so far, and very little else had changed.

He nudged Costas. "*Don't* say anything."

"Why not? Somebody should. How can anyone take that seriously?"

Jack turned and gazed at him pointedly. Costas was wearing baggy shorts, an outsized Hawaiian flowered shirt, aviator sunglasses, and a precarious lopsided turban he had made up out of the keffiyeh scarf. "Have you looked at yourself recently?"

"What?" Costas pushed up his sunglasses and adjusted his turban. "Desert chic."

"*Not.* As Rebecca would say."

"She would never, *ever* diss Uncle Costas like that."

Hiebermeyer bounded up and shook hands with both of them and then slapped Costas on the shoulder. He gently pulled the dangling end of the keffiyeh, and the entire cloth unraveled and dropped around Costas's neck. "*Mein Gott,*" said Hiebermeyer, eyeing Costas critically.

"You need to get yourself a stylist." He pursed his lips. "And Hawaiian is so *out* this year."

"What did you just say?" Costas exclaimed, smoothing his shirt down and pulling off the cloth. "So *out*?"

"Aysha's sister runs an haute couture chain in Cairo. She keeps me abreast of the latest fashions. They've even employed me as a consultant, to develop a line of evening wear based on Nefertiti's robes in the Akhenaten relief carvings we found at Amarna. It's always good to diversify." He grinned at Costas, then turned and strode off through the wadi in the direction of the river. "Come on, you two. Too much to see, too little time. I've got the inspectors coming in a couple of hours."

They followed quickly behind, barely keeping up.

"And speaking of Akhenaten, Jack, that's a fantastic discovery. *Wunderbar.* The sarcophagus of Menkaure. I can't believe it, found after almost two hundred years. If you can raise it, I'm going to see whether I can have it put back in the pyramid. I was there only the other day. It'd be a logistical challenge, but it might be fun to see if I can get a team of Egyptian students to do it the authentic way, with ropes and logs. I'm into experimental archaeology like that at the moment. And that plaque. Marvellous. I showed the image to Aysha and emailed it to my team at the Institute in Alexandria. It looks like some version of the Aten symbol, but nobody's ever seen anything quite like it. They're doing a full database check against every known wall painting and carving to see if we can come up with a match. As a wedding present Lanowski gave me a program he'd developed based on fingerprint recognition technology used by the FBI in America. It's revolutionized our study of Egyptian iconography. If we can't find a match using that, it doesn't exist."

Costas stumbled up alongside him. "Lanowski gave you that as a *wedding* present?"

"And this hat. A twelve-gallon hat from his home state. I always loved the cowboy stuff. He's a good man. The best. Never appreciated him until he told me that

Egyptology had been his passion before he turned to computer nanotechnology at the age of twelve. His new wife and Aysha get on like a house on fire. We're planning a joint delayed honeymoon to the pyramids at Giza to test a new program he's devised to study the alignments. It's going to blow all that astrological nonsense out of the water."

"Hang on, Maurice. A joint delayed honeymoon? You and Lanowski? Something not quite right there."

"*Everything's* right. It's the dawn of a new era in Egyptology."

Costas dropped back, shaking his head. Jack smiled to himself as they trundled forward. He loved being with Maurice when he was on a roll. He knew there would be a lot of discussion ahead about the shipwreck find, but now was clearly not the time.

They came to a halt on a ridge overlooking the river. Costas had recovered his elan, and slapped Hiebermeyer on the back. "Okay, Maurice. Give us the lowdown."

Hiebermeyer pointed to the river. "You have to imagine the Nile before the construction of the Aswan Dam in the 1960s caused the level of the water to rise, inundating all the features that made the Semna cataract so famous in history. Where we're standing now would have been a cliff about forty meters above a wide pool at the base of the cataract. Above that the river was constricted within a narrow defile only about forty meters wide, bounded by large granite promontories that stuck out into the river on either side, almost damming it. During low water in the winter months, the entire river was channelled through the constriction, pouring down from the rocky rapids to the south into the pool below us. You can get a great sense of its appearance and the drama of the place from sketches made by British officers when they were here in 1884."

"Come again?" Costas said. "British officers?"

Jack turned to him. "During the expedition to relieve General Gordon in Khartoum. A British force camped here on their way upriver during the final weeks of December that year, as the level of the Nile was dropping."

"Okay. Got you. What I was reading in that book of yours on the plane."

Hiebermeyer turned to the south, gesticulating grandly as he spoke. "To anyone coming here—the ancient Egyptians, the Romans, the Ottomans, the British in 1884—this place would have seemed like a gateway to another world, the last point you could reach before the cataracts ahead would force you to leave your boats and strike out across the desert. But the image of it as a portal to the riches of the south was only ever an illusion. Even today, standing here and looking south, it can seem a forbidding landscape, an endless expanse of desert with only jagged black basalt hills here and there to break the horizon. Imagine how it would have looked with the veil of spray rising above the cataract beyond that constriction and with a rolling tide of dust from the desert, and you can see why for a lot of people who came here, this place wasn't a gateway but the last outpost of civilization, the beginning of a no-man's-land where many who ventured beyond never returned."

"So what's the date of these ruins?" Costas asked.

Hiebermeyer beamed at him. "Follow me." He bounded along the edge of the wadi to higher ground, where a rectilinear excavation had taken the overburden of sand and dust down to bedrock, revealing the lower courses of a small square structure in stone about three meters across. A tarpaulin lay over one edge, and Hiebermeyer leaned down and carefully removed it, his back to them. "Prepare to be amazed," he said.

Jack gasped at what had been revealed. It was a beautifully smoothed statue head of a pharaoh, life-sized and broken at the neck. Above it, protruding from the wall, was a plinth with a pair of sculpted feet in the same dark basaltic stone. The head was strikingly individualistic, with bulging eyes, sunken cheeks, and a downturned mouth, the face of a hard man of war rather than the beatific image of youth so common among statues of the pharaohs. Jack stared at it, racking his brains, then remembered the report he had read from the first excavations that had taken place here back in the 1920s. "Sesostris III?"

Hiebermeyer raised his arms in mock despair. "Typical Jack Howard to choose the Greek name over the Egyptian one."

Jack grinned at him. "You'll never change me."

"One day, *one day* I'll make you realize that ancient Egypt was the origin of Western civilization, rather than that bunch of overwrought Greek musclemen in the Aegean and their mystical bards and philosophers, living up poles and in barrels."

"I thought excavating at Troy last year had won you over."

"Only because I proved that Troy had been ruled as an Egyptian vassal during the New Kingdom."

"If you hadn't found those hieroglyphs of Akhenaten carved on the entrance passage into the underground chamber we discovered, you wouldn't be here today. They *specifically* mentioned the Nubian Desert and the fort at the cataract."

"I was coming here anyway," Hiebermeyer huffed. "Aysha had already agreed to conduct renewed excavations at Semna for the Sudanese government, which wants to open up more sites along the Nile to attract tourists."

"Before we went to Troy, I distinctly remember Aysha saying that you had agreed to come here not to interfere with her site but to look after the baby."

Costas guffawed. "Dr. Maurice Hiebermeyer, director of the Alexandria Institute of Archaeology, the world's preeminent Egyptologist, forced to become a nursemaid. Oh, how the mighty have fallen."

"It was payback," Jack said, grinning, "for Maurice spending three months during her pregnancy sealed up inside the main chamber of the Great Pyramid at Giza."

"You did *what*?" Costas exclaimed.

Hiebermeyer looked defiant. "I'd been desperate to do

it for years. It was a chance in a million, while the pyramid was closed to tourists for restoration work. For ages I'd wanted to see what the conditions would have been like for ancient artisans inside the tomb, to see whether it would have been too damp for wall painting. Experimental archaeology. Living in the past. I couldn't turn it down."

"Yeah, right," Costas said.

"Anyway," Hiebermeyer said, turning to Jack, "there's nothing more important than my son. He's the future director of the Institute, and I've already gotten him to trace hieroglyphs with his fingers."

"But he might be a marine archaeologist, specializing in ancient Greece," said Jack, a mischievous glint in his eye. "After all, I *am* his godfather."

"And so am I, remember?" Costas said. "Last time I saw him, he gurgled just like a remote-operated vehicle itching to dive. I see a future submersibles engineer."

Jack grinned. "Okay. Back to Sesostris III. Or should I say *Senusret* III?"

"That's better," Hiebermeyer said, squatting down beside the statue. "The fifth pharaoh of the twelfth dynasty of the Middle Kingdom, ruling in the nineteenth century BC. He set up a string of forts and other defensive structures in the Nubian Desert, with Semna as the hub. Most of the ruins around us here are from a fort dating to his time, and you can see a second fort on the opposite side of the river where the excavation teams are concentrating their efforts today. Aysha thinks there was a garrison of perhaps five hundred men, as well as a workforce based on the riverbank, where there was probably a harbor structure for supply boats coming up the Nile from Egypt. Senusret presided over it all, or at least his statue did, from this shrine. It was a pretty belligerent enterprise, focused on presenting the strength of Egypt to the kingdom of Kush to the south. Senusret gave the forts aggressive names like 'Destroyer of the Nubians,' but he doesn't seem to have advanced farther south than here, and the forts were abandoned soon after his reign."

He took out his iPhone, pressed the screen, and passed it to Jack. It showed a fragmentary papyrus document covered in cursive script, faded and illegible in places. "This is one of our best finds, from only two days ago, flown back immediately to the Institute in Alexandria for conservation. It's one of the so-called Semna Despatches, and fits with others found in the temple of Ramses II at Thebes over a century ago. They're administrative reports sent back to the pharaoh's officials by the garrison commanders at the fort, and they mostly present a rosy picture, as if all the affairs of the pharaoh's dominions are safe and sound. This one is different, and may reveal the truth." Hiebermeyer reached over and pressed the screen again, and a fragmentary translation came up:

> On the fourth month of the second year . . . my troop, called Repeller of the Nubians, went out on patrol with food to the outpost of . . . but all there had been slain and mutilated; a great drumming was heard from the south, a wave of darkness descended, we heard the shrieks of the enemy and the lamentation of the women . . . we have returned to Semna, and the river descends in full fury, bringing with it the bodies stripped and mutilated of the other outpost garrisons at Akhet-re (?), Semionate and . . . I recognized my own brother among them . . . darkness descends again, the pool blackens and boils, the god snarls forth . . . All business affairs that take place here (Semna) are prosperous and flourishing.

"Pretty grim stuff," said Jack, pursing his lips. "All was definitely *not* prosperous and flourishing."

"That's probably why this dispatch wasn't sent in the end," Hiebermeyer said. "I think it was written after the commander came back from a particularly arduous reconnaissance patrol, and then a few days later he thought better of it and binned it. To present anything other than a rosy picture was perhaps to risk his own neck, even though this makes it clear that naming the fort 'Destroyer of the Nubians' was wishful thinking. It's impossible to date precisely, but my guess is this was written soon after the death of Senusret, who seems to have been the only one who could hold things together down here. Shortly after that the forts were abandoned, perhaps overwhelmed by the dark force the commander describes here."

Jack stared again at the statue. "That face reminds me of another pharaoh with similar features."

Hiebermeyer nodded enthusiastically. "You mean Amenhotep IV, who became Akhenaten. He lived more than five hundred years after Senusret during the New Kingdom. He was another individualist, and may even have modelled his statues on those of Senusret, perhaps to show continuity in this place with a feared pharaoh of the past, but also because he was attracted by Senusret's individuality, by how he seemed to have broken the mold. Akhenaten was trying to do the same throughout his younger life, culminating in his obsession with the cult of the Aten and his attempt to convert Egypt to faith in the one God. To me he's the most fascinating of the pharaohs, and seeing that inscription at Troy awoke a desire I've always had to come down here and trace his quest into the Nubian Desert. He had the same determination as Senusret but was a different kind of warrior: a seeker of truth rather than a king bent on conquest."

Hiebermeyer paused, looking at them both expectantly, and Jack returned his gaze. "I know that look. The statue's great, but what have you *really* found?"

Hiebermeyer seemed to hurl himself out of the trench and disappeared over the rocky plateau behind them. Jack and Costas followed, coming down in a wide gully bound on either side by ridges some three to four meters high. One section of the far ridge had been excavated down to bedrock, and Hiebermeyer was already inside the trench, gesturing for them to come over. They followed him and squatted down on the edge as he clambered down a wooden ladder and made his way across to the base of the rocky bank. He picked up a piece of shaped stone and held it up so they could see it. "This is green schist, part of a saddle quern, a grinding stone. We've found lots of fragments of broken querns in this trench." He put the stone down and then pointed to a section of the trench that had been left unexcavated, a layer of dust and sand filled with white chips and whitish streaks in the dust. "That's what they were doing. Grinding down stone." He searched the exposed face of the bank and pulled out a fist-sized lump of rock, turned it over and inspected it, then dropped it and pulled out another, repeating the inspection. He nodded to himself, and then tossed it to Jack. "What do you make of this?"

Jack caught the rock and turned it over in his hands, Costas peering alongside. It was cloudy quartzite streaked with dark green and sparkly mineral inclusions. Costas lifted up his sunglasses and looked more closely. He pointed to a streak of color in the rock. "Is that what I think it is?"

Jack held the quartz up to the sunlight. The streak of color shimmered and sparkled, and he saw another vein on the other side. "Well I'll be damned," he murmured. "It's gold."

Hiebermeyer nodded enthusiastically. "It's all along the edge of the wadi. There's a vein of it running through the metamorphic rock that makes up much of this plateau. There are ancient excavation pits all along the wadi to the south. This was a gold mine."

Costas took the stone from Jack and stared at the streak of yellow. "Is this what really drew Senusret here?" he asked.

Hiebermeyer shook his head. "This gully seems to have been deepened by Senusret's quarrymen cutting blocks from a sandstone deposit that ran along the center, in the process exposing the metamorphic gneiss on either side. But our geologists think that it was only after a few centuries of erosion that the quartz veins would have been exposed. The gold workings *were* ancient Egyptian but later than the Middle Kingdom." He picked up the fragment of quern stone again, then walked up to Jack and handed it to him. "Turn it over."

Jack did as he was instructed, feeling the gritty surface of mineral inclusions that would have made the rock so abrasive. He caught his breath as the base was revealed. In the center were twin cartouches surmounted by royal symbols, and above them the crocodile hieroglyph of a pharaoh. The forename and name contained within the cartouches were clearly visible, with distinct symbols: the scarab and sun in one, the ibex in the other, with other symbols clustered around. They were the same cartouches that he and Costas had seen three days before inside the sarcophagus at the bottom of the Mediterranean.

"Even I recognize those," Costas said. "It's Akhenaten."

Hiebermeyer was flushed with excitement. "You've got it. Here he is again. Gold mining would have been tightly controlled by the pharaoh's overseers, so even the grinding querns were stamped with his official cartouche."

"Do you think that's what brought Akhenaten here?" Costas said. "Not some mystical revelation in the desert, but the lure of gold?"

Hiebermeyer knitted his brows. "That's what I'd assumed, but then Aysha made me think otherwise. She believes that after Senusret abandoned this place and retreated north, these forts would have become forbidding places to the ancient Egyptians, ruins haunted by the ghosts of soldiers who had failed to broach the desert, places that may even have been cursed. For Akhenaten to have persuaded a force of soldiers to return here might have taken a special incentive, perhaps a discovery he himself had made when he came here alone as a rebellious teenager before becoming pharaoh, the expedition when he may have first experienced the revelation that drew him back a few years later. Perhaps the gold they found here secured the loyalty of his soldiers and helped them to overcome their fear. We know he was successful, because enough of a workforce came with him to build a temple complex at Sesebi, near the third cataract to the south of here. That's the only temple of Akhenaten previously known in the Nubian Desert."

"You say *previously,*" Jack said, eyeing Hiebermeyer. "Have you got something more up your sleeve?"

"Well, it might soon be up *your* sleeve. With the help of IMU equipment."

Costas sprang up. "You mean diving? I'm ready."

"There's some other stuff first." Hiebermeyer turned to Jack, beaming. "How's your Victorian military archaeology these days?"

Jack peered back at him and suddenly felt himself course with excitement. Since boyhood, he had been fascinated by the weapons and wars of the Victorian period, and during holidays from boarding school, when Hiebermeyer had stayed with him at the family home, he had dragged him to the range as he test-fired every antique military rifle and musket that had been accumulated by his ancestors over the years. He stood up and grinned. "That sounds right up my street. Lead on."

CHAPTER 4

HIEBERMEYER LED JACK AND COSTAS ALONG the ridge beside the Nile to an awning over a trestle table covered with plastic finds trays. He picked out an object and handed it to Jack. It was a spent rifle cartridge, the brass blackened with age; the shape was distinctively bottle-necked, with a wider lower body than most modern rifle cartridges, and the primer was dented where it had been struck by the rifle's firing pin.

Costas peered at it. "I wouldn't want to be on the receiving end of that. It looks as if it could take out an elephant."

"It's a Martini-Henry cartridge, .577 necked down to .450 for the bullet," Jack said. "It was the last of the big British black powder cartridges, designed to put down a fanatical enemy running at you at full tilt. Even so, there are many accounts of tribesmen out here taking multiple hits and still charging screaming into the British lines with their spears levelled and swords raised."

Hiebermeyer nodded. "Probably spurred on by the fact that there was no provision for treating the wounded in the Mahdi's army, and death in battle for a jihadist guaranteed an exalted place in heaven."

"How closely can you date this?" Costas asked Jack.

"The Martini-Henry was the main British service rifle from the early 1870s until 1888. To be archaeological about it, there's a *terminus post quem* in the fact that this particular cartridge is drawn brass, essentially a modern-style cartridge. The earlier cartridges of rolled brass foil were found to be deficient during the Zulu War in 1879 and were replaced soon after that. Given what we know about the chronology of British military deployment in the Sudan in the 1880s, I have no doubt that this cartridge dates from the time of the Gordon relief expedition of 1884 to 1885."

"I can be even more specific," Hiebermeyer said. He rummaged in a satchel on the table, pulled out a battered book, and opened it at a marked page. "This is Colonel William Butler's *Campaign of the Cataracts: Being a Personal Narrative of the Great Nile Expedition of 1884 to 1885*. The relief force under General Wolseley was divided into a river column and a desert column, with most of the effort until quite late in the campaign— really too late to save Gordon—being put into the river column. The plan was to drag over eight hundred whale boats up the Nile against the flow through the cataracts. Once they had reached open water, they were to be filled with British troops and used to break through the Mahdist lines besieging Khartoum."

"Come again?" Costas said. "Dragging boats *against* the flow of the river for hundreds of miles? What was wrong with going across the desert?"

"Exactly the question that many asked at the time, not least Gordon himself," Jack said. "Wolseley had done something similar in Canada in 1870 when he took an expedition up the Red River against a rebellion led by Louis Riel, a mixed-blood Métis. The expedition was a remarkable success and ended without bloodshed after Riel capitulated. Wolseley conducted much of his subsequent campaigning career by precedent, and the Nile expedition was to be his tour de force. He even brought over the same Canadians he'd used on the Red River expedition, including more than fifty Mohawks from the Ottawa valley, as well as West African Kroomen from the Gold Coast, because he had campaigned there against the Ashanti in 1873 and had admired their boating skills."

Costas shook his head. "It's hard to know who was more unhinged, Gordon in Khartoum going stir-crazy, or Wolseley insanely dragging boats upriver to rescue him."

Jack gave a wry smile. "By the time the river column reached this point, Wolseley had finally been persuaded to create a separate camel corps to advance across the Bayuda Desert and cut out the bend of the Nile, and it was that force that finally did reach Khartoum in the steamers that Gordon had sent downriver to wait for them."

"But too late," Costas said.

Jack nodded. "By two days. But there have always been bigger questions about the expedition, about whether Wolseley ever realistically intended to relieve Gordon. He and his superiors in Cairo and London seem to have convinced themselves that Gordon had gone off on a loop of his own, that he had become insane. But I've never really bought that. Gordon was certainly an individualist, to put it mildly, but he was also an exceptional administrator and a committed Christian. He was horrified by the plight of those besieged in Khartoum, who had come to rely on him for the dispersal of food and medicine, and he refused to leave them. The idea that he was a self-appointed messiah may even have been encouraged by the government in London, who knew they could never rescue him and were apprehensive about losing face. There must have been those who would rather he died and became a martyr, especially with the fear that he might be captured by the Mahdi and paraded in front of the world, a complete humiliation for the British."

Costas gestured at Hiebermeyer's book. "So what happened at this place?"

Hiebermeyer checked his notes. "The river column reached Semna on the twenty-third of December 1884." He took out a folded photocopied sheet from the book.

"Here's the official War Office report: 'At the head of this rapid is the great "Gate of Semna," a narrow gorge between two rocky cliffs, partly blocked by two islands about equidistant from the shores and from each other. Through the three passages thus formed, the whole pent-up volume of the Nile rushes as through a sluice gate.'" He pulled out another folded sheet and passed it to Costas. "And that's a contemporary print from the *Illustrated London News* based on a sketch sent to them by an anonymous officer. You can see the central channel, and the ropes used by the Royal Navy sailors to haul up the boats, with the voyageurs paddling and steering them. It shows what a monumental task this would have been. The river column was encamped here for several days, waiting for the boats to come up from the previous stretch of rapids and then for them to be taken one by one up through that narrow defile, now completely submerged by the effect of the Aswan Dam."

Jack leaned over and examined the print. "The detail on these drawings is astounding. It's easy to forget the training in draftsmanship and survey these officers had, especially the engineers. This looks good enough to be used for range-finding."

Costas took the cartridge from Jack and peered at it. "So we've got a guy up here shooting a Martini-Henry rifle, probably one day in December 1884. Is there a chance he was one of the enemy, the Mahdi's men? In Afghanistan, the tribesmen were good at getting hold of British rifles from battlefields and by stealing them, and their own gunsmiths were skilled at making copies. I remember seeing a photograph in the news a couple of years ago of a cache of arms seized by U.S. Marines from the Taliban, and as well as old Lee-Enfields there were a couple of Martini-Henrys."

Jack shook his head. "The Sudanese tribesmen hadn't yet had the opportunity. They'd first encountered the British army less than a year before, and even though the battles were generally bloody stalemates, the British were left in control of the battlefields and were careful not to lose their arms. The Egyptian army as well as the Sudanese irregulars under Gordon were armed with Remington rifles; thousands of these were captured after the first big battle against the Mahdi in late 1883. Some of the Egyptian soldiers spared by the Mahdi, those who promised to convert to his cause, served as musketry instructors and even produced halfway-competent snipers. The Remington took a .43 caliber round, so that would have been a further disincentive to acquiring Martini-Henrys, as they used different ammunition."

Costas looked at Hiebermeyer. "Where exactly did you find this?"

Hiebermeyer straightened up and pointed. "About fifty meters to the west, on the edge of the cliff overlooking the river. Let's go there now." Jack and Costas followed him, making their way over the bare sandstone and igneous rock and then through a shallow dusty gully full of dried-up camel dung that led to the cliff. They stopped beside a freshly excavated square about three meters across where the bedrock had been completely exposed, along with the lower courses of a finely constructed masonry wall that blocked off access to the cliff face to the southwest. Hiebermeyer jumped into the trench, moved aside a measuring rod, and squatted by the wall, pointing at the worked stone. "This is part of the fort complex built by our friend Senusret in the early second millennium BC. It's the final part of the lookout he ordered constructed on either side of the cataract. There were further outposts to the south, as we saw in that papyrus dispatch, but I think a veil of mist rose above that torrent in the river, and beyond was a land of darkness, a place they feared."

"The British in the river column must have begun to feel the same," Jack said. "This was their biggest obstacle so far, and everything ahead must have seemed almost insurmountable. They hadn't experienced battle yet, but they'd begun to encounter the odd dervish sharpshooter."

"You'll be interested to see where I found the cartridge." Hiebermeyer vaulted out of the trench and onto the ancient wall, and then disappeared over the other side only a few meters from the cliff edge. The other two followed and joined him in a pit about four meters across and two meters deep in the center, eroded around the sides but clearly man-made. The edge forming a parapet beside the cliff had been excavated down to bedrock in a section about a meter wide, exposing the construction sequence. Hiebermeyer got inside and turned around so he was facing the other two, and pointed at the section. "Here you can clearly see the pharaonic wall, in five surviving courses. This was a blockhouse attached to the larger complex we were standing in earlier, overlooking the river. But above the masonry you can see unworked slabs of gneiss and smaller stones, as well as compacted clay that must have been brought up from the river shore. There's clearly an amount of wind-blown fill inside the pit, but as you've seen, there isn't much sand in this part of the desert and certainly not enough to explain that material on top of the wall. I have no doubt it was built up by the British in 1884."

Jack looked around. "It's a sangar," he murmured. "That's a Pashtun word the British picked up in Afghanistan, meaning a protected built-up pit, basically a firing position or sentry post." He shaded his eyes and scanned the far bank of the river, where a group of Hiebermeyer's team could be seen excavating another complex of ruins. "My guess is that there would also have been one of these on the other side, and that they were temporary sentry posts established above the pool while the column was camped here during December 1884."

"The sentry post on the other side also served as a heliograph station," Hiebermeyer said. "We found smashed glass from the reflective mirror, which must have been damaged while they were putting it up or taking it down."

Jack continued to gaze at the cliffs opposite, moving slightly so that he was looking southwest. "If I were a dervish sharpshooter, I'd be in the rocks over there, above the gorge," he said, pointing. "That would give me a clear line of sight to the work being carried out on the river, as well as to this sangar. The distance to here is four hundred, maybe four hundred and twenty yards, within range of a Remington."

"And presumably of a Martini-Henry, from this side," Costas said.

"Could you do it, shoot accurately at this range?" Hiebermeyer said, looking at Jack.

"I've had a go with a Martini-Henry, 1883 vintage," Jack said. "It's difficult as the sights take a lot of getting used to, but it could be done. I've shot accurately at this range before with a Lee-Enfield, no problem."

"I've seen that," Costas said, squinting at Hiebermeyer. "Four years ago, in the Panjshir Valley in Afghanistan, when Jack used an old British rifle loaned to him by an Afghan warlord to take out a guy who'd been stalking us."

Jack continued staring at the cliffs, saying nothing. Hiebermeyer leaned over a finds tray and picked up a labelled plastic bag with a small lump in it, then pointed at the other debris in the tray. "This material came from inside the pit and shows that British soldiers were here for some time, several days at least. You can see the rusted lid from a tin of army-issue bully beef, and the paper wrapper from a package of Wills tobacco. Of course the conditions here are as elsewhere in the desert, and organic material survives very well." He handed Costas the bag. "Take a look at this."

Costas peered at the lump bemusedly and then handed it to Jack, who opened up the bag and carefully rolled the object out onto his hand. "Fascinating," he murmured. "It's a spent bullet, only partly compacted, so fired from a considerable range, conceivably from those cliffs opposite. And that's a little bit of fabric with it. This bullet went through a clothed human body." He weighed it in his hand and then peered closely at it. "This isn't heavy enough for a Martini-Henry bullet, but I'd swear it's from a Remington. The base is still intact, so we'll be able to measure it."

"Already done," Hiebermeyer said, beaming. "I've got an electronic caliper measurement of .445 inch, just right for a .43 caliber Remington. The bullet wasn't loose in the pit but had penetrated the clay on the side of the sangar. Fortunately I was here supervising when it was revealed, and I had the student stop excavating while the bullet was still *in situ* so that I could measure the angle of trajectory. You're right, Jack. It had been fired from the opposite cliff and had penetrated the sangar below the maximum possible line of sight of the shooter, so it was coming in on an arching trajectory. I used a laser range finder and got a range of four hundred and thirty-five yards to an opening on the upper ridge where a sniper could have been positioned. I then did a little research of my own with a friend in Germany who is a military reenactor, and he told me that the drop of a bullet from a regulation Remington cartridge in dry desert conditions over that distance would be about twenty-nine inches. That allowed me to find the exact spot on the opposite cliff where the sniper sat when he took the shot that hit the British soldier."

"And the spot where the sniper may have died," Jack said.

"How can you know that?" Costas asked.

Jack picked up the Martini-Henry cartridge again and turned to Hiebermeyer. "Did you find any more of these?"

Hiebermeyer shook his head. "That came from where you're standing, and we swept the entire sangar with a metal detector. My friend told me that the British generally didn't collect their cartridges after use. Any expended cartridges here would probably quickly have been trampled into the dust underfoot and not been visible to locals who might have come scavenging this place afterwards."

Costas looked around. "Yet if this was a sentry post, there'd be at least a couple of guys here at any one time, and if they were being sniped at, you'd expect them to fire a barrage of rounds at that cliff."

Jack narrowed his eyes. "I think there was someone here who knew his business and got them to hold their fire. I think he was a skilled sharpshooter himself. He would have known he had only one chance before his opponent moved. One shot, one kill."

"One down on each side," Costas said. "Even score, nobody wins."

Jack looked pensively back at the cliff. "A single sniper up in those cliffs could have held back the British column for hours, inflicting officer casualties and battering the morale of exhausted men who must already have been questioning the worth of what they were doing. So despite the casualty here, I think that if the dervish sniper was killed, then it was one up for the British."

Hiebermeyer replaced the finds tray and stood up. "Except that two men were killed that day in this sangar."

Jack stared at him. "How do you know?"

Hiebermeyer made his way out of the section and into the pit, and then leapt up on the wall again. "This is where it gets really fascinating, because what we've found takes us back from 1884 almost three thousand years. But before then, we're going to meet up with Aysha and hear her take on all this. After all, it *is* her site."

Jack climbed up to the rim of the sangar and stared to the south. He could hear the helicopter drumming along the course of the Nile, and he wondered how much deeper the echo would have sounded a hundred and thirty years earlier, before the Aswan Dam had been constructed and the river level raised. He looked into the waters now, imagining the gorge as it had been then: the rocks with the torrent in between, the boats queuing up awaiting their turn to be hauled through the cataract, the shouts and singing of the men below, British and Canadian, West African and Egyptian and Sudanese. He turned back and looked at the sangar again and thought about how thin the veil of dust was that lay

over the detritus of the past in the desert, how quickly
it reduced everything to the same level: the remains
from that day in 1884 could be as old as the ancient
Egyptian walls that surrounded them. Yet the absence of
any overburden, of any stratigraphy, also meant that the
past was immediate, and he could almost put himself
back there on that fateful day, hear the screams of the
soldier who had been hit and lay dying in the dust in
front of him, and see the man with the rifle who had lain
against the parapet and fired at the far cliff. In the blink
of an eye their modern clothes could become the khaki
of a hundred and thirty years earlier, and in another blink
the skirts and sandals of the ancient Egyptian soldiers
who had manned this outpost three thousand years
before that, all of them sharing the same apprehension
about what lay through the pall of dust beyond the
horizon to the south.

He took a deep breath, smelling the tang of the desert
and the acrid odor of camel dung, even imagining he
had caught a sulphurous whiff of gunpowder. He felt as
if another deep breath would suck in that veil and he
would take the past within himself and step out into
that day in December 1884. For a few moments he had
not only seen the sharpshooter but become one with him,
focused on the only things of importance at that moment: the balance of the rifle, the view through the
sights, the measured pace of his breathing, the touch of
his finger on the trigger. Jack wondered who the man
had been, whether he would ever know his name.

He took a water bottle from his leg pocket, unscrewed
the top, and offered it to the other two. Costas took a
mouthful, and then Jack drained the rest and replaced it
in his pocket, screwing back the top as he did so. The
drumming of the helicopter became a roar as it settled
into its landing site, the whirling rotor blades just visible
through the storm of dust created by the downdraft. It
powered down, and Jack turned to the others. "I'll give
Ibrahim about an hour to off-load the equipment with
the crewmen. It's his operation and I don't want to inter-

fere. But as soon as he calls through, I'm onto it. I'm itching to dive."

"Roger that," Costas said.

Jack turned to Hiebermeyer. "Does that give us enough time?"

Hiebermeyer paused. "I hope so. There are rogue elements in the regime here who could shut us down at any moment. There's a lot simmering just beneath the surface in the Sudan: warlords, fundamentalism. We're just trying to pack as much as we can into every day while we're still able to work here."

"Where's Aysha?" asked Jack.

"At the Senusret shrine," Hiebermeyer replied. "Once we've talked to her, I'll finish showing you what we've found. It's fabulous stuff, one of the most exciting discoveries ever made in Egyptology. Follow me."

PART 2

CHAPTER 5

MAJOR EDWARD MAYNE OF THE ROYAL ENgineers pushed his white cotton scarf up over his nose, leaving only a narrow gap beneath his headdress to see through, and pressed his heels into the flanks of his camel. He lurched forward as it swerved into a shallow gully, picking its way among the exposed bedrock that provided a surer footing than the loose shale and dust of the surrounding desert. Over the last two weeks Mayne had learned to move in rhythm with the beast, becoming one with it as his guide had taught him, leaving him swaying like a sailor on land. He dismounted to take measurements and sketch the rocky course of the river through the cataracts, noting the places where boats might be hauled up against the current. The day before, a messenger had reached him with orders to return to the main camp of the river expedition and report to headquarters, and he and his guide had ridden hard that morning to reach the camp before the midday sun made travel intolerable. He knew that Corporal Jones would be waiting for him in the sangar dugout, where he had left him with the sentries overlooking the camp beside the Nile. As he got closer, he had made sure to avoid the deep gullies so that he was always exposed to view. Over the past weeks Mahdist sharpshooters had begun to inflict casualties on the river column, and he knew there would be jittery trigger fingers at the sight of anyone wearing Arab dress approaching on a camel.

He looked back to the east, where he had parted ways with his guide, Shaytan Ahmed al-Abaid, a chieftain of the Dongola people of Upper Nubia, who had accompanied him on his foray into the desert. The previous evening they had huddled over the embers of their fire beside the wells of Umm Bayaid, concealed within a rocky gully from prying eyes, and had talked together until the last vestige of heat had left the rocks and they had lain to sleep on the hard ground, keeping close to their camels for warmth. Shaytan had been an interpreter for General Gordon in Khartoum and had left only three weeks before, when Gordon had ordered him out of the city for his own safety. The Mahdi's forces had blocked the main exit routes, and Shaytan had made it through only by disguising himself in the patched *jibba* robe of an Ansar warrior, the most fanatic followers of the Mahdi. He had travelled to General Wolseley's headquarters at Wadi Halfa, some two hundred miles north on the Egyptian border, and offered his services to the expedition that was now inching its way south along the Nile in a forlorn attempt to relieve Gordon. In the careful ways of desert dialogue, in a wide-ranging discussion over cups of strong tea, Mayne had extracted from Shaytan all he could about Gordon's state of mind. Shaytan's account was dispassionate, the most up-to-date he had, and was not clouded by the prejudgments of British intelligence officers that had made it difficult for Mayne to get a good grasp of the man. That evening's discussion had been the most valuable outcome of his foray into the desert; forward reconnaissance of the Nile had seemed of dubious value anyway in light of the probability that the river column would never reach Khartoum in time to save Gordon.

The camel snorted and tossed its head; Mayne knew he was close to the sangar now, just off to the west. Beyond that he saw the flash of the heliograph on a rocky outcrop above the far bank of the river, the signallers tilting the mirror in the sunlight to send out the long and short dashes of Morse code. The telegraph line from Khartoum had been cut as soon as the Mahdi's forces had surrounded the city; some said that Gordon himself had done it in a fit of pique over the delay in sending a relief expedition to get his Egyptian and Sudanese staff and their families out of Khartoum before the Mahdi made escape impossible. The heliograph could be used only for the most basic information, for requests for supplies or reports of daily progress up the Nile; the Mahdi's spies were perfectly able to read Morse code, and anything more sensitive would soon reach the ears of the sheikhs who commanded the force that the British troops knew was waiting in the desert somewhere to the south. The only way to communicate securely was by courier, using local Sudanese tribesmen, who could ride swiftly and knew how to avoid the thieves and murderers of the desert oases. For weeks now it was the only way that messages from Gordon had reached them, messages that had infuriated Wolseley in their fickle vacillation between optimism and fatalism and in the obscurity of Gordon's intentions. Even the authenticity of the messages could be suspect, brought by messengers whose loyalty could never be certain. In the desert, the truth shifted like the sands, changing subtly in complexion with each gust of wind, then being swept away by storms that left a whole new landscape of reality to understand and navigate.

Mayne steered the camel towards the flashing light, knowing that the sangar now lay directly ahead above the near bank of the river. The message being sent out would be relayed down the heliograph posts to Korti, the advance camp on the Nile where the camel corps was assembling, and then on to Wadi Halfa. He smiled wryly to himself, remembering what Corporal Jones and the other soldiers had called Wadi Halfa: *Bloody Halfway*. It had become a standing joke for the men of the river column to ask one another how far they had gone at the end of each day, after another few hundred yards of backbreaking toil, hauling and rowing the boats to the next obstacle; the answer was always the same: *bloody halfway*. The joke had become strained as the level of the Nile had steadily fallen through December, and the channels he had spotted during his reconnaissance trips upstream had become trickles by the time the boats reached them. Sometimes it seemed as if they were caught in a Greek myth of the underworld, where no matter how hard they tried, their goal remained forever elusive. Yet Mayne knew that if this were the underworld, then they were in only the first circle of hell; somewhere ahead was an invisible barrier beyond which lay a deeper reach, a place where a force of darkness was marshalling that could obliterate them with the speed and ferocity of a sandstorm. And in the eye of that looming maelstrom was General Charles Gordon, their sole purpose for being here, a man whose future seemed increasingly doubtful as the chances of the relief expedition ever reaching him faded hour by hour.

Mayne turned and watched Shaytan receding noiselessly in the distance, his camel wavering in the heat haze as it sauntered away. The sun glinted off the brass-covered flintlock pistol with a handle like a rat's tail that Shaytan had taken from the dismembered corpse of an Ottoman Turkish official they had found in the desert a few days previously; whether the work of the Mahdi's men or brigands was unclear. With his golden gun and his belted dagger, Shaytan seemed from another era, yet Mayne had learned that the desert had a timeless quality in which the past seemed to live with the present. It had seemingly rebuffed every attempt by the British to introduce new technology: the railway his fellow engineers had pushed as far as they could beyond Korti, until the supply of track and their own energy had been sapped; the river steamers that Gordon had used in the upper reaches of the Nile near Khartoum, constantly breaking down and immobilised for want of wood for fuel; the

Gatling and Gardner machine guns that should have assured their supremacy on the battlefield but that jammed
in the dust and the heat. They had learned through bitter experience that the only way to broach the desert
was to adapt to it and learn the ways of desert survival
as Mayne had done from Shaytan, yet even that put in-
terlopers at a disadvantage against those who had been
born to it. It was impossible to know where Shaytan
would go next, or which side he would now join. What
was certain was that his time with Mayne had come to
an end, and they both knew that if they were to meet
again, they might be trying to cut each other's throats. It
was the way of the desert, and signified nothing more
than that they were both part of the eternal course of
history in these lands.

Shaytan had called Mayne "Nassr'ayin," meaning
"Eagle Eye." It was the same name he had been given in
Iroquoian by the Mohawk Indians when he had spent a
year living among them as a boy on the Ottawa River in
Upper Canada, when his uncle had been in charge of a
Royal Engineers detachment maintaining the canal from
Lake Ontario to the new capital. The Iroquoian name,
"Kahniekahake," had stuck when he had returned to
Canada as a newly commissioned subaltern and joined
the Mohawk scouts in Wolseley's expedition up the Red
River in 1870 to quash the rebellion of Louis Riel. It
was an extraordinary fact that some of those same men,
including his boyhood friend Charrière, were here today,
employed by Wolseley for their expertise with river craft
to help haul the hundreds of whaleboats to be used to
transport soldiers up the Nile towards Khartoum.

To the followers of Islam, the eagle was a perfect creation of Allah; to the Mohawks it was the spirit of a
young warrior on a vision quest. Yet Mayne knew that
Shaytan wore Islam as lightly as his ancestors had worn
the beliefs of others who had passed through the desert
in the distant past, and that for the Mohawk the spirit
world required no special belief; it was simply the world
they inhabited. Spending time with Shaytan had allowed

Mayne to understand the desert people in a way that the staff officers in Korti and Wadi Halfa never would. The call to jihad that lay at the core of the rebellion was not the main motivation for the majority of the Mahdi's army, a vast and motley gathering of tribesmen drawn from all quarters of the Sudan, some of them from the deepest reaches of the desert, where the influence of Islam was peripheral at best. For many, their instinct was to fight each other rather than join in a common cause. And yet this truth, that they were not all converts to militant Islam, was not a weakness; in the hands of the Mahdi, it was a strength. The Mahdi himself was one of them, born on the Nile, and he knew what drove his people. He knew how to use his holy vision to attract and rally his core of fanatical followers, the Ansar, and how to use their suicidal courage to draw others to follow his banner. And the tribesmen were not simply fighting to expel foreigners—Turkish and British and Egyptian and even Arabs—in order to defend their families and their traditions. The Mahdi knew how to stir them so that they were fighting because they relished it, because their pulses quickened at the sight of blood, because they could not resist following when the Ansar surged forward screaming and brandishing their spears at the enemy. Mayne had realised that the war had become self-fuelling, and that the only hope the British would ever have of containing it would be to return with an army large enough to mount a campaign of attrition and annihilation.

Mayne looked back one last time at the wavering form in the distance. A gust of wind took one end of Shaytan's head scarf and unfurled it like a banner, until it seemed to join the distant streaks of black cloud that appeared above the horizon; his camel appeared to stretch outwards and upwards like a mirage, and then was gone. It was like this in the desert, a place of mirages, of illusions, where desperate thirst could feel like dust in the throat, where there was no moral compass, where cruelty could be as casual and transient as the

camaraderie he had felt over the last few weeks. Of all
the places where he had been on campaign, he had never
experienced the insidious draining that he had felt in
the desert. The worst of it was when your body dried up
until you were like a camel; they said that if you survived that without going insane, you learned to feed it
with just what was necessary to keep from collapsing.
Mayne knew he had been there often over the past few
days, that Shaytan had made him experience it to show
him how to survive; but it had left him with a desiccated
feeling that would take days to resolve, and he knew
that his body would try to convince him he was sated
when he needed to drink more than he ever had done
before in his life.

He turned back, pulled hard on the reins to keep the
camel's head in the direction of the river, and kicked its
flanks again. He found the animal strangely reassuring,
as if its plodding gait were taking him out of that world
of mirages and anchoring him back in reality. Seeing the
patches of solid bedrock under the sand reminded him
of the ancient ruins that Shaytan had shown him, Nubian and Roman and Egyptian, some of them from the
time when the pharaohs had ventured this far south
and tried to tame the wilderness they believed had been
the homeland from which their civilisation had sprung.
The ruins had been vestigial, elusive—the tamped-down
floors of desert corrals, crumbled watchtowers, temporary forts—and there had been no stratigraphy to them;
with seeming whimsy the wind would blow sand away
to reveal ruins that were three thousand years old, or so
recent that Shaytan could remember those who had
lived in them. As soon as people passed on, the desert
seemed to swallow their history and reduce it to the
same desiccated imprint, the fate that seemed to lie in
store for their own endeavours just as it had for the expeditions of the pharaohs who had preceded them on
this trek into the shadow lands of their own history.

Yet in those few elusive ruins, Mayne had found a
human presence stronger than he had ever done among

the towering monuments of Giza or Luxor or Abu Simbel that he had visited on his voyage south through Egypt. The day before, he had seen strange pyramidal forms rising from the sand, sheer-sided outcrops of basalt from some ancient volcanic eruption that had resisted the wind and stood stark above the desert like the backbone of the Earth itself. In a flash of insight he had understood the origin of the man-made pyramids of ancient Egypt, an interest spurred by his time spent visiting the archaeological sites of the Nile after his first posting to Cairo. Those people who had gone north, the ancestors of the first pharaohs, had taken with them this vision of their ancestral landscape and had attempted to re-create it in their burial monuments. He realised why he had found the wonders of ancient Egypt curiously unmoving, for all their grandeur and technical marvel. They were no more than imitations of nature, like the walled gardens of European aristocrats, constructed by a people who could bear to inhabit a world that only they controlled. To those who rebelled, those like the heretic pharaoh Akhenaten, that world must have seemed artificial, claustrophobic, unbearable; Mayne could see why Akhenaten had come here in search of truth, rejecting the religion of the pharaohs and finding deeper meaning in the one God, the Aten.

He remembered something and reached under the fold of his desert robe into his tunic pocket, taking out a small package. Shaytan had given him a *hejab,* a pouch containing an amulet on a leather necklace with verses of the Koran wrapped around it. He released the reins of the camel and untied the leather thong that kept the bag shut, dropping the amulet into the palm of his hand. The wrapping was diaphanous, insubstantial, and when he took it off, it seemed lighter than air. As he held it in his other palm, a wisp of wind suddenly took it from him. He snatched at it, but it was gone. For a moment he thought of dismounting and chasing it, but it was flying high above the desert, and it would he hopeless. He did not even know whether it truly had been verse from the Koran or some more ancient wisdom of the Dongola transcribed into Arabic. But the amulet seemed more substantial, and he peered at it closely. He realised that it was an ancient carving in the shape of a scarab beetle, like those he had seen for sale in the alleyway markets of Cairo, pillaged from ancient tombs. It was jet black, carved from hard volcanic stone, probably from some outcrop in the desert itself. Embedded in the wings were lines of gold wire and two tiny gemstones that he recognised as peridot, the beautiful green stone that the ancient Egyptians mined on St. John's Island in the Red Sea. The scarab must have been a prized possession in antiquity. Perhaps Shaytan had picked it up in one of those ruins, or it had been passed down to him through the generations of his ancestors since the pharaohs had turned their eyes away from this place. On its base Mayne could feel the ridges and indentations of carving, and turning it over he saw that it was hieroglyphics. When he had time, he would dig out the notebook he had filled with hieroglyphic symbols during two days of enforced leisure waiting for supplies when the expedition had encamped at Akhenaten's ruined capital of Amarna, and see if he could find a match.

He saw a flash of reflected light up ahead, and quickly hung the scarab around his neck. The light had come from a bayonet poking above the wall of the sangar about two hundred yards away above the river gorge. He saw a wisp of smoke from a billycan fire, the universal sign of British soldiers brewing up. He pursed his lips. They were going to have to be more careful. Shaytan had spotted movement among the rocks above a few miles upstream, and Mayne knew that the British sentry posts would be prime targets for the Mahdi's sharpshooters. He squinted at the western horizon beyond the smoke, just making out the distant ridge above the far bank of the river, but he could see nothing. He remembered the last time he and Shaytan had been this close to the Nile, when he had taken the Martini-Henry rifle out of its leather cover in front of the saddle and fired at a derelict *shaduf*, a water-lifting device, adjusting the sights for the range until he had shot the top of the pole away in three successive rounds, enough to know that the sights were correct should he have to do the same to a human target on the opposite ridge of the river as they worked their way up the cararacts. That was when Shaytan had called him Nassr'ayin, Eagle Eye, and it was for the same reason that he had acquired the name from the Mohawk years before. He had relished shooting the rifle in this elemental place, free from the superimpositions of civilisation. It was his constant, a tunnelling of his vision that excluded everything else, just as the river and the burning sun were the constants of the desert. And it was what he was here to do. He picked up the reins, ready to yank them. It was time he made his presence known.

CHAPTER 6

MAYNE PULLED HARD ON THE REINS, STEER-ing the camel towards the sentry post overlooking the Nile. The wind-graded dust and gravel of the desert had given way to *hamada*, the hard igneous plateau that skirted the river where it had cut its way through the bedrock on its course north towards Egypt. He could see the Nile now, a hundred feet or so below the level of the plateau, sinuous rivulets of brown that curled around the outcrops of black rock that broke up the river as it ran down the cataract, the twists of white water showing where it was fast and dangerous. The men working below were not yet visible, but he could hear their cries echoing down the gorge as they hauled the boats past the rocks: the bellowed orders of the British sergeants and corporals; the undulating chant of the West African Kroomen singing in unison; and the distinctive nasal lilt of the Mohawk Indians, who spoke the archaic French of the voyageurs they had guided for generations through the Canadian wilderness.

He slid off the camel, took his saddlebag and rifle, and left the beast snorting and chewing on some desert grass in a shallow gully about fifty yards from the sentry post. The sangar was a natural cleft in the cliff top, surrounded by the remains of an ancient masonry wall that the soldiers had fortified with rocks and mounded gravel to form a parapet around the edge. As he approached it, he could see the khaki pith helmets of half a dozen men and the long bayonets of rifles that had been left propped against the parapet. He had not yet been spotted, and he stopped for a moment to listen to the murmur of voices, among them the distinctive West Country burr of Corporal Jones, the sapper who was his servant, holding forth as usual to a rapt audience. "Camels," he heard Jones say. "Can't stand 'em. My officer loves his, made me try to ride it. Horrible it was, spitting and belching and eating its own vomit. All those men volunteering to join the camel corps for the desert column, they don't know what they're in for."

Another voice piped up. "Tell us more about the dervishes, Jonesy."

Mayne heard the suck of a pipe and saw a ring of tobacco smoke rise above the steam of the billycan that was boiling in the fire. Jones knew how to play his audience, how to build anticipation. He heard the pipe being knocked out, slowly, deliberately. "It's the spears that puts the fear of God in a man," Jones said quietly. "As long as a lance they are, with metal points the length of your arm, sharper than those bayonets. After they've done with the killing, they go over the battlefield and dip their spears in the wounds, and then smear the blood all over themselves. That's Johnny Fuzzy-Wuzzy for you." He paused, and Mayne heard the striking of a match and then the suck of the pipe again. "Like the devil in battle they are, mark my words. Saw them myself, at El Teb in February. Like one of those medieval church paintings of the seven circles of hell, with little black demons serving Satan. That's where we're all going, I tell you, up this river to the gates of hell itself."

"I heard Colonel Burnaby speak of the battle when he arrived to join the desert column after recovering from his wounds." Mayne recognised the voice of the impressionable young infantry subaltern who had been left in charge of the sangar. "He was there as well, at El Teb."

"And he saw to them, hundreds of them," an Irish voice pitched in. "We've all heard the stories."

"Too right, mate," Jones asserted. "The colonel did for them good and proper, standing there on a rock above the battle wearing a Norfolk jacket and a stalking hat, looking for all the world like a country gent on a Sunday shoot. He had a fearsome weapon, a four-barrelled howdah pistol, like the ones they use in India to shoot tigers from the backs of elephants. It fires the same cartridge as the old Snider rifle, big enough to blow a hole clean through a man so you can see out the other side. Saw it with my own eyes, I did, the first dervish Burnaby killed, his innards flying and twirling out behind him like he was on fire, and still he kept coming. They're devils, I tell you. Then the colonel drops his pistol and fires pig-shot point-blank with his double-barrelled twelve-bore. The dervishes knocked him up bad, but he kept on blasting. Twenty-three shells he fired, and he killed thirteen of them. And when his ammunition was finished, he laid about him something fearful with his sabre and killed as many again. Saw it all with my own eyes."

Mayne smiled to himself. Jones was a born raconteur who could reduce himself to the level of the coarsest of the soldiers, but as a street urchin in Bristol a benefactor had paid for him to go to the Bluecoat School, where he had picked up enough to converse more articulately with Mayne than some of the officers. He was in his late twenties, some ten years younger than Mayne, but he had already bounced up and down the ranks several times, his natural abilities almost exactly counterbalanced by his transgressions, usually for speaking his mind in the presence of a less accommodating officer. He had been in India with the Madras Sappers and Miners and had served in an arduous jungle campaign in the south before going to the war in Afghanistan in 1880, where he had picked up the surveying skills that had first brought him to Mayne's attention. Before being despatched to the river column by an exasperated commanding officer, Jones had been in a Royal Engineers company attempting to build a railway into the desert from Suakin on the Red Sea coast; they had been present at the first major encounters of British forces with the Mahdi army at the bloody battles at El Teb and El Sid earlier that year. Whether he had actually seen Burnaby in action with his own eyes was a moot point that Mayne did not wish to explore, though there was enough corroboration to show that his account was essentially accurate.

"Now there's a soldier's soldier for you, sir, Fred Burnaby, make no mistake," he heard Jones say. The pipe was sucked, and he caught a waft of tobacco smoke. "Some say old Burnaby has more brawn than brains, but mark my words, if he were in charge here, he'd hoick us out of the river and march us across the desert to where we could stand up to the fuzzy-wuzzies like real British soldiers, not like the sewer rats we are here. You can tell that to all your fancy friends in the press and your staff officers with their maps and plans, begging your pardon, sir."

Mayne smiled again in spite of himself. El Teb had been part of an abortive attempt to establish a Red Sea beachhead in order to approach Khartoum from the east, a plan that had bogged down in the fetid coastal swamps when the local Baggara tribesmen had rallied to the Mahdi's cause and inflicted a series of disastrous defeats. But even that had not been enough of a wake-up call for some of the officers on the staff. One of the more tedious colonels, a man who had never been on the receiving end of a dervish charge, had heard stories of Burnaby's Norfolk jacket and the shotgun and had said it was not sporting. *Not sporting.* Few of them realised what they were up against. Even General Wolseley had assured the press that the appearance of a few dozen redcoats on a river steamer at Khartoum would cow the enemy into submission and relieve General Gordon and his Egyptian and Sudanese garrison. Yet it was Wolseley who had devised the plan they were currently executing, a scheme of astounding logistical complexity to inch a rescue force up the Nile against the flow, almost guaranteeing that they would not get there before the Mahdi's forces overwhelmed Khartoum. Corporal Jones was right. If the will really existed to relieve Gordon, then the only course of action was a bold move across the desert, though whether a maverick like Burnaby was the right man to lead it was another moot point.

Mayne scraped the ground noisily with his boot and climbed the parapet. The knot of soldiers inside jerked their heads toward him, clutching at their rifles. He cleared his throat. "Speaking of more brawn than brains, I thought this was meant to be a lookout post." It hurt to talk, the first time he had done so in hours, his throat dry and coated with dust. The subaltern stood up quickly, disconcerted, straightening his tunic. "We never thought an enemy would come from that direction, sir. I have two sentries in the rocks with their eyes trained on the cliff above the opposite bank. That's where we saw the dervishes watching us yesterday."

Jones stood up, like Mayne a few inches over average height, put his hands on his hips, and looked Mayne up and down, then shook his head. "You look a sight, sir. Every bit of you. I don't know where to begin."

"Don't bother." Mayne let the saddlebag drop, pulled off his headdress, and tried to push his fingers through his thick dark hair and then through his beard. He looked at his hands and knew his face must be the same, layered with a dark orange crust of desert like the bedrock he had just been riding over. He hardly dared think of his odour; fortunately he seemed to have lost his sense of smell after a few hours on the back of the camel. He swallowed hard, trying to wet his throat. "The messenger reached us yesterday evening at the Kordofan wells; I'm due at Korti tomorrow afternoon for a conference with General Wolseley. That's thirty miles downriver, and there are about six hours of daylight left. There's no moon at the moment, and even the voyageurs won't paddle through the cataracts when it's pitch-dark. I don't have time to wash and change."

"You mean you don't *want* to, sir. You know the general's going to send you out into the desert again, and you don't want to lose that look. It takes a while to grow a convincing beard. A few days' stubble is a dead giveaway, as none of the Arabs have it."

Mayne said nothing, but unwound his headdress and scarf and stuffed them into the bag, then took off his hippo-hide belt and his robe. The robe had been another layer above his uniform and at first he had objected to it, but it had kept him cool while he was riding, the white cotton reflecting the desert sun. Beneath it he wore the standard attire of an officer in the desert campaign: a Sam Browne belt with a holster for his Webley-Pryse revolver, an ammunition pouch containing twenty rounds, a bag with his tinted sun goggles, and a leather water bottle; and below that a grey serge jumper, yellow ochre corduroy riding breeches, puttees wound up to his knees, and brown ankle-length boots, all of it adapted from kit he had worn on the North-West Frontier of India. His pith helmet, dyed with Nile mud and acacia bark and with a cloth neck veil, was attached to the saddlebag. He would have liked to carry on wearing the headdress and scarf in this heat, but he needed to remain inconspicuous, keeping spying eyes from seeing anything singular about him. And there was another factor now too: the dervish sharpshooters who might be in the cliffs opposite. A headdress would show that he had been in the desert, probably gathering intelligence, and would suggest that he was an officer, which would make him a prime target. He did not want to invite a bullet before his mission had even begun.

Jones pointed to a khaki-coloured canvas roll-up the size of a cricket kit bag among their surveying gear on one side of the sangar. "I kept that beside me all the time, sir, as I promised you. Your special equipment."

Jones knew what the bag contained, though not its true purpose. On the face of it, a sporting rifle was an unremarkable piece of gear for a British officer travelling abroad who might expect opportunities to hunt along the way; there were officers fired up by tales of African game who had brought with them entire arsenals of every imaginable type and calibre. But Mayne's gun was a make rarely seen on this side of the Atlantic, and he did not want to draw attention to himself. The wooden box inside the bag was sealed and weatherproofed so that it was not damaged in any way. He suspected that the time to test-fire and sight it in would be soon, perhaps immediately after his visit to Wolseley, so he would take it with him when he left the sangar for the river. He nodded his acknowledgement to Jones. "Is my boat ready?"

"The bow was stoved in on a rock during the passage from Korti, and the sappers down below are patching her up. They're going to signal me when they're finished. Meanwhile Mr. Tanner and Major Ormerod of the Canadian contingent have discovered something they thought you might want to see. They know about your interest in the ancient ruins, and they've come across some carvings in the cliff face below us."

Mayne squinted at the ridge on the opposite side of the river. "I'll stay up here, I think," he murmured. "If there are dervishes watching us, I'd rather try to do something about it than make myself a target at the base of that cliff. Judging by the difficulties I saw ahead in this cataract, the river column will probably still be camped here when I get back. Plenty of time then for exploring ruins."

Jones looked at him shrewdly. "You've been away sometimes for weeks on end, and that's just carrying out reconnaissance upriver. If General Wolseley wants you to go into the desert for him, then you'll probably be away for a long time. We won't be seeing you back here at this spot, sir, that's my guess."

Mayne pulled the Martini-Henry rifle out of the holster attached to his saddlebag and picked up the cartridge box. "Then I'd better make the best use of my time while I'm here. My spotting scope and binoculars are in the saddlebag. Bring them to the parapet and we'll see if we can't spy out those dervishes of yours."

"You're having something to eat and drink first, sir."

Mayne grunted, then dropped into the sangar and leaned his rifle against the parapet. Jones was right. He was not yet ready for hardtack biscuit and tinned bully beef, but he took the proffered leather *mussak* water bottle gratefully, wetting his lips and then swilling the water around his mouth as he had learned to do from the Dongolese, taking small sips before slaking his thirst. He left the bottle half full and passed it back, taking his first proper look at Jones, who was wearing regulation khaki but sporting a colourful bandanna under his helmet, its knotted end hanging down his back like a pigtail. Mayne recognised the cloth pattern of the Hudson's Bay Company; it must have been given to him by one of the Canadian voyageurs recruited by Wolseley to navigate the boats up the cataracts. Unlikely friendships had formed among the motley crew assembled for this task.

Mayne waved away an open tin, but Jones succeeded in thrusting a rock-hard fragment of biscuit into his hand. "Was it as you expected, sir? The river, I mean?"

Mayne slumped back against the parapet. "The next stretch of open water begins about seven miles ahead. I've mapped out a possible route through the cataract in between, but the river was too muddy to see any underwater obstructions even from my vantage point high above the bank. It'll be down to the Mohawks to navigate the way forward."

"They've got an uncanny ability, sir. We've been watching them in the rapids below us here. Your friend Charrière, he's the best."

"Rivers are in their blood, and the canoe is like a second skin to them," Mayne replied. "They can sense the slightest change in the current, allowing them to detect rocks underwater as if the river had been stripped away." He wiped the sweat off his forehead with the back of his hand and took the water bottle again from Jones. "I've identified the best landing point for the flotilla when it reaches the foot of the next cataract at the end of the open water. It's on the far bank, but the obvious route beyond that is a dead-end alley, and they'd have to back-track if they tried going up it, losing hours. They'll need to cross the river and work their way up below the cliffs on this side. I'll pass my sketches on to General Earle's adjutant before I leave."

"Is the next cataract going to be as bad as this one, sir?"

Mayne took another swig. "Worse, probably. And there are four more stretches of cataract before the clear passage to Khartoum. That's more than two hundred miles ahead, and by the time open water is reached, the river level will have dropped so much that even the clear sections between the cataracts will be full of shoals and exposed rock. Time is most definitely not on our side. At best it's going to be a close-run thing."

"And a few good marksmen on the cliffs could slow us down even more," the subaltern said.

"I thought the dervishes couldn't shoot worth a damn," the Irish soldier said, leaning up on his elbows from where he had been lying, staring intently at Mayne.

"Don't count on it," Mayne replied. "The true *jihad-diyah*, the Ansar, have forsworn modern weapons and despise firearms as the tool of the infidel. But the Mahdi's been very astute. He knows that the traditional tribal warrior of the Sudan equates courage and manliness with the sword and the spear, and by extolling that tradition he's been able to recruit more tribal men to his cause. But the Remington rifles they captured from the Egyptians have been put to good use too. The Mahdi has raised a cadre of sharpshooters to provide long-distance fire over the heads of the advancing Ansar. The few Egyptian soldiers who were allowed to survive capture have taught them how to clean and maintain the rifles and how to shoot."

"Soldiers that we trained ourselves, turning what we taught 'em back against us," the soldier grumbled.

"Can't say as I blame them," Jones said. "The Egyptian soldiers we massacred back at Tel el-Kebir when we first arrived in Egypt wanted only freedom from Turkish rule, and we put the survivors in chains and sent them down here to the seventh circle of hell to get slaughtered. Joining with the dervishes isn't just about saving their own skins; it's about carrying on their fight against the Ottomans. I'm not saying as we should sympathise with the Mahdi, heaven forefend, sir, but I've seen the Ottoman officials on the way down here and the way they lord it over the Egyptians, and I can see their point."

"The Ottomans are our allies, Corporal Jones," the subaltern said. "Watch what you say."

"Begging your pardon, sir, I'm only saying what Tommy Atkins thinks, that is when he's allowed to think, when he's not digging holes and hauling on ropes and dodging crocodiles."

"Well, from what Major Mayne says about the work ahead, we're going to need a lot more of that. And we can't have you thinking, Jones."

"No, sir. Most definitely not, sir."

Mayne grinned tiredly. "It's not the Egyptians we have to worry about, it's the Mahdists. And they don't yet use firearms as we do in massed volleys, or employ handguns at close quarters."

"Colonel Burnaby put them to rights on that score," Jones said. "He showed them what a pistol in the right hands can do."

Mayne slumped back, suddenly dead tired. At close quarters, a gun was only as good as the speed with which you could reload the chamber, and he knew that any battle with the dervishes would see these soldiers quickly reduced to bayonets and rifle butts and bare hands. He thought again of Burnaby, a man whose legend was matched by his physical stature and deeds. As a subaltern he had wreaked havoc in the officers' messes of Aldershot and London, pushing the boundaries of boisterous play and earning the dislike of senior officers who had dogged his career ever since. He was an officer

in the Household Cavalry, the Blues, a regiment that had
seen no foreign service for decades but afforded its officers five months' leave a year, and therefore scope for
an energetic man with connections to appear on the
spot wherever action was hotting up. This Burnaby did
with flamboyant regularity, finding himself some tenu-
ous attached position that allowed him to exercise his
freewheeling nature while seeking out the thick of the
action. After recovering from his wounds at El Teb, he
had become one of the hotchpotch of officers attached
to the river column, just as Mayne was now; and then he
had found himself a position on Lord Wolseley's staff,
edging ever closer to where they all knew the next flash
point would be, somewhere in the desert on the way to
Khartoum. Burnaby had his admirers, Wolseley among
them, Queen Victoria another, and he was the darling of
the press, the epitome of the military hero in the popular
imagination. But above all he was loved by the men.
Tommy Atkins expected his officer to lead from the
front, and if he did so with the bravura and dash of a
Burnaby, he would follow him anywhere.

Burnaby had another role too, one that had brought
him into contact with Mayne on missions known only
to a select few in the War Office intelligence department.
They had last met in the field four years earlier, during
the final months of the Afghan War, in a desolate frontier outpost in Baluchistan. Forays to Khiva in Russian
Asia and to the eastern frontier of Asia Minor during
the Russo-Turkish war of 1877 had made Burnaby an
expert on the Russian military, a specialisation that
suddenly had huge cachet as Russia and Britain veered
towards a proxy war in Afghanistan. When Mayne
questioned him for the intelligence department in Baluchistan, he found him sharp and perceptive, inclined to
cut to the point, qualities that were paramount for an
intelligence observer in the field.

And Burnaby had been in the Sudan before, using another of his long leaves ten years earlier to report for
The Times on Gordon's first period as governor general

in Khartoum. Mayne wished he could quiz him now on Khartoum and his time with Gordon, but in so doing he might be entering dangerous waters, leaving himself open to questions on his own role that even a fellow intelligence officer was to be denied. Mayne worked only in isolation, answering to one superior alone in the War Office; he never knew whether there were other operatives who were party to his missions, though he suspected it—those sent to take over if he failed, others perhaps tasked to execute the same directive as his own if his mission were to be compromised, to prevent him revealing the truth of a role that would shock the army and the nation if it were ever to come out.

He ran yet again over his own cover story, thinking of everything he had said and done since he had last taken stock, finding no new chinks in his armour. Corporal Jones had suspected that his missions into the desert might be preparation for something bigger, but he had no reason for thinking that it might be anything more than a deeper penetration of the desert ahead of the camel corps that was now assembling at Korti. Among his fellow officers, Mayne was unremarkable, a thirty-eight-year-old whose name had gone steadily up the gradation list until reaching major earlier that year, with none of the brevet promotions and temporary commands that singled out the rising stars. As a Royal Engineer, he was one of a corps of almost a thousand officers posted around the world who had trained and served together and often returned to their headquarters at Chatham for refresher courses and periods of study; as a survey officer specialising in forward reconnaissance, he was known more widely still among the officers of infantry and cavalry and artillery he had served alongside in the field. The utter secrecy of his role was best served by his familiarity as a skilled officer with a reputation for toughness and resilience who would go behind enemy lines and return without making a show of it.

His cover extended as far back as the beginning of his

military career. As a subaltern in 1870, he had been plucked by Wolseley from the School of Military Engineering to join his expedition to Canada against Louis Riel. Back in Chatham, he had been visited by a Captain Wilson from the War Department, who had heard of his survival skills and his exceptional marksmanship, learnt as a boy from the Mohawks, and recruited him for a top-secret role. By the time he met Burnaby in Baluchistan, he had spent almost three years in Central Asia, living in disguise for long stretches in the mountains of the Hindu Kush while the Afghan War raged below, watching and waiting in case the British were routed as they had been forty years before. He had been with Wolseley for the invasion of Egypt in 1882, and with another river expedition in prospect, it was natural that Wolseley should call on him once more. Wilson was here too, acting as Wolseley's intelligence chief. If Mayne were to be activated, there would be no word, no secret conference, just a handshake and a small folded code. Wilson's presence was enough to put him on high alert; he knew that the call he had received to attend Wolseley would decide his role here one way or the other.

He looked at the medal ribbons on the tunic of the soldier nearest to him, among them the Khedive's Star for the invasion of Egypt in 1882. The Khedive was the Egyptian puppet of the Ottoman Turks, the sultanate in Constantinople that ruled an empire stretching from Cairo and Jerusalem to Damascus and Baghdad. The British were forever tottering towards war with the Ottomans, but for the time being they were allies, for as long as the Ottomans provided a buffer against the Russian threat. When the British had invaded Egypt in 1882, it had been to secure their interests in the Suez Canal, to ensure that their new gateway to India was kept open and free from the venality and financial mismanagement of the Ottoman regime in Cairo. Yet after defeating the dissident Egyptian army at Tel el-Kebir, they had propped up the old regime, reinstating the Khedive and ostensibly handing back the reins of power to the Ottomans; they had even supported the Khedive in his renewed attempts to control the Sudan, an exercise that had begun ten years before when the War Office in London had allowed Colonel Charles Gordon to be appointed governor general in Khartoum, supported by the motley collection of European and American adventurers that Gordon gathered around himself.

The Sudan had been the last great bastion of the African slave trade, and Gordon's appointment had met with approval among the moral crusaders of England, among them no less a person than Queen Victoria herself. If anyone could sort it out, it was Gordon, a man of near-suicidal courage who as a young officer had stood exposed on the parapets in the Crimea in order to attract Russian fire and pinpoint enemy positions, and whose Christian fervour seemed to match the growing evangelical mood of the country. Yet as Gordon himself realised soon after taking up his appointment, supporting Ottoman expansionism in the Sudan was a recipe for disaster, with ominous consequences. The slave trade may have been abhorrent to Victorian sensibility, but it was a mainstay of the Sudanese economy and so deeply embedded in tribal loyalties and hierarchies that to suppress it suddenly would require massive military intervention. To the horror of his admirers, Gordon had come out in favour of maintaining the trade in the short term. He had realised that the tribes of Sudan were a complex mosaic of alliances and visceral enmities; the one thing they shared in common was a hatred of Ottoman rule, a hatred that had spread among some to include all outsiders, providing a fertile breeding ground for fundamentalist Islam and a new cry for jihad fanned by the emergence of a charismatic local Sufi known as the Mahdi, the chosen one.

Yet it was Gordon, not the Mahdi, who was now the nub of the problem, and the reason why Mayne was here. The British imperial system that had so often succeeded by giving free rein to talented individualists was also prey to their whims, to their occasional instabilities and bouts of insanity. Much depended on the shared culture of moral decency and gentlemanly behaviour, of unswerving loyalty to Queen and country that allowed the Colonial Office to send out men to administer vast tracts on their own, confident that their discretion and judgement would accord with the wishes of Her Majesty's government. The men who occupied these positions of power with restraint were the genius of the British system, but where restraint fell away, they could be its greatest weakness. With the expansion of the empire, a secret office had been established in Whitehall under the remit of military intelligence to develop a safety net, a series of checks and balances. Much of the work involved intelligence-gathering, character assessment, advice to government on whom to appoint and where, but there was also a contingency for what to do if things went wrong.

For six months now, all eyes had been on Gordon in Khartoum, and everything hung in the balance. The British government had supported the Egyptian Khedive's regime in the Sudan, but Prime Minister Gladstone's new Liberal government had no intention of dispatching a military force of the size that would be required to defeat the Mahdi. There was, however, a need to evacuate Europeans and Egyptian officials and their families from Khartoum, and Gordon was the man for the job. He had seemed to agree to this brief, but then something had gone wrong. He had become increasingly cut off in Khartoum, holed up in the governor's palace. The messages that came out were terse, infrequent, increasingly erratic. Whitehall began to fear the worst. Gordon's highly individual form of Christianity allowed him to empathise with Islam in a way that some found disturbing, to the extent of wondering whether he himself might go over to the Mahdi, as some Europeans captured by the dervishes had done. The prospect was a nightmare for Gladstone's government and would be a catastrophe for Britain's reputation abroad. If rescue were impossible, better that Gordon die a martyr.

Mayne took a swig of water and shut his eyes. He thought of the men below the cliff struggling up the river, the nearly impossible nature of the task; not for the first time he wondered whether there were other forces at play here, whether this excruciating exercise was deliberate, a very public attempt to rescue Gordon that was surely doomed to failure. At the moment, the likely success of the expedition and the nature of his own involvement hung in the balance, but he knew that with the clock ticking and Khartoum starving, something would have to give way very soon.

He himself was as deeply implicated in empire as any of them. His father had been an Irish indigo planter in Behar, in the shadow of the Himalayas. As a small child Mayne had thought nothing of the thousands of men and women they employed like slaves in the crushing mills, and the opiate splendour of their villa and the gardens where he had played. It was the only world he had known, and it seemed the natural order of things. When he was eight, at boarding school in England, his parents and brother and sister had been hacked to death by mutineers of the Bengal Army in Cawnpore, their bodies thrown down with those still living into a well. His beloved ayah had survived long enough to tell the story of their brutal torture and deaths to the British soldiers who had arrived too late to rescue any of them but who had exacted a terrible vengeance. Mayne thought of Burnaby's four-barrelled howdah pistol and the slaughter at El Teb. Any lingering sense of chivalry and sport in war was long gone now, expunged by the Zulu slaughter at Isandlwana and Rorke's Drift, by the bloodbaths of Colonel Hicks's last stand and the Red Sea battles, which could be only a foretaste of what was to come.

He opened his eyes and raised himself up so he could see over the parapet to the ridge opposite. He was looking for a telltale flash of light off a blade or a gun barrel, but he knew that the reconnaissance scouts of the Ansar were too good for that; they had blackened the barrels and receivers of their Remingtons, and with the sun behind them on that ridge they would give off no reflection. He squatted on his knees, keeping his head below the parapet, feeling better after his rest. The soldier tending the fire below the billycan took his pipe out of his mouth and spoke. "General Wolseley came to talk to us last week. He claimed that no number of dervishes could withstand the smallest of our columns."

"Bosh," exclaimed Jones, propping himself up from where he had been lying against the parapet. "Hicks's army of ten thousand two years ago was annihilated. *Annihilated.* All the wounded were murdered with those spears, and the prisoners they took had their eyes gouged out and their manhoods ripped off before being crucified, when the dogs ate them alive. I heard it myself from a Dongolese who had been there and seen it all."

Mayne tightened his bootstraps and paused. It sounded like a typical soldier's exaggeration, except that it was true. "Hicks's army was made up of Egyptian conscripts, fellahin from the Nile valley," he said. "About the least likely soldiers you can imagine, and terrified of the desert. Quite a few of them had been in the rebel Egyptian army that we defeated at Tel el-Kebir when we first invaded Egypt in '83, and some of them were still prisoners in chains when they were conscripted for the Sudan. But we have to hope that Wolseley is right. After all, he was talking about British soldiers. About the best. About soldiers like you, Jones."

Jones stiffened. "Johnny Fuzzy-Wuzzy won't take me without a fight."

"Indeed. Now let's get cracking and set up a fire position on that parapet. I want to be ready when the sun drops out of our eyes and we can see that ridge clearly."

CHAPTER 7

MAYNE LAY AGAINST THE PARAPET OVER-looking the Nile and extended his telescope. High above him he heard the sound of birds flying north, huge flocks of flamingos migrating from the desiccated marshlands below Khartoum, a whistling and whoosh-ing that followed the flow of the river rather than work-ing against it, as the expedition was. For a moment he felt a chill down his spine, as if he were watching the remaining life force of that place bleeding away past him. He shook off the thought and scanned the opposite cliff top with his telescope, tracing the jagged line of rock from the crag where the signallers had set up the heliograph to the farthest point he could see in the dust haze to the south, well beyond rifle range. The after-noon sun was arching west and framed the line of the ridge with absolute clarity, but made it impossible to see through the cracks and gaps where Mahdist sharp-shooters might be lurking. He lowered the telescope and shaded his eyes. In this light all they could hope to see was a puff of smoke, and that would give them less than a second before the bullet whined overhead or smacked into the rock, or into one of them. Shaytan had told him that some of the Madhi's men had become highly profi-cient with their Remingtons, and they would have the advantage of the sun behind them. Mayne realised that he might be watching and waiting interminably. He would give it half an hour longer, until the sun had dropped below the level of the hills on the horizon, and then he would leave the sangar and make his way down the scree slope below the cliff towards the river.

He left the two sentries at the parapet and slid down a crack in the ancient masonry wall that concealed him from the opposite cliff but gave a clear view of the scene below. A pair of rocks jutting out into the river formed a natural gateway into the cataract, constricting the river to a muddy torrent as it flowed into the pool where the whaleboats were collecting. Confronting the torrent was a solitary man in a canoe inching his way up against the flow, a hawser line coiled behind him. Once he had made it through, he would find a place to tie the rope off, and then teams of men would use it to haul up the whaleboats, dozens of which were now milling below the cataract, waiting their turn to follow. Mayne could tell that the man in the canoe was a voyageur from his measured stroke along one side of the boat, the paddle twisted each time to act as a rudder, rather than the frantic paddling from side to side of the British soldiers, who had little idea how to control a canoe. He well remembered his own first efforts as a nine-year-old boy on the Ottawa River, and that moment when he suddenly realised he was one with the boat, that he could use it as an extension of himself.

As he watched the voyageur work his way up the torrent, unswerving and utterly focused, he saw a man on the jutting rock above him hurl a stone trailing a thin line to the rock on the opposite side, where it was caught by another man and then passed to a team of sailors, who hauled across a thick hawser that had been attached to the line, then looped it around a rock and made it fast. At the same time, a procession of soldiers stripped to the waist, followed by West African Kroomen, shiny black and wearing only loincloths, made their way up among the rocks to the point where the canoeist would shortly attach his rope, beyond the torrent and in the first pool above the rapids that would provide the next staging post. On a rock above it all, the sergeant major in charge of today's efforts had positioned himself ready to bellow orders and encouragement as the first whale-boat was brought into position. After weeks of trial and error they had brought the procedure to a fair state of perfection, but even so every day brought new challenges, new obstacles to overcome in the rocky bed of the river, and all the time the level of the Nile was dropping inexorably, making any kind of progress a challenge at best.

Mayne recognised the man who had hurled the line as his friend Charrière, the foreman of the Mohawks. He was wearing the corduroy trousers and checked shirt that Wolseley had provided for them, and his long black hair was braided down his back. Among the Mohawks, Charrière was known by his Iroquoian name, Teonihuapataman, meaning "he whose blood flows like the river," but he also bore the French name he had inherited from his grandfather, a voyageur who could trace his ancestry back to the first adventurers from France who'd gone to the New World more than two centuries before. As part of the Iroquois Confederacy, the Mohawks had fought alongside the British in the American War of Independence, and again in the war of 1812, but since then their reputation for brutality had softened as they intermingled with the Algonquian people of the Ottawa valley, becoming voyageurs in the fur trade and log men on the river. To Mayne, though, who had lived with them and watched them hunt and explore, they still had an edge to them, men whose forefathers had been steeped in the blood of savage war.

Mayne remembered Charrière's disquiet when they had met again on the Red River expedition. Mayne had been away at school and then at the military academy in England, and he had cut the long hair that he had grown as a boy. To the Mohawks, hair retained memories, and to cut it was to sever a link with a past in which Mayne had been adopted into the tribe and shared the coming-of-age rituals with Charrière as they became adolescents. Their friendship had endured and had been rekindled here in this most unlikely of places, but there had been a distance between them; Charrière had never again called him by the Mohawk name that Mayne had been given as a boy.

He watched a sailor curl his body around the hawser and begin to pull himself across the gorge towards Charrière, inching his way over the torrent. On Charrière's belt he could see the coiled *kurbash,* the hippo-hide whip that Shaytan had given him when he joined Mayne on a previous foray into the desert. It had belonged to Shaytan's ancestors, passed down from distant antiquity; in return, Charrière had given him a polished stone mace head he carried in his leather bag, a weapon his grandfather had used during the American War of Independence. Where the whip had once had a metal tip, long since rusted away, Charrière had spliced in a razor-sharp flint he had brought from Canada.

Something had distracted Charrière's attention from the sailor on the hawser. Mayne watched him unhitch the whip from his belt and uncoil it, and then saw the tip flicker across the pool below and snap against the surface, causing a ripple to spread out towards the boats around the edge. Mayne raised his telescope and trained it on the pool, uncertain whether he had seen a dark shape beneath the muddy surface where the whip had struck. Two shots rang out from below, the bullets hissing into the water to no obvious effect. No one had yet with certainty seen a crocodile in this pool, but the soldiers believed one was lurking there, making washing and drawing water a hazardous enterprise. Mayne was not entirely convinced, but it was another reason why he had decided to forgo any attempt to cleanse himself before setting out for Wolseley's camp at Korti.

Jones came up beside him and peered down. "I'm sure I saw it," he said in a hushed voice. "It's the monster the Sudanese river men talk about."

"You can't be sure," Mayne said. "It could have been a whirlpool or one of those giant river carp."

Jones shut his eyes, reciting. " 'When he raiseth himself up, the mighty are afraid. Round about his teeth is terror. In his neck abideth strength, and terror danceth before him. His neesings flash forth light, and his eyes are like the eyelids of the morning. Upon earth there is not his like, that is made without fear.' The leviathan, sir, from the Book of Job."

Mayne lifted his eyebrows. "You remember that well. You've missed your vocation. You should have been a preacher."

"The leviathan's not some ancient mythic creature, sir, it's a crocodile. That word *neesings,* in King James's time it meant snortings, well almost. I recited it to our Egyptian interpreter, and he said that's what crocodiles do; they have a habit of inflating themselves and discharging heated vapour through their nostrils in a snorting kind of way, and in the sunlight it sparkles."

"It seems you've become a natural historian too. You ought to take care. Natural history and preaching rarely mix, I find. Your congregation will want the fire-spitting dragon of the deep, Satan at hell's mouth."

"It's that picture Mr. Tanner showed me, sir. I just can't get it out of my head."

Mayne turned back to the river, amused. One of the officers, Lieutenant Tanner, the engineer in charge of the boatbuilding detachment, had brought along a small library of Greek and Latin literature dealing with the Nile, and one evening the more literary among the officers had amused themselves looking up references to crocodiles in Pliny and Plutarch and Herodotus. Several of them, including Mayne, had left the expedition camp on the way south through Egypt to explore Akhenaten's capital at Amarna and had been shown a towering image of the crocodile god Sobek carved into a rock face. Since then it had been imperative among the more sporting officers to bag one, as yet to no avail. Mayne had invited Jones to join them that evening because of his encyclopedic knowledge of the Bible, virtually the only literature he had been exposed to as a boy, and he had quoted those lines from memory. As the port wine flowed and he grew bolder, he told them a story he had heard of how a giant Nile crocodile thrashing its tail to pick up speed had leapt on land and chased a woman up a tree, and then dragged her down and into the water, never to be seen again. Tanner had gone one better and pulled out a print cut from *The Life and Explorations of David Livingstone,* hot off the press when he had left London; entitled *"A Frightful Incident,"* it showed a voluptuous naked woman swooning on her back on a rocky islet in the Nile, a crocodile the size of a dinosaur poised as if to ravish her. Jones had sat speechless, staring at the image with his mouth open, and then had rushed with it down to his mates around the fires a safe distance from the river, all of them in equal measure terrified of crocodiles and starved of female company in the six weeks since they had been allowed to visit the dens of Cairo on the voyage south.

There was a yell from the rocks, and Mayne looked back at the gorge. The sailor crossing the hawser had slipped and was hanging by his hands, his feet bouncing off the torrent below. The hawsers had been taken from Royal Navy ships at Alexandria and were impregnated with tar, a constant problem as the scorching sun melted it into a slippery mess. With another yell he dropped into the torrent and disappeared, swept into the pool below. Charrière kicked off his boots and dived in after him, arching powerfully off the rock and plunging in close to where the dark shape had appeared. It was not the first time he had rescued sailors of dubious swimming ability, but this time Mayne knew there was a special imperative: just out of sight downriver was a vicious whirlpool that would suck anyone caught in it to their death. He quickly scanned the edges of the river, hoping that the crocodile, if that was what it was, had been given enough of a bloody nose by the whip to keep out of the way.

Charrière and the sailor surfaced simultaneously, the man thrashing and yelling, and Charrière grabbed him by his chin and began to swim hard across the pool. He did not try to fight the current but let it take him, edging diagonally towards the far shore, reaching a rock just before he would have been swept beyond Mayne's sight. A cluster of soldiers who had been running along the bank abreast of them reached in and pulled the two men out, lay the sailor down, and left Charrière to strip off his shirt and walk back towards the boats.

It was an unremarkable incident, repeated every day or two in some form as they toiled up the Nile, but Mayne was thankful that his friend had not given his life in such a trivial way only hours before he was due in front of Wolseley; the message Mayne had received in the desert had also told him to bring Charrière along. Yet these episodes seemed like a warning, a reminder that the river was not just an impediment but was also treacherous, lethal; it was as if the Nile itself were pushing them to turn with the flow and go north like the birds, to leave this land where river and desert ruled all. Mayne had heard the Mohawks talk about it among themselves in Iroquoian, not wanting the English to overhear, but he remembered enough of the language to understand. Many of them had already left the expedition, their contract with Wolseley having expired, and only a few of those who remained wished to stay longer. They had said that with each cataract they felt slower, heavier, as if the earth itself were pulling them in, and to go farther would be to reach places where men who fell into the water would no longer be rescued, where the invisible enemy along the cliffs would make the river into a gauntlet of death, where they would pass into another, darker world from which few could ever return.

He took another swig from the bottle. With the worst of his thirst now slaked, he could let the water linger in his mouth, and he tasted the mud of the Nile. It was always a risk drinking water from the river; it was less safe than water you had drawn yourself from a well but safer

than water offered to you by a stranger, water that might
be tainted. In the desert, it was no slight on hospitality to
refuse an offer of water from a passerby, and to wait instead until the next well or cistern. The river water he was
drinking had washed past Gordon, had drained something from Khartoum, though whether it was lifeblood or
something malign, a seeping poison, he could not tell. He
stared at the pool where Charrière had rescued the man,
trying to see through the depths as a Mohawk would, to
sense the shape of the riverbed. He had often wondered
what it was like beneath, whether it still harboured any
of the history that had passed this way or whether it was
just a rush of blackness over a scoured bottom, everything cleansed by the annual flood that irrigated Egypt
and kept the river uncluttered by human debris. Shaytan
had told him that only when the river had been tamed
would the land to the south ever be conquered by outsiders, or the forces unleashed by the Mahdi spill out to
the north and threaten the world beyond. It was only the
saying of an old Sufi mystic, but it held a kernel of truth,
and that truth was the advent of new technology: just as
plans were afoot to build a dam at Aswan to control the
Nile, so railways were being driven ever farther south
into the desert from Egypt and the Red Sea that would
allow an army to move in rapidly, and at the same time
provide weapons and communication that would enable
the jihadists to break free from their medieval world and
spread their fire to places that many of those with the
Mahdi today scarcely knew existed.

When he had first arrived in the Sudan, Mayne had
been taken by the extraordinary clarity of the gorge, as
if the water that had swept away the sand to reveal the
carapace of rock beneath had also cleansed the air above
the river, leaving it visible from a distance as a shimmering, glistening snake coiling its way through the desert
from the lowering darkness to the south. In the early
weeks, when he had little to do, he had occupied his
time making sketches of the river column, sending them
to the *Illustrated London News,* where they had been

inked up and published as the work of an anonymous officer. Those images had given the British public what Wolseley had wanted them to see: visions of heroic endeavour, of soldiers and sailors and colonials working together for a noble cause, of the allure and danger of the desert beyond.

Then, the limpid air had seemed to extend far over the river to the south, magnifying everything and foreshortening the distance they had to cover, drawing them on in a fever of activity. Now he saw the illusion for what it was; it felt as if they had been seduced, lured deep into the desert by a promise on the horizon that was forever receding, as if in a bad dream. The air beyond the cataract was obscured by the same sand mist he had seen in the desert, and the silvery stream of clarity had been reduced to a bubble above the men and the boats, one that seemed to close in the farther they went on; it was as if the light they had taken with them as they pressed south could no longer penetrate the dust and obscurity, and now only illuminated their own toil. He felt that if an ill wind from the south were to sweep over the scene and obscure it, he would look again and they would all be gone, swept from history like the ancient army of the pharaohs whose traces remained only where they had carved their marks deep into the rocks of the river gorge.

"Major Mayne, sir." Jones lay down beside him again. "The boat looks close to being ready. Seems your friend got there a bit faster than he might have liked."

Mayne glanced towards the river. Charrière had made his way along the shore to the landing point where the boat had been repaired and was now wading around it in the water, inspecting the hull. Mayne raised his telescope and peered along the cliffs yet again, still seeing nothing. He felt uneasy, but there was nothing he could do. With the whaleboats now assembling in greater numbers, a sharpshooter could have his choice of targets; with more troops coming into the camp, he might be waiting until more senior officers appeared. General Earle fortunately was out of the picture, having left to join Wolseley at

Korti the day before. And it was always possible that
there was no sharpshooter at all, that the movements they
had seen among the rocks were mere tricks of the light or
perhaps curious local tribesmen, not necessarily with anyone in their sights. Even if there were a danger and Mayne
could make a difference, it was only a matter of time before they would scout ahead and see not just a solitary
marksman but a horizon filled with dervish spears and
banners. The soldiers in the sangar beside him who had
only ever heard Corporal Jones tell of battle would soon
experience the full horror for themselves. That was to
be their war; his was to be another, far to the south. He
knew that Jones could look after himself, whether in the
thick of battle or more sensibly occupied in support work.
He would have a word with Tanner before leaving to
ensure that the corporal was attached to an engineer company, to keep him from being remustered as infantry
when the time came for a fight.

He rolled against the parapet and stared back out over
the desert. The pellucid light of the early morning when
he had woken at the wells with Shaytan had given way
to a dusty haze, a mist of sand that lay low over the
desert floor; it seemed to cut off anything that rose above
it, leaving the pyramidal outcrops he had seen earlier
hanging in the distance like a mirage, and his camel
standing fifty yards away partly disembodied, as if its
head were peering above a diaphanous veil of red. It was
a disconcerting effect, part reality, part mirage, but it
was also alluring, and he could see how men had been
tempted to ride off into the desert and disappear, caught
in an embrace that only those who knew what they were
seeking and had learned its ways could survive.

The heliograph flashed above the opposite bank, and
he snapped back to reality. He turned to the river and
saw that the boat was now being rowed out, tested
by the sappers who had repaired it. He peered at the line
of the cliff one last time. He could not wait any longer
and he would have to take his chances. He retracted the
telescope, put it in its case, and slung it round his neck

beside the binoculars, then handed the Martini-Henry rifle and the cartridge box to Jones. "Take this. It's the most accurate rifle the engineer quartermaster could find for me when I arrived. It's sighted for four hundred yards over the river."

"Nobody up here could take a shot like that except you, sir."

"Then you'll need to keep your heads down." He stooped over and picked up the khaki bag that Jones had been looking after for him, checking that it was wrapped and secure.

Jones watched him, his voice hesitant. "So you really are leaving us for good, sir?"

Mayne paused. "I don't know. But look out for me."

"Sir." The subaltern offered his hand, and Mayne shook it. "We'll be on guard next time, sir. The next time a British officer appears out of the desert disguised as an Arab."

Mayne turned to Jones. "That reminds me. My camel."

"Sir?"

"I won't be needing her again. She's yours."

Jones stared at Mayne, then out at the chewing, grunting form beyond the parapet, then back at Mayne, his face a picture of horror. "But *sir*."

"A little desert grass, some water. You'll find she's very loyal. Once you feed her, she won't look at any other man. And if you get cold at night, hobble her and snuggle up tight. You won't notice the smell after a while."

The Irish soldier jostled Jones. "Go on, Jonesy. You was telling us how good you was with the Egyptian ladies in Cairo. Well, here's one for you now, and a chance for you to show us what you're worth."

Jones's face had turned from horror to despair. Mayne grinned at him, then picked up his saddlebag and slung the khaki wrap over his back, feeling the hard wooden case inside, and turned towards the parapet.

He had delayed long enough.

He needed to leave now.

CHAPTER 8

"GET DOWN, SIR!"
There was a crack as a bullet whined by, so
close that the air it displaced pushed Mayne off balance
and sent him tripping and stumbling back into the sangar. The report of the gunshot echoed and rumbled
down the gorge below, and he heard yells and commands from the men on the river as they took cover. He
quickly doffed his bags and crawled to the parapet
beside Jones, who handed back the rifle he had taken
from him only moments before. The other soldiers
had dropped what they were doing and crouched with
their heads under the parapet. The sound of the report
had come about half a second behind the bullet; for a
.43 calibre Remington that meant the shooter was about
four hundred yards away, perhaps five hundred over the
river where the air was cooler and less dense, slowing
the bullet by a fraction. He twisted his head to one side,
listening as another bullet whined by. He could also
gauge the distance a Remington bullet had travelled by
its noise, whether a snap or a buzz or a whine, and what
he heard confirmed his estimate: four hundred, perhaps
four hundred and fifty yards, exactly the distance from
the ridge opposite where he had expected a sharpshooter
to appear. He whipped out his telescope and trained it
on the ridge. Another bullet whined over, followed by

another sharp report, the noise overlaying the distant echoes of the previous report and resounding through the gorge. He lowered the telescope, searching for the telltale puff of white smoke. Another shot rang out, but he could see nothing. The man had waited until there was enough haze coming off the desert to obscure the smoke, and until the sun was directly behind him, dazzling any onlookers from the opposite bank. He was good, too good to allow himself to be caught by the soldiers who would already be clambering up the rocks from below to search for him, but likely to hold his ground until he had inflicted serious casualties among the men by the river or here in the sangar.

"It's a harassing fire," the subaltern said, his voice high-pitched with excitement and fear. "They can't be aiming at us individually from that far off."

"There's only one of them," Mayne replied. "The dervish sharpshooters only work alone, like any good marksmen. And I wouldn't be sure it's just harassing fire. He's going to get his range soon enough, and then we might be in for some trouble."

The subaltern slid farther down into the sangar, holding his helmet on to his head. "What do you propose to do?"

"He's using the sun behind him as cover, but he's left it a little late in the day. Pretty soon the sun will drop and we might have a chance of seeing him on that ridge. Until then we sit tight."

"Do you intend to have a go? At this range?"

Mayne pursed his lips, looking at the others. "Everybody hold their fire. I'll have only one chance. As soon as he knows we've spotted his position, he'll be gone and that'll be it." He glanced at the wrapped box and then dispelled the thought. The Sharps was more accurate at a longer range, but he had yet to sight it in, and to use it now would be to compromise himself, to open himself to questioning that he did not want. The Martini-Henry would be at the limit of its effectual range, but he had got to know its foibles in the desert, and he felt confident with it. He glanced through the crack in the parapet masonry and saw the men of the river column running around and diving for cover, sheltering behind rocks and overhangs, the sentries fixing bayonets and holding their rifles at the ready, blindly scanning the rocks above them. He glanced at the subaltern, who had taken out his revolver and was gripping it hard, his knuckles white and his hand shaking, popping his head up to look and then quickly slipping down again, breathing fast and hard. Mayne opened up his cartridge box. "At the moment he's targeting us because he knows he's got us at a disadvantage in this light, and it's always good to put the wind up a sentry post like this so that the men inside keep their heads down and fail to see what's coming next."

"What do you mean?" asked the subaltern, alarm in his eyes. "The Mahdi army?"

Mayne grunted, not listening, eyeing the river again. "We don't want him shifting his position behind a rock where we can't see him but he can shoot at the river column below. Their progress is slow enough as it is, but being under fire will seize it up completely. The Kroomen and voyageurs are not members of Her Majesty's armed forces, and I doubt whether being shot at was in their contract with Wolseley."

"How long?" asked the subaltern, his voice hoarse.

Mayne narrowed his eyes, looking towards the orb of the sun to the west, beyond the ridge. He remembered the days he had spent with Shaytan, observing everything about the desert, learning to gauge the remaining daylight by the position of the sun above the horizon, a crucial survival skill. He had needed to prepare himself for what might lie ahead in the days and weeks to come, but it was paying off here as well. "About half an hour," he murmured. "We need to catch him just as the sun drops and before he realises he's visible. That might be a matter of moments."

The subaltern had slid down the sloping edge of the parapet on his back and was now gripping the revolver with both hands, trying to control his shaking. "I'm going to watch the desert on this side. He could be distracting us while others sneak up from the east."

Mayne looked at the subaltern, a terrified young man under fire for the first time, his back to the enemy, trying to convince himself and his soldiers that he was not a coward. Every soldier had to go through his trial by fire, and it was especially hard in the sangar, where there was nothing they could do except wait. "All right," he said. "Corporal Jones, watch the southern flank."

Mayne trained his telescope on the opposite cliff once more, seeing only the glare of the sun, then lowered it and turned over, his back against the parapet. Two of the soldiers were still crouched at the rear of the sangar, vulnerable to bullets that would be falling in an arched trajectory at this range, and he waved them urgently forward, making space so that they could squeeze up alongside him. Another bullet whined overhead and struck a rock, moaning like a spent firework as it tumbled off into the distance. The rock was only yards from where his camel stood in open view, munching away oblivious to the danger. He thought for a moment. Exposing himself would be an additional risk, but he was sure the marksman had not yet pinpointed the range well enough to shoot accurately. He would need to hit a visible target before he had done that, and repeat his point of aim. Mayne turned to Jones. "I'm going out. I won't be long."

Jones stared at him, horrified. "Where?"

"The camel. *Your* camel. A good camel like that's worth its weight in gold."

Jones seemed incapable of response. Mayne crawled to the ancient masonry wall at the far end of the sangar, quickly vaulted over, and ran below the ridgeline of the cliff until he was some thirty yards away and about the same distance from the camel. He dropped below a slight rise in the plateau that put him out of sight of the opposite side of the river, then threw himself flat, hugging the ground, and crawled across on his elbows. Just

as he came within range, the beast emptied its bowels
in a vile spray, filling the air with a brown mist; then
it bent its neck round, staring down at him with that
expression of disdain and indifference unique to the
camel. A bullet struck with a deadening thud somewhere
in its midriff, only a few feet above Mayne's head. He
rolled over just as another whined by, and saw where
the first bullet had embedded itself and flattened into the
camel's harness, the bone-dry leather already beginning
to smoulder with the heat of the lead. He whacked the
harness with one hand to extinguish it and swivelled
round to kick the camel hard behind its front right knee,
bringing it down with a groan on its forelegs. He quickly
did the same to the hind legs, then took a coil of braided
leather rope from the harness to hobble it. The camel
was still vulnerable to falling bullets and ricochets, but
at least it was no longer a visible target. He crawled back
the way he had come, feeling the brush of air as another
round buzzed past. The marksman was getting better;
these seemed more like targeted shots. He reached the
wall and leapt over, then quickly crawled up beside
Jones and peered out through the embrasure in the parapet. Jones stared at him, wincing and going red in the
face, then let out a loud exhalation. Mayne stared,
alarmed. "Are you all right? Are you hit?"

"No, sir." The voice sounded strangulated. "It's you,
sir. It was bad enough when you first joined us; now it's
a lot worse. That smell, sir. That *stench*."

Mayne sniffed, smelling nothing, and then glanced at
the sleeve of his tunic, seeing the spatter of brown. "Ah.
Occupational hazard for the cameleer, I'm afraid. You're
going to have to get used to that, Corporal Jones."

He positioned his rifle against the parapet and took a
round from the ammunition pouch, examining it carefully, and wiped around the narrow upper end of the
brass case that clenched the bullet to ensure that it was
free from dirt. He pulled down the lever of the rifle to
open the breech, put the cartridge on the loading block,
and pushed it home with his thumb, then closed the

breech with the lever. As there was no safety on the Martini-Henry, it was now cocked and ready to fire. He lay on his front, nestled against the edge of the embrasure, and slid the rifle out until the muzzle was resting on the parapet, invisible to an observer four hundred or more yards away; then he shouldered it and aimed along the sights, traversing across the stretch of ridge where he would have positioned himself had he been the sharpshooter, where the profile was broken up by jagged spurs and ridges that would provide good concealment. He relaxed, breathing in deeply a few times, focusing his mind, remembering how good he had always felt when he had a target in his sights and knew he could kill, how it had made him feel when he had first done it and all the grief and anger at the death of his parents and brother and sister had finally seemed to lift from him, if only for a precious moment.

"Sir, I'm going for ammunition." He heard the Irish soldier speak to the subaltern, and then a shuffling noise as the man crawled across to the stack of gear at the back of the sangar. He felt uneasy for a moment, knowing that the man would be vulnerable to a bullet on an arching trajectory, but he was in position now and did not want to lose his concentration, even to shout out a warning. The sun was dropping, and he knew he would have only one chance.

Suddenly there was a deafening metallic clang beside him. A bullet had smashed into the receiver of the rifle of the soldier next to him and ricocheted off in fragments, peppering the loose folds of his tunic but miraculously missing flesh. The soldier knelt up, stunned, head and shoulders above the parapet, and Jones screamed at him to get down, but it was too late. A bullet burst out from him in a spray of blood and shredded cloth, and he fell backwards with a neat black hole in the front of his neck, his eyes wide open and lifeless. Behind him Mayne heard the sickening thump of lead striking flesh, and then another few seconds later, followed by a blood-curdling cry and a string of Anglo-Saxon curses. He kept focused on the ridge, his right forefinger feathering the trigger, panning the rifle in a tiny arc to cover the twenty to thirty metres of cliff where he thought the shooter would be. Another round whined overhead and crashed into the rock behind. The sharpshooter had got their range and was firing fast, dropping rounds into the sangar as quickly as he could work the lever of his rifle and reload. Mayne knew that this was his chance: there would be small movements in the rocks, moments of incaution as the shooter exposed himself, misplaced confidence that there could be nobody opposite to match his skill.

He sensed something different, a barely perceptible change in the light. He blinked, and it was still there. *The sun had dropped.* And then he saw it, a minuscule wobbly reflection among the rocks, the white of a head-dress, a briefly elevated rifle barrel. He held himself steady, staring down the sights, both eyes open, focusing on the target. There was no wind, and he could aim dead-on. He adjusted infinitesimally to the left, an instinct, no more, and then slowly exhaled until there was nothing left, and squeezed the trigger. The rifle jumped and cracked, and through the smoke he saw the figure rise upwards as if standing, but then crumple sideways and hang headfirst over the ledge in front of him, arms dangling, blood gushing and splatting down the cliff and his rifle falling to the rocks beneath.

He was conscious of a ragged cheer from the men by the river below. He barely felt the need to breathe, and when he did so it was as if he had taken a lung full of the strongest tobacco, leaving his heart pounding and the blood rushing to his head. It had been a long time since he had done that. He let go of the rifle and turned to look at the scene in the sangar. The man who had been beside him was lying on his back in a pool of blood, already coagulating and dotted with flies. The other two bullets had hit the same man, the Irish soldier who had gone back for more ammunition. He was surrounded by a group of men, with his trousers torn off, his legs drenched with blood and shaking convulsively. One round had ploughed into a calf, shearing off the muscle and leaving it curled up in a lurid yellow and red mass below his knee. The other had gone through both thighs and severed the arteries, leaving him bleeding to death in agony. The subaltern was propping his head up while the other men worked feverishly to staunch the blood, Jones holding his hand and feeding him dribbles of water from his bottle. The soldier was moaning and weeping, his face deathly grey and contorted, his lips saying something that only the subaltern could hear. Mayne could have told him that he had got the man who had shot him, but it seemed irrelevant. He swung open the loading lever on the rifle to eject the spent cartridge, and then closed it up and laid it beside Jones's gear. He watched as the man's face relaxed and his eyelids drooped and his breathing became a rasping, snoring rattle, and then he was dead.

The subaltern remained hunched over, unable to move, and the two men beside his legs sat back, their arms and tunics dripping blood. Jones got up and came over to him, offering the water bottle. Mayne took it gratefully, drinking in great gulps, feeling suddenly very much alive. "That was a good shot, sir," Jones said, eyeing him. "Not even the Afghans could shoot like that."

Mayne wiped his mouth and handed the bottle back. "It's what we soldiers are out here for, isn't it, Jones? To kill the enemy."

"Kill the enemy," Jones repeated thoughtfully. "That's right, sir. To kill the enemy." He jerked his head towards the others in the sangar, all of them sitting in various stages of shock, two of them with their heads in their hands. "Don't worry about them, sir. I well remember the first time it happened to me, when a mate died in my arms. It was at Maiwand in Afghanistan, back in '80. Now there was a battle for you."

"I know. I was there. In the mountains, watching."

"Forward reconnaissance, sir?"

"Something like that."

Jones paused. "I'll tell my story to the others, then."

Mayne picked up his bags again and shouldered them. "I'd give it a while. Let them get over this little battle first."

"This time you're leaving for good, sir?"

"The boat's waiting, and I've already lost time. There's nothing more I can do here. I'll pass the word to send up a burial detachment. And Jones?"

"Sir?"

Mayne jerked his head towards the recumbent snorting form in the desert. "Don't forget."

Jones closed his eyes for a moment. "Sir."

"She's hobbled by her back legs. You'll need to take a bayonet to cut her loose."

Jones eyed him suspiciously. "Rear legs means rear end, right? Up close?"

Mayne took out his head scarf and tossed it over. "Wear this. It'll protect you."

Jones caught it, sighed, and then held out his hand. "Godspeed, sir."

Mayne shook it. "And to you." He shifted his load and started up the edge of the parapet. It had been a half-hour delay that he could ill afford, but he felt better for it. His mind was sharp, focused, and everything he had been doing over the past weeks, the preparation in the desert, suddenly seemed worthwhile. He was itching to be downriver at Korti and ready for whatever Wolseley had planned for him.

CHAPTER 9

Mayne PICKED HIS WAY OVER THE PARAPET and began to descend the rough path the soldiers had made up the slope from the river, scrambling down the rocky abutments that became more sharply angled the closer they were to the cliff face on his right. The friable rock of the plateau gave way to the hard igneous substrate of the river gorge, providing a surer footing as he followed the small piles of rock the soldiers had made to mark the trail. At the base of the rocky outcrop was a sandy scree slope angled at forty-five degrees towards the river and curving round to the base of the cliff about a hundred yards from the water's edge. As he began to slip and slide down the sand, he saw two men making their way in his direction among the boulders between the river and the base of the scree, occasionally stopping to watch his progress. They were both officers, dressed in khaki and pith helmets, and as he neared them he recognised Lieutenant Tanner of the engineer detachment and Major Ormerod, the commander of the voyageurs. He came to a halt in a cloud of dust in front of them, then unslung his saddlebag and the khaki wrap and laid them on the sand. Ormerod, a burly Scotsman with a handlebar moustache, proffered his hand. "Christ, Edward, you look as if you've been through the wars."

"Just the desert." He shook hands with both of them

and then drew his fingers over the matted mass of his hair. He regretted now giving Corporal Jones his head scarf; he would get another at Korti. He jerked his head up towards the top of the slope. "They need a burial detail."

"It's on its way," Tanner said. "We saw the soldier at the parapet get hit. A damned poor show."

"There are two dead," Mayne said, uncorking his water bottle and sipping from it, then squinting at the river, where Charrière was still up to his waist beside the boat. He gulped, wiped his mouth, and pointed towards him. "He should watch out for the crocodile."

"It won't attack him," Tanner said. "Not after he gave it a bloody nose with his whip."

"You saw it?"

"I know it's there. We all do."

"The moment it rears its ugly snout, it's mine," Ormerod said gruffly. "I've got a double-barrelled express rifle mounted on a tripod overlooking that pool, and a servant watching day and night. I don't want my voyageurs to return home and say one of their number was taken by a leviathan of the deep. That would be the last time we'd see them on an imperial adventure, and probably the last time we'd see them in church. The Mohawks would probably put their buckskins on and disappear back into the forests."

Mayne capped his water bottle. "Corporal Jones is convinced that the leviathan of the Bible was not a satanic monster but a Nile crocodile."

"That's bad enough," Ormerod grumbled. "A twelve-foot killing machine."

"And you?" Tanner asked.

Mayne looked at him. "Me?"

"What do you think?"

Mayne paused. "I think this expedition needs to disencumber itself of as much baggage as possible, and I think we are in danger of being weighed down by a leviathan of the mind."

Ormerod grunted, then gestured towards the cliff top. "If that was you, it was a hell of a shot, Mayne. The

Mohawks talk about your shooting from the Red River expedition, but that's the first time I've seen it."

"Service rifle, that's all," Mayne said. "It shows what our soldiers could do if we trained them properly in long-distance marksmanship." He reslung his water bottle and reached for his bags, but Ormerod put out a hand to stay him. "There's something we want you to see first. At the base of the cliff."

"Jones told me. But I don't have time."

"You've got half an hour. The boat leaked during the trial, and Charrière's caulking it with some foul mixture the Dongolese concocted from camel dung and grass. There's nothing you can do to help, so you might as well take a look."

Mayne glanced at the green-brown smudges from his camel's greeting on his tunic mingling with the dark spots of blood from the soldier who had been shot beside him. He had probably had enough of camel dung for one day. "All right. But let's make it quick."

He followed them about twenty yards along the base of the cliff, stopping where a cluster of shovels and picks had been leant against the rock beside a portable gas lantern. Tanner, in the lead, pointed to an opening about two yards wide and a yard deep, evidently revealed by recent digging. It was the upper part of an ancient doorway hewn out of the living rock. He picked up the lamp and sat on the sand, then slid himself feet first into the entrance. "It was completely buried when we arrived, but one of the officers' dogs got up here and dug his way to the slab covering the entrance," he said, his voice edged with excitement. "I don't think it had been opened up since the time of the pharaohs. Follow me."

Mayne sat down on the sand beside Ormerod and they pushed themselves in after Tanner, ducking under the rock. It was suddenly cool, so much so that Mayne caught his breath, and the air was damp. They were on a slope of sand that had evidently poured into the chamber since it had been opened, cascading down to the floor and nearly filling it. Inside, the only light came from the narrow slit at the entrance, and as they slid farther down they descended into gloom.

"There's about two feet of water at the bottom," Tanner said from ahead of them, his voice sounding distant and hollow. "It's below the level of the Nile, and would have been in antiquity too. I think it was deliberately built that way. The water's surprisingly clear, and I'm sure there's a lower entranceway buried under the sand that must come out on the edge of that pool in the river, though I haven't found it yet."

Mayne caught a waft of gas as Tanner opened up the lamp, and heard the clicking of the flint as he tried to ignite it. The hiss turned to a roar and suddenly they were bathed in orange light, too dazzling to see anything. Tanner turned down the flame until it was white, and then Mayne could make out the walls, their own forms looming as shadows cast by the lamplight, giant and overarching. The chamber was about the size of the nave of an English country church. Where the walls had been cut from sedimentary rock, it was eroded and covered in green slime, but the right side directly in front of Mayne was black basalt, polished smooth and free from growth.

He stared at what he suddenly saw, astonished. "Good God," he murmured. He took the lantern from Tanner and slid down the sand closer to the wall, sloshing in the cold water that filled the edges of the chamber. The wall was covered in relief carving, deeply etched into the stone. He put his hand on it, feeling the cool, clammy surface, and drew his fingers along the lines. He remembered from his geology instruction at the School of Military Engineering how difficult it had been to chisel igneous rock, and he marvelled at the ancient masons who had managed such a prodigious feat in this desolate place, so far away from their homeland in the lush floodplains of the Nile to the north.

He backed off a few steps to take in the whole image, and sat down on the sand. It was unquestionably carved by the ancient Egyptians, its shapes and hieroglyphic symbols familiar from others he had seen at Luxor and

Amarna to the north. It showed a procession of skirt-clad Egyptian soldiers heading into battle; ahead of them was a naked enemy, with spears and little round shields, running and lunging at the Egyptians. Tanner slid down beside him. "That's what first amazed me when I came down here," he said. "I was at El Teb with Burnaby. Those look just like the Beya we were fighting."

Mayne raised the lantern and peered closely. Tanner was right. The enemy had their hair in plumes and rat-tails, exactly as the Beya wore theirs, greased with animal fat. These were Corporal Jones's fuzzy-wuzzies, fighting off intruders three thousand years ago just as they were now, and just as terrifying. The scene seemed suddenly immediate, as if past, present, and future were caught together in one image. But there was more, and he moved a few steps to the right, slipping back and holding up the lamp to stop it from falling into the water. The next scene showed men with raised hatchets and swords hacking at a jumble of bodies and at prisoners with arms raised in supplication. The victors were exacting their usual price; in the register below was a ghastly melange of severed heads and limbs and genitalia, the carvings half submerged by the edge of the water, as if they were floating in it.

But there was something wrong. This was not the usual picture of Egyptian conquest. It was not the Egyptians who were the victors; it was the enemy. The prisoners were receiving the same treatment they were shown inflicting on enemies in countless other wall reliefs in Egypt, depicting conquests real or glorified. And yet this had clearly been carved by Egyptian hands, by masons who had toiled here in this chthonic place under instruction from someone who wanted to celebrate defeat, not victory. *What was going on?* Mayne stared at the awful image in the lower register and remembered Jones's account of General Hicks's last stand two years before, of the Mahdi's men ripping the genitalia off Egyptian prisoners before they fed them to the dogs. Seeing this image sent a chill through him, as if he were looking not at the ancient past but at history foretold, at the fate that lay ahead of them now.

And there was yet more. Tanner pointed farther along, and Mayne raised the lantern. Filling the entire wall at the head of the army was the huge figure of their leader striding forward. It had none of the usual appurtenances of kingship, but Mayne instantly recognised the bulbous belly and distended chin he had seen on wall carvings at Amarna. He remembered the scarab he had been given by Shaytan, hanging round his neck now, and where he had seen the inscription on the base before: it was the hieroglyphic cartouche of Akhenaten, the heretic pharaoh shown here wearing nothing but a robe and sandals. Akhenaten had led his army south and yet seemed divorced from his soldiers, turning away from the carnage of defeat and striking off alone, his eyes determinedly ahead. And in front of him, radiating from the corner of the chamber, was his most characteristic symbol of all, the Aten sun disk, its rays extending outwards towards the pharaoh and seeming to embrace and draw him forward, each ray ending in a hand with palm outstretched.

Mayne stared at the image. He had seen the fragmentary remains of a wall carving like this somewhere else, two weeks earlier, near the wells of Jakdul, not in an underground chamber but scattered over a windswept ruin scarcely visible above the surface of the desert, its walls reduced to foundation courses and the spread of rubble buried in dust and sand. Shaytan had told him that eight years earlier he had guided Gordon Pasha himself to the place, when Gordon was touring the Sudan during his first period as governor general and had a burning passion to discover the antiquities of the place. He had been accompanied by a flamboyant American, Charles Garner Wright, an army officer and adventurer who still wore the uniform of the Confederate South, one of several Civil War veterans who had sought employment with the Khedive's army, and by a German archaeologist who Mayne realised from Shaytan's description was Dr. Heinrich Schliemann, the discoverer of

Troy, a man greatly admired by Gordon. The three men had spent days at the site, digging into the sand yet revealing little more than the fragments that were almost completely buried when Shaytan showed it to Mayne.

Tanner nudged him. "You haven't seen the best. Look at the wall opposite the entrance."

Mayne turned and raised the lantern, and then gasped. Leering out of the gloom high above was the head of a giant standing sculpture, or more accurately the snout. He could see that it was a figure striding forward, carrying a staff in one hand and the ankh symbol in the other, a statue in the round carved out of the living basalt. But it was the head that was extraordinary. It was not a man's head, but the head of a crocodile, with eyes carved deeply on either side and jagged teeth encircling the mouth, the fourth incisor from the front on either side lodged in the upper jaw.

"It's Sobek, the Egyptian crocodile god," Tanner said, his voice hushed. "The built-over recess behind it is cracked at the top, so you can see inside. It's filled with mummies. *Crocodile* mummies, that is. I think this was a temple that adjoined the pool in the river, with a channel running into it. During the annual flood of the Nile, it would have provided refuge for crocodiles from the rushing water of the cataract. I think crocodiles actually lived here."

Mayne stared at the statue. He remembered the evening he had spent with Tanner and Jones picking through the ancient sources for mention of crocodiles, and what Plutarch had said about them: *the Egyptians worship God symbolically in the crocodile, that being the only animal without a tongue, like the Divine Logos which stands not in need of speech*. They had checked it themselves on a rotting carcass they had found downstream, and it was true: the Nile crocodile had no tongue, and a top jaw that could detach itself to accommodate prey far larger than itself, like a snake. *The divine word that shall not be spoken*. It struck him that the early Christians who reviled the Egyptians for making idols, and all those since who thought they worshipped animal deities, were wrong and should return to the ancient authors to seek the truth. Sobek was not a god but the divine presence manifesting itself through the crocodile. Just as the Mahdi and his followers saw Allah in the works of man, so the ancient Egyptians perceived the divine presence in all the facets of nature. In his mind's eye, Mayne saw Akhenaten, the pharaoh who had experienced the revelation more strongly than any other, marching ever southward to free himself from the shackles of the priests and the old religion that had empowered those images, drawing from them and taking with him the divine presence. Perhaps he had built this temple on the very edge of the Egyptian world beside the crocodile pool as a last gesture to the old ways before leaving it all behind and plunging into the desert. It was out there that the archaeologists should be searching for him, not at Amarna or in the monuments to the north, yet Mayne knew it was a place where little evidence of his passing would ever be found: no ruins or statues or temples, only the distilled desolation of the desert and the brilliance of the sun.

Tanner turned to him, his face flushed in the lamplight and his voice edged with excitement. "I have a theory, Mayne. I think they were doing something here that they couldn't do in Egypt, something that the priests would have banned, an ancient ritual from their prehistoric past. I think that's why Akhenaten came here and had this place carved out far beyond the control of the priests, back in the land of his ancestors. I think this was a sacrificial chamber. And look at those images of dismembered bodies. I mean *human* sacrifice."

Mayne stared at the wall, his mind reeling. *Human sacrifice.* Did that scene of violence show a real battle, or was it allegorical? He looked at the procession of soldiers again, and then at the image of the pharaoh. He realised that there was something missing: images of Egyptian military expeditions always showed priests. There were none here, and the image of Akhenaten lacked the usual priestly equipment of a pharaoh, the staff and the ankh symbol and the crown. Had he cast them off and come to the desert already divested of the old religion? Or had he done so here, beyond the borders of Egypt, having reached a place sacred to his early ancestors where only the river and the desert held sway? *Had the sacrificial victims been the priests?*

Mayne remembered Corporal Jones and the leviathan, his description from the Book of Job: *His neesings flash forth light, and his eyes are like the eyelids of the morning.* He strained to see the head of the crocodile, raising the lamp as high as he could. The eyes were made of crystal, a deep red, perhaps agate, but the nostrils were crystal as well, brilliant pellucid stones cut in facets that reflected a dazzling light even from the sputtering flame of the gas lamp. He looked back at the slit of light through the entrance, realising that the chamber was aligned east-west. Now, with the sun on the horizon, the light was shining high above the statue, close to the roof. But an hour ago, about the time he had been waiting for the sun to drop enough to see the sharpshooter, it would have shone directly into the eyes and nostrils of the crocodile, reflecting a brilliant, shimmering light, as if the crocodile itself were emitting a beam towards the sun. He thought of what this place might have been like three thousand years ago: down below, beneath the sand that now obscured it, a passageway through the rock to the river for the crocodiles, and up above, far above the reach of anyone sealed in the chamber, a slit just wide enough to let that flash of light through, a beam of red and green that those watching outside might have seen as the beginning of a new dawn, as the last ray of a godhead who had consumed the victims needed to release his energy in one flash towards the divine light of the Aten, allowing the chamber and the last exhalations of the old religion to be sealed up forever.

"Good Lord," murmured Ormerod after they had stood in silence for several minutes, hearing only the drips of condensation from the walls, tiny splashes magnified in the chamber as they fell into the water. "Not a word of this to the men. They're jittery enough about crocodiles as it is."

Mayne heard a hollering outside; it was Charrière calling his name from the river. Tanner and Ormerod began to make their way up the slope towards the entrance, but he lingered, staring at something he had seen in the wavering light of the lantern. It was a small slab of stone about eight inches square and partly detached from the wall; it had once been fixed into a depression below the image of Akhenaten, but the mortar around its edges had evidently crumbled in the dampness of the chamber. The decoration on its surface seemed continuous with the surrounding image, a series of radiating lines from the sun symbol, and in the top left corner an acute angle overlaying the lines that corresponded to the lower hem of Akhenaten's robe. Yet with the slab detached from the wall, it also seemed as if it might form part of something else, one quarter of a larger square with lines that radiated out from a shape in the centre formed from the acute angle. He picked it up, feeling the weight of the basalt. He remembered Shaytan's account of Gordon and Schliemann and the American excavating the temple in the desert. They had been looking for a carving, something that might be like this. On a whim he decided to take it. Someone at headquarters might know its meaning, perhaps Kitchener, another engineer officer who had been close to Gordon and shared his archaeological interests.

As he pocketed the slab, he accidentally caught and broke the thong around his neck that held the scarab that Shaytan had given him. He cursed under his breath, scrabbling around where it had fallen into the water at the edge of the sand, knowing that he was probably only digging it in deeper. He heard the hollering again and looked up to the sunlight streaming in from the entrance, seeing the silhouetted forms of the two men waiting for him. He would look for it when he returned. *If* he returned. He held the weight of the slab in his pocket and struggled upright in the sand. He seemed to be taking one artefact at the expense of another, the one in his pocket of uncertain meaning and the other a sacred relic from a man he rated highly, a gift to protect him in the desert. It was as if something within was pulling him away from the bonds that tied men to each other; ever since his parents' death he had been destined to live as an outsider. He had begun to understand better what had made him sit at night with his back to the fire while Shaytan was asleep and stare into the darkness of the desert, wishing he could walk out and let it enfold him, to disappear forever from the affairs of men.

He felt himself sink farther into the sand. Below him the ground was saturated, and he realised that there was no certainty that the floor of the chamber continued at the same level, that it might be a deeper pit full of quicksand that could suck him down. He hauled one leg out, then the other, and began to make his way laboriously up the slope. He remembered what the Mohawks had said when he overheard them talking apprehensively about the river ahead, about the feeling of heaviness; perhaps that was what they had meant. He laboured on, making little progress, his heart pounding. It occurred to him that Tanner and Ormerod could dislodge the sand and it could slide down like an avalanche and engulf him, entombing him forever with the crocodile god. He remembered his mission to Wolseley; disappearing in a place like this was decidedly not the fate that he had envisaged.

He took one last look back, then released himself from the grip of the sand and scrambled up to the chamber entrance until he stood outside beside the other two, blinking in the waning sunlight. He walked over to his gear, opened up his saddlebag, and pulled out the robe he had been wearing in the desert, then unsheathed the knife he kept on his belt and cut into one edge of the cloth. After replacing the knife, he tore off a strip, then took the stone slab out of his pocket and wrapped it in the material, tied it with a length of cord from his pocket, and handed it to Tanner. "See that this gets to

Corporal Jones, would you? He looks after my belongings. We'll have a good look at it when I get back. And I'd like him reassigned to the Railway Company at Korti. You'll be the senior remaining Royal Engineer with the river column after I've left, so he's your responsibility. Can you see to that?"

Tanner took the package and tucked it into his tunic. "Right away. I'm heading up to the sangar now." He paused, gesturing back at the entrance to the chamber. "What do you think of it?"

Mayne nodded towards the river. "I think with what might be lurking in the pool, that's one god you can't afford to ignore."

Tanner grinned, shaking his head. "If I survive this little jaunt, I might just try to wangle a number like the one Kitchener had in Palestine and come back here as an archaeological surveyor. If there's more like this to be found, we might be on to the greatest treasure trove from antiquity."

Mayne shouldered his bags and shook hands with Tanner. "Soldier first, engineer second. You remember what they drummed into us at Chatham? And archaeologist third. But I wish you the best of luck. The cataract ahead will be hard work, but by the time I'm back, the column should be well past it. And that sharpshooter won't be the last. Where there are sharpshooters, there's an army somewhere beyond."

Tanner nodded, his smile gone. He was ten years older than the subaltern in the sangar, due for promotion to captain that year, and had been in Afghanistan. "We've posted more piquets along the riverbank ahead of us, and a company of infantry has been put on alert to act as skirmishers should the need arise. Before he left for Korti, General Earle instructed us to proceed with extra caution. Direct orders from Lord Wolseley."

Mayne shook Ormerod's hand and watched the two men trudge up the scree slope. That was the problem with this expedition: too much caution. High overhead, half a dozen vultures circled, smelling the blood of fresh corpses. On the opposite cliff, two soldiers had reached the body of the marksman and tipped it off into the river. It came floating by now, down the torrent between the two rocks and into the pool, where soldiers crowded along the edge, peering at it as it rolled over and over in the current, unmolested by crocodiles. The sharpshooter had undoubtedly been disguised as a desert Arab, just as Mayne had been on his travels with Shaytan, but he had revealed his true colours before opening fire: the body was wearing the patched jibba of the Ansar, the white robe with the embroidered patches that made it look like the dress of a poor Sufi; and above the gaping hole where his face had been, Mayne could see that the man had been shaven-headed. He had seen the Ansar before, fleetingly with Shaytan far to the south when they had watched a Mahdist force surge by in the distance, a storm of dust with banners above and the occasional flash of white as men disengaged from the main force to get out of the dust, riding their camels along the near flank. But seeing a jibba this far north was unnerving, as if the man had broken through the invisible membrane that still divided their world from the darkness ahead.

He looked at the two rocks again, where Charrière had been standing when he had first seen him from the sangar. Down here, close to the river, the rocks looked more impressive, like sentinels guarding a gateway to an unknown world. Through them he could see where the pellucid light over the pool, with everything sharply delineated, gave way to a haze and then an impenetrable miasma, the rocks of the cataract seeming to wobble and shimmer and then disappear from view entirely, as if he were looking into a mirage. He knew that his destiny lay somewhere out there, but for now he was glad to be turning north for a day or two for a respite. He was desperately tired, and struggling up that slope in the chamber had given him a raging thirst.

He heard a shout, then turned and saw Charrière standing in the boat in the pool, waving at him.

It was time to go.

PART 3

Chapter 10

Jack Howard followed Hiebermeyer and Costas along the ridge from the sangar towards the site where they had seen the sculpted head of the pharaoh Senusret beside the square structure of the shrine that had been revealed in the excavation. It was midafternoon, and despite being November it was still hot enough to send rivulets of sweat down his face and make a dive in the Nile seem more appealing by the minute. He could see the figure of a woman on top of the shrine, picking her way slowly around and squatting down to inspect something more closely. Below her in the wadi, a jeep with a child seat strapped into the front passenger side was parked up against the ridge. A young man was leaning against the bonnet, smoking and talking on a phone. He saw them, pushed off, and waved languidly, a holstered sidearm clearly visible.

Jack waved back. "A bodyguard?"

"Aysha's cousin," Hiebermeyer replied. "He's just finished his national service in Egypt and was at loose ends. His military police unit was stationed at the frontier and liaised closely with the Sudanese border guards, so there was no problem getting him a temporary permit to carry a firearm in Sudan."

"You expecting trouble?" Costas asked.

Hiebermeyer shrugged. "You can't be too careful. There's always been a bandit problem in the desert, and there's a growing fundamentalist presence in Sudan. The bandits think any excavation is after gold, and the fundamentalists get itchy over anything they think might disturb Islamic history. Aysha's cousin may be a one-man show, but the Sudanese police helicopter squadron at Wadi Halfa is only half an hour away."

They walked towards Aysha, who saw them and waved. Jack always relished spending time with her, not only for her sharp intelligence but also because she seemed to have walked straight out of the past; she had a face like one of the lifelike portrait plaques of the Hellenistic period found on mummies in the Faiyum, where Hiebermeyer had first met her. She was wearing a man's keffiyeh headdress, a loose white long-sleeved shirt, and a long skirt, but with robust desert boots and a workman's belt with pockets and loops for tools. On her front was a swaddled bundle attached by cords around her waist and over her shoulders. Costas surged forward and peered at the face just visible beneath the protective sunshade at the front. "How's my favorite small person?" he asked.

"Ahren's fast asleep," Aysha said. "He'll sleep for another hour and then be bright and perky all night."

"This is his first taste of an archaeological excavation," Hiebermeyer said, beaming.

Jack smiled at Aysha. "I was with Maurice at Heathrow when he bought him some blocks to build a model of an ancient Egyptian temple."

"Correction. Maurice bought *Maurice* some blocks to build a model of an ancient Egyptian temple. It was the centerpiece of the excavation tent until our lovely son brought it tumbling down."

"Earning his archaeological credentials," Hiebermeyer said proudly. "Far more interested in ruins than standing structures. That's my boy."

Aysha walked carefully over to an awning on one side

of the shrine and sat down on a folding chair. The others joined her. Jack, who had been thinking hard since seeing the evidence from 1884 in the sangar, glanced at Hiebermeyer. "Do you remember I promised to look for some material I had in the Howard family archive related to the Gordon relief campaign?"

Hiebermeyer looked at him keenly. "Your ancestor, the Royal Engineers officer?"

Jack nodded. "My great-great-grandfather, Colonel John Howard. He wasn't part of the expedition, but he was in charge of a committee at the Royal Engineers headquarters at Chatham that looked after Gordon's collection of antiquities. Howard passed through Egypt in March 1885 on his way back home from India and picked up a crate of material in Cairo that had been sent down from the Sudan. I know it contained some archaeological finds that Gordon had dispatched from Khartoum the previous year, including ancient Egyptian artifacts from the desert. Those mostly went to the Museum of the Royal United Services Institute in London, and when that was disbanded in the 1960s they were dispersed around various museums in England."

"You told me there was some material related to Semna."

Jack nodded. "Just two envelopes in the collection of his private papers that I have in that old wooden sea chest in my office on *Seaquest II*. But it's frustrating because both are empty. One has the sender's address as 'River Column, Semna,' dated the twenty-fourth of December 1884, and it's from Lieutenant Peter Tanner, a sapper friend of Howard's from his time in India. I know they shared an interest in archaeology, and I've always imagined that was what the letter was about. Sadly Tanner was killed in battle alongside General Earle six weeks later, when the river column had its first major engagement with the Mahdi's army, at Kirbekan, some sixty miles south of here."

"And the other?"

"That one's a real puzzle. It's a scuffed brown manila

envelope about twenty centimeters across that had once been tied around, as if it had contained something heavy, an object the size of a large floor tile. It's addressed to Howard at the School of Military Engineering and was from a sapper in the 8th Railway Company, Royal Engineers. It was posted in May 1885 from a British army field hospital at Wadi Halfa. The 8th Railway Company wasn't meant to be a combatant unit, but they did fight one of the last battles of the campaign, when they were besieged at the fort of Ambikol at the end of the railway line and held off wave after wave of dervish attacks. The sapper must have been badly wounded to have been at that particular hospital. His name was Jones, and I realized I recognized him from his regimental number on the envelope. He'd been a sergeant with Howard in India during the Rampa Rebellion in 1879, and a bit of research showed that he was a corporal with the river column in 1885 before being transferred to the Railway Company. Sometime after that he must have lost his corporal's stripes and been reduced to sapper, not for the first time in his army career, it seems. It was common for engineer officers and NCOs to have close friendships, as they often worked together for months on end with no other soldiers present. When Jones had been with Howard in the Rampa jungle, they made some major archaeological discoveries. That might explain why he chose to send Howard what looks to have been some kind of artifact from the desert."

"Is there any chance of following the trail further?"

Jack nodded. "The sea chest contains only papers that happened to be among my father's material when he died. But another couple of boxes of my great-great-grandfather's papers were found when restoration work was carried out in the attic of the old hall on our estate last year. My grandfather was in serious debt following the Second World War and had to let the house, and it seems that he put a lot of family material into storage in the attic and then forgot to tell anyone about it. I've managed to look through only a few boxes so far, but

I'll go straight to it when I get back to the IMU campus after we finish our diving here. The attic is going to be converted to rooms for visiting scholars, and I need to supervise removal of all the material to the library before the end of next week. If Jones's artifact came from Semna, which seems possible, then maybe it's something that can shed light on the archaeology of this place. I'd love to go through the whole collection properly, but until now I hadn't seen myself having the time. A retirement project maybe."

Hiebermeyer peered at him over his glasses. "Retirement? Jack Howard?"

Aysha shifted the baby. "Why not put Rebecca on to it? John Howard's her ancestor too."

Jack gave her a rueful look. "I don't think family history is her cup of tea. At the moment she's toying with applying to study theoretical physics at Caltech."

Aysha waved her free hand dismissively. "That's just an act of rebellion against you. If you told her there was some kind of archaeological trail in those family papers, she'd be onto it like a shot. Remember, I've spent weeks sitting beside her in the finds lab cleaning bits of broken pot. I can assure you that she has the Howard genes. Anything to get out of drudgery, and she'll do it."

"Okay. I'll set it up. But I want to have a look again as well. Especially after having seen this place."

"The Royal Engineers played a major part in the development of archaeology out here," Aysha said, gently rocking the baby. "It's fascinated me since you first suggested that I study it for my master's dissertation project in London."

Jack looked at Costas. "It's one of the unsung aspects of the development of archaeology in the Victorian period. One of the main jobs of the Royal Engineers was survey and mapmaking, and in the course of their explorations they laid the groundwork for archaeological research in many areas of the world that came under British influence, including Palestine and Egypt. A lot of them were also keenly interested in biblical history and archaeology in its own right. That was the period when people were really beginning to put facts behind the time line and geography of the Bible. The Royal Engineers attracted many men who today might well have become professional archaeologists."

"A case in point is Lord Kitchener," Aysha said. "I made a special study of him because I felt that his role in the archaeology of Egypt had been overlooked. We think of him chiefly as the man who avenged Gordon, who led the British in the reconquest of Sudan and the final victory against the Mahdist army at Omdurman in 1898. But in so doing he opened up the whole of the Nubian Desert to archaeological exploration, including the first investigations that took place here at Semna. I always felt that if he hadn't been so obsessed with avenging his hero, he would have been able to carry out more exploration himself in the desert, as that was really his calling.

"General Gordon is another example. When he was first made governor general of the Sudan in the 1870s, he travelled around the country extensively, accompanied by some colorful European and American characters he'd appointed to his staff. He managed to visit many archaeological sites and amass a large collection of antiquities and ethnographic material. I ended up arguing in my dissertation that if it hadn't been for Gordon's insistence on staying to evacuate Khartoum in the face of the Mahdist uprising, then he wouldn't have died and Kitchener might never have been spurred on in his career of reconquest, leaving the archaeology of the Sudan virtually unknown. So in one way or another, Gordon is the linchpin of the whole story, and without him we might not be here as archaeologists today."

"The Mahdi was the bin Laden of the 1880s, right?" Costas asked.

"There was more to him than that," Aysha said. "For starters, he wasn't a spoiled rich boy with a whim for jihad that became obsessive. The Mahdi was the real deal, and he lived the life he preached. He was a Sudanese boatbuilder with Arab ancestry who became a Sufi holy man. He had visions and was highly charismatic, leading people to think he was a kind of messiah. His followers included many Sudanese tribesmen who were disaffected with Ottoman rule and wanted their own freedom; these were the enemy the British and the Egyptians fought, the warriors they called dervishes. The Mahdi died in the same year as Gordon, in 1885, probably poisoned, and his revolt ended with the defeat of his successors at Omdurman in 1898, but he was certainly seen as a role model by bin Laden and his cronies. Growing up as a Muslim in southern Egypt, I can assure you that the influence of the Mahdi's family and his chosen line of successors remain strong. You do not use his name in vain in this part of Sudan without risking your neck."

Jack turned to Costas. "Gordon was also a Royal Engineers officer. So you can see the link with Kitchener and with my great-great-grandfather. After the Royal Military Academy, they'd all done the same two-year course at the School of Military Engineering at Chatham, and they were a tightly knit corps. And many of them not only had archaeological interests but were strongly committed Christians influenced by the evangelical movement. They were most interested in the archaeology of the Holy Land, which for them included Egypt."

"And that ties them to the Mahdi as well, especially Gordon," Aysha said. "Gordon was a real maverick, an iconoclast, not very good at taking orders, something he shared with Kitchener. But in Gordon's case his iconoclasm extended to his religious views as well. The evangelical movement liked to claim him as one of their own, to see him as a devout crusader who had gone to Khartoum to confront the Islamist threat, but in truth that was far from Gordon's own attitude. His view of religion was very inclusive, and his focus was on the common tradition from which Islam and Judaeo-Christian beliefs sprang: the same God, many of the same prophets, a similar take on the idea of a messiah. He knew that the Mahdi had visions of Jesus as well as of Muhammad and that he shared Gordon's fascination with the Old Testament prophet Isaiah. And both men would have had an interest in Moses and the origin of the idea of the one God."

"Which brings us neatly back to Akhenaten," Jack said. He pulled a small paperback book out of the side pocket of his combat trousers and tossed it to Hiebermeyer. "Have you ever had a go at reading that?"

Hiebermeyer looked at the cover and raised his eyes knowingly. "*Moses and Monotheism,* by Sigmund Freud. Yes, I have attempted this. A great deal of psychobabble, but the kernel of it contains some sound ideas."

Jack grinned. "I had a look at it on the plane on the way here; I'm glad I'm not the only one who struggled with it." He turned to Costas. "Freud was putting his own particular spin on the well-established theory that the pharaoh of the Old Testament Book of Exodus was Akhenaten, and that it was he who was associated with Moses and the idea of the one God. This theory gained real bite during the late Victorian period when archaeologists began to understand more about the cult of the Aten, the sun god that Akhenaten tried to foist on Egypt at the expense of all the old gods. Because this vision of one God happens to Moses in the Bible as well, Freud toyed with the notion that the two men were really one, that Moses was Akhenaten. Personally I'd discard all that in favor of what you actually read in the Bible, which seems a perfectly plausible picture of a pharaoh and a Hebrew slave sharing the same vision."

The baby cried, and Aysha quickly undid the cords and passed him to Hiebermeyer, who put down the book and began feeding him with the bottle she gave him, sitting awkwardly but with a beaming smile on his face. "I agree with Jack. We're talking about real people, not some kind of mystical union."

Costas grinned at him. "You're a hands-on kind of guy, aren't you?" The baby coughed, spraying milk over

Hiebermeyer's face and neck, and Costas stiffened, looking past Hiebermeyer's shoulder. "Can you handle a camel as well?"

Hiebermeyer tried to wipe his face on his sleeve while shoving the bottle back in the baby's mouth. "What do you mean, a camel?"

"I mean, a *camel*." While they had been talking, the camel that they had first seen from the Toyota had loped over and was now craning its neck down so that its face was directly behind Hiebermeyer, its jaws chewing from side to side and its hooded eyes looking out indifferently, apparently disconnected entirely from the scene. Suddenly its tongue came out and wrapped itself around Hiebermeyer's face, drooping down over his chest to lick up the milk and then withdrawing again. The animal licked its lips contentedly and backed off with a sigh. Costas guffawed, and Hiebermeyer spluttered, trying to wipe his face again while still holding the baby. Aysha quickly took Ahren from him, and Hiebermeyer got up and stumbled towards an open water barrel behind them, dunked his head into it, and shook it vigorously before returning, sitting this time a good few meters away from the camel. He blinked and wiped away the water, then eyed Costas. "Watch it, Kazantzakis. Next time it'll be you."

"That camel's become the expedition mascot," Aysha said. "The locals say it's descended from a camel that was left here by a British officer during the Nile expedition and is still waiting for him to return. So we feel kind of sorry for it. And it's taken a particular liking to Maurice."

"So I can see," Costas said, grinning at Jack.

"I think it's time you earned your keep as godfather," Hiebermeyer said. He went over to Aysha, carefully took the baby from her, and gave him to Costas, whose expression had changed to one of frozen horror. Aysha passed him the bottle, and they all watched for a moment as the baby fed contentedly, his eyes closed. "You look as if you were made for it," Aysha said, then turned to Hiebermeyer. "Have you remembered our visitors?"

Hiebermeyer snorted with annoyance and looked at his watch. "I could do without them. When Jack and Costas have gone to kit up, I have to get to the excavation on the other side of the river and make sure everything's shipshape there too."

Costas looked dubiously at the river. "How do you get there? Swim? Watch out for crocodiles."

Hiebermeyer shook his head. "We took a page out of the 1884 expedition. We rigged a cable across the river just like the ship's hawsers used by the Royal Naval contingent to haul whaleboats up the Nile. One of those pictures from the *Illustrated London News* shows a cable strung between those two jutting rocks that formed the narrowest point of the cataract, now completely submerged. I use the one we set up to pull a boat over the pool below us to the other side."

"Who's coming, exactly?" Jack asked.

"We're expecting a visit from the Sudanese Ministry of Culture. It's a scheduled inspection, and I welcome that. Our team here is almost entirely Sudanese, and I'd love to see this develop into a permanent program. Ever since the Aswan Dam construction, this area has been written off by archaeologists assuming that the interesting sites have all been inundated, but as you can see, there's a lot still to be found on higher ground above the river. Perhaps the program could have IMU backing."

"I can certainly propose it to the board of directors," Jack said. "Especially if our dive produces good results."

"What I'm apprehensive about is the new guy they're bringing with them. He's been specially appointed to increase awareness of recent Sudanese history, especially the Mahdist period. As a historian, I have a lot of sympathy with the idea. The Mahdi was an extraordinary character, and the way in which the Sudanese people rose up in support of him, mainly fighting for their own independence from foreign interference rather than out of religious fanaticism, should be looked on positively as a basis for nation-building today. God knows, this place needs it."

"Has there been any progress yet?" Jack said.

"Things got off to a bad start when Kitchener desecrated the Mahdi's tomb after the Battle of Omdurman in 1898; from then until the end of the Anglo-Egyptian regime in 1956, the Mahdist era was not exactly a focus for celebration. Even the period of Gordon's rule quickly passed out of visible history, because there was so little left to look at and a great desire to sweep away the horror of that time and look ahead. The only significant building to survive the Mahdist destruction of Khartoum, the palace where Gordon was holed up, was demolished after the British returned in 1898. The only other substantial survivors are two of the river steamers that he used to make contact with the advance force of the British on the Nile. The *Bordein* was restored in 1935, the fiftieth anniversary of Gordon's death, and was something of a tourist attraction until it fell into disrepair after the British left. One of the new appointee's first jobs has been to oversee its restoration. He wants it to appear as it did when the Mahdi ruled Khartoum and took over the steamers for his own use."

"I'd go along with that," Jack said. "Virtually all we know of the place during those years of Mahdist rule after 1885 comes from the account of Rudolf von Slatin, the Austrian officer who had been one of Gordon's staff and later returned under British rule as a special inspector for the Sudan. It is extraordinary that a former boatbuilder from the Nile should have ended up ruling a country three times the size of France, and anything that can be done to put that period into visible history is very worthwhile, in my book."

Costas knitted his brow. "Wasn't there another steamer, one that was wrecked? I flipped through Jack's books on the plane on the way here and that caught my interest. Gordon sent one of his officers downstream with a lot of his personal papers and artifacts, but the steamer foundered and the officer was murdered."

"Colonel Stewart," Jack said. "The steamer was the *Abbas,* wrecked in the fifth cataract, about five hundred kilometers upstream of here, in September 1884. It was the event that really seems to have sent Gordon into a downward spiral."

Costas turned to Aysha. "Has anyone ever dived on it?"

She shook her head. "Not to my knowledge. The Mahdi's men ransacked her and salvaged what they could after Stewart was murdered. They'd been persuaded that there was gold on board, and that's what the locals still believe. They're pretty hostile to anyone going near the site. There's a local warlord who runs the place like a private fiefdom."

"Any truth in it?" Costas asked. "The gold?"

"Gordon wasn't that kind of treasure hunter. But he does seem to have sent a good part of his archaeological collection away in the *Abbas,* and that must still be lying on the riverbed. We thought it might make a good IMU project."

Costas turned to Jack. "What do you think? Sounds like another case of the *Beatrice,* digging up a nineteenth-century wreck to find ancient antiquities."

Jack pursed his lips. "It'd have to be a pretty big prize for me to go diving at a site guarded by a Sudanese warlord and his private army who might be hankering to relive the murder of a British officer on the site a hundred and thirty years ago."

Aysha nodded. "I think you'd have to get them on your side."

Costas turned to Hiebermeyer. "Would that project come under the aegis of this new guy? Excavation of the steamer would put that period of history into the limelight, with the added attraction of ancient artifacts. Who knows what kind of things Gordon might have collected."

Hiebermeyer looked uncertain. "I'm keeping my distance. I haven't told you about this man's background. He's not a career politician, but he's from an immensely wealthy Sudanese family based in Egypt. Everyone on his father's side is originally from this part of the Nile in Upper Sudan. They claim descent from the prophet Muhammad through his grandson Hassad."

"The same as the Mahdi?" Jack asked.

"The man's name is Hassad al'Ahmed. His family were boatbuilders, just like the Mahdi's. He's never openly claimed a connection, but my contact in the Ministry says it's an unspoken assumption."

Costas whistled. "Now that *is* living history. Maybe he's intent on not just celebrating the history of the Mahdi but is also a jihadist himself."

"You have to ask that question of everyone you meet out here," Hiebermeyer said. "But I don't think it's as straightforward as that. When Aysha and I gave our briefing on the Semna project for the Ministry people in Khartoum, I noticed that he seemed completely uninterested and was texting most of the time until I mentioned my particular interest in Akhenaten, when he suddenly pocketed his iPhone and began furiously taking notes. I mentioned this to my Ministry friend, and he said that both this man and his father had plagued the Ministry with requests to excavate a number of sites up and down the Nile with evidence for ancient Egyptian occupation. They'd been rebuffed because the family had an ugly reputation for treating any project they'd been allowed to develop in the Sudan as their own private enterprise, using bribery to corrupt officials sent to police them. The Ministry had been obliged to accept Hassid's appointment with great reluctance after he'd made a cash donation of thirty million dollars to the Khartoum museum in return for the role. Officially he has nothing to do with ancient sites, but it's no surprise that he's managed to shoehorn himself into the inspection today. Ostensibly he's here to look at the evidence we've found from 1884, but I'm sure what he's really interested in is the pharaonic remains and anything else he might wheedle out of us about ancient

Egyptian discoveries. Why he should have that special interest, I don't yet know."

He looked at his watch and stood up. Aysha went over to Costas and took the baby, now fast asleep, and sat down again. Hiebermeyer turned to Jack and Costas. "I promised to show you how I know that two soldiers died up here that day in 1884. And how that's led to a fabulous ancient discovery. It's the reason why you're here. Aysha, we'll be back in half an hour. Let's go."

CHAPTER 11

HIEBERMEYER LED JACK AND COSTAS FROM the shrine over about two hundred meters of bare rock towards the beginning of a large gully that opened out into the desert to the east. They dropped a few meters below the level of the surrounding rock and walked towards an off-white tent some fifty meters into the gully, at the end of a dirt track from the main road where several of the expedition vehicles were parked. The tent was the size of a small marquee, with a pitched roof and guy ropes pegged out and anchored against the wind. Hiebermeyer opened the door flap and ushered them inside, where the air was noticeably warmer. "It's something of a greenhouse in here during the day, but it's the price we pay for keeping the dust out of the excavation," he said. They followed him over to a square trench about three meters across and two meters deep, with measuring rods along the sides and a plastic sheet laid over the bottom.

Costas squatted close to the edge of the trench, being careful not to let the loose dust and stone crumble inside. "This looks like a crime scene investigation," he said. "An ancient burial?"

Hiebermeyer nodded. "During our preliminary recce, Aysha spotted two low piles of rocks about two meters long, evidently man-made. As you've seen, the plateau is largely exposed rock—gneiss and granite with some sandstone—and this gully is one of the few collecting places near the river for wind-borne dust and sand, the only place with stable sediment deep enough for a burial. But the two burials we found under the stones weren't ancient. Beneath that tarpaulin are the semi-mummified remains of two British soldiers."

Jack stared, his mind reeling. "Are they from the Gordon relief expedition?"

"The khaki uniforms are correct. They have the shoulder badges of the South Staffordshire Regiment, one of the units with the river column. And one of them has a letter dated early October 1884 from a woman in Dublin in his front tunic pocket."

"So this is why you think a second soldier was killed in the sangar."

"We've left the bodies *in situ* but did a full forensic analysis. They were clearly both buried at the same time and with some care, undoubtedly by their comrades. One was killed by a single gunshot wound to the upper chest and probably died immediately. The other, the one with the letter, was hit twice, once in the lower leg and once through both thighs, severing the artery in his right thigh. He probably bled to death in agony."

Costas stood up and backed away. "I don't want to see."

Hiebermeyer put a hand on his shoulder. "Don't worry. We've reburied them exactly as they were, and we're about to infill the trench. We've arranged that the Commonwealth War Graves Commission, which administers the Khartoum War Cemetery, will take charge of the site. They mainly deal with Second World War casualties from the desert campaign against the Italians and the Germans, but they also have charge of First World War casualties from the war against the Turks as well as any bodies discovered from the 1880s and 1890s. We know the names of these two soldiers from their personal effects, and the Sudanese authorities have allowed the Commission to build a monument at this spot."

"So that closes the chapter on that fateful day in December 1884," Jack murmured, looking pensively at the tarpaulin.

"It closes that chapter, but it opens another one," replied Hiebermeyer, his eyes gleaming. "Just like in the sangar, when they dug down here the soldiers cut through something else, something ancient. They probably thought it was the remains of earlier human burials, but when Aysha and her team removed the surrounding sediment, they found something unexpected. Prepare to be amazed." He lifted a flap of canvas dividing off part of the tent beyond the trench, and they stared in astonishment. On a hospital gurney at one end was an intact mummy, the crisscrossed strips of linen clearly visible beneath the hardened resin on the surface. The head was in the form of a stylized mask, with eyes and other features picked out in paint, the colors faded to pastel shades of green and blue and grey. Only it was not the mask of a human being. The mummy was lying on its front, and the head tapered to a snout, jutting out and ringed with painted teeth. Jack whistled. "Well I'll be damned," he said. *A crocodile.*

He gently put a hand on the resin, feeling the warmth where it had absorbed heat from the sun, a disconcerting sensation, as if the mummy were still alive. "Is it real? Inside, I mean?"

Hiebermeyer nodded. "We took it to the Khartoum School of Medicine for a CT scan. It's a fully mature adult male *Crocodylus niloticus.* There was a scarab in part of the wrapping that we unravelled dating to the reign of our friend Senusret III, about 1850 BC." Hiebermeyer moved to another hanging curtain. "Now, get a hold of this one." He pulled the canvas away, and they stared in even greater astonishment. A second gurney held another crocodile mummy, this one in fragments, with only the snout and head and the lower part of the tail intact. But the head was huge, at least twice the size of the first mummy's head. And instead of painted features, the mask was picked out with gold leaf and encrusted jewels, black stones like jet for the eyes and a beautiful translucent green stone for each of the nostrils. Jack leaned forward and gently touched one of the stones, seeing the reflected light turn his finger a watery green, a shade he had never seen before.

"The nostril stones are peridot, from St. John's Island in the Red Sea," Hiebermeyer said. "The Egyptians sailed there specially to mine it. In the sunlight they reflect an amazing beam of light, almost too dazzling to look at."

"It's huge," Costas said in a hushed tone. "I mean the crocodile. I've never seen anything like it."

"Despite the richness of the embellishments, it was pretty crudely mummified and hasn't survived so well, even taking into account the damage to the torso caused by the British soldiers digging through it," Hiebermeyer continued. "Our analysis of the wrappings shows that the smaller mummy was encased in linen and papyrus characteristic of the reeds grown along the banks of the Nile in upper Egypt, whereas this one is local desert grass mixed with Nile clay probably from the pool below, as well as scraps of papyrus documents that seem to have been discarded from the fort."

"This is where you found the Semna dispatch you read to us earlier?" Jack said.

Hiebermeyer nodded. "The smaller mummy was undoubtedly brought here from Egypt, whereas we're sure this one is a crocodile that lived here and was mummified on the spot. And yes, it's big. *Huge.* The largest known Nile crocs are those recorded in the nineteenth century by European hunters. Maybe there were leviathans among them, but this one now stands as the largest Nile crocodile ever recorded. I sent Lanowski the CT scan, and his computerized reconstruction of the bones gives its length. Most fully grown male Nile crocs average about four to five meters. This one is almost nine meters, the size of a bus."

"Ibrahim was telling us about local stories of a leviathan in the river here," Jack said. "This seems to bear them out."

"Lanowski calculates the crush strength of the jaw at twenty-five kilonewtons, enough to split a cow in half," Hiebermeyer said. "But like all crocs, the muscles that open the jaws are weak, and you'd be able to hold them shut if you wrestled it down. Lanowski says the IMU medicos will be particularly interested in the integumentary sense organs on a crocodile of this size, as they may reveal ways of sensing pressure that have applications to diving technology. But you'd have to catch one live."

Costas stared at him. "Don't even think about it. I'm not acting as fishing bait for one of Lanowski's experiments. He wants a live crocodile, he can catch it himself."

Jack gazed back at the trench. "What are they doing buried up here, so high above the river?"

"That was my first question too," Hiebermeyer replied. "Nile crocs lay eggs in November and December, the time of year when the level of the river was already well down, and yet they instinctively nested above the summer high-water mark in order to prevent their nests from being inundated as the river rose again when the eggs were due to hatch. It was the reason why the ancient Egyptians thought crocodiles could foretell the future. They'd choose a sandy spot where they could bury their eggs and stand guard. Where we are now is one of the few locations with any depth of sand close to the cataract, even though it would have meant a lumbering climb for them up the slope. It's an exposed location but open on all sides, so it would be difficult for anyone intent on stealing the eggs to sneak up unobserved. Given the size of the crocs that lived here, anyone chancing on them would have kept their distance. On open ground like this, a croc can move faster than most people can run. In the water, one this big would be even faster, up to forty kilometers per hour in bursts."

"I'm glad you used the past tense," Costas murmured. "*Lived*, not live."

"Don't be too sure. Absence of evidence isn't proof of absence. At night our workmen who sleep in the open claim they sometimes hear deep breathing from the pool, a snorting sound."

"Oh great," Costas muttered. "This gets better by the moment."

"Do you think there are more mummies here?" Jack asked.

Hiebermeyer shook his head. "You can see the lower courses of a masonry enclosure beside the trench with the soldier burials. We think the two crocodile mummies were buried side by side as offerings, one a tamed crocodile carefully mummified in Egypt, the other an untamed leviathan from this place. Perhaps there was some meaning to the double burial: the one to demonstrate that the priests could subdue the creature, the other to show respect for the primordial beast, here at this place on the very edge of civilization."

"You mention priests," Jack said, peering at Hiebermeyer intently. "At all the other places where crocodile mummies have been found, they've been discovered in large numbers, stashed in temples to the crocodile god Sobek. At Crocodilopolis, for example."

Costas looked horrified. "At *where*?"

"Crocodilopolis. Crocodile town. On the Nile near Memphis."

"They had a place called that?"

Hiebermeyer snorted impatiently. "That's Jack being Greek again. The ancient Egyptians called it Arsinoe. The priests there kept a crocodile embellished with jewels and gold in a special pool, replacing and mummifying him when he died. They called him Petsuchos."

"*Pet*suchos? You're kidding me. They kept a pet crocodile?"

"Not a pet exactly," Jack said. "More like a personification of a terrifying monster god. I don't think you stroked it and took it for walks."

Costas stared at the mummy. "I'm beginning to get it.

You think the same kind of thing was going on here, don't you?"

Jack peered at Hiebermeyer intently. "The cult of Sobek was always associated with a temple. That's the one thing missing here. I may be wrong, but I think you have something more to show us."

Hiebermeyer's eyes gleamed, and he dropped the flap covering the mummy. "Back to the plateau where we started. We should get moving. We haven't got much time."

"One final question," Costas said. "How did the crocodiles here get so big?"

Hiebermeyer's phone went off, and he read a text message. He clicked it shut and put it away. "That was Aysha. The inspectors have arrived at the opposite bank. *Scheisse*. They were supposed to come here first. We're not ready for them yet over there." He snorted in annoyance, glanced at his watch, and charged out of the tent, then stopped and looked at Costas. "Did you say something?"

"How did the crocodiles get so big?"

Hiebermeyer scratched his chin, looked thoughtfully down, and then peered at Costas, a glint in his eye. "Oh, human sacrifice, I should imagine."

"What? *Human* sacrifice?"

"The priests couldn't do it in the civilized heartland of Egypt, where that sort of thing was a no-no. But I've always thought there were those among the Egyptian priests who were itching to do it. Thank God they couldn't know what the Aztecs used pyramids for; otherwise Giza would have been a bloodbath. But out here, where no one was looking, they could have had a field day. There were all those awkward foreign prisoners of war: Hittites, Canaanites, Hebrews, Nubians. Perhaps even the odd Greek too as a tasty morsel." He eyed Costas mischievously. "So instead of summoning up a mythical monster, they create a real-life leviathan. What better way to placate the god than to keep him happily engorged in his pool of death here rather than letting him go hungry and swim south to bring darkness over Egypt?"

"Pool of death," Costas said miserably. "That's where we're going diving."

Hiebermeyer grinned at him. "And where it's been waiting for three thousand years. Pretty hungry by now."

Costas groaned, and Hiebermeyer strode on ahead. A few minutes later they stood on a rocky plateau about the size of a tennis court overlooking the Nile, just beyond the site of the sangar. Aysha appeared over the ridge and joined them, holding the baby. Jack could see that Hiebermeyer was bursting to tell them what he had found. "Well?"

Hiebermeyer pulled a folded sheet out of his pocket. "Extra-high-frequency ground-penetrating radar," he said, beaming. "Another little project with my friend Lanowski, developed for a new search I'm planning in the Valley of the Kings. The new technology can penetrate deeper into rock than ever before, and I'm certain it's going to give us another find to rival Tutankhamen's tomb. But this is the first chance I've had to try it out for real. And it came up trumps. *Big*-time."

He unfolded the sheet and passed it to Jack, his hand shaking slightly with excitement. Jack opened it out, and Costas peered over. "Holy cow," Costas murmured. "There's something really big down there."

Jack stared at it, his heart pounding. The printout showed the ghostly image of a square chamber beneath the rock some twenty meters across. "How deep under the surface is this?" he asked.

"Our geophysicists agree with Lanowski that the ceiling of the chamber is at least eight meters below ground level. Before you ask, there's no chance of getting to it from here, at least not without explosives and mining equipment. This whole outcrop is solid pre-Cambrian rock, as hard as iron. It must have taken the ancient Egyptians decades to dig out that chamber."

"You're sure it's that old?"

"I'm certain of it, Jack. You said it: there's one thing missing in the archaeology of this place, and that's a temple. Finding those crocodile mummies clinched it for me. I knew it had to be to the crocodile god Sobek. I used our database to check the dimensions of known Sobek temples elsewhere in Egypt, and what we have here looks bang-on. It would have opened up beside the river and had access to that pool."

"Do we know what the cliff face looks like?"

Hiebermeyer produced another sheet of paper. "Ibrahim's been hard at work over the last few days. He was desperate to tell you, but I asked him to wait until I'd put you in the picture. He took a Zodiac out on the river and used an echo-sounding imager he'd brought from his Red Sea equipment store. It couldn't penetrate the mud in the center of the pool, but it did produce this." He handed Jack the sheet. It showed a graduated profile image of the underwater cliff and the former rocky shore in front of it. At the base of the cliff Jack could clearly see the outline of a massive doorway, the jambs and pediment carved out of the living rock. Maurice was right. It was an incredible image, an ancient temple carved into the cliff, the entrance submerged completely under the waters of the Nile.

"The door looks shut, and it's probably stone," Hiebermeyer said. "But below it you can just about see what I think is a rock-cut channel that led out to the pool. That also fits with other temples of Sobek: a channel to allow tame crocodiles to swim between the river and a sacred pool within the temple. It's just possible that you might be able to get inside that way. The channel is about thirty meters below the present level of the Nile."

"What about before the Aswan Dam?" Jack said. "At low water before the 1960s, the temple would have been exposed. Has it ever been reported?"

Hiebermeyer shook his head. "The photographs show a huge drift of sand and rocky debris coming down from the plateau below the sangar and concealing the entire entrance. It might have been possible for someone to slide into the upper part of the doorway, where there was usually a narrow triangular opening above the actual door to let in air and light. But it looks to me as if there's been a rock fall that's blocked up any opening that might have existed. If the locals know anything about a temple here, they're keeping quiet. They seem to be terrified of this place."

"Can't say I blame them," Costas murmured.

"Can you do it?" Hiebermeyer asked Jack. "Can you dive here?"

Jack slapped him on the back. "We can certainly try."

"That's great," Costas mumbled. "First you violate the sacred crocodile mummies by excavating them, and now we plan to swim right into their lair. Just great."

Jack gestured at the printout. "Have you told your Sudanese inspector about this?"

Hiebermeyer pulled down his hat and stood up. "We haven't told anyone except you and Costas and Ibrahim. And I'll be doing my very best to avoid him. I don't get on with him, and I'm liable to say something that will scupper us. Aysha's the official permit holder and site director here, and she knows how to deal with men like that."

Costas watched Hiebermeyer's shorts sink dangerously below his waistline, and then stared as he hitched them up and tightened the lederhosen suspenders. He shook his head. "Well, if Aysha can deal with you, she can deal with any man."

Aysha waved dismissively. "Maurice is a piece of cake. Dangle an Egyptian mummy in front of him and he's putty in my hands."

"Even a crocodile mummy?"

"Just one mummy," Hiebermeyer said, gazing fondly at Aysha and the baby, then glaring at Costas. "Just remember, not all the crocodiles around here are mummified."

Costas suddenly looked dismayed, and Jack grinned.

"While the inspection's going on, my aim is to be underwater. It's always the best place to be."

Costas looked doubtfully at the river. "*Usually* the best place to be." He checked his iPhone. "Huh. A message from Sofia."

"She reminding you about that dinner date?" Jack said.

"She says she's sending you her draft of the press release on the *Beatrice* for your approval. And she's come up with a name for the submersible: *Nina*. It was one of Columbus's ships; apparently its master was an ancestor of Sofia's. It means 'girl.' I like it. She wants us to do more exploration in the Americas."

Aysha peered at him. "Who's Sofia?"

"Oh, just a friend."

"A dinner-date friend?"

"I've sent her a picture of me with Ahren."

"Whoa," Aysha said. "That's diving in at the deep end."

"Just showing her my friends."

Aysha smiled. "You know how to touch a lady's heart."

Costas paused. "Will Sofia think I'm hitting on her?"

"Well, are you?"

"She and Costas met in a submersible," Jack said. "They plummeted to the depths together."

"You were there too, Jack!" Costas exclaimed.

"So, you're taking a page right out of Lanowski's book," Hiebermeyer said, smiling at Costas.

"I'd rather not take anything out of Lanowski's book," he muttered.

Hiebermeyer slapped him on the back. "You ever need any advice on the man stuff, you come to me."

"Yeah, you and Lanowski both," Costas said glumly.

"He'd be more than happy to help out, I'm sure," Hiebermeyer said. "We could do the male bonding thing, a weekend maybe, and combine it with the two-day seminar I know he's itching to give you on submersible circuitry. Or is it three days? He's told me all about it. I think he called it an idiot's guide. I might even sit in on it myself. I could learn a few things." He beamed at Jack mischievously.

"I think you've just been had," Jack said, turning to Costas. "No more jokes about his shorts, maybe?"

"No way," Costas said, suddenly determined, giving Hiebermeyer a steely look. "From now on, it gets serious."

Jack grinned, and then his phone rang. He answered it quickly. "That was Ibrahim. He's got the equipment stowed in the Toyota ready to drive to the river's edge. Time to saddle up."

"What do you mean, *saddle up*?"

"I thought we'd take a camel ride to get there. Immerse ourselves in desert culture before we immerse ourselves in the Nile. The full Sudan experience."

Costas stared at the camel, which had ambled over to the plateau and was gazing at him dolefully. "Oh no," he said. "That thing's got it in for me."

"It'll be all right," Aysha said. "If you mount it while it's lying down, you won't have to go anywhere near its orifices."

Costas looked at the camel, than back at the river. "Camel, crocodile. Camel, crocodile. Camel. Crocodile."

Hiebermeyer thrust a picture he had been carrying of a Nile crocodile in front of Costas. "Snap," he said.

"What do you mean, snap?"

"I mean snap, the card game. If you don't get on the camel now, I'll put another picture on this one and then when you get in the water, *snap*."

"*Snap*," Costas repeated feebly. "Okay. I get it. Crocodiles. A really bad joke. You can make up for it by helping me get up on this camel. Where's yours, Jack?"

Jack pretended to look shocked. "Oh, I'm not getting on a camel. No fear. I'll be walking far ahead, at the end of a very long lead." He took a deep breath and turned to the others. "Good luck with the inspection, Aysha. I thought I'd been pretty well everywhere, but I've never dived in the Nile. I'm itching to get in."

He turned and peered again at the plateau beside the river where the temple lay concealed. Only a few hours earlier, he had been flying over the Abu Simbel temples beside Lake Nasser, imagining diving into the submerged chambers in the cliff face where the statues of Ramses the Great had once stood. That would have been a remarkable dive, for the haunting atmosphere rather than the possibility of new discoveries; before the Aswam Dam, the inner chambers at Abu Simbel had been above the level of the Nile and had been scoured by treasure hunters and archaeologists for generations. Here, though, it was different. The temple at Semna had never been explored and may have been sealed up for millennia. They might be like Carter and Carnarvon in the tomb of Tutankhamen, entering a space that had been undisturbed since the time of the pharaohs, except underwater and with dangers that made the curse of the tomb seem lame. But they had dived on the very edge of possibility before—into an iceberg, down mine shafts, above a live volcano—and Jack would confront the risks here as he had done then, with Costas to keep him from straying too far into the unknown. He felt the adrenaline pumping already. This could be the dive of a lifetime. *If they could get inside.*

He looked at Costas. "You good to go?"

Costas picked up the camel's lead and handed it to him, a doleful expression on his face. "All I ever wanted to do was build submersibles. And here I am about to ride a camel across the desert in the Sudan, and then get eaten by crocodiles. And don't say it," he said, glancing at Hiebermeyer. He shook his head again and then turned to Jack, cracking a smile. "But you know I'll follow you anywhere, Jack. Even on a camel. And in answer to your question, *yes.*"

"Yes?"

"I'm good to go."

CHAPTER 12

JACK SLIPPED INTO THE WATER AT THE EDGE
of the river and felt the wonderful sense of relief he
always experienced at the beginning of a dive, when the
weight of his equipment disappeared and all he could
think about was the excitement ahead. The submersible
two days before had been a different kind of thrill, but
only because the extraordinary allure of their prize had
allowed him to overcome his dislike of confinement in
small spaces and his yearning for the freedom he was
about to experience now. He had been looking forward
to diving again since he had last donned equipment
more than a month ago at the IMU training facility in
England, and the fact that this was his first ever dive
in the Nile meant that the adrenaline was pumping at an
even higher rate than usual. He looked at Costas, who
was floating beside him with his visor already shut and
his headlamp on. They were wearing all-environment
e-suits, Kevlar-reinforced dry suits with fully integrated
buoyancy and breathing systems controlled by comput-
ers built into the back of their helmets. The contoured
backpacks contained three high-pressure cylinders filled
with gas tailored for each dive, in this case air for the main
part of the dive, a helium-oxygen mix for the deeper
part, and pure oxygen for decompression during their
ascent, all of it attuned to a dive with a predicted depth

of over sixty meters and a duration of at least an hour. They had no safety backup, but the equipment had been tried and tested in extreme conditions, and they both knew they could rely on each other's skill-set and the mutual trust they had built up over the years.

Jack snapped his visor shut and activated the intercom. "Good to go?" He could hear Costas's heavy breathing as he struggled with something underwater. He slipped under the surface and saw that Costas was attempting to adjust the weight of a large object on his waist belt. The increasingly frayed boiler suit that he had worn for years as an outer layer had finally given up the ghost during their dive the year before into the volcano at the site of Atlantis, and the new one still looked startlingly white, in need of a really dirty dive into a hole in the ground to give it credibility. Costas had transferred all his tools and gadgets from the remains of the old suit to the new one and had added a second belt to take more. He heaved it around, then gave the divers' okay signal.

"Good to go."

They dropped a meter or so below the surface and then turned in the direction of the channel. Jack checked the computer readout inside his visor, showing depth, available gas supply and suit temperature, and then looked around him. The water was clear but with a peculiar darkness to it, and he could not see the bottom. They had chosen to enter at a point some fifty meters upriver from the submerged rocks of the great gate of Semna, and to use the current that flowed through the narrow defile to take them into the pool below and then up to the location of the submerged channel that seemed to lead into the underground chamber. They knew that the flow near the riverbed was strong, and they were prepared for a rocky ride and the risk that the current might sweep them beyond their target; but there were no good entry points closer to the chamber, and this route was the better option.

A few minutes later they had descended to twenty

meters and Jack could see the two massive rocks of the great gates below him, their surface worn smooth by millennia of floodwaters, and between them the defile some twenty meters wide that had once channelled the entire flow of the Nile into the pool below. Costas swam vigorously ahead to position himself over the channel, and Jack followed, letting himself sink slowly into it. "Ready for a ride," Costas said. Jack looked down into the blurry flow of fast water and realized that he was being sucked in and his only choice was to go with it. Costas was suddenly drawn away from him at horrifying speed, spinning around as the current took him forward and down towards the rocky base of the channel. As Jack felt the water grip him, he instinctively resisted, and for a few moments felt a searing pain in his torso as the current dragged his body away from the calmer waters above. Then he relaxed, letting the current pull him under, sucking him along. He was at the mercy of the water, unable to control his movements, and could do nothing but watch as he came terrifyingly close to the rocky outcrops that loomed out of the side of the channel and disappeared as quickly behind him. The depth readout inside his visor plummeted from thirty to fifty meters in a matter of seconds, and he braced himself for the impact with calmer water beyond the channel that he knew would be like hitting the surface after jumping off a high board. He caught sight of Costas some ten meters in front of him, his headlamp beam spinning around crazily, and he sensed a darkness ahead in the deep water of the pool at the end of the channel. He checked his depth gauge again: almost sixty meters. The floor of rock below him was pocked with potholes but worn smooth by the water, devoid of visible life. It was as if they were being sucked into another world, the protean darkness from which the Egyptians believed all creation sprang; the channel was like the passage through which escape could never be possible, dooming all who allowed themselves to be taken by it to an eternity of swirling around the pit of the underworld.

Suddenly he felt the wind knocked out of him, as hard as if he had been hit in a rugby tackle, and he heard Costas gasp as well. They had been thrown clear of the channel, and he sensed the flow of the water decrease and his fins begin to find purchase as he kicked himself upright. He saw nothing but darkness, and switched on his headlamp. The beam reflected off particles suspended in the water, dazzling him, and he switched it off again. The glowing red readout of his depth gauge showed seventy-two meters, well below the level of the channel. He felt himself sinking farther and injected a quick blast of air into his buoyancy compensator to stop his descent. His limbs felt heavier as he moved them, as if they were pushing against some resistance, and he realized why. He had sunk into the silt on the floor of the pool, an accumulation that had been suspended here since time immemorial, swirling and settling beneath the channel, its bottom somewhere in the ooze far below him.

Costas's voice came over the intercom. "Jack. You there?"

"Roger that," Jack replied. "I'm here, though I don't know where that is."

"Try rising to sixty meters."

Jack kicked, but his foot jammed into something. He reached down with his right hand and felt a smooth shape with undulations, perhaps an eroded rock that had broken free from the channel and come to rest in the pool. He must be closer to the bottom than he had thought. He pulled his foot again, but it was stuck. He reached down with his left hand and felt the other side. It was big, at least a meter wide. He put his hand into a hole on one side, feeling a hollow space within, and then found a similar hole on the other side. He realized that the object was symmetrical, with the same shapes on both sides. He moved his hands forward where the rock narrowed towards his trapped leg, and then reached farther down, feeling sharp protuberances through his gloves. He tugged at his foot again, and then heaved. "Shit," he exclaimed.

"What is it?" Costas said.

"I've been bitten."

"What? I haven't seen anything living down here."

"You won't believe it, but it's a crocodile."

"*No way.*"

"Don't worry, it's not alive. It's a giant crocodile skull, wedged into the rocks at the bottom of the pool. But I can't get it to release me. My fin's caught in its teeth."

"Don't pull on it. I've been reading about these things. That only makes it clamp down harder. Try lifting the top jaw up."

Jack reached down, found a place between the teeth to slot his fingers, and pulled with both hands. It came away surprisingly easily, and he kicked his trapped fin until it was free. He dropped the jaw, letting it fall slowly back into the silt, and then swam upwards, rising until he could just make out the glow from Costas's headlamp beam and then his shadowy form a few meters away. He blasted air into his suit until he could see Costas clearly, his upper body poking out of the sediment into the clearer water above, and beyond that the turbulence of the current. "Thanks for the tip," he said. "I thought I was about to lose my foot."

"It gives me the jitters just thinking of that thing down there," Costas said. "You sure it was dead?"

"Long dead. Pretty well fossilized. Probably even a dinosaur. It was big enough, huge."

"You sure? Everything looks bigger underwater. You know, refraction of light through your mask. Add a bit of adrenaline, a bit of nitrogen narcosis . . ."

Jack measured the breadth with his hands. "I didn't see it. But it was this wide."

"Okay. That's enough for me. The sooner we're out of this primeval soup, the better." Costas pointed away behind them. "My terrain mapper's showing the entrance to that rock-cut channel about forty meters away at bearing two hundred and seventy-three degrees, depth twenty-five meters. The underwater river created by the current seems to flow around the lower side of the pool, but we might be able to avoid it by swimming beneath and rising up the other side, close to the edge of the pool. You good with that?"

"Sounds like a plan. You lead."

Jack followed Costas as he rose slightly and swam over the sediment in an easterly direction. He dropped down again to avoid the swirling waters of the channel, his form skirting the billowing mass of sediment like an aircraft flying in and out of a cloud. He stopped suddenly, raised his hand, and pointed at a jagged mass rising out of the silt. "Check this out," he said. "It's machinery from a river steamer."

Jack swam up beside him, close now to the rocky edge of the pool. Wedged into the mass of metal was a large upturned vessel like a rowing boat. "Amazing," he exclaimed. "The dimensions look bang-on. I'm guessing this is one of the whaleboats from the 1884 expedition." He stared for a moment at the wooden hull, as well preserved in the freshwater as if it had been sunk that day. He remembered the sangar with the evidence of the British soldiers, and for a moment it felt as if he would rise from the waters into the bustle of activity of those few days in 1884 when the expedition had passed overhead. He turned from the wreckage and looked at Costas. "Fantastic. This really brings history alive for me."

"How's your air supply?"

Jack had been monitoring his gauges since dropping beyond their expected depth threshold in the pool. "More depleted than I'd like. I think I was breathing a lot trying to right myself in that channel."

"Me too. Let's get going. At least from now on it'll be shallower."

They swam past the wreckage and up the rocky wall, its sides smoothed by the current but here and there covered with patches of green algae-like growth, the first signs of aquatic life Jack had seen since entering the water. A few minutes later they topped twenty-five meters depth and swam over the original surface of the riverbank beside the pool, as it had been at low water before the Aswan Dam was constructed. They followed the drop-off until they came to the feature they had seen in the sonar profile readout that Ibrahim had provided; it was a rock-cut channel leading away from the sub-merged riverbank towards the cliff base and the under-ground chamber they knew lay some thirty meters to the east, still invisible in the murky gloom. Jack sank down into the channel, stretching his arms out to either side and dropping to the floor. "Just wide enough for a croc-odile," he said.

"Don't," Costas said. "We've tempted fate enough as it is."

"The channel and the cliff face must have been buried in sand before the Aswan Dam, explaining why none of the earlier archaeologists saw this," Jack said. "Every-thing must have been swept clean when the river rose and flooded through. It shows how much more you can see underwater. I really need to get Maurice diving."

"You've been saying that for years. You'll never change him. And I dread to think where those shorts would end up if he dived in with them on."

Jack swam up the channel, and moments later they were at the base of the cliff. The channel disappeared inside, into a black cavity just large enough to fit his frame; its floor was carpeted with sand where it had evidently remained since the inundation, kept by the rock walls of the channel from being swept away. Jack sank down to the rocky floor, peering ahead through his headlamp beam as far as he could see. He noticed the sand slope upwards in a deeper accumulation until it seemed to fill the aperture some five meters ahead. He checked his pressure gauge. "I've got about twenty min-utes left at this depth. We may not be able to get past that obstruction. But I'm going to try."

"I'm on your tail," Costas said. "Go for it."

Jack swam forward using a gentle dolphin stroke with his fins, his arms by his sides. After five meters he came up against a bank of sand and put his hands into it. The sand was coarse-grained, easy to dig into, but there seemed little way of making progress. "I think we must be within a few meters of the chamber, but this could be as far as we go," he said.

"Don't give up so soon," Costas said. "Make way for Walter, and see what he can do."

"Walter?"

"My very latest gadget. A miniature water pump. He sucks away sand and deposits it down an exhaust tube into the current. When I heard we were going to the Nile, I thought 'sand,' and decided this would be a good dive to trial him."

Jack heard a whirring and raised himself to let a little vehicle about the size of a small dog drive under him and bury itself in the sand, sucking it away and disgorging it out a plastic tube somewhere behind. In a few moments it had burrowed deeper and disappeared. Jack followed, pulling himself through a hole in the sand just big enough for him to squeeze his way along. After about three meters the sand fell away to open water in front of him, and he saw Walter pause, leap out, and then bury himself in the sediment again a few meters to the right, like a rodent digging a hole. Jack wriggled out of the sand and then turned to see Costas do the same, his head emerging beside Walter's exhaust pipe. Costas quickly pulled himself along it and dived into the sediment after Walter until only his fins were sticking out. A moment later the whirring noise stopped and he re-emerged, holding the pump by the tube like a dog on a lead. "He's got a mind of his own," he gasped, looking up. "So where are we?"

Jack increased the intensity of his headlamp and panned it around. They were inside a large rectilinear chamber at least ten meters high and fifteen meters across. The sand that had partly filled the channel formed a large sloping bank against the side of the chamber facing the cliff, evidently where it had fallen in from the sandbank outside before that had been swept away by the rising waters of the Nile. He watched as Costas swam slowly up to a dark form at the rear of the chamber, his beam playing on its surface, and then come to an abrupt stop where the form protruded at the top. There was a gasp, and a sound like a whimper, and then Costas spoke in a whisper. *"Holy cow."*

Jack swam up to him and gasped himself as the image came into view. "Holy crocodile, more like," he exclaimed.

Maurice had been right. Only he could never have imagined anything like this. It was a statue of the ancient Egyptian god Sobek, half man, half crocodile, its snout flashing with jewels where their headlamp beams reflected off them. It faced directly towards the entrance to the temple to the west, towards the setting sun. Jack glanced at his air supply readout. "Fifteen minutes left: five for the chamber, five to get out, five to ascend, then pure oxygen for half an hour."

"Okay, Jack." Costas had pushed off and recovered his composure. "You take a quick look around. I'll reactivate Walter and get him to dig us out again. If he's got any battery left."

"I don't want to hear about it. Let me guess. You've never tried him before."

"Has to be a first time for everything."

Jack swam down to the center of the chamber and then panned his beam around the walls, starting at the buried entranceway and moving clockwise. He saw nothing but blank stone until he had passed the statue and was on the wall to his right when an extraordinary scene came into view. It was a relief carving of an ancient battle, or rather its aftermath, with a wild-haired enemy executing and dismembering their prisoners, a jarring scene because the prisoners were unmistakably Egyptian. He panned the beam farther on. A huge figure of a man came into view, the style different from the battle scene. He stared in amazement, barely able to think, memorizing as much of the detail as possible, features of the carving that he would have time to ponder later. It was the same pharaoh he had seen two days before, fifteen hundred miles away at the bottom of the Mediterranean. He could scarcely register it. *Akhenaten.*

"One minute left, Jack."

He saw something glinting in the sand below the image, hesitated, and then swam for it, in exactly the opposite direction from the exit route. He reached down and picked it up, clutching it as he swivelled around to swim back towards Costas. He looked at it for a second before shoving it in his leg pocket. It was a beautiful ancient scarab, carved out of green stone with a hieroglyphic cartouche on the base he recognized as that of Nefertiti, Akhenaten's consort. It seemed an extraordinary artifact to discover in the empty shell of a temple, and he wondered whether anyone else had been in here since antiquity, whether anyone had come through the sand in the upper part of the doorway before the river level rose. Yet perhaps Nefertiti herself had been here, part of some ritual in this temple with Akhenaten. It was a remarkable find, but it could scarcely prepare him for what he saw next, an object that Costas was holding up in both hands for him as he approached.

"Walter came up with the goods," Costas said, his face beaming through his visor. "He dug this up when he went for his little snout around near the entrance."

Jack took it from him. It was a heavy rod about a meter long, of solid gold, the heaviest golden object Jack had ever held. But it was more than just an astonishing treasure in gold. It was the royal scepter of an Egyptian pharaoh, the only one ever found. A pharaoh truly had been here, but for some reason he had left his greatest symbol of office on the floor of the temple, discarded in this most unlikely place so far from the royal palaces of Egypt hundreds of miles away down the Nile.

Costas pushed him towards the hole. "Now, Jack. No time left."

Jack held the rod close to him and dived into the sediment, his free hand forward, following the tunnel that had been created again by Walter. Five minutes later he was free, swimming down the channel into open water, Costas behind him trailing Walter, seeing the sunlight flickering on the surface of the river some fifteen meters above. He glanced at his readout again. They had been in the temple for only eight minutes. *Eight minutes.* And yet what they had found in those minutes would have been the discoveries of a lifetime for an Egyptologist. He could hardly wait to show what he was carrying to Maurice and Aysha. He turned to Costas, who had come up alongside him, a broad grin on his face. "I know what you want me to say," Jack said.

"Yes?"

"Well done, Walter. Well done, Costas."

"See? A team. All three of us."

"A team."

"I've never seen gold like that before, Jack. *Never.*"

"Nor me. It's one of the most amazing things we've ever found. I'm itching to get back in there again. We need to think about a team, logistics, a time frame."

"I'm onto it."

Half an hour later they were floating on the surface a few meters off their planned exit point two hundred meters downstream from the pool, their visors lifted and eyes closed, drained by the exhilaration of the dive but revitalized after the final fifteen minutes breathing pure oxygen.

Costas floated alongside, and Jack saw that his boiler suit was now suitably streaked with grime. Costas looked skeptically at him. "Did you *really* see a crocodile down there?"

"I told you, I didn't see it. I *felt* it."

"*Felt* it. You mean felt as in you somehow sensed it, you thought it was there? A fevered imagination, maybe?"

Jack raised his hands. "No, I mean felt as in touched." He lifted one leg out of the water, showing the white striations on his fin. "And you can see the bite marks."

"You could have scratched your fin against the rocks going through that channel."

"If you don't believe me, you can go down there and see for yourself."

Costas shuddered. "Not a chance. It's bad enough thinking it might be there, let alone actually finding it."

Hiebermeyer came bounding down the slope, Ibrahim following behind, and squatted down by the shore. "Well, how did it go?"

"We found it, Maurice," Jack said, his eyes gleaming. "You were right. It's a temple to Sobek, with a huge statue of the god at one end. But it's even better than that. There's a massive wall relief showing Egyptian soldiers defeated in battle. I think it must have been carved during those years after the death of Senusret when things were falling apart down here. Maybe they thought they'd offended the gods in some way. My guess is the temple dates to that time too. But it gets even better. At one end of the relief there's a huge image under a sun symbol, a pharaoh, but not wearing a pharaoh's crown or carrying the scepter, walking out as if he's striding off into the desert alone. It's Akhenaten."

"Mein Gott," Maurice said under his breath. "Lower your voice, Jack. Let's keep this to ourselves for now, the four of us here and Aysha. Was there anything else? Any clues? Anything like the image on that plaque in the sarcophagus?"

Jack pursed his lips. "In the lower folds of the skirt, the lines of the sun symbol seemed to create a pattern. At the point where the lines converge, a square block is missing, cut out as if someone's removed it. There might have been something in it, some recognizable feature, maybe some hieroglyphics."

Hiebermeyer exhaled slowly, shaking his head. "Still a missing piece of the jigsaw puzzle." He stared at Jack, narrowing his eyes. "You've found something else, haven't you?"

"I always thought you wanted to be a pharaoh, Maurice. Well, today's your lucky day." Jack heaved the golden scepter out of the water and placed it in the other man's outstretched hands. Hiebermeyer stared speechless and fell back against the slope, sitting and holding the scepter. As he turned it around, he noticed a cartouche. *"Akhenaten,"* he whispered. "It's Akhenaten's royal scepter. It's the most astonishing find in Egyptology in my lifetime."

"The question is, how did it get there?" Jack said matter-of-factly. "And I think the clues are in the wall carving and in the closed door of the temple. The carving shows Akhenaten stripped of ornaments, as if he's walking away as an ordinary man, not as some priest-king. That fits in with the image of a penitent man going in search of the Aten, like a pilgrim who has cast aside worldly goods. And the door suggests finality, as if he's closing the door on the old religion and walking away free of it. Let's imagine Akhenaten himself in there, carrying out some kind of propitiatory ceremony with the priests, maybe even something he's told them will reaffirm his allegiance to the old gods, but then abruptly turning and casting aside his crown and scepter and walking out, leaving his men to shut the door on the old religion forever, even the priests themselves."

"Good crocodile food," Costas said.

"What do you mean?" asked Jack.

"Well, Maurice himself said it. This was a place out of the way where they might have fed humans to the crocodiles, like the Hebrew slaves. What better way for Akhenaten to turn the tables than to release the crocodiles from this pool up that channel into the sealed temple, to feed on the priests themselves?"

Hiebermeyer pulled a keffiyeh out of his satchel and wrapped it around the scepter. "Not a word of this to anyone until we've finished here. If the locals get wind of a find like this, we'll be swamped by gangsters searching for gold, and before you know it this place will be a battleground. And not a word to our new Sudanese inspector, al'Ahmed. This scepter should go to the Khartoum museum, but I don't trust him." He glanced at

Ibrahim, who was standing beside him. "We'll take this away in the Toyota and hide it in the conservation tent in the camp."

Ibrahim nodded, took the bundle, and hurried away back up the slope. Jack held on to a rock by the shore, speaking to Hiebermeyer. "I want to get back in there tomorrow. Maybe we can find that missing piece of the relief carving. For starters, we need to establish a depot tent for our gear and hire a security guard."

Hiebermeyer shook his head. "That can wait. Did you find anything down there from the 1880s?"

Jack nodded. "A whaleboat and some steamer machinery. There's probably more. What do you mean, this can wait? What's more important?"

"Good. That's what I'll tell al'Ahmed about. The reason you're not diving here again tomorrow is that he's arranged for you to visit the wreck site of the *Abbas*, the steamer that foundered upriver in 1884 with Gordon's antiquities on board. It could be the only opportunity we get. It seems too good to miss."

Jack's heart pounded with excitement, but he forced himself to think carefully. "What about the security situation?"

"Al'Ahmed says he's sending in his own people to keep the local warlord at bay. I'm assuming he's talking about Sudanese Interior Ministry police."

"You said you didn't trust him," Costas said. "How can we?"

"You can't. But he talked about it while the other antiquities people were there, the ones we do trust. He said he was arranging a permit and fast-tracking the paperwork, and nobody there raised any protest; there was a lot of enthusiasm, in fact. They could all be in his pay, of course, but we have to take that chance. If this leads to a high-profile excavation and some spectacular finds, then it will justify his appointment and raise his status. It makes sense for him to want it to work."

"Or it could lead to us finding something he really wants, and then him booting us out," Jack said.

"It's your call."

Jack tipped over and floated on his back, smelling the Nile, enjoying the sun on his face. He thought of the site of the *Abbas*, upstream beyond the great gates, into the forbidding land that had terrified the Egyptians in the time of the pharaohs, and thousands of years later when a new force had risen to confront them in the desert. He thought of the men of the river column, of the unknown man with the rifle in the sangar who had so intrigued him, and how he and Costas now seemed to be dogging the footsteps of the relief expedition. Travelling to a site upstream, they would reach the place where the column had fought its first bloody battles with the Mahdi. And he thought of the lure of something else that had brought Akhenaten here, and perhaps Gordon too.

He thought of the sarcophagus and the plaque, and now the Sobek temple and the golden scepter: they were extraordinary discoveries that had made pursuing this trail more than worthwhile. He could end the season on a high and look forward to returning to both places next year, if nothing else got in the way. But right now, knowing that there might be more to be found, a potentially greater prize, put him on tenterhooks. He was on a roll, and he could not stop it.

He lifted his head and stared at Hiebermeyer. "Okay. I'll go with it. Let's get Ibrahim to load up the gear. We can leave this evening. It could be the only chance we'll ever have to find out what General Gordon might have hidden in that boat."

CHAPTER 13

MAJOR EDWARD MAYNE OPENED THE FLAP of the tent and stepped inside, his eyes smarting in the fog of tobacco smoke that filled the air. It had been hot outside, uncomfortably so in the late afternoon sun, but here it was like walking into the overheated parlour of a London gentlemen's club or one of the native sweat lodges that Charrière had shown him in Canada when they were boys. He envied Charrière remaining outside, sitting with the sentries in the shade of a palm tree close to the Nile. The British had not yet learned the Arab way of keeping a tent cool in the desert sun, and the heavy canvas was more suited to a Crimean winter than the furnace of the Sudan. To Mayne it was symptomatic of the campaign as a whole: the British had half adapted, wearing desert-coloured khaki instead of scarlet uniforms, riding camels instead of horses, some of them even ditching their pith helmets for Arab headdress, yet the tactics were those of earlier campaigns. Mayne knew that there were those in this tent now who had the originality of thought to break free, to adapt to the desert; yet with time running short and Wolseley in tight control, there seemed little chance of altering a course of action that had been fatally flawed from the start.

Two officers were hunched over a portable desk in the far corner of the tent, one busy with a protractor and ruler and the other taking notes. Five other men sat around a trestle table in front of Mayne, dressed in the idiosyncratic mix of uniform and personal clothing typical of British officers on campaign. Wolseley himself sat directly opposite, a short, dapper figure immaculately composed, peering at a map along with three of the others. The only man who had seen Mayne enter was sitting to Wolseley's right. There had been a decidedly exotic tang to the air, and Mayne remembered the taste for cherry tobacco that Burnaby had picked up on a recent sojourn in Morocco. He was there now, lounging sideways, cigarette held languidly and legs crossed, just like his famous portrait by James Jacques Tissot painted fifteen years before in London; only instead of the undress uniform of the Royal Horse Guards, he was wearing a kind of ersatz Scottish deerstalking outfit, with a giant howdah pistol holstered at his side. He nodded amiably at Mayne and took a deep drag on his cigarette, letting the ash fall in a shower on the floor and exhaling smoke rings upwards, watching them cascade against the tent roof and descend in a cloud over the other men.

Mayne saw another difference from the portrait: the supremely self-confident cavalry officer of Tissot's portrait had become heavyset, with dimmed eyes; he was a man who knew he could go no further in his military career and whose time for shoehorning himself into adventure would soon be curtailed by age and a new world with fewer places for freelancers like him. Mayne knew that the indifference Burnaby affected here cloaked an acute mind, yet he sensed too that the detailed planning that was preoccupying the others truly was an irrelevance for a man who had perhaps been drawn into the Sudan for something of the same reasons that had compelled Gordon himself to return, attracted by the darkness that lay to the south and by the promise of apotheosis in the battles to come.

"Ah, Mayne." Wolseley had spotted him and quickly stood up and extended a hand. Mayne leaned over and shook it, feeling the skin of his arm prickle with the heat under his tunic. "You know the others around this table. General Earle of the river column, General Stewart of the desert column. And of course Colonel Burnaby and General Buller."

Earle and Stewart both glanced at him and quickly turned back to the map, which Mayne could see showed the loop of the Nile surrounding the Bayuda Desert on the way south to Khartoum. Buller was sitting at Wolseley's left, a giant of a man with a face like a North American bison. He heaved himself up and extended a hand. "Edward, my dear boy. Had no idea you were here until Wolseley told me. You should have sought me out in my tent. You know there's always a bottle to be uncorked for you."

"Sir," said Mayne, shaking hands. "I should like that above all things. Perhaps when this is over." Buller was one of Wolseley's inner circle, his so-called "Ashanti Ring." Mayne had first met him in Canada, and despite his bovine exterior had found him an agreeable companion who spoke with refreshing candour. Like Burnaby, Buller had grown stout and heavy-jowled, fuelled by a prodigious appetite for alcohol; Mayne had seen his personal camel train arrive at Korti laden down with crates of Veuve Clicquot champagne, an outrageous indulgence that only Buller could pull off. But the men loved him because he was a soldier's soldier, a celebrated winner of the Victoria Cross in the Zulu War, a warrior who fought at the bloody forefront of battle and had a reputation for fearlessness surpassed only by Burnaby himself.

"Major Mayne has been attached to the river column," Earle said, peering at Buller over pince-nez spectacles as the other man sat heavily back down. "He's been surveying the riverbanks, carrying out forward reconnaissance ahead of the boats."

"Just like old times in Canada, eh?" Buller said, slapping his hand on the table. "And you've got the Mohawks with you too!"

Mayne turned to Wolseley. "I've brought along Charrière, as you requested. He's waiting outside."

"Best damned hunter I've ever seen," Buller rumbled, shaking his head. "Took me with him into the forest back in '70 above the Winnipeg River. Never seen a man fell a deer before with a throwing knife. He still got that squaw? She was damned good too. Could have led the expedition."

"His wife and child died in a cholera outbreak two years ago," Mayne said.

"Ah. Sorry to hear it." Buller paused for a moment, then turned to Wolseley. "Had Stephenson in for a few drinks last night, your old quartermaster-general. Told me about your pension arrangement for the voyageurs after the Red River expedition. Damned decent of you, if you ask me."

Wolseley looked briefly discomfited, then tapped his pencil on the map. "It was the least I could do. They gave their services to an expedition that achieved its goal without a single life being lost. I treated them as I would have done British soldiers, for services to Queen and Empire."

"Especially generous to Charrière, I gather," Buller said.

"He was my chief reconnaissance scout. He risked his life more than the others."

"Never knew when you might need to call on his services again, eh?" Buller said, eyeing Wolseley and slapping the table. "In the Sudan, of all places."

Mayne knew that the voyageurs were being paid handsomely for their work on the Nile, so it was hardly as if they were here solely out of loyalty to a patron. But it was typical of Wolseley, the type of act that drew men to him. He could be prickly, sometimes snobbish, an infuriating stickler for detail that was probably the undoing of this expedition, but he could also be generous to those under him in a way that seemed to go beyond expediency. Even though he looked something of an aesthete beside larger-than-life characters like Buller and

Burnaby, he was also a ruthless soldier who bore the scars of frontline fighting from his first action as a sub-altern in the Crimea thirty years before.

Buller peered at Mayne. "So, you've been surveying the Nile, eh? Too many damned engineers on this expedition, if you ask me. Mapping, planning, building. Old Charlie Gordon's a sapper, and General Graham at Suakin on the Red Sea, and those two in the corner," he said, jerking his head towards the figures hunched over the desk. "If you want my opinion, we're overengineered."

Mayne saw the twinkle in Buller's eye. He was right, as usual, but not necessarily in the way he meant. Sapper officers were trained to seek solutions to engineering problems, not to create them. In many ways this was an engineers' war: a war of survey, of intelligence, of logistics. And Buller knew perfectly well that the problem with overengineering lay with Wolseley, whose fastidious attention to detail and obsession with repeating his renowned river expedition had prevented the dash across the desert that could have seen a British force at the gates of Khartoum weeks ago. But Buller owed his career to Wolseley, and he was astute enough to couch his criticism in elliptical terms. In any case, they all knew it was too late for any change of strategy now.

The taller and younger of the two men who had been working in the corner of the tent came over to Wolseley, holding a map. He had chiselled, handsome features and a waxed handlebar moustache over a beard; a keffiyeh cloth was wound loosely around his neck, and with his sun-bronzed features he could have passed himself off as an Arab. He stared at Mayne, the cast in his right eye making it impossible to return his gaze comfortably. Wolseley glanced up at him. "Major Kitchener has just traversed the Bayuda Desert and come within two miles of Khartoum. He's my deputy assistant adjutant general for intelligence, though sometimes he thinks he runs the show."

Mayne nodded at Kitchener, knowing there would be

no handshake. Kitchener was an individualist who did not take orders easily; he was not one of Wolseley's Ashanti Ring, and had come perilously close on several occasions to overstepping the mark. He was saved by his indispensability as an intelligence officer and by the sheer force of his presence. He had become the eyes and ears of the expedition, a fluent Arabic speaker who had developed his own intelligence network as far as Khartoum and rallied loyal tribesmen around him, and who was the last man present in the tent to have spoken with Gordon. Mayne had encountered him three weeks earlier in the Bayuda Desert when Kitchener had swept down upon them like one of the Madhi's emirs, swathed in Arab dress and surrounded by a bodyguard of tribesmen.

Mayne looked into Kitchener's disarming eyes. "Congratulations on the survey of Palestine. I saw the first of your volumes at the Royal United Services Institute library in London before I came out here. It's a prodigious achievement, more than most survey officers would hope to achieve in a lifetime. It puts the study of biblical geography truly on the map."

Kitchener kept staring. "Palestine interests you? You were not part of the biblical archaeology society at Chatham."

Mayne held the steely gaze. He remembered the group of evangelical officers who believed that the scientific survey of biblical lands was their true calling, the most noble use of the skills they were learning as engineers. Charles Gordon, an individualist who professed allegiance to no church or movement, was not among them, but they revered him for his morality and because he seemed to live his life to the utmost by Christian principles: a man who would now seem poised for the ultimate Christian act, willing to sacrifice himself for those in Khartoum who depended on him.

Mayne shook his head. "My interest is purely professional. Before coming out to the Sudan, Lord Wolseley asked me to discover everything I could about Gordon, his possible motivations for being here, his recent state of mind. I read the book he wrote about his time in Jerusalem in 1883. He seemed to retreat into himself in much the same way he has done in Khartoum, and as he did in China twenty years ago before leading his army to victory there. But he also carried out some useful survey work. He used your maps and notes to identify to his satisfaction a number of New Testament sites. Together your work provides a most valuable basis for intelligence on Palestine should we ever come to confront the Ottomans there."

"My opinion, decidedly," said Kitchener, his stare unwavering.

Wolseley gestured towards the other man at the desk. "In which case you will also be familiar with the work of Kitchener's superior and my deputy adjutant general for intelligence, Colonel Sir Charles Wilson."

Mayne looked over, seeing a slight man of about Wolseley's age who also wore the lapel badges of the Royal Engineers. Wilson put up a hand in acknowledgement while continuing to write in his notebook. It made sense that Wilson should have been appointed to the expedition. He had recently been military adviser to Sir Evelyn Baring, British agent in Egypt, and had even been considered for Gordon's role as saviour of Khartoum. He and Gordon knew each other well, and Wilson shared his passion for the Holy Land. Like Kitchener, Wilson was not one of Wolseley's Ashanti Ring, yet Mayne sensed no palpable tension between the two men. They were united by an overwhelming common purpose, the relief of Khartoum, and Wilson's personal friendship with Gordon as well as his expertise on the Sudan meant that he could be at the centre of Wolseley's operations with no questions being asked.

Wilson finished writing and came over, looking at Mayne with his penetrating blue eyes. Mayne extended his hand over the table. "Sir Charles. While I was reading General Gordon's *Reflections in Palestine,* I chanced upon a description of the ancient arch that bears your name under the Temple Mount in Jerusalem. I should very much like to have your opinion on its purpose."

Wilson shook his hand, keeping his gaze. "It's always gratifying to find an officer with an interest in archaeology, especially a fellow sapper. Perhaps when this expedition is over, we can meet up again and discuss it."

Mayne withdrew his hand. There had been no hint of recognition in Wilson's eyes. Yet Wilson had been Mayne's superior in the intelligence department for almost fifteen years now, the man who briefed and debriefed him in the hidden complex of rooms under Whitehall. Mayne felt a rush of certainty course through him. In the past, his immediate contact had always been someone else, a middleman, an anonymous officer on the staff, someone who would secretly make his presence known and wait to pass on the signal to activate his mission. But this time was different. For the first time, Wilson himself had come, a man who was not only intelligence chief for the Nile expedition but also head of the most secretive department in Whitehall, an officer charged by the highest authority in the War Office to send out missions essential for the security of the Empire, missions that would shock the British Establishment to the core if the truth were ever to come out.

Mayne thought hard, his mind racing. Everything that was happening now, the relief expedition, the planning around this table, was the culmination of involvement in the Sudan that had begun before the British invaded Egypt three years earlier, going back to Gordon's appointment by the Ottoman Khedive as governor general of the Sudan in 1875. At that date Wilson's official role was as consul general in Constantinople, a brief that allowed him to travel widely and gather intelligence on the Ottoman Empire. It was no surprise that his interests came to cover the southern limits of Ottoman control, in Egypt and the Sudan. With the completion of the Suez Canal in 1869, Egypt had become the pivotal crossroads of the Empire, the gateway to India. For the British and the French, the other main shareholder in the canal, the lands of Egypt and the Near East also held huge historical resonance. Eight hundred years ago, the first crusaders had reached the Holy Land, confronting the forces of Islam that had laid claim to Jerusalem. Now those forces were once again rearing up, and standing at the apex of that gathering maelstrom was the figure of General Charles Gordon. Mayne knew now that his own future was wrapped up in that man's destiny; that this was to be the ultimate mission for which Wilson had been preparing him.

Wolseley beckoned Mayne over. "You know why you are here?"

"I await your instructions, sir."

"Then listen closely. What I am about to tell you will not only determine Gordon's future, it will shape the future of the Sudan and Egypt and our prestige in the eyes of the world. What I am going to ask you to do must remain top secret. There will be no medals, no public accolade. Only those of us around this table will ever know. Are you willing to serve your Queen and country?"

Mayne caught Wilson's eye, then gave Wolseley a steely look. "It's what I'm here for. Tell me what I have to do."

CHAPTER 14

W OLSELEY PICKED UP A TATTERED PIECE of paper from the table and showed it to Mayne. "This is Gordon's last communiqué. It reached me through Kitchener's network of spies, carried by fast camel through the desert. It's dated the twenty-ninth of December, two days ago. He says: 'Khartoum all right, and can hold out for years.'"

Kitchener opened the notebook he had been holding. "General Gordon has been sending his journals down by steamer to Metemma for safekeeping, and I have read the most recent entries. This is one for the fourteenth of December. 'If the expeditionary force does not come in ten days, the town may fall; and I have done my best for the honour of our country.'"

Burnaby tapped his cigarette ash onto the floor. "Lord Randolph Churchill has suggested to me that we collect together a group of big-game hunters with African experience and send them to rescue Gordon," he said. "A posse, as I believe they would call it in America."

"With you at their head, doubtless," said Buller, giving Burnaby a jocular look.

"The thought had occurred to me," Burnaby said with a smile, leaning back and exhaling another cloud of smoke.

"Out of the question," Wolseley said forcibly. "This is

not the Wild West, and Her Majesty's army does not appoint deputies to do its dirty work." Kitchener shut the notebook, and Wolseley stared at Mayne. "You see our dilemma. Gordon was in a perilous situation in November, and yet two days ago he said he can hold out for years. Clearly the latter cannot be the case. We must question his state of mind."

"Can you not *order* Gordon to leave?" Earle said. "You outrank him."

"Officially he works for the Khedive of Egypt, as governor general of the Egyptian province of Sudan. If I bring the Queen's Regulations to bear, he will resign his commission in the British army and be out of our orbit completely. He has tried to resign before, and only the intervention of Gladstone kept him on our books. It is the only thread of control we have with him and we cannot jeopardise it."

"The man only ever treated orders as a basis for discussion," Earle said. "They even say he consults the prophet Isaiah before giving his approval."

"Orders as a basis for discussion? That sounds familiar." Wolseley raised an eyebrow at Kitchener. "Except that some of us operate without the need to consult any prophet other than ourselves."

"Is there any hope of negotiation with the Mahdi?" Earle persisted.

Kitchener snorted. "As self-appointed ruler of the entire Muslim world, he answers only to Allah."

"Only to God?" Buller mutterered. "That sounds like Gordon."

"General Gordon answers to *himself*," Kitchener snapped.

"That also sounds like someone else, Major Kitchener."

Kitchener's look hardened, but he kept his counsel. "General Gordon's intentions are tied to his sense of responsibility towards the people of Khartoum. In China he was there to defend the mercantile interests of the

West, and in Khartoum he is here to defend the liveli-
hood of the Sudanese."

"By all accounts it is a pestilential place, a veritable
Gomorrah," Earle said forcibly. "Why Gordon should
choose to make it his cause is beyond me. They say
that half the population are slaves, the other half slave
dealers."

"A trade that Gordon has allowed to continue, to the
consternation of the prime minister *and* the Queen,"
Buller added.

"He allowed it to continue because it is in the best
interests of the Sudanese people," Kitchener retorted.
"General Gordon abhors the corruption of the Ottoman
viziers who control the Sudan, and the venality of the
Arab and Egyptian merchants. By banning the slave
trade he would have lost sympathy with both the Ottomans and the Sudanese. By allowing it to continue he
has established his reputation among them and increased
his chance of quashing the trade when the time is right.
His actions are sorely misunderstood, even by his erstwhile friends. His decision was made with noble intentions." Kitchener opened a marked page in the notebook
and read from it. " 'November the ninth. I declare positively, and once and for all, that I will not leave the
Sudan until everyone who wants to go down is given
the chance to do so.' " He paused. "The next line is written by General Gordon in capital letters. He states that
if any emissary comes up ordering him down, 'I will not
obey it, but will stay here, and fall with the town, and
run all risks.' " Kitchener shut the journal and put it
down. "He reiterates his intention to stay many times,
with great vehemence."

"At that date he was incensed by the murder of his
friend Colonel Stewart, whom he had sent down from
Khartoum to supposed safety in the steamer *Abbas* a
few days before," Wolseley said. "Now perhaps he will
be less agitated and see more reason."

"Or see no reason at all," Buller said. "He has been
under fire since the end of October, when the Mahdi ar-

rived with his army outside Khartoum. Kitchener tells
me that his garrison lives on tree gum and tobacco
dregs and bread made from the pith of palm trees. As for
the civilians, they must have eaten the last of the rats
weeks ago. The dead will be strewn in the streets, and
one shudders to think what the living eat now. There are
those who say that Gordon has rigged the palace to ex-
plode if it is taken; ever the engineer. They say that he
sleeps by day and stays up at night, sitting framed by his
window in the palace deliberately backlit by candles, as
if he's asking for a bullet. I ask you: are these the acts of
a man who can any longer see reason?"

Kitchener snorted. "General Gordon is an officer of
the Royal Engineers. He will have calculated the distance across the Nile to the nearest sharpshooters, and
know perfectly well that their Remingtons would stand
little chance of hitting him at that range. And he will
also have calculated the uplifting effect on his Egyptian
and Sudanese garrison of seeing him night after night
seemingly impervious to gunfire. If it makes him seem a
god in their eyes, then it can be only to the good in his
present situation."

"It's not their perception of his godlike status that
matters to me; it's whether he has that perception himself," Buller rumbled. "Gods don't need to be rescued by
mere mortals like us."

Wolseley tapped his pencil on the table. "Twenty years
ago I watched him deliberately expose himself above
the parapets at Sebastopol in the Crimea. He was drawing the fire of Russian sharpshooters so that the smoke
would reveal their positions. He's not the only one
among us who seems to relish a dice with death." He
glanced at Burnaby, who flicked the ash of his cigarette
and looked impassively on. "In February, Gordon arrived in Khartoum alone, like a penitent holy man. He
presented himself to the people of Sudan as their saviour, and also as one who was at their mercy should they
choose to disbelieve him. He depends for survival on his

own heroic self-image. That is how you garner loyalty among these people."

"Heroic, or foolish," Buller muttered.

"He has the heroic qualities of authenticity and honour," Kitchener replied. "He will not be swerved from what he thinks is right, and he will not let down those who have given their loyalty to him. He will *not* leave Khartoum without his people," he reiterated.

"The fate of that place and its people is beyond our control," Wolseley replied.

"Then so, it seems, is the fate of General Gordon," said Kitchener.

Wolseley waved the piece of paper again. "But our latest intelligence suggests otherwise. This message was written only days ago, and is buoyant."

"We would be wrong to believe such assurances," Buller rumbled. "With Colonel Stewart gone, Gordon no longer has Europeans to advise him, only Egyptians and Sudanese who regard him not as a general but as a holy man, their own version of the Mahdi. He even wants a slave trader to be his deputy, I tell you."

"Zubayr of the Ja'aliyyin," Kitchener said. "A venal man by the standards we suppose that we have, but the Sudanese tribesmen understand a slave trader and respect him more than they do the Ottoman and Egyptian officials."

"It's just as it was in China," Wolseley muttered. "He has always surrounded himself with mavericks and foreigners. His closest confidants have never been men of his own background we can trust, but others like himself who take him even further from our control. In China he locked himself away and brooded for two months before finally capturing Soochow and killing the rebel leaders. He may be in the same state now, and have a surprise in store for us yet."

Buller grunted. "From what Kitchener tells us, he is now very far from the logic that we propose to apply to his rescue. He may even wish to dig himself deeper into that pestilential hole that looks as if it will become his tomb."

"He has done everything to increase his isolation," added Earle. "Even before the telegraph line was cut, he packed up his cipher book and sent it away with his belongings in the steamers. Why did he do that, deliberately cutting himself off from us?"

"A fit of pique," Buller said. "Disgust that he was being made a sacrificial lamb."

"It would take someone with a saint's powers to endure what he has gone through without cracking."

"It is a test he's set himself. He's dragging his own cross through the streets to Calvary. No wonder he was so interested in finding the location of Golgotha on his recent trip to Jerusalem. He was pacing out his march to apotheosis."

"Gordon's isolation began before he left England," Wolseley said. "His furtive departure from Waterloo station in February, with the commander in chief packing his bag for him and Lord Baring handing him money, like parents sending off a miscreant son to exile in the colonies. The die was cast the moment that train pulled out of the station. And then the brief for his role at Khartoum that everyone knew he would discard in favour of his own mission, to save the people. I cannot help but see Mr. Gladstone behind this."

"Gladstone does not want a martyr," Buller said.

"It might serve him for Gordon to make a fool of himself."

"There is a fine line between a fool and a martyr."

"That's Gladstone's gamble, and perhaps Gordon's too."

"This rescue mission has been hampered from the start by Whitehall," Buller said, slapping the table. "Who, I wonder, could be behind that? And there is another possibility. Gordon could go down in flames with his city, or he could survive and be captured. That would be the worst of all outcomes for Gladstone. The image of

Gordon standing alongside the Mahdi in chains must keep him awake at night."

"Or *not* in chains," Wolseley said. "*That* would be his worst nightmare."

"Then we must do everything we can to prevent it."

"That is why we are here, gentlemen. On with the planning."

Mayne felt the sweat prickling on his face. He glanced at Wilson, who appeared to be concentrating on the map. The conversation had veered dangerously close to their own secret purpose in being in the Sudan, and he was beginning to feel on edge.

Buller banged his hand on the table again. "The longer he strings it out, the more intractable he becomes. If he has gone seeking personal redemption like the children of Israel, then I fear he may have become lost in the wilderness."

"This is a military and logistical matter, not one requiring us to delve into the mind of a latter-day prophet," Wolseley said sharply.

"In that you are, in my opinion, entirely wrong," Kitchener said quietly.

Wolseley glared at him and then put a finger on the map. "We are here to discuss a rescue mission. We are at Korti on the Nile. From here, the column under General Stewart will advance across the Bayuda Desert, rejoining the Nile where it loops around some hundred miles to the south of us. Meanwhile the column under Earle will continue to make its way up the river through the cataracts." He swept one hand across the desert and the other over the eastward loop of the Nile, bringing them together on the river at a point about halfway between Korti and Khartoum. "The two columns will meet here at Metemma. Stewart's column will arrive first, and an advance force will be sent forward to Khartoum in Gordon's three river steamers that should be waiting for us. When Earle's river column arrives, the rest of the force will embark on the whaleboats and follow. If the advance contingent in the steamers is successful in retrieving Gordon, then the rest of the force will turn around and withdraw to Korti and the Egyptian border. If we do have to go forward into Khartoum and raise the siege, then so be it. But our intention, gentlemen, is not to save Khartoum or the Sudan. It is to rescue General Gordon."

"The Mahdi's army will not stand idle," Kitchener said. "There will be battle in the desert, mark my words. Days spent dithering and planning now will advance our cause to hopelessness. Time is of the essence."

Wolseley tapped his pencil irritably, then leaned forward. "After discussion with Colonel Wilson, I have decided to send a man forward to Khartoum in advance of the steamers. His job will be to persuade Gordon of the utmost gravity of his situation, and the imperative for him to leave with our forces when they arrive. Colonel Wilson himself will then accompany the flotilla of steamers up to Khartoum to escort Gordon out. Gordon must be made to understand that the steamers will have room for him alone, and not for the entire damned population of Khartoum as well. If he wishes to save his own skin, he must abandon them. The man I have selected for the job is you, Major Mayne. If Gordon chooses to stay, then his fate is no longer in your hands. Do you understand?"

Mayne remained stock-still. "Yes, sir."

Wolseley put down his pencil and arched his hands together. "Time has run short for us, gentlemen. Colonel Wilson has received intelligence that Russian forces have advanced over the Oxus River near Panjdeh in Afghanistan. It's the most dangerous escalation since the end of the war in Afghanistan four years ago. If it comes to renewed war now, we will be siding with the Afghans against the Russians. Mr. Gladstone has ordered an emergency session of Parliament, and the army in India has begun to mobilise. And this won't be just a British war to curb Russian imperialism on the borders with India. The French will become involved, as they did in the Crimea. The web of alliances across Europe will draw in other nations, some of them itching for an excuse to get at each other's throats. The greatest fear is that Germany could enter as a belligerent against us and even against the Russians too, and that she could emerge supreme if we overextend ourselves in the east. Gentlemen, for the first time since the war against Napoleon, we could find ourselves leading armies across the English Channel to Flanders and Picardy and Normandy."

"So Egypt and the Sudan becomes a sideshow," Buller rumbled.

"We could be withdrawn at any moment," Wolseley replied. "We must attempt to reach Khartoum without delay."

"The Mahdist jihad is as much a threat as the Russian menace," Kitchener said.

Wolseley shot him an annoyed glance. "We are here to rescue Gordon, not to put down a desert rebellion that would scarcely concern us were Gordon safe and away."

"It should concern us," Kitchener replied forcibly. "It threatens Egypt and the entire Arab world. The fires of fanaticism will spread to India. There will be bombings and outrages in Europe."

Wolseley waved one hand dismissively. "The Mahdi will die, and the rebellion will wash against the borders of Egypt and dissipate. The tribesmen have neither the appetite nor the ability to prosecute war beyond their homeland. They are riven by internal jealousies and feuds that will consume them. Beyond the present question of Gordon, the revolt is of little moment to us as we have no interest in occupying the Sudan."

Mayne watched Kitchener bristle but keep quiet. He reflected on the absurdity of a situation where a flash point two thousand miles away in Afghanistan had finally lit a fire under Wolseley, when for months now Gordon's situation had presented the utmost urgency to all other onlookers, up to the Queen herself. Not for the first time he wondered whether Wolseley's sluggish operation had been deliberately engineered because the relief of Gordon was always going to be problematic;

better to be unsuccessful this way and blame the obstinacy of the man himself rather than fail spectacularly in a risky dash across the desert to Khartoum.

Wolseley turned to Mayne. "You will impress upon General Gordon the urgency of his situation."

"Mayne will be able to impress *nothing* upon General Gordon," Kitchener interjected. "As you yourself are aware, he is a man of the strongest convictions."

"*Major* Mayne will follow my orders. *Brevet* Major Kitchener will remember his rank and focus his attention on the map," Wolseley said, his voice strained with controlled anger. He waited until Kitchener had resumed sketching in the lines and then turned again to Mayne. "You will impress upon General Gordon the urgency of his situation," he repeated. "This may well be his last chance of escape. Kitchener himself carried out a reconnaissance of the shoreline at Khartoum in October, and I have used his information to devise a plan. Kitchener?"

Kitchener appeared to ignore Wolseley, concentrating on tracing a line on the map.

"Major Kitchener, *if you please,*" Wolseley exclaimed impatiently.

Kitchener carried on for a few seconds more until he had completed the line, and then pointed to a small structure he had drawn on the bank of the Nile opposite the palace. "This is a ruined fort," he said. "It dates from the time of the Egyptian foundation of Khartoum in the 1830s, but it is remarkably similar to a fort of the pharaoh Akhenaten I observed farther down the Nile. Studying the ancient fort has helped me to understand its function."

He eyed Wolseley coldly, then laid his ruler on the map just south of the fort, on a line running across the southern point of Tutti Island to the shoreline of Khartoum just northwest of the governor's palace. "To the south of this line, the shore opposite Khartoum is unoccupied by the Mahdi's forces. At this point the river is some eight hundred yards across, beyond the effective range of their Remington rifles. Instead they've occupied

Tutti Island, close enough for them to fire accurately into the city."

"So the fort is abandoned," Mayne said, peering over Earle's head at the map.

"It should be your objective," Kitchener said. "If you arrive under cover of darkness, you should be able to get into the ruins unseen, and from there plan your trip across the river to the governor's palace."

Wolseley tapped his pencil on the fort. "This fort is where you will take Gordon. If you succeed in spiriting him away in disguise from the palace and return across the river without being seen, you can hole up in there until our river steamers arrive. Captain Lord Beresford of the Royal Naval contingent will be under instructions to send a landing party to the fort simultaneously with putting a half company of troops ashore at the governor's palace."

Kitchener had folded his arms and stood aloof, his face set impassively. "You may as well order all the troops to make for the fort, as any British soldier who attempts to land at the palace will be shot down by the marksmen on Tutti Island."

"Or by the marksmen on the palace roof, if Khartoum has already been taken," Burnaby added, dropping his cigarette on the floor and crushing it.

"If Gordon agrees and comes away to the fort, Mayne's role in his rescue will be exposed once the steamers arrive," Earle said. "We had agreed to keep his mission secret."

Wolseley nodded. "Beresford will find Gordon alone in the fort, because Mayne will have disappeared into the desert once they see the steamers round the bend of the Nile at Tutti Island. Gordon will go along with the secrecy, as the last thing he will want is for the world to see that he has agreed to be spirited away. It must seem as if he crossed the river alone in disguise to await our arrival once he had spotted our steamers coming, from a place where he could then direct an assault against Tutti Island and return back into the city at the head of our troops. He must be given the opportunity to see that this could happen, even if events turn out otherwise. The press can then report that his move to the fort was in fact an attempt to rescue Khartoum, and if he leaves with us it was not of his own volition. His reputation would remain untarnished."

Buller snorted. "Old Charlie Gordon doesn't care about his reputation anymore. All he cares about is his people in Khartoum and the promises he has made them. He's their messiah. He'll go down fighting rather than scuttle out with his tail between his legs. That's where this plan falls asunder. We've left it too late. He won't want to be rescued."

Wolseley pursed his lips and looked at Wilson. "Your opinion? You are my intelligence chief."

Mayne held his breath. Suddenly his mission was on a knife edge. Only he knew the thoughts that would be running through Wilson's mind, the urgency of keeping Wolseley's plan on course. Wilson looked up. "I defer to Kitchener. He's the last man here to have seen Gordon."

Wolseley pursed his lips again and looked up at the tall man standing impassively opposite him. For once Kitchener was silent, staring at Wolseley with those disarming eyes, his moustache barely twitching. Wolseley turned away and looked at the others.

"Mayne?" he said.

Mayne did not dare to glance at Wilson. He could not allow Wolseley to be dissuaded, even though he knew Buller was right. Buller's scenario was precisely the one that had brought him here. Gordon might die defending Khartoum, but he might also survive and be captured. That could not be allowed to happen.

He spoke confidently. "It can be done. Charrière and I can reach the Blue Nile, and I can make my way across to the palace. I know what to say to General Gordon."

Wolseley nodded curtly. Kitchener leaned over and continued transferring his notes to the map as they watched in silence. When he had finished, he stood up, and Mayne pointed at a series of crosses that he had put along the course of the Nile. "What do these mark?" he asked.

"Ancient ruins from the pharaonic period," Kitchener replied. "A passing interest."

"A passing irrelevance," Wolseley said irritably.

Kitchener pointed to one cross. "Not an irrelevance, sir. This cliff face had a bas-relief showing slaves pulling boats over rocks in the river, apparently undertaking the same exercise as General Earle's river column, without of course the benefit of Mohawks or Kroomen but with many different dark-skinned men among the team."

Earle looked up incredulously. "Are you saying that the ancient Egyptians attempted the same exercise, dragging boats through the cataracts?"

"The next scene shows them having abandoned the boats and setting out across the desert. Of course, they had no camels then, the camel having been introduced by the Arabs, but they have horses and chariots, and even the slaves are shown striding off confidently."

"A lesson for us there, perhaps," Buller rumbled, peering at Wolseley.

"Precisely my plan in ordering out the desert column, though we hedge our bets by keeping the river column going," Wolseley said tartly.

Mayne picked up Wolseley's pencil and put another cross beside the Nile to the southeast of Korti. "Yesterday I was shown an underground chamber found by our sappers beside the third cataract," he said.

Kitchener looked at him sharply. "Any inscription?"

Mayne thought for a moment and decided not to describe the scene showing the destruction of the Egyptian army. "At the far end of one wall was the image of a sun disk, with its rays carved over the entire relief. In front of it was a man with a distended belly and an elongated face, a pharaoh."

"Akhenaten," Kitchener breathed, looking over at Wilson. "It must be."

"I believe so," Mayne said. "I saw the same disk when

we stopped at Amarna on the voyage south through Egypt and visited the excavations there."

Kitchener spoke directly to Wilson. "I will visit this site tomorrow morning."

"Right now, you will finish tracing the desert route," Wolseley said, his patience clearly wearing thin. "You still need to show Mayne a track from Metemma to Khartoum."

Kitchener stood back from the map. Wolseley tapped the pencilled lines between Korti and Metemma, and then between Metemma and Khartoum, and looked at Mayne. "If all goes to plan, Wilson will reach Gordon within a day of your meeting with him, giving Gordon as little time as possible to change his mind if you are able to persuade him to leave. Meanwhile the Mahdi might force our hand by ordering the final assault on Khartoum. But we must take our chances. Whether you succeed or fail, Mayne, you will not wait to return on the steamers but will make your own way back along the Nile to rejoin General Earle and the river column. If we fail to save Gordon, and one of the press correspondents gets wind of the fact that a British officer had managed to reach him beforehand, then there will be hell to pay. Do you understand?"

"Yes, sir."

"It would look like a desperate measure that could have been ordered only by the expedition commander. I would rather the blame went higher up the chain of command in Whitehall. Scapegoats will be sought, gentlemen, you can be sure of it. The press and the public will bay for blood, and those on whom the blame should fall for delaying the despatch of the expedition will be seeking any sign of weakness in our conduct. If my reputation is tarnished, then so is that of every one of you around this table. Major Mayne's mission must remain secret, known only to those of us in this tent and to Charrière, who will go with you."

Mayne stared at Wolseley. He had guessed as much, but he still had to try. "Most of the Mohawk contingent has left for Canada. Their job was mainly done after the third cataract, and their contract finished. Charrière will want to go too."

Wolseley gave him a thin smile. "They're anxious to get back to their wives and families. As you told Buller, Charrière has nothing to go back to. I want you to operate together just as you did on the Red River expedition fifteen years ago, when you observed Louis Riel and his rebels from your hideout for days before the rest of the column arrived."

Buller slammed his hand on the table. "Come on, man. You should relish it. You were a team. He can be your bodyguard and your tracker."

"Colonel Wilson will brief him after this meeting," Wolseley said. "You are agreeable to this?"

"Sir." Mayne returned an unwavering gaze. He well remembered the two of them lying with their rifles on the ridge above Riel's encampment. He had been there as Wolseley's reconnaissance scout, with Charrière as a runner to report back should Riel strike camp and return to the American border. Had Riel mustered his men in preparation for a fight, then Mayne had an entirely different mission, one so sensitive that nobody else knew of it. His friendship with Charrière had always been predicated on what he had been briefed to do that day.

Wolseley carried on. "I requested you for this expedition because I anticipated just such a mission. I had General Earle send you on long reconnaissance forays into the desert not only to acclimatise you but also so that your fellow officers in the column will not think it unusual if you return a few weeks from now after a particularly long absence, dressed and bearded like an Arab and doubtless the worse for wear. And if you do not return, you will not be the first British officer to ride out into the desert and disappear without a trace."

Mayne said nothing but nodded. He knew who really pulled the strings here. Wolseley had played into Wilson's hands in almost every detail. The absolute imperative of any mission Mayne carried out for Wilson was anonymity. And he knew that there was one message, one simple code that Wilson could give him that would make his disappearance afterwards a necessity, his ultimate act of duty to Queen and country. The message that would show that he had been given a license to kill.

Wolseley stood up. "Kitchener will give you the maps to memorise. You must take nothing with you that could be traced back here."

"Sir."

Buller reached over to shake his hand. "Good luck, Edward. Give Charlie Gordon my regards. If he doesn't agree to come out, then he can have the damned place as far as I'm concerned."

Burnaby lit another cigarette and gave Mayne a languid smile. "Best of luck, old boy. Perhaps we'll meet on the other side."

Mayne nodded at him and then turned to follow Wilson and Kitchener to the entrance flap of the tent. Wilson looked back at him intently. "You have everything you need? *Everything?*"

"I have everything."

"Kitchener will answer any questions you might have. Good luck." Wilson shook his hand firmly. As he did so he passed him something, a folded piece of paper, which Mayne kept in his hand without looking at it. Wilson turned back into the tent as Kitchener came out. Mayne tensed, the adrenaline coursing through him at last, his hand held tight around the paper. He knew there was no turning back now.

CHAPTER 15

MAYNE OPENED THE TENT FLAP AND STEPPED outside, waiting for Kitchener to collect the map case and join him. He walked a few paces into the desert, relishing the fresh air after the smoky atmosphere inside, breathing in deeply and smelling the coppery tang the sand exuded after a day in the burning sun, a smell like blood. After the heat of the afternoon the encampment beside the Nile was beginning to stir again, and the soldiers who would make up the desert column were preparing for departure the next day. In the marshalling ground to the south he could hear the snorting and bellowing of more than three thousand camels, along with curses and yells that showed the inexperience of the men who had been detailed to handle them. Beside the river the naval contingent was cleaning and oiling their Gardner machine gun, an unwieldy weapon mounted on a carriage that had already shown its vulnerability to sand and dust. In the distance he could hear the crackle of musketry from the rifle range as the infantry sharpened their skills for what might lie ahead. The piquets of dismounted cavalry he could see on the ridges were a reminder that although Khartoum and the Mahdi were two hundred miles away, dervish spies were everywhere and the troops were vulnerable to sharpshooters and suicide attacks. It was a lesson that the soldiers in the river column had learned all too well the previous day, and one that the desert column would confront soon enough as they struck out across the desolate wasteland to the south.

The sand turned bloodred as the rays of the setting sun streaked across from the southwest. Soon it would be a dazzling spectacle, deep oranges and maroons, the ridges and knolls of the desert framed black as the orb of the sun dropped below the horizon. He remembered first seeing a desert sunset three years before, one evening alone at the pyramids of Giza, when he had arrived in Egypt to carry out intelligence work in the wake of the British invasion. That was when he had first come south too, though only as far as the border of Egypt at Aswan, before the first cataract of the Nile. The ruins he had seen at sunset there had seemed to draw him farther on, and he had tried to imagine what it had been like for those who had gone before, for the ancient Egyptians, the Romans, the Arabs, what it was that had made them go against the flow of the Nile and travel into the land that would so often become their grave. During evenings sitting above the ruins, he had felt as if the red rays were reaching out across the sand, pulling him towards the setting sun and into the dangerous darkness that followed. He thought it had helped him to understand Gordon, to see what it was that could take a man like that and put him in a place that seemed beyond the edge of the world.

He thought about how the archaeology of the Holy Land had motivated those among the officers who were steeped in biblical history. Twenty years before, Wilson had carried out the Ordnance Survey of Jerusalem, intent on improving the water supply but in the process revealing much of its archaeology. He had then worked for the newly formed Palestine Exploration Fund on the survey of Western Palestine and the Sinai, work so highly esteemed that it earned him a Fellowship of the Royal Society. Kitchener's exhaustive four-year survey of Palestine had made his name before he had any military reputation. And Gordon had been fascinated by Palestine all his life, culminating in the year's leave he had spent in Jerusalem in 1883 exercising his engineer's eye to pinpoint to his satisfaction the site of the crucifixion and key locations of the Old Testament. It was a point of similarity between Gordon and the prime minister, also a fervent biblical scholar, except that Gladstone's religion made him bridle at Gordon's messianic status in the eyes of the people, and the two men would never publicly acknowledge their shared fascination as scholars.

For these men, the southern desert represented the great unknown: the place of exile, the possible location of the lost tribes of Israel, and the ancient hiding place of the Ark of the Covenant. They were fascinated by Akhenaten, whose venture into the desert three thousand years earlier seemed to mirror their own, a pharaoh who had seen the one God, the Aten. The desert seemed a place where those who were lost might be found, a place of redemption. Perhaps these men were not just enthused by the archaeology they came across, but like Akhenaten were seeking a revelation, a flash of insight that might give them a personal vision of God.

Kitchener came up alongside and handed over the map case. "Colonel Wilson and I have prepared this for you. Memorise it and return it before you leave. You will take the desert route behind Stewart's column, aiming for the wells at Jakdul and Abu Klea, and then on to the Nile at Metemma. Cross the river to the east bank, as the Mahdi's forces occupy the west bank on the approaches to Khartoum. It should take you four days by foot to reach Khartoum from Metemma. You should be able to keep one day ahead of the river steamers carrying Wilson and the rescue force, as there are cataracts that will impede their progress. At Khartoum the river will be low and the mud banks treacherous. You will arrive on the opposite bank from the governor's palace, beside the island of Tutti. You would do well to find a *nuggar* boat and make your way across at night. The palace is guarded by Gordon's Sudanese irregulars, but there are plenty of Arabs milling about, and your features are sufficiently dark that you should be able to pass yourself off as a native, with your beard and a headdress."

"Tell me, Kitchener. We're out of earshot of the tent. What do think of our chances?"

"You've seen my high regard for Gordon and my belief that his rescue is possible," Kitchener replied pensively. "But I am fully aware of the odds against it. In the two years since Hicks set out on his doomed expedition, the Mahdi has captured seven thousand Remington rifles, eighteen field guns, a rocket battery, and half a million rounds of rifle ammunition. More than sixteen thousand Egyptian troops have been killed or captured, and our own casualties are now in the hundreds. Only two weeks ago another force of a thousand Egyptian soldiers and *bashi-bazouk* policemen were annihilated. Every week more tribal leaders are defecting to the Mahdi. Gordon is defended by Sudanese soldiers whose officers have betrayed them. The telegraph line is cut, there is no heliograph, and he is surrounded. The noose is tightening. It would be hard not to believe that he is done for."

"Your opinion?"

"My opinion will not change the course of events. I advise you to look out for yourself. In the desert I carry a cyanide tablet, in case I'm captured."

Mayne looked towards the clump of palms where Charrière was sharpening his hunting knife on a small whetstone he carried on his belt. "That will not be necessary. My bodyguard will see to it that neither of us is captured alive. And he will also spot anyone who tries to follow us."

"The desert is different from the forests and rivers of Canada."

"It's the mind of the tracker that matters." Kitchener stared at him, and Mayne held his gaze. In some ways Kitchener was the more obvious man for the job, a flu-

ent Arabic speaker who had travelled in disguise deep
into the Mahdi's territory, who had earned his desert
credentials. But he had become too visible amongst the
tribesmen for a covert operation; Gordon would have
been forewarned of his arrival, the element of surprise
would have been lost, and Gordon might have re-
trenched and refused to budge. Wolseley had been astute
enough to keep Mayne out of the limelight, to give him
extensive desert experience but ensure that he was unknown in Khartoum. And yet Wolseley was a pawn in
the hands of a more powerful directive. In reality Mayne
was not Wolseley's man, but Wilson's.

And there was another factor. Mayne's appointment
might conflict with Kitchener's desire to be in the thick
of it, but Kitchener was ruled by intellect rather than
instinct; he did not have the near-suicidal disregard for
his personal safety of a Burnaby or a Buller.

Kitchener tapped the map case. "Gordon will be expecting an officer to try to reach him before the relief
force arrives. As you will be disguised as an Arab, you
will need a convincing entreaty to gain an audience with
Gordon once you reach the palace. I suggest you take
along your Royal Engineers cap badge and ask for it to
be sent to him. He won't turn away a fellow sapper."

"He might think it comes from you."

"He knows well enough that Wolseley will keep me
back."

"Do you still have spies in the desert, your Ababda
bodyguard?"

Kitchener remained expressionless. "The Mahdi's
forces have nearly sealed off the city. The east bank of
the Blue Nile, where you are heading, is the last remaining point of access, and the river crossing will be perilous. Nobody could do it in daylight without being shot
down either by Gordon's men at the palace or by the
dervishes on Tutti Island. In answer to your question, I
have not had any firsthand intelligence from Khartoum
for days."

Kitchener had *not* answered his question. Mayne remembered him at the military academy, aloof and uncommunicative. It was impossible to tell whether he was being evasive or simply addressing the issues that he felt to be significant. He was giving Mayne the latest intelligence, that was all. Mayne knew that the networks of spies would now be focused on the opposing armies themselves as they crystallised for war in front of Khartoum or somewhere in the desert as the British column advanced. With all eyes on troop movements rather than the odd Arab traveller, he might stand a better chance of passing through the desert without being reported by spies of the Mahdi.

"The Mahdi has fuelled the uprising by playing on the grievances of the tribesmen. None are to be trusted except my Ababda men." Kitchener paused. "On another matter, but related. Do you know Captain John Howard?"

Mayne paused. "A few years below me at Woolwich. Out with the Madras Sappers in India putting down the Rampa rebellion, and now back at the School of Military Engineering to instruct in survey."

Kitchener nodded. "He's another who shares my interest in the archaeology of the Holy Land. Colonel Wilson and I have recommended that he be entrusted with the safekeeping of Gordon's antiquities when they are sent to Chatham, including any from Khartoum that we can salvage. Howard is a scholar and a safe pair of hands. I met him before coming here, and he told me that the Rampa rebellion began as a protest by tribal people against a tax on alcohol, was then hijacked by the nationalists who wanted it to be seen as an uprising against the British, and by the second year had simply become violence for its own sake, with the brigands burning and killing because they enjoyed it. The longer a rebellion is allowed to string out, the more it will become self-fuelling. Men who have been persuaded to become killers learn to love it and do not put down arms easily."

"The warrior tradition is strong in the desert."

"We must strive to equal it. We are a worthy adversary to warriors of the Mahdi army, whereas the Egyptians and Ottomans are not. The Ansar despise the fellahin of the Nile as poor soldiers who have no taste for war, and in that they are right. An Egyptian army like the one led by Hicks they can wipe out in an easy afternoon. A real army like ours they will throw themselves on with fanaticism, because there is a chance that we might defeat them. The more they encounter us in battle, the more they will return. It is the way of war: the fight becomes the end, not just the means. We may stem the tide temporarily with a good fight or two, but attrition is the only way to stop them, and we do not have the manpower."

"Wolseley intends us to leave the Sudan to its own devices."

"That would be a profound mistake," Kitchener said. "The jihad could engulf North Africa and the Middle East, just as it did thirteen hundred years ago. It could prove a bigger threat to us than Russia and Europe combined."

Kitchener closed his empty map case and straightened up, then suddenly held Mayne by the shoulder, his eyes boring into him. "If any harm should befall Gordon, I will take a life for each hair on his head. Even if it takes the rest of my career, I will gain vengeance. You mark my words."

Mayne stared at him, discomfited. They said that Kitchener's eyesight had been permanently affected by the sand and the desert sun, but his eyes also showed that he had been seduced by the cruelty of the desert, a place where the value of a man's life was less than that of the camel he rode on and the handful of grain in his saddlebag.

Kitchener released him. "When Khartoum falls, we should expect the worst. The Ansar are a medieval army and will behave like any other medieval army when they stormed a city. They will rape and pillage, mutilate and torture. The fair-skinned Egyptian women will be the first, the wives and daughters of the Ottoman officials still in Khartoum. They are the ones that Gordon will not leave behind. And then they will kill everyone."

"All in the name of Islam."

"For the dervishes baying for blood on that day, Muhammad will be about as far from them as Christ was from the crusaders when they took Acre."

"Could he convert to Islam? I mean Gordon? Others have done it among the Europeans captured by the Mahdi. The Austrian von Slatin for one."

"Von Slatin converted out of desperation to boost the loyalty of his Sudanese troops. It did him little good as they were massacred anyway, but after he was captured his conversion kept him alive. Others among the captured Europeans have done so under duress. Convert, or have your hands and feet chopped off."

"You have not answered my question."

Kitchener paused. "The Sudanese credit Gordon with *baraka,* with mystical healing powers, just as they do the Mahdi. Gordon and the Mahdi are closer than many might think. The Sufi version of Islam that the Mahdi was born into is tolerant and inclusive. The fundamentalism he espouses now is for the jihad, and in person he and Gordon would find common ground. They share a passion for the prophets common to both religions, for Isaiah in particular."

"The Mahdi has invited Gordon to join the jihad. My Dongolese guide told me that he even sent him a present of a patched jibba of the Ansar to wear."

Kitchener snorted. "Gordon kicked it across the room in disgust."

"And yet he kept it, along with the Mahdi's other presents."

"What are you asking me?" Kitchener demanded, suddenly haughty again.

"If Gordon is pushed, which way will his pendulum swing?"

"You mean has he built his own crucifix, is he standing on a holy rock reaching out to Allah?"

"Either way he is flying very close to the sun."

Kitchener squinted at the reddening orb on the horizon. "That's easily done in the desert. You can forgive a man out here for thinking like a pharaoh."

"Or like a Mahdi."

Kitchener pursed ·his lips. "As Christians we have been more savage to those within our faith who do not follow our path than we have been with the infidel. The Mahdi is playing the same game. He has persuaded his followers that the Turkish Muslims are unbelievers because they do not follow the jihad. He knows that in future the jihad will gain strength from this war with moderate Islam. And he knows perfectly well that the true Ansar, his most fanatical followers, number only a small minority now among his army, and that the majority are tribesmen who have been swept up for reasons other than faith. The basis for their fervour in battle is to be sought deep within the history of the desert itself. To keep that fervour stoked, the Mahdi must satisfy the warrior urge for blood and keep them wanting more. It is a precarious edifice, with weaknesses that one day we might exploit to turn the tide."

"Yet not in this campaign."

"Each battle for the Mahdi has a parallel in the battles that the Prophet Muhammad fought twelve hundred years ago. As his power develops, the Mahdi is able to shape his own history so that it becomes even more similar. His ultimate aim is to restore the caliphate as he believed Muhammad envisaged it, to discard modern progress and take the world back twelve hundred years."

"Using Remington rifles and Krupps field guns."

"Means, not ends. Necessary evils to counter the weapons of the unbelievers. All will be discarded when the jihad is over, and the blade and spear will rule supreme again."

"Do you think Gordon sympathises with this view of history?"

"Gordon stands apart from history. But like the Mahdi, he inhabits the world of the foundation of our religion. His time in Jerusalem three years ago was a spiritual journey back to the final days of Christ. And since first arriving in the Sudan ten years ago, he has been absorbed by the world of the Old Testament, the time of Moses and Pharaoh and the Exodus from Egypt. He believes that Akhenaten was the pharaoh of the Bible and that Moses received his vision of one God from him. He believes that the vision came to Akhenaten somewhere out here in the desert."

"Those relief carvings I saw, of Akhenaten and the sun disk," Mayne murmured. "That's why you were so interested in them. Have you seen something similar in the desert?"

Kitchener gave him a stony stare. "Why do you ask?"

"Because I know Gordon was searching for images of Akhenaten, and excavated sites in the desert with Heinrich Schliemann during his first period as governor general. My Dongolese guide worked as an interpreter for Gordon before joining me, and his last act before leaving Khartoum was to load crates of antiquities and artefacts onto the steamer *Abbas* for its voyage to safety. Among them was a stone slab that Gordon had insisted be double-crated and cushioned in cloth. My guide knew of my interest in the ruins and inscriptions we passed in the desert, and he drew me a sketch of the slab showing hieroglyphics and radiating lines like those of the Aten sun disk."

Kitchener's eyes bored into him. "Can you reproduce it for me?"

Mayne shook his head. "It was a sketch made with a stick in the sand."

"You say this slab came from Khartoum?"

"Gordon himself supervised the loading. Whether it was from Khartoum or from one of Gordon's expeditions, I do not know."

Kitchener shook his head, knitting his brow. "If he had made such a find earlier, he would have told me. This must be a recent discovery, very recent."

"Why would he have thought to tell you? Surely there

were far more pressing concerns than antiquities and archaeology."

Kitchener's eyes were ablaze. "*Nothing* more pressing, I can assure you."

"My guide had left the steamer before Colonel Stewart was murdered, but he watched from the far bank as dervishes swarmed over the wreck and dived into the water. They brought up all the crates they could and prised them open, but threw everything back. He thought they were searching for gold and had no interest in the artefacts."

"The stone slab?" Kitchener demanded.

Mayne shook his head. "Apparently it was hidden beneath the boiler, where Gordon insisted it be concealed. It seemed to be his prize possession. My guide saw nothing like that raised before the wreck slipped into deeper water."

"So it is still there," Kitchener said quietly, more to himself than to Mayne.

"In the River Nile near Abbas Kortas, close to the west bank, so under the Mahdi's control, I fear. If you're thinking of attempting to recover the steamer and Gordon's belongings, that will have to wait until you are able to lead your army of reconquest into the Sudan."

"It is an artefact of the *utmost* importance," Kitchener murmured.

Mayne gazed at him. "What is going on? Who else knows about this?"

Kitchener stared at him intently. "It is a discovery that is the concern of the *highest* echelons of power. All I will say is this. Many who support Gordon regard Prime Minister Gladstone as a malign force; but do not do so. He has a great interest in Gordon's discoveries in the desert. He has taken a gamble with Gordon, one of which Wolseley has no knowledge. For months Gladstone pulled every string to prevent Gordon being reappointed to the Sudan; he was working against what he saw as Gordon's self-destructiveness. But then Gordon went in private to see Gladstone to tell him about something archaeological he needed to find in the desert that he had come close to tracking down during his previous period in the Sudan, an ancient Egyptian temple. He took me and Colonel Wilson into his confidence. Gladstone was won over by his zeal and agreed with great trepidation to let him go."

"And yet he is at loggerheads with Gordon in public."

"Gordon did not keep his end of the bargain. He should have left Khartoum as soon as he had located the inscription, but he did not."

"This discovery must have been a pretty large prize."

Kitchener stared at him, began to speak, but then thought better of it. He straightened up and tucked the map case under his arm. "If you reach Gordon, he may choose to reveal more. If you do not reach him, then there is no value in you knowing."

"I need every point of sympathy with the man and his motivations if I am to persuade him to leave."

"If that is truly your purpose."

"I follow Lord Wolseley's orders. You know what those were."

Kitchener grunted. "Do you speak the language?"

"My guide taught me some of the Beja language, Tu-Bedawi, and I know Arabic."

Kitchener's eyes narrowed. "An Arabic speaker. You are well prepared."

"A war out here was always in the cards. I'm a surveyor, Kitchener, just like you. Learning the language is an essential tool of the trade."

"And you have been preparing for this ever since Gordon first arrived in the Sudan a decade ago."

"I go where I am ordered."

"Tell me, Mayne, who do you really work for? It is not Wolseley, is it?"

"The same as you. Queen and country."

Kitchener paused. "You will need Bishari camels. You had better find them before every last camel in Lower Sudan is snapped up for Stewart's desert column."

With that Kitchener swivelled and abruptly left. Mayne

remained for a moment, thinking about what Kitchener had said: *If any harm should befall Gordon, I will take a life for each hair on his head.* It was heated, emotional, but it was a warning. He thought of Kitchener's questions about Gordon's artefacts. He had seen men of reason become irrationally secretive about a shared endeavour, and there was doubtless some trail of discovery that had enthused Gordon in his early days in the Sudan, and with which he had infected Kitchener. But there were now larger matters at hand, and he put the thought from his mind.

He began to walk towards Charrière, remembering his assurance to Wilson that he had everything he needed. The box he had carried from the cataract was among his belongings. In it was a present his uncle had brought him from the American West: a beautiful Spencer rifle with a 34-inch barrel in .50-90 calibre, designed for long-range buffalo shooting. With custom-loaded cartridges using diamond-grade Curtis & Harvey powder, Mayne would be able to hit a man-sized target at over a thousand yards.

From his reconnaissance he knew a place on the river just south of the second cataract that closely replicated the width and conditions of the Nile at their destination; he would go there tomorrow morning, alone. He needed to plan with the greatest of precision when the most accurate shooting was possible: just after dawn, when the air over the river was cool and settled and less likely to disrupt the flight of the bullet. He would need to adjust the Creedmore aperture sights for the range he had seen on the map that Kitchener had shown him. Afterwards he would disassemble the rifle and pack it tightly in its case, with the sights protected against the jolts of the trip ahead. The success or failure of the mission could depend on it.

Mayne's resolve hardened as he thought again of Gordon. They had something in common, daunting tasks with little hope of rescue. For Mayne, to succeed was to do his job; to fail was unthinkable. He had always known this, and it was part of the draw. But this time the stakes were higher than they had ever been before. This was not just about one man and a standoff that had riveted the world; nor was it just about Egypt and the Suez Canal, or British prestige in the eyes of Russia or Germany or the Ottoman Empire. It was about something more terrifying than that, about the resurgence of a force from the desert that twelve hundred years before had swept to the very gates of Europe, that would do it again and this time know no bounds.

He remembered the piece of paper Wilson had slipped him as they shook hands. He knew what it was already, but even so he felt his heart pound as he opened it and glanced down. It was a black spot, a smudge of ink, the oldest form of code. He looked up and stared at Charrière. It meant there was no coming back, for either of them.

He crushed the paper in his hand and looked out towards the desert, his eyes narrowing against the dust and the setting sun. He thought about Kitchener's warning. Sometimes vengeance was possible, sometimes not. That was another thing Wilson had seized on when he had recruited Mayne: the need of a young man to seek retribution, to find meaning and justice for his parents' death when he knew it never could be found, when all that was left was a yearning to kill.

He remembered Wolseley's words. *If Gordon chooses to stay, then his fate is no longer in your hands.*

Wolseley could not have known how wrong he was.

PART 4

CHAPTER 16

MAJOR EDWARD MAYNE BLINKED HARD, wip-
ing his eyes as they watered, squinting in the intense sunlight and the dust. Two hours earlier he had sat
shivering under his blanket, watching the first streaks of
dawn ignite the desert in shimmering patches of amber
and then spread into a uniform orange-red haze. It had
been like that every morning in the desert, as if the first
reflected heat off the land caused the dust to rise, creating a miasma that the sun could then penetrate only dif-
fusely; to be crossing the desert was to be submerged in
it, to be at the whim of the eddies and tides of history
that swept over it like the violent dust storm they had
endured the day before. He had felt it since they left
Korti twelve days ago, a sense that they were moving
deeper into a place where colour had become monochrome and the light dispersed and opaque, increasing
his foreboding about what lay beyond the loop of the
river over the rocky plateau ahead.

He tried to stop shivering. He had still not shaken off
the chill of the night, but it was becoming hot, uncomfortably so for the camels; they needed water badly.
He knew that the wells ahead would be no more than
trickles of muddy water at the bottom of pits in the
ground, but it would be enough. He lay forward over

the boulder and extended his telescope, jamming his elbows into cracks in the rock and peering through the eyepiece. The desert in this part of the Sudan was not like the dunes he had seen in Egypt; instead it was what the Arabs called *goz*, a vast undulating plain of low gravel ridges broken by jagged rocky outcrops, brown and grey and dull maroon. The occasional patches of desert grass and thorny scrub could seduce the unwary into thinking that the *goz* was more life-sustaining than the dunes of the Sahara, a dangerous illusion borne out by the bleached camel bones and half-mummified corpses they had seen poking out of shallow graves along the way. He had come to realise how so many who had descended this way from the north—the ancient Egyptians, the Romans, the Ottomans—had found themselves mired in this place, drawn in and then checked by some invisible force that enclosed and drained them, making return impossible. And now he was watching history repeat itself, following a modern army that seemed perilously close to foundering in this harsh land as so many had done before.

He trained his telescope on the rise in the middle distance, perhaps two miles to the south. He had recognised Abu Klea from Kitchener's sketches, the last watering place before the Nile; they had last seen the river ten days ago at Korti, before they began the trek across the desert that cut off the loop to the east. He panned to the right, to a dust cloud that hung over the slope, and saw the flash of polished steel, then a blur of camels' legs and khaki tunics folding in and out of the haze. He and Charrière had followed Brigadier General Stewart's desert column all the way from Korti, but this was the first time he had seen it in broad daylight. To the left of the column was Stewart's *zariba*, a defensive encirclement of thorny scrub, camel saddles, and commissariat boxes where the soldiers had bivouacked the night before; to the right, a mile or so away where the slope merged with the flat desert, lay the patch of green that marked the wells. Between his position and the column was a wasteland of rocky knolls and low ridges, with undulations that made it difficult to gauge distance. He estimated that the wells were four thousand yards away, almost due south, and that the dust cloud was a thousand yards nearer, precisely on the path that he and Charrière would need to follow to get to the Nile.

He heard something in the far distance and held his breath, listening. He had heard the same noise once before, at the cataracts on the Nile, when the jihadi tribesmen had shadowed the river column, taunting them. It was the sound of tom-toms, dervish drums, irregular, wild, rising to a climax and then tapering off again, relentless. It seemed to be coming from all directions, an unnerving feature of distant sounds in the desert; it reminded him of hearing noise when he had swum underwater, impossible to locate and making it seem as if he were surrounded. But he knew it must be coming from a dervish force beyond the wells, the object of Stewart's advance that morning.

The Mahdist army might not yet be visible, but he knew they would be battle-ready. Kitchener had predicted that there would be a fight in the desert before they reached the Nile. That night there had been a crescent moon, and just before dawn the planet Venus had been visible on the horizon, omens the emirs always sought before unleashing war. But for Mayne, predicting battle was more than just a matter of augury and superstition. For more than a week now he had watched Stewart's column trundle forward excruciatingly slowly. They had marched by night, making more laboured progress than they would have done by day, exhausting both men and camels; both slept poorly in daylight, and the camels had less chance of foraging and finding water. When Stewart had reached the rocky crater of Jakdul and its wells at the midpoint of the desert route, he had lingered for days. To Mayne it was almost as if he were willing the enemy to meet him in the field by giving ample time for spies to reach the Mahdi's camp outside Khartoum and tell him of Stewart's advance; the Ansar warriors would have been itching for a fight, forcing the Mahdi's hand. This was truly a battle foretold. Mayne frowned, snapping shut the telescope. Getting to the Nile was going to take more time than he had bargained for, and with Gordon's status in Khartoum more uncertain by the day, time was of the essence.

The camel hobbled beside him grunted and belched, emitting an odour so foul it made Mayne's eyes smart again. It shifted on its forelegs and stared in the direction of the wells, chewing its cud. The bags of *dura* wheat slung over its back were nearly empty, and its hump was sagging. Both their camels had traversed the Bayuda Desert many times and knew exactly where they were, that the oasis ahead contained expanses of desert grass they could graze on as well as the puddles of muddy groundwater where they could slake their thirst. They had hobbled the camels the evening before to prevent them from wandering off on their own, and that night they had been restless. Mayne felt his own cracked lips and was beginning to sympathise. Their breakfast of lime juice and biscuit had still not allayed the chill of the night, and he was looking forward to getting on the move again.

A figure materialised beside him, silent as ever. Over the past days Charrière's skin had darkened with the sun and the dust, accentuating the deep grooves that scored his cheeks and forehead. The desert of the Sudan must seem a world away from the rivers and forests of Canada where he had been brought up, but he had relished the challenge to his tracking and survival skills. He tossed back the Arab robe he wore over his woollen trousers and checked shirt, took out a hunk of dried meat from a pouch on his belt, cut off a strip, and passed it over. Mayne had acquired a taste for the jerky carried by the voyageurs on the Red River expedition fifteen years before; this time it was camel rather than moose meat, but he took it gratefully. Charrière cut himself a piece and the two men chewed and sucked for a few minutes without talking. Then Charrière raised the depleted water skin that had been hanging from his shoulder, letting a trickle pour into his mouth before passing it to Mayne, who did the same, taking only a mouthful, knowing that the wells ahead were under dervish control and the tepid water might be their last for some time. They had been warned about thirst blindness, and he had wondered about the wavering images he had been seeing on the horizon the day before, whether they were mirages of the desert or tricks of the mind, or both. Today he would need all the clarity he could muster. He took another swig, leaving a few mouthfuls as a reserve, then passed the skin back. Charrière plugged and re-slung it, then pointed ahead, his voice slow and deliberate, with its distinctive French-Canadian accent. "That is no longer an army on the march."

Mayne looked out again. "About a quarter of an hour ago they began to form a square. They've dismounted and corralled the camels inside. They've only just left the *zariba* where they spent the night, so it's too early for them to be setting up camp again. You can see the glint of steel where they've fixed bayonets. They must be able to see something closer to the wells that we can't."

Charrière squinted at the low hills behind the wells, then slid off the rock and lay splayed in the dust beside the camels, his ear to the ground. "We may not be able to see it," he said, "but I can hear it. There is a pounding, a great pounding of human feet, many thousands of them. And something else I can hear in the air too, a beating sound, like a thousand drums."

Mayne shut his eyes for a moment. The soldiers in the square were not just preparing for a skirmish to repel a suicidal attack by a few jihadi horsemen like those who had beset them since they had entered the desert. What they could hear and see ahead of them now was barely imaginable, terrifying, a storm from the south, the edge of a sweeping darkness that would stir up an atavistic fear in the hearts of men whose crusader ancestors had faced it eight hundred years ago when they had come to reclaim the Holy Land. Mayne remembered how the tom-toms had so terrified the Egyptian soldiers with the river column on the Nile; he hoped the British would have more resolve than the Egyptian fellahin, men with an ancestral fear of warriors from the south. But what the men in the square must be able to see now would shake anyone, a mass advancing from the horizon against which victory might seem inconceivable.

Charrière picked up the telescope and peered through it. "I can see puffs of rifle fire near the square. Mahdist sharpshooters must have come up among the rocks. These folds and gullies in the desert will provide them with cover."

"When you see volley fire from the square, then you know the Mahdi army is attacking," Mayne replied. He turned over and sank back against the rock, forgetting for a moment the chill and the hunger and thirst, retracing the brief for his mission. He and Charrière had left General Wolseley's base at Korti dressed as Arabs and riding the best camels that could be found for them as they shadowed Stewart's desert column. The column had been sent south across the Bayuda Desert towards Metemma on the Nile, a direct route of 176 miles that cut off the wide loop of the river to the east. Once at Metemma it was to meet up with General Earle's river column, and a small vanguard under Colonel Wilson would embark in the river steamers that had been sent there by Gordon from Khartoum, 98 miles to the south. The plan then was either breathtakingly audacious or astonishingly naïve. The arrival of a few dozen British redcoats would cow the enemy, who would disappear back into the desert. Khartoum would be relieved, and Gordon saved. The expedition would be the greatest triumph of British arms since Queen Victoria had come to the throne.

Mayne knew that the chances weighed astronomically against any of this coming to fruition, not least the time factor: Gordon had issued a last plea for help weeks before, and already Stewart's column had lingered for ten days longer than was necessary at the wells of Jakdul in the middle of the desert. The chances of the river column reaching Metemma before February were vanishingly small, with the falling level of the Nile at this time of year making the cataracts more treacherous by the hour. Yet Mayne's own mission to get to Gordon just before the steamers arrived at Khartoum depended on Gordon knowing that the relief expedition had reached Metemma and that rescue for himself and his people was possible; only then, Mayne knew, would he stand any chance of convincing him to leave. It had meant dogging the tails of the desert column, waiting until now, with the Nile less than twenty-five miles ahead, when the arrival of Stewart's force at Metemma within two days seemed a fair certainty; he and Charrière could then bypass the column and make their way to Khartoum to reach it just ahead of the steamers and the relief force.

Following the column had hardly required Charrière's tracking skills. More than a thousand British soldiers mounted on camels and horses, a thousand more camels carrying disassembled mountain guns, a Gardner machine gun, ammunition and supplies, and the usual trail of followers and servants had created a veritable dust storm visible for miles. The enemy would have known about it even before the force had departed Korti. The question in Mayne's mind for days now had not been whether the Mahdi would detach a force from the besieging army at Khartoum to confront Stewart, but when. This morning he had the answer. The Mahdi had ample forces at his disposal, at least 250,000 men according to Kitchener, an army growing daily as the local tribesmen lost faith in British resolve and threw in their lot with the jihad. Mayne could only hope that the detachment of a large force would show that the Mahdi had not yet decided to take Khartoum by storm but that he would starve the city into submission; that might give Mayne a better chance of reaching Gordon in time. Or it could mean that Khartoum had already fallen and that the entire Mahdi army had been released to move north. If so, his mission was over and the survival of Stewart's force, of Mayne himself and of Charrière, would be hanging in the balance, with Egypt itself the next to fall as the Ansar surged north.

He remembered Charrière's morning foray and peered at him. "Are we still being followed?"

The other man nodded. "The same distance behind each day. I circled back to find their tracks. They bivouacked last night behind that ridge visible back along the trail on the horizon. Four men, with camels."

Mayne grunted, pursing his lips. Charrière had spotted them on the first night after leaving Korti. To begin with, Mayne had thought little of it; the desert track was well used and local tribesman plied it even in times of war. But the four men had remained behind them for the full ten days it had taken Stewart to leave Jakdul, and he had become suspicious. They were not simply waiting their turn to use the wells, as Stewart's men would have let local tribesmen through and there would have been no need for them to remain concealed. They must either be brigands or Mahdist spies, or both. It had been impossible to be stealthy with two snorting and kicking camels under them, and the tribesmen of the desert were as adept at tracking as Charrière was. But Mayne wanted to shake them soon, once they had left the exposed wasteland of the desert route. Kitchener's map had shown an area of dense mimosa and acacia scrub in the final miles of the journey towards the Nile, beyond Abu Klea; that was where Mayne planned to leave the camels and make their move.

Charrière thrust something at him, a scrap of paper. "I found this in their tracks." Mayne turned it over, staring. It was a torn piece from a tobacco wrapping. He could read the label: *Wills Tobacco Co., Bristol*. He shrugged. "There's plenty of British stuff like this lying around. There would have been a haul from the dead officers when the Mahdi annihilated Hicks's Egyptian army two years ago. And brigands could have rifled tobacco from British soldiers in the desert column while they slept." He thought for a moment; the Mahdi had expressly forbidden smoking among his followers. He looked at the scrap again, feeling a tinge of unease. He thought back to Korti, to the faces around the conference table with Wolseley. In this world of spies, of cat and mouse, Mayne surely occupied the deepest fold; he was the spy, not the one spied on. He thought of Kitchener, who had been with the desert column but had been ordered back by Wolseley from Jakdul, fuming at not being in on the action. He remembered Kitchener's words to him outside the conference tent: his warning about Gordon, his suspicion of Mayne, and his evasiveness when Mayne had asked him about his spy network. It was possible that Kitchener had secretly ordered him to be followed, exercising his self-appointed authority in the desert beyond Wolseley's reach. He thought too of his own secret superior, Colonel Sir Charles Wilson, caught up now in that battle square ahead of them, an intelligence officer seeing action for the first time in his career and a hovering presence over Mayne's mission. Surely Wilson was the linchpin of all subterfuge and would not tolerate any others interfering in his game, whether sanctioned by Wolseley or by Whitehall. If he had known, he would surely have told Mayne about any possible impediment to his mission. Mayne knew there was little to be gained from further speculation, but it nagged at him. *What was going on?*

Charrière gestured ahead. "Our followers will be watching us now from that ridge behind and will be able to see what we can see now. They will know that if we carry on forward we must go off the track to avoid the battle, and if so they could lose us. If they are intent on waylaying us, they may choose to make their move before that."

Mayne took the telescope and stared at the British square, seeing sporadic puffs of smoke from rifle fire. He hoped that the Ansar ranged against them was not the main force of the Mahdi army; if so, they would annihilate the square and swarm over the Abu Klea hills, mak-

ing his own progress to the Nile virtually impossible.
But even a British victory could have adverse consequences. If Khartoum had not yet fallen, a victory could
persuade the Mahdi that a British force to be reckoned
with was on the way and that he should storm the city
without delay. Either way, what happened today was
going to decide the fate of Gordon. He snapped the telescope shut and stood up. "Agreed. We move now."

Fifteen minutes later they dismounted beside an exposed
knoll a thousand yards closer to the square. The dervish
force was now clearly visible, and Mayne trained his
telescope on the approaching mass. He could make out
individuals beneath fluttering banners, surging forward
behind emirs on horses and camels, their blades glinting.
He had been shown dervish weapons by his guide Shaytan weeks before in the eastern desert, and he knew
what the British would soon be facing: ten-foot-long
leaf-bladed spears, razor-sharp and as lethal as a Zulu
assegai, as well as shorter throwing spears, straight,
double-edged, cross-hilted swords, and a few special-
ist weapons—the hippo-hide kurbash whip, lethal in
the right hands if wrapped around a man's neck, and
boomerang-like throwing sticks embedded with slivers
of razor-sharp obsidian that could hobble the legs of
camels and men alike. He peered closely, scanning the
front ranks. These were not the wild-haired, semi-naked
warriors Corporal Jones had seen on the Red Sea coast
the year before, the Baggara tribesmen who had been
the first of the Mahdi's supporters to meet the British in
open battle, where Colonel Fred Burnaby had cut such
an extravagant figure with his shotgun. Here, the front
ranks were dominated by Kordofan Arabs from the
Madhi's heartland south of Khartoum, men who wore
skullcaps and the patched jibba tunic, who eschewed the
elephant-hide shields carried by the Baggara; they were
the Ansar, the most fanatical supporters of jihad. The
Mahdi had astutely celebrated their traditional ways of

war, stoking their self-esteem as warriors, knowing that in overwhelming numbers at close quarters their weapons could win the day against the bayonets and bullets of the British. But he also knew the power of the rifle, and had equipped select Kordofan warriors with the Remingtons that they had taken from the slaughtered Egyptian soldiers of Hicks's force two years before. Mayne could see their ragged fusillades today on the ridge behind the main force, and knew that among them would be the captured Egyptian and Sudanese soldiers who had chosen the Mahdi over execution and had trained select Kordofan to become expert marksmen.

He watched the force assemble in front of the British, their standards with Arabic slogans held high above the front ranks. It was an extraordinary image, half buried in history, a medieval army marching out of the folds of time to confront the might of modern firepower, yet still it sent a cold shudder through him. The sheer numbers could prove overwhelming; it had happened at Isandlwana in Zululand six years before, and it could happen again here. Everything depended on the resolve of the British soldiers in the square: on the years of parade-bashing and field drill that made the Grenadier Guards and the Household Cavalry the most disciplined soldiers the world had ever seen; on that stoicism and grim humour that Mayne had seen in Corporal Jones and every other seasoned British soldier he had encountered; on the determination of the officers to play the game for Queen and country, to lead from the front and be seen by their men in the thick of the action, to sell their lives dearly and take as many of the enemy with them as possible.

Mayne steadied his telescope, watching the men ululating and dancing in the front ranks. The Ansar still had faith in their own inviolability; they had not yet encountered the volley fire of Martini-Henry rifles and had no reason to disbelieve the Mahdi's promise that bullets would not harm them. They were driven by an unswerving belief in divine purpose and in the power of their leader; they also believed they were defending their way of life and their families, and would fight with a savagery that seemed natural in a desert world where life was cruel and death often came whimsically.

He cast an expert eye over the marksmen's position in the rocks behind the main force. Like the sharpshooter at the cataract, the best of them should be able to pick off a man from six hundred yards; if they had been well taught they would also understand the principle of high-trajectory volley fire and be able to land bullets with lethal velocity in the square from a range of fifteen hundred yards or more. The fact that the bullets would be indiscriminate, hitting friend and foe alike, would be irrelevant. Even if their inviolability proved to be a shaky promise, the Ansar were still convinced that greater glory awaited them in heaven if they gave their lives for the jihad, and whether they were felled by a bullet from a Martini-Henry or a Remington would be a matter of supreme indifference when their time came.

Charrière eyed Mayne. "Our camels will not last long without water."

"The camels will be found soon enough. Whichever way this goes, the battlefield will be swarming with scavengers once the soldiers have departed. If we tether the camels here beside the trail, they'll be found. They'll be someone's prized possessions."

Charrière put his hand up to the cheek of his camel, which flinched and then stared at him with limpid eyes, chewing contentedly on the last twist of desert grass they had cut for the animals the previous day. Mayne untied his saddlebag, pulled it off, and then peered at Charrière. "Are you thinking you'd like to take your camel back to Canada?"

Charrière said nothing for a moment, taking his hand from the camel's face and untying his own bag; then he stopped and narrowed his eyes at the southern horizon. "This is a long way from the Ottawa River."

Mayne followed his gaze, imagining the shimmer

from the Nile where it snaked its way through the desert some twenty-five miles off, and remembering the untouched wilderness far up the Ottawa River: two great arteries whose course could take the unwary traveller into enveloping folds of darkness, where the river seemed to purge them of history and they became one with it, disconnected from their past lives and the motivations that had brought them there. He turned towards Charrière as he began disassembling his bag, selecting what was necessary for the trip ahead. "Almost all of your fellow Mohawks from the river column have returned to Canada. Why did you stay on?"

Charrière looked at him, his eyes dark, unfathomable. "Fifteen years ago we were hunting Louis Riel. Now it is General Gordon. Then, it was Colonel Wolseley. Now he is a general. Different quarry, same master."

"Is it Wolseley you serve?"

Charriere gazed back at him. "I could ask you the same question. Who do you serve?"

Mayne paused and gave a wry smile. "Queen and country."

"Then I will tell you. *Moi, je préfère la chasse*. I like to hunt."

Mayne eyed him. "Do you prefer to hunt men?"

"I like to track my quarry, to wait for the right moment, and to kill cleanly."

Mayne nodded towards the dust cloud over the wells. "There's going to be plenty of killing before long. And unless we're lucky enough to get through before the battle starts, we're going to have blood on our hands, and perhaps end up as bloody heaps in the desert."

"*Insha'Allah*."

"What did you say?"

"*Insha'Allah*. It is the will of God. My Arab friends taught me this expression at the cataracts."

Mayne pulled out the contents of his bag and cracked another smile. "You should be careful, my friend. You're going native."

Charrière spoke slowly. "An American officer serving

Gordon out here who fought the Lakota after the Battle of the Little Bighorn called the Dongolese tribesmen the Indians of the desert. I find that these people and my people have a lot in common."

Mayne stared at the horizon. He thought of the cruelty of this place, of the hardened faces of the tribesmen, of the decisions the desert forced on them that could mean life or death in an instant, and also of the humanity he had experienced travelling with them, the intensity of life for a people constantly on the edge. He remembered the year he had spent with his uncle in Canada after his parents had been killed, a damaged boy seeking meaning, and the comfort he had found in the forests with Charrière and his father, the moments of pleasure that were possible only with the danger and excitement of the hunt. He knew what Charrière meant. And he had seen enough of the Sudanese tribesmen over the past weeks to understand his empathy.

He turned back to his bag and took out the wrapped leaves containing the last of the biscuit, enough for two days. The lime juice had been finished that morning, and he left the empty bottle in the bag. He transferred the biscuit and his telescope to the pouch on his belt, along with a pencil, a roll of paper, and a small leather wrap containing gold sovereigns and his Royal Engineers cap badge. He felt for the revolver on his belt, a Webley New Army Express .455, harder-hitting than the old Webley-Pryse he had carried at the cataract, took it from its holster, and broke it open to check that it was loaded, then snapped it shut and reholstered it. He felt for the extra box of cartridges he kept in a separate pouch beside his knife, a gold-handled blade his Dongolese escort had given him three weeks ago before they had parted ways. He pulled the empty water skin off the camel and slung it round his neck, and then did the same with the coiled blanket. He had weighed up the blanket in his mind, an extra burden he could ill afford, but the nights had been bitterly cold, and with barely enough food or drink they would be feeling it more keenly from now on. Finally he slung on his back the wrapped wooden box containing his Sharps rifle, the barrel and stock tightly packed inside to ensure that the sights were not knocked out of place during their trip.

He watched Charrière finish his own packing, swirling back his robe to check the large hunting knife he had brought with him from Canada. Charrière tightened his blanket roll over his back and deftly tied the camels' front legs together with lengths of leather cord, to ensure that they did not bolt and attract attention from the British lines, then he stood up and pointed to a low rise in the gravel plain about half a mile away, midway between their position and the British square. "Let's get to that knoll," he said. "Then we'll decide whether we can follow the trail between the two armies. Are you ready to run?"

Mayne shifted his burden until it was comfortable, leaving his arms free to swing, remembering how the Mohawk hunters preferred to run rather than walk along the forest trails in Canada. He took a deep breath and nodded. "You lead."

CHAPTER 17

TWENTY MINUTES LATER, THEY STOOD PANT-
ing on a rocky outcrop less than a thousand yards
from the British square. To their left lay the rough
ground flanking the low plateau of Abu Klea that was
their chosen route, and ahead of them was a dried-up
watercourse they had spotted between the two armies
that was their fallback option should the other route
become unviable. At the moment they could not risk
moving, as they were within rifle range of the square;
the British soldiers would be jittery, likely to shoot at
anyone in Arab gear. They would have to wait until all
eyes in the square were on the advancing Mahdist army
to their right, until the moment when battle was about
to be joined. And there was another factor: if the men
somewhere behind who had been shadowing them since
they had left Korti decided to break cover and ride them
down now, it might force them to risk running, fully
exposed to British fire, to seek shelter in the gullies in
front of the square, hoping that their pursuers would
rein up once they saw that they were being led into a
murderous dead end. Mayne glanced at the angle of the
sun in the sky: it was about 10:30 a.m. The watercourse
gully had become visible to them only in the last few
yards of their run, and would be invisible to anyone following them until they reached this point. He had to

hope that their pursuers would never guess that one option open to the two men was to run a gauntlet that would appear suicidal to anyone bearing down on them from a distance.

He wiped his face with the cloth of his headdress; it had become hot, and he had cast off the chill of dawn. With his telescope he could see the British square more clearly now, the soldiers wearing pith helmets and khaki tunics with bandolier cartridge belts, their rifles at the ready. They were standing four deep, three hundred or three hundred and fifty men to a side, their sword bayonets thrust out like pikes, the slight curve in the blades reflecting wickedly in the sunlight. It seemed an image straight out of the Napoleonic Wars, a garish anachronism in this modern age of rifles with a range and volume of fire many times that of the muskets of Waterloo. The American Civil War twenty years before had shown the horrific consequences of infantry fighting as their forefathers had done in close formation but with modern rifles, and the tactic had been all but dropped from the training manuals for a European conflict. Yet it was precisely that concentration of firepower that made the square such a devastating tactic in this kind of war, that could even the odds for the British in the face of seemingly overwhelming disparity in numbers. And as the Zulu wars had shown, massed assaults by an enemy with weapons little changed since the days of the Romans could still crush a modern army, and firepower was only as good as the resolve of Tommy Atkins to stand his ground in the face of an opponent who was terrifying precisely because he did not play by the rules of modern war.

He thought of those men now: the bluejackets of the naval division manning the Gardner machine gun, the artillerymen with their mountain guns, the sappers who had built the zariba and were now standing stolidly in the square with the rifles, and above all the infantry and the cavalry, the Grenadier Guards and Household Cavalry who made up much of the camel regiments, men whose normal duty was the most intimate defence of the realm, safeguarding London and the Queen. He remembered the fatalistic humour of Corporal Jones and his mates, the intense camaraderie that fortified them against the devilry without. For those men now facing the test of their lives, the true purpose of the expedition, the reason why they were here in the depths of the Sudan and not in their barracks at Knightsbridge, would by this hour have become an irrelevance; all that would concern them was not letting their comrades down. Mayne watched the square bow outwards at the rear as the camels corralled within tried to force their way out but were pulled back and hobbled in the centre, a great mass of grunting and foaming beasts. They could prove the greatest strength of the square, something the soldiers at Waterloo did not have, an imperturbable mass that might break the dervish charge if the front lines of soldiers should collapse.

He thought of the officers he knew well, bunched together around Stewart in front of the camels, their field glasses glinting as they scanned the enemy lines: Colonel Wilson, who had been sent with the column by Wolseley to go ahead and communicate with Gordon; and Fred Burnaby, in his element again, who had hunted out war and would fight like a lion, whose yearning seemed almost a death wish. There would be other officers there too for whom the objective of the expedition would now be secondary, for whom the chance of battle would be a welcome certainty; it would give them a hope of glory little different from the aspirations of the dervish warriors, and freed from the murky uncertainties of Gordon and the opprobrium that would fall on them at home if they failed in their mission to rescue him. Whatever happened here, whether it was a last stand against impossible odds like Isandlwana in the Zulu War or a victory like Rorke's Drift, their names would be immortalised as soldiers and not as pawns in a political game.

Charrière suddenly cocked an ear towards the ground and then twisted round to look behind them. "Our pursuers. They're coming."

Mayne turned and raised his telescope. Over a low knoll they had traversed not long before, he could see a knot of four riders, wavering in and out of focus like a mirage. The camels were tall, gaunt, spectre-like, their legs seemingly elongated in the heat haze, cantering in a line abreast directly at them. The riders wore robes and headdresses and had unholstered their rifles, carrying them angled out with the butts resting against their thighs. They were perhaps twelve hundred yards distant.

Mayne's mind raced. He could set up his Sharps rifle, and it would be four rifles against one. But to use it now would almost certainly be to compromise his mission: he had adjusted the sights minutely for his expected range when he had test-fired it over the Nile near Korti, and he was loath to risk jolting it. As long as there was still a chance of reaching Khartoum, the Sharps would remain packed in its case. And even if he were able to shoot one of them, the other three would dismount and could pick them off at their ease. Their best chance still lay in the torrent beds and gullies around the plateau of Abu Klea to the east of the square, the escape route they had devised a few minutes before.

A percussive report resounded from the direction of the square, and he looked back in time to see a cloud of white smoke above the screw gun. The round exploded in the front rank of the dervish line, creating a gap that was immediately filled with spearmen in jibbas who joined in the dance, stamping their feet rhythmically. They were now formed up like an ancient Greek phalanx, in a serrated line, with an emir on camelback holding a standard at the apex of each serration. Sharpshooters on both sides were beginning to find their mark, with men falling in the front ranks of the square and the phalanx. For the first time Mayne could see that Stewart had sent out a force of skirmishers, men who were now scurrying back under fire towards the square.

He pursed his lips; that had been a tactical mistake. The value of skirmishers was as sharpshooters, and the phalanx was easily within range of the massed riflemen in the square. The minutes needed for their withdrawal would forestall the first volley, as the British would not shoot as long as the skirmishers were still in the line of fire. Stewart had taken a frightening gamble. The closer the phalanx was allowed to get, the more likely it was to overrun the square without being held back by volley fire. Even with the speed of reloading a Martini-Henry, they would have the chance of only a few volleys before the enemy was upon them. If the commander of the Madhist army had any sense, he would see that the British were exercising the kind of restraint to save their own men that would never occur to him, and would order his forces to charge now.

Mayne snapped his head back. A bullet had zinged overhead and slapped into a boulder, ricocheting off into the plain. He turned and squinted and could just make out one of the riders with his rifle levelled. He had fired mounted on his camel from perhaps eight hundred yards; *he was good*. Not even the best of the Egyptian army marksmen who had gone over to the Mahdi were that proficient, and they had only Remingtons. Mayne recalled being with the soldiers above the cataract when the sharpshooter from the opposite bank had found his range; he remembered the distinctive whine of the Remington bullet at about the same range. It was a lighter bullet than the Martini-Henry, .43 rather than .45 calibre, and made a different noise. The Martini-Henry was the rifle of the British army, the best service rifle in the world, one they did not even let their Egyptian allies use and the Mahdi had not yet been able to capture. Yet the bullet he had just heard was unquestionably from a Martini-Henry. He had that cold feeling in his stomach again. *Who were they?*

Two of the riders broke off to the right, and he watched them slowly pick up speed as they brought their camels to a gallop, whipping them hard as a cloud of dust rose behind. Mayne cursed under his breath. They were heading towards the hill of Abu Klea behind the square, cutting off their planned escape route. That left only one choice, the dried-up torrent bed between the opposing armies. He swiftly calculated the distances. The ground ahead of them was flat and unimpeded, and they would be able to run fast. They were perhaps two thousand yards now from the British square, and the gap between the armies was no more than eight hundred yards. If they ran now, they would be targeted by sharpshooters from either side, and by their pursuers. But if they waited until the moment the Mahdists began their charge, when all eyes would be on the opposing armies, they might have a chance of getting through. And their pursuers would know that if they followed, they would be caught up in the maelstrom as the armies converged.

Another bullet tumbled by and ploughed into the dust ahead of them. He gripped the bag with the rifle on his back and crouched down ready to run, watching Charrière do the same. Suddenly, the only meaningful time was measured in seconds. The Mahdi army must launch their attack now.

Then he heard it. A low noise, different from the stomping of feet, different from the drumbeat, a shrill, insistent chant, ten thousand men in unison: *La illaha la illa ras Muhammad*—there is no God but Allah and Muhammad is his Prophet—repeated over and over again until it became like the rushing of a mighty river.

A great flash swept the front line as a thousand spears were brandished. The standards of the emirs were lowered like lances. The chant was lost in a rumbling that shook the earth, a pounding of feet that set Mayne's teeth on edge. The dervish army was like a coiled spring, ready to strike.

His heart was thumping. What happened next would take place with terrifying speed: the two armies were like beasts bent on death or victory, warily sniffing out their opponent's weaknesses and strengths, tensed for a pounce that when it came would be of appalling savagery and violence. And he knew they might not make it to the gap in time to get through. They might be running headlong into a wall of death.

A trumpet sounded, high and shrill. He looked at Charrière. *Now.*

CHAPTER 18

MAYNE RAN FORWARD AS FAST AS HE COULD, crouching low, his right hand behind his back clutching the strap on his rifle case, his left arm extended and ready in case he should trip over one of the black clinker rocks that were strewn on the desert floor. Charrière was slightly ahead and to the left, loping more than running, his Arab robe tied up around his waist and the long sheath of his knife poking out below. Ahead of them lay the gap between the British and the dervish lines, and in the centre of that the low torrent bed that was their objective. Already Mayne could see that it was shallower than he had hoped, that to run along it would leave them exposed to fire from both sides. They would either have to risk it or get down on their hands and knees and crawl, an option that was rapidly closing given the speed of the dervish advance.

A bullet whistled between them, ploughing into the gravel ahead. He dared not look behind for fear of tripping, but the accuracy of the fire showed that their pursuers had kept within range. They zigzagged, keeping low, jumping into gullies and using any natural cover they could find. They were no more than three hundred yards away now, and the noise was suddenly overwhelming. The clap of the mountain gun was followed by the drone of the shell and then a krump as it burst in the Mahdist lines, throwing up bodies and limbs in a haze of red. The Gardner machine gun erupted in staccato fire, shooting over the heads of the crouching infantrymen, and then stopped abruptly, evidently jammed. He could hear the bullets now from the Mahdist sharpshooters zipping and droning overhead, and saw khaki forms in the British line fall back and crumple. The dervishes surged forward, keeping phalanx formation behind the emirs on camelback. The gap was narrowing alarmingly, now no more than two hundred yards, but still the British held their fire. They were close enough now to hear the hoarse goading and swearing of the soldiers, the grousing of camels, the sergeants and corporals bawling at their men to remain steady, to fire only in volley when the order came. A bullet zapped by dangerously close, not from their pursuers but fired from the square by some clear-eyed British marksman who thought he had seen two fanatical Arabs running at them from the north.

Mayne grabbed Charrière and pulled him to a halt. It was no good. They were not going to make it. It had been a calculated gamble to go for the gap, but it had closed faster than he had hoped. To continue that way now would be to run straight into the jaws of death. He dragged Charrière into a low gully in front of a boulder, protected from the rear, and they crouched down together, panting hard. They could not run around the rear of the square, as the soldiers there would be ready for an attack on that side and would gun them down instantly; nor could they try to run through the dervish line, as they would be trampled. They were going to have to veer left, to ride the tide of the dervish advance and head straight into the side of the British square in the hope that the troops would stem the tide long enough for them to get through to the other side and safety. Their chances were vanishingly small, but it was better than certain death. Once inside the square, they would aim for the far left corner: Mayne had seen it fall back and open to let the skirmishers in, a risky move on the part of the officer in charge of that section of the line that could have put the entire square at jeopardy. He had a sudden image of Burnaby, of self-imposed heroic duty, of how such a man in his perfect milieu might make a pact with death to save his men; but all that mattered now to Mayne was that the disorder in the line at that point might allow them an escape route if they survived that far.

A trumpet blared, and suddenly the dervish shooting ceased and the phalanx came to a halt, like some great beast pausing for breath. All Mayne could hear was a sound like a distant rushing wind, the low chanting of a thousand voices that had been in the background since the start of the dervish advance. Then the lead emir raised his standard and cried out, a deep, beautiful voice like a muezzin calling the faithful to prayer. The moment he stopped, a thousand throwing spears were launched from the front line, silver streaks that reflected the sun like a shimmering rainbow, flying in a low arc and then falling to cries in the British line as those thrown the farthest found their mark. Then the chant was drowned in a cacophony of drumming and the pounding of thousands of sandalled feet, the dervishes marking time like parade-ground soldiers about to march forward, making the earth beneath Mayne tremor and shiver. The air was rent by shrieks, not of fear but of exaltation, by men who would soon be with the Prophet in heaven and would beckon more to join them, drawing the jihad inexorably on until it swept away all who did not believe in the divine wisdom of the Mahdi.

Just as the dervish line surged forward, Mayne heard an order being bellowed from the British square, and then a deafening crack as three hundred and fifty Martini-Henry rifles fired in unison. It was as if a sudden hurricane had hit the dervish front line, blowing men back. Seconds later another volley thinned out the next wave, but still they kept coming. The British had cut it fine, holding their fire until every bullet would strike flesh, hoping that the piles of bodies would stem the dervish advance; and when there was no more time for reloading, the enemy would still face a glittering palisade of bayonets, wielded by modern riflemen trained to use cold steel as murderously as their predecessors who had confronted the forces of jihad in an earlier age.

A bullet whanged off the boulder and punched Mayne in the neck, bowling him over. Charrière crouched down and felt for the wound. There was no blood, thank God; the bullet was nearly spent and had not penetrated. He caught sight of two distant camels about a thousand yards to the east of the square, their riders kneeling down and shooting. They were the two pursuers who had ridden away from the others to cut off their likely escape route, but they had now seen that they were not going that way and had turned back. Mayne knelt up, peering back along the desert track to the north. The other two men had also dismounted and were firing at them, the noise of their bullets lost in the din from ahead. He turned back to the square. The dervish line had now extended outwards, the phalanx having been split by the volley fire, the northern mass wheeling round to come in on the flank of the square in front of him and Charrière. The dervishes seemed to be coming directly at him, a surging wave of screaming men and shimmering spears that tore down upon them with a roar like the sea, the low hill behind them sparkling all over with jets of flame from rifle fire.

They were in a death trap. He crouched forward, ignoring the throbbing in his neck, and nodded at Charrière.

They dashed forward towards the square, swept in by the dervish advance. Dust swirled and lashed at Mayne's face, a storm that sucked him in like a vortex. And then it lifted as they came close, and he saw detail with astonishing clarity. The first wave of dervishes seemed to bound into the square like animal predators, lunging into the British bayonets, screaming. One man was running so hard that the barrel of the soldier's rifle went through the hole in his stomach made by the bayonet, thrusting out like a bloody pike and discharging into the press of dervishes behind. Men with hideous wounds from British rifle fire kept running forward, some so badly injured that they gargled blood when they tried to scream; they knew there would be no succour for the wounded from either side, and that to fall before they had expended their last drop of life might be to forfeit their promised place in the afterlife.

The British soldiers held their ground, dying where they stood rather than being pressed back. But the dervish tide was sweeping in like surf over rocks, surging and climbing over the soldiers, and then the first few were inside the square. Mayne saw one Ansar run screaming into a bayonet and be lifted bodily over the soldier's head, a jet of flame bursting through his body in tendrils of blood as he cartwheeled away; the soldier fell backwards and was immediately speared under the chin by the next dervish, the broad blade slicing his face off and throwing it into the air. Dervishes tumbled and scrabbled over the bodies that cluttered the line, hacking and stabbing their way forward, following the emir whose camel had galloped through a gap into the square unscathed, spitting and snorting as it halted. Just as the emir planted his banner, a soldier shot him from below, the bullet ripping through him from the groin and blowing his head open like a flower, his body dropping like a stone. Beside the dead emir Mayne saw the sailors frantically trying to clear the Gardner machine gun being cut down to a man, speared in the back and the neck, their throats slit. A dervish throwing stick came scything in, slicing through the legs of two camels at the leading edge of the corralled mass in the centre of the square, causing them to fall with a bellow and crush the man who had been holding them. The first of the dervishes was at the camels now, the spearhead of a phalanx that seemed bound to envelop them and wash over the rear of the square just as it had done the front. And yet the

camels stood solid and the square held, rent with gaps
where the phalanx had struck but still unbroken.

And then Mayne too was inside, stumbling over bodies, everything in a blur. Dervish bullets zipped overhead
like insects, whacking off metal and thudding into flesh,
slapping into the flanks of camels. He heard the clash of
blades, the dull thwack of swords on sweaty tunics, the
screams and shrieks of the dervishes. And then he heard
the bellowing of the British sergeants at the rear, revers-
ing the line so that the soldiers could fire into the square,
aiming on either side of the knot of camels in the centre
and into the melee at the front where almost all the British soldiers had fallen. There was an immense crack of
rifle fire and a rushing of bullets overhead, and then another volley. The mountain gun joined in, a thunderous
clap as it fired at point-blank range. Mayne ran on, stag-
gering, his ears ringing from the gunfire. Another team
of sailors raced up to take over the Gardner machine
gun and got it into action, a juddering, hammering sound
as it spat rounds from its multiple barrels, the men
crouched behind the carriage wheels lifting the wooden
trail and panning the gun along the line of the approaching dervishes. Then the gun jammed again and the bluejackets frantically tried to clear it, only to be swept away
and hacked down by the tide of dervishes who overran
the position. Seconds later the force of the assault was
broken by the mass of camels in the centre of the square,
imperturbable as ever despite the bullets thwacking into
them and the tide of humanity pressing up against their
flanks. In that instant of lost momentum the British soldiers were among the dervishes, the officers firing their
revolvers and laying about them with swords, the men
thrusting and slashing with their bayonets. Dervish bullets fired from the distant ridge whistled and rasped by
as they plunged into the melee. More soldiers came up
from the rear bayonet-fighting, desperately parrying and
thrusting, slashing at necks and heads when they could
with the points of their blades. Mayne saw an officer
empty all five chambers of his revolver into a screaming

dervish before the man ran him through with his spear
and collapsed in a bloody heap on top of him. Another
officer with a knuckle-duster grasped a dervish in a
headlock and punched his nose upwards so that it shattered into the man's brain; he then was caught by an
emir with a whirling kurbash whip who snared him
round the neck and decapitated him with a sword.

Mayne was conscious of Charrière beside him, pulling
him close to his ear. "To the camels!" he yelled, dragging
him forward. But then a dervish came screaming at him,
his curved knife held high, and Mayne dropped to the
ground and lifted a discarded rifle, pulling the trigger
but hearing only the jar of the spring in the receiver. He
dropped the loading lever and frantically tried to prise
the spent cartridge from the breech, but he was knocked
violently sideways as the dervish ran straight into the
bayonet; he saw the bone and cartilage protruding from
the man's hips where he had been hit as he ran into the
square. He had been a dead man running, and for a horrible moment Mayne realised that most of the dervishes
who had made it this far would be like that, the living
dead, fuelled only by adrenaline and faith. He struggled
upright and tried to pull out the bayonet, but the man's
abdomen muscles had clenched it tight and he saw that
the blade had snapped where it had hit the backbone.
He looked up and saw a British soldier staring at him,
aiming, and then a hand grabbed his shoulder and Charrière pulled him violently away, towards the camels.
Charrière had picked up a sword and was slashing and
hacking on either side, cutting a way through to the centre of the square. The mountain gun a few yards away
erupted in an immense clap and belch of flame, leaving
Mayne reeling as Charrière dragged him on. The throng
became too tight to move, and he dropped the sword
and whipped out his knife, using it to parry a spear and
then twisting his assailant off balance and slicing through
his neck, nearly severing his head. Ahead of him Mayne
saw a bullet take off the lower jaw of a camel and the
bones and teeth fly into the soldier who had been hold-

ing it, ripping off his ear and leaving him screaming and clutching at the ragged hole. Another bullet burst through his head and sprayed blood and brains over the flank of the beast, which remained standing and making chewing motions with its upper jaw as if nothing had happened.

And then they were through and among the camels. They stumbled beneath the first beast's legs, crouching down and slithering through the faeces and urine as they made their way forward. The din of battle was muffled for a few moments but then intensified as they came towards the other side and out into the melee again, dodging among screaming and shrieking men, hearing the thwack of blades on flesh, the whine and whistle of bullets and the thuds as they found their mark. Mayne slipped in a pool of blood and fell face-to-face with a British soldier lying on his back with a fearful wound to his head; his eyeballs had protruded from their sockets and burst, the liquid glistening like bloody tears on his face. "Water," the man croaked, reaching for him blindly. "*Water.*" Before Mayne could think of acting, Charrière had heaved him up and dragged him on. A bullet nicked his arm and ricocheted into Charrière's shoulder, lodging in the flesh. Charrière flicked the bullet away with his knife and then stood facing two dervishes who ran at them screaming, their spears levelled. He pulled the spear from the hands of one of them, reversed it, and ran the man through until he was nearly embracing him, then pushed the body away as it went limp. Mayne drew his revolver and shot the other man, the gun jumping back in his hand as he fired; then he picked up a Martini-Henry rifle and slammed the butt into the man's neck as he went down. A few yards ahead of him Charrière had found another sword and was slashing and stabbing, cutting a path through the mass of dervishes, allowing space for a British sergeant to order a ragged volley at point-blank range that dropped a dozen of them in one go. Mayne ran behind, crouching low, sensing the British soldiers on his left and the dervishes to the right, and the two sides closing together again behind him in the shrieks and yells of hand-to-hand fighting.

As they approached the far edge of the square, Mayne saw a huge man propped with his back against a rock, surrounded by dead dervishes, his tunic drenched with blood. He blinked, wiping the sweat from his eyes, and stared again. It was Burnaby. He had taken a fearful spear thrust to the neck, a gash wide enough to put a hand through that had somehow missed the jugular but had sliced deep into his windpipe. Above his thick thatch of dark hair, the top of his skull had been sliced clean off by a sword, exposing his brain. His left arm was twisted horribly under his back, but with his right hand he was fumbling to load the massive four-barrelled howdah pistol on his chest, spilling the big .577 rifle cartridges out of a pouch on his belt. His eyes were strangely askew, but they flickered with recognition as Mayne came over to him. "I say, Mayne old chap." His voice sounded strange, reedy, and the gash in his throat frothed as he spoke. "Nearly took you for Johnny Arab in that attire. You couldn't help me, could you? Trying to load this damned thing. I'm afraid that dervish bowled me over an awful crumpler."

Mayne knelt down and reached for the cartridges. He and Burnaby had been to the same school, and that peculiar expression was one he himself had used countless times on the playing fields, holding his cricket bat with the wicket knocked out behind him. For a second it seemed a perfectly normal thing to say out here, where war for a man like Burnaby was simply a continuation of the contests of his youth. It was a thought that instantly evaporated when he looked again at Burnaby's horrific wounds. He grasped the barrel of the pistol and dropped four cartridges into the breech, then snapped it shut and clamped Burnaby's hand around the grip, putting his finger on the trigger. "I say, Mayne," said Burnaby, his voice weaker. "You couldn't light me one of my cigarettes, could you? Really could do with it now." He seemed to be struggling for words, and Mayne knelt down. Burnaby's voice was now little more than a whisper, and his neck was seeping bloody froth. "Listen here, Mayne. You know I work for Wilson too. I know your true mission. Watch your back. Don't trust anyone. *Anyone*. Now, out of my way."

Mayne had blocked out the battle for the last few seconds, but threw himself sideways just in time to see a half-naked dervish rush at them, his spear held high. Burnaby raised the pistol with a wobbly hand and fired. The round hit the dervish square in the face, blowing his head backwards in a haze of blood and brain. Burnaby suddenly jerked back and blood erupted from his nose. He had been hit in the forehead by a spent bullet that had caved in his sinuses and lodged in the bone of his forehead. The force of the blow had knocked him unconscious, and his head was lolling, his eyes half open and sightless and his breathing coming in terrible rasps. The bullet had been a small mercy, but not enough. There was only one thing Mayne could do for him now. As he pulled out his revolver, he saw a soldier who had detached himself from the melee and was hurtling towards him, bellowing for him to stop, his bayonet poised. Mayne remembered Burnaby's comment about his desert attire; to the soldier he would look like a Mahdist about to finish off their beloved colonel. There was a shriek from in front, and another dervish came hurling forward. Mayne wrenched the howdah pistol from Burnaby's hand and fired all three remaining barrels in quick succession, the massive recoil kicking the gun high above him each time. The rounds hit the dervish in the centre of his chest, blowing his heart out and leaving a hole large enough to see through. The man fell in a gory heap on Burnaby, whose eyes were now glazed over in death. Mayne sprang back to face the soldier, dropping the pistol and raising his Webley, but before he could aim it and shout a warning that he was British, the other man had tumbled backwards as a bullet struck him.

Mayne turned and ran forward, slipping over the gore from a man's abdomen and driving his right knee painfully into the ground, then picked himself up and leapt over the stacked wooden crates that formed the edge of the zariba. He saw Charrière waiting, then glanced back, hearing his own rasping breath, the pounding and ringing in his ears, the shrill whistling he experienced after gunfire. Hearing those things, he realised that something was different. The shooting and shrieking had stopped. And then he saw a most incredible sight. The dervishes had turned and begun to walk silently out of the billowing gun smoke in the direction they had come, their spears and swords held down. The ferocious energy that had propelled their advance had suddenly been expended, and the British had stood their ground. He was astonished by the dignity of their departure, by its utter disjunction from the savagery of a few moments before; it was as if they were mere tribesmen again, no more than people passing through, a timeless imprint of humanity in the desert that made the battle seem just a passing storm. The last of them disappeared out of sight, and for a moment the British troops slumped and exhausted in the zariba seemed agape with disbelief, stunned into immobility. It had been less than fifteen minutes since the dervish charge had begun. *Fifteen minutes*.

Then there was a rippling noise, a ragged cheer that quickly became a snarling frenzy of rage. The soldiers picked themselves up and surged forward, hacking and stabbing at the fallen dervishes, yelling profanities in voices hoarse with gunpowder and adrenaline and thirst. Mayne heard the crack of rifle fire and the sliding and crunching of bayonets in bodies. They had seen dervishes feign death and leap up with knives, and they were taking no chances. Ever since Hicks's army had been annihilated, they had known they would be given no quarter in defeat, and now they were doling out the same in return. It was war unchanged from the days of the first jihad over a thousand years before, war without morality. Mayne saw a soldier bayonet a dead dervish over and over again in the face, bellowing maniacally. Another was on his knees bashing a head to pulp with a rock, his arms drenched with blood like a butcher's. An officer appeared, waving his revolver and trying to restore order, but Mayne knew he would be able to do nothing until the bloodlust had run its course.

He sat alongside Charrière behind a rock. They were outside the zariba now, but it was safer to hide until the officers had regained control and there was less risk of being mistaken for dervishes and shot. The officers would want to capture any surviving dervishes, yet would probably be unwilling to give chase until they were certain that the enemy was routed. Mayne and Charrière would have to rely on their speed to escape once they had revealed themselves. Mayne lay close to the earth, panting hard, regaining his breath. His sense of smell was returning, and he recoiled from it: the acrid sulphureous reek of black powder, the sickly latrine stench of spilled bowels, the coppery odour of blood, the smell on his own body of sweat and fear and adrenaline. He caught a whiff of roasting flesh and saw a dervish a few feet away who had been shot at point-blank range, the powder burns encircling the wound and wisps of smoke rising from the hole. The smoke of battle was clearing now, and he sensed sunlight through the haze. He heard a bugle and the shouts of the sergeants and corporals ordering the men to re-form the square in case of fresh attack. He stared back at the ground. The earth was cracked and blackened, parched as it always had been, the dark patches of blood already sopped up by the dust. The desert was beginning to absorb the residue of battle even before the frenzy of killing had died away.

He listened hard. He realised that the background sound had gone, the chanting, the drumbeat, the pounding of feet; the dervish army had abandoned the wells and was retreating. Soon the soldiers he could now see standing and moving about slowly in the swirling dust would snap back to reality; the square would consolidate and the advance would be ordered. But for the moment they were caught by the shock of battle, as dazed as he was. Colour was returning gradually, as if he were looking at an old-fashioned daguerreotype where the iodine and mercury had created a maroon monochrome but the artist had touched it up with crude streaks of colour to give a semblance of reality.

Mayne looked at his hands, blackened by the greasy grime of gunpowder, and felt the throbbing bruise on his neck where the bullet had struck him before they had entered the square. He stood up and looked around him, trying to calm his breathing. He saw blood and brains spattered on faces, and the cracked lips of dying men, their bodies no longer producing saliva, their tongues swollen and off-white with mucus. One man missing the top of his head convulsed and juddered and then went still. A soldier lying on dead comrades pulled a spear from his own neck, as he did so releasing a gush of arterial blood that pumped out of him like a geyser, his face whitening as his body drained. He fell back, alabaster among the grey. Another who had been too close to the muzzle blast of the screw gun was lying obscenely exposed with his clothes blown off, his skin lacerated in a crazy pattern like a cracked pavement. It was the first time Mayne had registered the instant aftermath of battle. Ten minutes ago these men had all been alive, and the shocking speed of their deaths seemed to leave a lingering aura over them, like the warmth on a fresh corpse; but he knew that with each rasping final breath that aura would dissipate and the colours would go, sucked into the desert and extinguished by the burning heat of the sun, leaving only a monochrome image of desiccation and decay.

He remembered something his Dongolese guide Shaytan had told him at the cataracts, about the wind created by a desert battle: that if you listened hard enough, you could hear the distant shrieks and sighs of banshees who performed a wild dance in the sky high above the fight, mocking both the victors and the vanquished. He remembered the carving of the desert battle he had seen in the underground chamber beside the cataract: the Egyptian soldiers advancing hieratically, Akhenaten at their head, then their bodies splayed below, the vast disk of the sun and its rays dominating all. Had Akhenaten sensed this too? Had he fought battles against an enemy from the south where the desert seemed the only victor, where the sun seemed to eclipse all? Had he turned back to Egypt, bringing with him a new God and a belief that the power of the Aten might release men from conflict that could give only the illusion of victory?

He remembered crouching beside Burnaby, an event that seemed impossibly long ago, and Burnaby's whispered warning to him: *watch your back*. He looked at Charrière, sword still in his hand, the blood congealing on his arm where he had prised out the bullet. He could barely think of his thirst. They would both need water, soon. There was no chance now of reaching the wells of Abu Klea, which would soon be under British control; they could not risk being seized and questioned. It would have to be the Nile, more then twenty miles off. They had to hope to find another source on the way if they were to have any chance of surviving the marathon run that now lay ahead of them.

He remembered their pursuers. Had that been the purpose of Burnaby's warning? He looked beyond Charrière to where the clearing smoke had revealed the rocky knoll to the east, the rising ground that had provided a defensive position for the British encampment overnight. That was the direction their pursuers would have taken if they had decided to outflank the battlefield and regain the track to the Nile on the other side. More likely they would be lingering in the valley, waiting for the British to march down to the wells, intent on picking over the battlefield and checking the dead so they could tell their paymaster that their job had been done for them. But it would be only a matter of time before they realised that Mayne and Charrière had survived, and that with camels they had the advantage of speed. Mayne knew it was essential that the two of them cover the open ground on the way to the shrub and mimosa forest before their pursuers regained their trail. The forest would be a maze of danger and dead-end passages in the dark, and they needed to get as far through it as they could while it was still daylight.

And there was added urgency. The dervishes who had melted away from the battle would soon pass word of their defeat to the Mahdi himself, which might lead him to order the final assault on the city, losing Mayne precious time in his attempt to reach Gordon before it was overwhelmed. Abu Klea would show the Mahdi that the British were a force to be reckoned with, that they were superior to the Egyptian army he had terrorised and routed two years before. If the British were to stay in the Sudan, the jihad would not be the walkover his early successes had promised. But the victory might ultimately be a hollow one. The Mahdi knew that the British were there under duress, and if he were to order the assault on Khartoum now, to remove Gordon from any hope of rescue, they would abandon the Sudan and withdraw to Egypt. He knew they were not present in numbers sufficient to defeat his main force in a set-piece battle; yet if word of Abu Klea were to reach tribesmen of wavering loyalties, it might tilt them towards the British, whilest the news might cause the garrison at Khartoum to redouble their resolve to stand firm, thinking that a British force was finally on its way to defeat the Mahdist army and relieve the city.

Mayne stared in the direction of the Nile to the south, seeing only the haze of an approaching dust storm on the horizon, and below that the undulating rocky plain that extended to the dark smudge marking the beginning of the tangled mass of shrub. He could see no sign of humanity, no flickering lights, no crumbled ruins, not even the camel trail that must lie somewhere in the folds of the ground ahead. He felt as if by passing through the battle he had entered a darker place, a shadowland, a world beyond knowledge where even the pharaohs had feared to tread. This was the land that Gordon had made his own, and it was only here that his motivations could be understood. He swallowed hard, trying to rid his throat of the taste of battle, then twisted round to look one last time. There was no sign of their pursuers, for now. He nodded to Charrière, who dropped the sword and sheathed his knife. Mayne holstered his revolver and grasped the wrapped rifle that was still on his back, knowing that the instant they stood up in their Arab gear they could still fall prey to a trigger-happy British soldier. They crouched forward, readying to leap up and run.

A bugle sounded, and he heard the stomping noise of soldiers falling in. Now was their chance. All eyes would be down the slope towards the retreating Mahdist forces and the wells where the soldiers and their camels would be desperate to slake their thirst.

They needed to move fast. Mayne put his hand forward to signal Charrière. He tensed, his heart pounding.

They began to run.

PART 5

CHAPTER 19

THE TOYOTA BOUNCED AND JOLTED ALONG the track towards the Nile, through growths of desert grass and plots of vegetables and fruit trees enclosed by low mud-brick walls. They were approaching the site of the wreck of the *Abbas,* some sixty kilometers south of the Semna cataract along the Nile towards Khartoum. The surrounding land was more low-lying than at Semna, more suited to agriculture, and every available area of sandy soil had been turned to arable. The track ran beside an irrigation channel that extended over a kilometer from the river; ahead of them on the bank they could see a pair of pivoting *shaduf* water-raising devices, the oldest and simplest equipment for getting water from the river into the channels, used since early antiquity. Two scruffy boys who had been operating the devices left them and ran up to the Toyota as it sped by, and chased it through the cloud of dust they left behind. Ibrahim turned to Jack and pointed at the window. "Keep it wound up," he said. "This isn't a good place. When we get out, watch your pockets."

Jack glanced at Costas in the backseat, and then kept his eyes glued ahead as they tore down the final few hundred meters of the track and came to a skidding halt only a few car lengths from the water's edge. "Thanks, Ibrahim," he said.

"Rocket man, that's what I'm going to call you," added Costas.

"Apologies for the speed," Ibrahim said. "It's a habit you pick up around here. I learned to do it when I was with a Sudanese naval attachment in Mogadishu. You go fast everywhere there, and avoid stopping at all costs."

"So what's the lowdown here?" Costas said, peering out the closed window beside him.

"There's a local warlord who runs this district. His boys belt around in 'specials' like those we used to see in Mogadishu, openly carrying AKs. It shouldn't happen in Sudan anymore, but it does. Basically they're a continuation of the tribal fiefdoms that dotted this territory at the time the British arrived here, concentrating especially on these precious cultivable patches of land. Back in the old days, they made their loot from the slave trade. When you see how these places are run, you can understand how General Gordon found it so difficult to stamp it out. These days of course it's drugs rather than slaves, and that's why you don't look over those mud-brick walls. It's mostly poppies, but high-grade marijuana too."

"How does al'Ahmed fit in with this?" Costas said. "The new official who got us here."

"Officially he's a special appointee to oversee enhancement of the historical and archaeological evidence for Sudan in the period immediately before British rule, especially the era of the Mahdi, which is celebrated by many Sudanese as a time of independence between the Egyptian and the British regimes. That's why he's summoned you here, as a convenient way of getting the world's top archaeological diving experts to have a look at the *Abbas* site. And he's secured this area by promising police if needed. But you won't be seeing any of those when we arrive, because unofficially his family controls most of these drug-producing areas, providing protection from inter-gang warfare and an assured market in return for a substantial cream of the profits, usually eighty percent. One word from al'Ahmed and these people bow to his will. Those shifty young men you can see sitting on the wall ahead of us, the two with Kalashnikovs, those are our police. But we have to remember that al'Ahmed wears his official hat too, and he has the authority to call in the real police if he decides he doesn't need us anymore."

"Great," said Costas, staring at the children who were banging at the door of the car. "Why do I have a bad feeling about this?"

Jack pursed his lips. He had felt uneasy all the way from Semna, and now, seeing this place and sensing the atmosphere, he was beginning to question his decision to agree to a visit. He looked at the riverbank a few meters ahead. "How far out is the wreckage?"

"The most likely site's about two hundred meters out and thirty meters deep," Ibrahim replied. "It should be a quick dive straight from shore to see whether there's anything worth looking at. We can be in and out within two hours and back on the road to Semna."

Jack tapped the dashboard. "Okay. Let's do it."

"Watch the kids."

They all got out of the car at the same time, and were immediately swarmed by about a dozen children. Jack firmly pushed two boys away and prevented another from looping his finger around his watch. The two young men with Kalashnikovs sauntered over, and one of them raised his rifle in the air. There was a deafening crack and the children quickly dispersed, scattering into the irrigation ditches and alleys surrounding the fields. One of the men swaggered up to Jack and put out his hand, grasping Jack's in an iron grip. "Hassid Saib told us to look after you, and we will. No more trouble from small boys, eh? Or we shoot them, see, like little pigs." The man aimed his rifle here and there, laughing, the other hand still firmly holding Jack's. "You give us a little *baksheesh*, huh, and maybe we give you something from our fields, eh? You Americans always like our hashish."

"Nobody said anything about money," Costas said.

Ibrahim walked up to the man, and they spoke in Sudanese. He turned to Jack. "I'm sorry. I hadn't anticipated this. Can you do a hundred dollars to share between them?"

"Then no more?" Jack said.

Ibrahim spoke again to the man. "If any more men come asking for money, they will shoot them."

"That's not exactly what I had in mind," Jack said.

"It's posturing. I'd give him the money from our cash box, but it's best that he sees you doing it. He knows you're the boss."

Jack produced a roll of notes from his back pocket and handed it over. The man released his grip, smiled and took out an enormous spliff from his front shirt pocket, licked one end, put it in his mouth, and then lit it. He took a deep drag and passed it to Jack, who patted his chest and declined. Ibrahim spoke to the man again. "I told him it's the diving. You should never smoke before a dive."

"Okay," Jack said. "Let's get moving." The two men sauntered back to their companions, split the roll of notes between them, and resumed their seats on the wall, passing the spliff between them. Ibrahim opened the back of the Toyota, and Jack and Costas quickly donned their equipment, then lumbered down to the shore and stepped into the muddy sludge on the edge. The river here was very different than it was in Semna, more heavily silted and sluggish, and they were going to have a more difficult time seeing underwater. Jack pushed the men with guns from his mind and tried to focus on the excitement of being the first since 1884 to dive on the *Abbas,* with the possibility that they might find antiquities that had been left by the local salvors, who would have had little interest in them. He flipped down his visor, watched Costas do the same, and then slipped into the water and swam out on the surface until he reached a point close to the edge of a small island. The river bore little obvious resemblance to the descriptions of this place in 1884, when Colonel Butler of the river column had visited it and seen wreckage on the foreshore, but Jack and Ibrahim had compared a satellite image with the sketch maps from the time and estimated that a position about fifty meters off the southern tip of the island would land them on any wreckage, if it still existed.

He stopped in the water, gave an okay sign and a thumbs-down to Costas, and then raised his arm to signal their descent to Ibrahim on the shore. He could see that the men were now ranged along the bank; he watched as two more Toyotas hurtled into the parking place, screeched around, and disgorged their occupants, all of them carrying guns. Jack remembered the murder of Colonel Stewart and his party on that fateful day when the steamer had run ashore here in September 1884, when a duplicitous local official had offered them hospitality and they had all been killed. Ibrahim was right. This was definitely not a good place. He turned to Costas, who was still on the surface, watching the shoreline as well. He clicked on his intercom. "Let's get this done as quickly as possible. I want out of here."

"Roger that."

Jack dropped below the surface. Seeing that the water visibility was no more than three to four meters, he swam close to Costas so that they were within visual range. He bled his buoyancy compensator and they quickly descended almost twenty meters to the river bottom, a dark brown bed of mud and sludge. "Compass bearing fifty-two degrees," he said, monitoring the directional readout data inside his visor. "We'll do one transit for twenty meters, swim five meters southwest, do another transit, and call it a day if we don't find anything."

"Let's hope we do," Costas said. "I want to make this worthwhile."

They began to swim slowly forward, three to four meters apart, scanning the riverbed for any anomalies. Almost immediately Costas sank down and pointed at a feature poking out of the sludge. "I may be wrong, but I think that's a gun mounting," he said. Jack swam over to take a look, suddenly excited again. "Probably a four-pounder, a typical deck gun for a steamer. That's promising."

"Look ahead, Jack."

Out of the gloom a large section of wooden planking came into view, curving around to a rudder and up to a railing that had rusty metal slabs attached to it, evidently armor plating. "That's *got* to be it," Jack enthused. "Gordon had all his river steamers armored to the point where they became top-heavy, but it kept them pretty well protected from the Mahdi's guns. You can see the dents of bullet impacts all over the place. This thing has really been through the wars."

They swam through a gap in the frame and over the deck of the vessel. A good deal of planking had been removed, and the deckhouse superstructure was largely flattened, but the vessel was in surprisingly good condition considering that it had been exposed to salvage at low water. Jack had to remind himself that he was no longer in seawater, that unlike the *Beatrice* in the Mediterranean, this was a wreck where much of the wooden and metal structure could survive in the freshwater of the Nile in a good state of preservation. In the middle of the collapsed deck structure, they swam over the large rotund mass of one of the boilers, collapsed sideways but remarkably intact. Jack stared at it, remembering how they had been a mixed blessing in 1884, providing steam power that made the boats the only screw-propulsion vessels on the upper Nile but requiring such quantities of wood that they quickly outstripped the meager local supply, forcing crews to demolish houses and even shaduf devices in their insatiable demand for fuel.

Jack sank down to the silt, leaving Costas to explore

the other side of the boiler, and looked around. It was immediately apparent that any attempt to discover smaller artifacts and spilled crates would require a major excavation project, with airlifts and dredges to remove the overburden of sludge that had buried much of the wreckage. If there were antiquities from Gordon's collection here, they were unlikely to find them today. He tapped his intercom. "I think we've got the result we want. We found the wreck, it's in good condition, and it could be excavated."

"Jack, come around here." Costas had gone headfirst into a corroded hole in the deck below the boiler, leaving only his fins protruding. "There's something wedged under the boiler plate. It's a large slab of stone. I think it might have markings on it. Come down beside me and see if you can help me push it out."

Jack swam around and squeezed through the hole, coming upright beside Costas. The slab looked perhaps a meter by a meter and a half in area and about ten centimeters thick. He pulled himself past Costas and inspected it as closely as he could. The edges were coarse and uneven, as if the slab had been hacked away from a larger piece. But the few centimeters of upper surface he could see were smooth and polished. He pushed his hand in farther and felt incised lines and a definite cartouche. There was no doubt about it. This was from an ancient Egyptian wall relief, far larger than any other that he knew of this far south in the Sudan, from a major temple or other monument. It looked as if it had been packed in multiple wrappings that had largely perished, leaving a compacted mass of burlap and cordage jamming the slab firmly beneath the boiler.

"I don't think we're going to move it, Jack," Costas said. "I think this was deliberately wedged in here by someone who wanted to hide it."

"That could be only Gordon," Jack said. "He might have been fearful of something this large being pilfered or damaged."

"It's certainly kept it free from looting until now," Costas said.

"Let me try to get closer," Jack said. "There's a hieroglyphic cartouche in there, and I may be able to make it out." He wriggled past Costas and put his hand farther into the gap over the slab, feeling more of it. He found the cartouche again and felt it as if it were Braille, his eyes shut. His knowledge of hieroglyphics was not that of an Egyptologist, but he had learned to identify this one. "It's our old friend Akhenaten," he murmured. "Now where does Gordon get a slab like this with Akhenaten's name on it?" He had a sudden hunch, and he felt the lines that extended around the cartouche, imagining in his mind's eye how they might cover the entire slab and a larger original depiction. He remembered the carving he had seen in that fleeting second in the wreck of the *Beatrice*, on the slab inside the sarcophagus. He was certain it was the same pattern. Then he remembered the depiction of Akhenaten in the crocodile temple, the missing slab in the center that he was convinced was the key to understanding these images, to seeing them for what they really were. He pushed his hand in to a point where he felt the center of the image might lie, but it was completely sealed beneath the packing material. "We're going to have to come back," he said. "This is really important. As big as anything we've found yet." He withdrew his hand and pushed back from the wreckage and then rose alongside Costas out of the hole. "I'm not saying anything about this to al'Ahmed. We'll tell him about the wreck, which is supposed to be his main interest. If we talk about antiquities, then this site will be stripped bare before we're back."

"If he sends down divers of his own, they'll find this anyway," Costas said. "Keeping mum would just be staving off the inevitable."

"If we play our cards right, it'll be us doing the excavation," Jack said. "Then we can reveal this find first to the Khartoum museum, and bring it up under controlled conditions so that nobody else walks away with it. Antiquities like this are worth millions and are used to lubricate drug deals. And we know al'Ahmed has a special interest in Akhenaten. He may even know about this slab and just be using us to find the wreck and establish its existence. We need to play a very careful game."

The high-pitched whine of an outboard motor approached at high speed from some distance away. When it was over their location, it turned around and idled. "Sounds like a Zodiac-sized outboard, sixty to eighty horsepower," Costas said. "The only guys out here I can imagine having those will be the police. That's encouraging if they've finally arrived, though I don't want to ascend into a revving outboard if there are other people who don't know we're here. I vote we swim up along the riverbed to shore."

Jack nodded, and they set off underwater. After about a hundred meters the riverbed rose to less than ten meters' depth, and then it became too shallow to justify remaining submerged. The sound of the outboard was still some distance away, over the site, and it seemed safe to ascend. Costas gave the thumbs-up sign, and they both rose together face-to-face only a stone's throw from shore.

Jack knew something was wrong even before they broke the surface. Pulsating orange lights seemed to revolve in the water, and they heard a loudspeaker in Sudanese. Three police cars with flashing lights were parked beside the Toyota, and the inflatable suddenly revved up and gunned towards them, sweeping around dangerously close and coming to a halt. Two policemen in combat gear were sitting at the back carrying assault rifles, and in between them a Sudanese man in a suit and tie with a police badge on his belt stood up with his hands on his hips, staring at them. Jack flipped back his visor. "Do you speak English? Is there a problem?"

The man shook his head and motioned them to shore. Costas was already struggling out of the sludge, and

Jack joined him. Unclipping their helmets, they walked into a blaze of lights. Jack shaded his eyes, spotting Ibrahim sitting in a car with a policeman taking some form of statement. "Ibrahim! What's going on?"

A policeman moved up to him and raised his rifle, and Jack immediately put his hands up, followed by Costas. He felt his harness being roughly unclipped and his backpack drop to the ground. Someone grabbed one wrist and then the other, handcuffing them behind his back. He could see that Costas was receiving the same treatment, and they were both pushed forward into the glare. "What the hell is going on?" Jack said angrily to the nearest policeman. "Why are we being arrested?"

Ibrahim appeared in front of him, followed by two policemen. "Listen to me, Jack. They're not going to arrest me. I'm going to drive back to Semna immediately. They've stripped the car and taken your mobile phones, everything. I've seen this before. All you'll get back when they dump you across the Egyptian border will be your passports. But I'll be waiting for you."

"Why are we being arrested?" Jack said. "What for?"

A policeman stood between Ibrahim and Jack, patting a truncheon, but Ibrahim spoke to him quickly in Sudanese and the man stepped aside grudgingly, a scowl on his face. Ibrahim turned to Jack. "I'm not supposed to be talking to you. You're not supposed to have contact with anyone until you cross the border. Once you remove all your gear, they'll blindfold you and take you in separate cars. Nobody will tell you anything. But you've been arrested for diving on an archaeological site without a permit, and for attempting to steal antiquities. That carries a statutory sentence of ten years. You're getting off lightly."

"But we had a permit," Jack exclaimed.

"We had *permission*, not a permit. There was nothing on paper. Everything was at the whim of al'Ahmed, and he's clearly decided to revoke his support. It was always going to be a risk."

"We find it for him, and then he deports us," Jack said. "It was a setup."

"Be cool, Jack. And you too, Costas. Go with the flow and don't provoke them. You can shout as much as you like after you've crossed the border. But one thing you can be sure of is that you won't be allowed back in the Sudan while this man holds the strings of power in the antiquities department."

CHAPTER 20

MAJOR EDWARD MAYNE LAY AGAINST THE crumbling mud-brick wall of the fort peering through his telescope over the Nile at the low buildings of the city some eight hundred yards away. He took a deep breath, then dropped his head down and swallowed hard to stop himself from retching. They had smelled the city from miles off, an occasional waft in the air, then a rancid backdrop that had tainted every breath, and finally the sickening, honey-sweet smell that assailed him now, a stench of decay combined with the fetid odour of the river, which was too sluggish to wash away the filth that oozed into it, leaving it mouldering and fly-ridden on the mud banks that lined the shore. From a distance they had seen flocks of vultures wheeling over the city, and as they approached they watched the birds drop down and pull indescribable trophies from the river mud—lumps of gristle and strings of bones barely hanging together—and fly off with them to their desert feasting grounds to the west. Four weeks ago at the cataract he had mused on the fact that they were drinking water that had flowed past here, past Gordon, but now it made him sick to his stomach. He had known that Khartoum would be a city on its last legs, a place of starvation and disease and death, but nothing could have prepared him for this.

He lay still for a moment, listening for Charrière's return from the riverbank. The exposed riverbed was as wide as the Thames foreshore in London at low tide, but instead of hard gravel was a muddy effluvium that was already beginning to dry and crack; the river itself continued to flow through a narrow central channel, but on either side it was reduced to brown trickles and pools between mudflats. They had spotted one place where a boat crossing looked feasible, an irregular channel that ran past Tutti Island some four hundred yards to the west and then towards the far shore, its waters visibly diminishing even in the short time they had been there. Charrière had gone half an hour ago to investigate a cluster of boats that had been drawn up nearby, their owners evidently awaiting the winter runoff from the mountains to the south that would once again cause the Nile to flood.

It had been a week since they had left the battlefield of Abu Klea, a week during which they had kept to their plan, staying one day ahead of the three steamers that were chugging the ninety miles up from Metemma. They had moved fast through the desert, keeping close to the course of the river but far enough away to avoid being spotted, travelling in the cool of the night under a full moon and hiding in rocky gullies during the day. If all went according to plan, the steamers would arrive some twelve hours from now, soon after dawn tomorrow morning, providing they survived the barrage of artillery and rifle fire that the Mahdi's men would undoubtedly throw at them. Even so the only approach would be up the channel opposite the palace where the river still flowed, and they would have to use duckboards and ropes to get across the mud banks to Mayne's present position in the fort, the rendezvous point where they would pick up Gordon. The plan had worked so far, but barely. Had he and Charrière arrived a day later, there would have been no chance of getting a boat across, and his only hope would have been to mingle with the Mahdi's men on the far shore of the White Nile

and attempt to get into the city from there, a virtually
suicidal venture as his Arab disguise was bound to be
rumbled close-up. His mission still hung in the balance;
everything about it had been a close-run thing.

He heard the croak of frogs and the buzzing of mosquitoes. Away to the left an emaciated cow with its eyes
sewn shut was circling round and round a wooden post,
pulling a wheel that raised and lowered a shaduf water-
lifting device over the bank of the river. The harness
creaked and groaned, and the beast wheezed. Someone
had taken potshots at it, probably the Mahdist sharpshooters on Tutti Island; it had two black holes in its
upper flanks and a gaping hole in its stomach where a
bullet had exited along with a string of entrails, now
hanging from it and swarming with shiny fat flies. Yet
still the beast lumbered round, the shaduf dipping into
an imaginary river that had dropped below its reach
many days ago. The ravenous people on the opposite
bank must have been tortured by the animal's existence,
but it had been saved from butchery by the danger of
crossing the river within range of Tutti Island, and the
torpor Mayne had seen through his telescope: of men
and women too far gone to move, let alone launch a
boat. Charrière had promised to despatch it with his
knife once the sun was down and it was safe to do so
without being seen.

Around the cow lay stacks of sun-dried bricks and
piles of mud, solidified masses that dotted the shoreline like collapsed termite mounds. Mayne realised that
the shaduf had been used to bring up water for brick-
making and that the deep pit behind him inside the
ruined fort had been excavated for its mud. Its bottom
was a festering slurry, alive with hatching insects, and he
felt his sandals dig into it now, the mud oozing between
his toes. The caked layers of sweat and grime on his skin
had kept the mosquitoes at bay, a lesson he had learned
from the Mohawks in Canada, but Charrière had protected himself further by daubing his face and forearms
with liquid mud from the pit; afterwards he had seemed

barely visible, as if he had emerged from the banks of
the river like some Nile wraith. Mayne had forgone the
treatment, caring little about the discomfort of insects
and the risk of fever. He needed to look half present-
able if he were to stand any chance of getting past the
gate guardians at the palace and being allowed to see
Gordon.

He raised his telescope and studied the palace now. It
was the only building of any grandeur, a low two-storey
affair with twelve large French-style windows on each
floor facing out over the river, and an external staircase
on the left-hand side that led from an upper-floor balcony to a forecourt enclosed by a perimeter wall and the
gate to the street outside. He stared at the front of
the structure, scrutinising the approach from the river
while there was still enough light. A retaining wall and
low balustrade lay along the top of the riverbank; below
that was a stairway leading down to a small dock. The
present level of the river was some fifteen feet below that
and fifty feet out, but duckboards had been laid over the
mud from the stairs to the water's edge. Anchored in
the mud was a series of upright posts of indeterminate
purpose, probably for mooring. He could see yet another reason why tonight was the only possible time
to go. A gap had already appeared between the duckboards and the water, and another few hours would
make it impassable, an expanse of ooze and quicksand
that would terminate his mission within a stone's throw
of Gordon's upper-storey windows.

He looked at them now. They were shuttered and
dark. For a moment he wondered whether the whole
exercise had been in vain, whether Gordon was in there
at all. Then he remembered Buller telling him that Gordon slept during the day and was up during the night;
despite the onset of darkness, it was still only about five
o'clock, and he might not yet have risen. And there was
something else, clinching evidence. Mayne looked at the
duckboards again, seeing how the planks had been laid
alongside one another in threes and lashed over trans-

verse timbers placed on the mud about four feet apart. It was exactly how they had been trained to construct them at the School of Military Engineering, practising on the tidal banks of the river Medway. He shook his head, remembering Buller's remark about Gordon: *ever the engineer*. The lowest extension of the planking nearest the water had been built in the same fashion, so Gordon must have been out there supervising the work a mere matter of hours before. He must still be alive.

He scanned along the shoreline as far as he could to the east. He could just make out the ditch and parapet that enclosed Khartoum on its landward side, earthworks that Gordon himself had had built yet could have no hope of defending with his few hundred remaining Sudanese troops, many of them by now surely on the brink of starvation and reduced by disease and untreated wounds. Within the walls lay a straggling line of mudbrick huts leading up to the more substantial residences close to the palace where the Egyptian and Sudanese officials and their families must be holed up, barely surviving on Gordon's dwindling food supply, paralysed by fear.

He cocked an ear, thinking he had heard footsteps, but it remained unsettlingly quiet. His Dongolese guide Shaytan had told him that the Mahdi ordered his entire army to prayer just before dusk, and the Ansar enforced it with an iron fist; anyone caught transgressing had their hands lopped off. A quarter of a million men had been down on their hands and foreheads facing Mecca, their chanting too far off to be heard. But now somewhere in the distance he heard the single beat of a drum, nothing more, as if one of the drumbeats from Abu Klea had been captured somehow on the wind and spirited here, an ominous portent of things to come. He heard the thump of artillery, the shriek of a shell, and the whoomph as it fell somewhere beyond the palace, raising a cloud of dust that joined the pastel-red pallor lying over the city. A rifle shot rang out from the island to the right, and he saw a dark figure scurry for cover below the balustrade of the palace. It was the first gunfire he had heard, and it was strangely reassuring. When they had arrived from the desert, it had been not only the deathly quiet he found unnerving but the absence of smoke and burning; it was only when he looked with his telescope that he realised the reason: everything flammable in the city—the wooden frames of the mud-brick houses, the shaduf water-lifting devices that should have lined the shore, the thatched roofs, the palm and fruit trees, the barrows and carts—was long gone, destroyed in the weeks of bombardment or chopped up and used for fuel. It was a city reduced to a skeleton, where even high-explosive shells failed to make much impact, with nothing left to splinter and shatter other than the fragile human beings who still clung to life in the streets.

The few people he had seen were like the wretches he had once watched sifting through rubbish on the Thames foreshore on a foggy London morning, only here they were naked and there was no tide to wash away the filth of the river. It was as if the city had collapsed in exhaustion during the day, and what little energy remained— for scouring the alleyways yet again for anything edible, for raising ever more fetid water from the river—came out in a brief burst at dusk before it dissipated again and the nighttime bombardment of the city resumed. The people had been living in the shadow of death for too long to care what tomorrow might bring; they knew as Mayne knew that this day could be their last, that the arrival of the steamers with the relief force would surely provoke the Mahdi to order a final assault in which everything squalid would be cleansed, in which the city would be cleared of its suffocating pallor and the divine light would be allowed to shine through, in which all those who did not see it and who still clung to Gordon would be raped and mutilated and butchered.

He turned again to the foreshore and spotted a group of women and children dragging two corpses down to the river; they left them in the mud and scurried back up the bank. He looked at the dark pool below the bodies

and wondered whether the vultures were the only ones
here with a taste for human flesh. Shaytan had told him
that the slave traders had captured crocodiles from the
Nile and kept them in special underground tanks, feeding them with those who had crossed them. Perhaps
these women were doing the same, leaving offerings to
beasts that had been set free in the river but still lingered
nearby, expecting a feast of death. He remembered the
underground chamber beside the cataract and the image
of the ancient Egyptian crocodile god Sobek. Perhaps
these people, in this place too shrouded in horror for the
divine light to break through, had reverted to worship-
ping the beasts the ancients believed radiated the divine
presence. He wondered whether Gordon had seen that
too when he had first come here, and whether his zeal
to lift the shroud and bring light to these people had
brought darkness down upon himself, a darkness that
Mayne could now see swallowing up the city, leaving
only the lights of the palace flickering in the gloom.

He put his hand on his forehead, feeling the sticky
dampness his fingers had picked up from the mud-brick
wall. Everything seemed to be covered in a viscous over-
lay, as if the city were decaying and its putrescence seeping out around the edges, over the Nile and into the
desert beyond. He remembered what this place had been
before: a city whose population was either slave dealers
or the slaves themselves, people who had either discarded morality or whose morality had been destroyed
when they were put in chains. A city like that had been
in a state of decay long before the siege had begun, its
rotting core concealed perhaps by the bustle of trade
and the thin carapace of civilised normality provided by
the governor and his administration. With those gone
it was as if the horror had been allowed to surface,
the decay to ooze out. The darkness he saw now in the
corners and alleyways was not merely shadows but
something more substantial, a malaise that would soon
swallow the skeletal houses and leave nothing there at

all, a decaying mound eviscerated of life, like the ancient city mounds he had seen in the desert to the north.

Seeing the emaciated forms of the people had made him conscious of his own body, of the sparseness of muscle in his forearms, the gaunt cheeks beneath his beard. It was as if all that had hardened him, toughened him up for the desert journey, had in reality been preparation for Khartoum, reducing him to a state where he could be absorbed by the city and stand alongside others as a supplicant to the man who had arrived in their midst like a prophet. But the spareness of his frame scarcely registered against those he had seen on the other shore. This had been a city without food for weeks, apart from the dwindling supply of grain that Gordon must have kept for his own people. The only conceivable sustenance could have come from the corpses that mounted every day, dead through starvation or disease or gunfire; even so, their withered bodies could scarcely have provided palatable nourishment. He caught himself up, suddenly horrified by the ease with which he had assumed the worst. But contemplating Khartoum was like looking at one of the medieval paintings of hell that so fascinated Corporal Jones, where imagining the concealed horrors was worse than the visible images. He wondered how many other cities had gone this way, their inhabitants reduced to living without meaning, solely for survival, until they were mere shadows; and how many of the stark white ruins that he had visited, places like Akhenaten's capital Amarna, had ended their days not in quiet abandonment but in squalor and amorality and putrescence, reeking of decay.

He heard a footfall outside the wall, and Charrière slid alongside him and squatted down. "I've found a small reed boat about the size of a canoe. I've used my knife to make you a paddle from a piece of plank. It's crude, but it will do. The channel will take you to within a hundred yards of the island, so you will need to go without making a sound, just as we used to when we crept up on deer on the shore of our lake in the forest."

It was the first time Charrière had spoken of their past. Mayne had a sudden vision of the two of them as boys half a lifetime ago in Canada, of the birch-bark canoe that Charrière's father had made him, of the trust they had had in him that he had betrayed by leaving. He started to say something, to tell Charrière how much he wished they were back there now, how sorry he was for letting him down all those years ago, but then he looked into Charrière's eyes, cold, hard, dark, and said nothing. He raised himself up, keeping below the level of the walls. "A reed boat is good. There will be no noise if I go over a rock."

Charrière looked back out over the desert, scanning the gloom and frowning.

"What are you thinking?" Mayne asked.

"There are no camels, but I sense it. There are others there."

Mayne stared at him. "Our pursuers? There's been no sign of them since Abu Klea."

"I have not been able to backtrack at night and look for them. We have been on the move continuously."

Mayne looked around. "There might be others hiding here in these ruins, people who have made it across from the city." He remembered Shaytan telling him that on the way out from Khartoum on the steamer, he had spotted figures along the banks of the Nile, scarcely human forms with distended bellies and bulbous eyes, crawling over the mud and catching fish with their bare hands, eating them raw.

"When you have gone across the river, I'll look around. If there is anyone here, I will find them." Charrière handed him a cut section of reed and pointed to the hollow inside where he had pushed out the pith. "If you are shot at while you are on the river, you can drop over the side and breathe through this. Bullets are stopped after only a few feet underwater. You will be safe."

Mayne thought of the women and children he had just been watching, and of the crocodiles. He would rather lie on the boat and be like a crocodile himself, become one with this reed boat as he had once done with a canoe, slide stealthily below the line of vision of anyone watching until he reached the other side. He pointed to the case with the rifle he had laid beside the wall. "If I come back without Gordon, I'll set that up. My job is to protect him until Wilson arrives with the steamers and gives Gordon a final chance to leave. Until then I am to shoot any Mahdists that attack the palace."

Charrière peered at him, and then at the palace opposite, narrowing his eyes. "Kahniekahake will have his work cut out for him. He may be able to take down a few attackers, but if the Mahdi comes, he will not be able to save General Gordon."

Mayne was stunned. It was the first time he had been called by his Mohawk name since he was a boy: Kahniekahake, Eagle Eye. He swallowed hard. Now of all times he needed to keep focused. He looked at Charrière. "A few may be all it takes. It may keep Gordon alive until the morning."

"You need to leave now," Charrière said. "By the time you reach the boat, it will be dark enough to cross."

Mayne followed him out of the pit, keeping below the ruined wall of the fort and then behind a ridge of mud that lined the riverbank. He felt a surge of feeling he had never felt before, a sudden overwhelming need to pour out emotion he had kept bottled up since his parents had died all those years ago, a need to reach out to Charrière and tell him the truth. He took a deep breath and held it, ingesting the smell and taste of where they were, the horror of it and of what he was about to do. He was letting Charrière down again: he had lied to him about the rifle and about his mission. He remembered the slip of paper with the black spot that Wilson had given him. Should he be required to enact the ultimate directive, there was one final deed he must do, a deed that would require him to shut off his emotions entirely and never return to them. He remembered Wilson's last words as they parted ways in London three months ago, words that had drummed at him over the past few days like a headache. *Nobody must know*.

They reached a narrow muddy creek in the foreshore opposite the island. A line of planks led over the mud to the water's edge, and Charrière pointed to the boat pulled up alongside. It was made from a single bundle of reeds, about twelve feet long, lashed around every foot or so and ending with a slightly upcurved stem and stern. It was pristine, almost luminescent against the brown and black of the creek; Mayne knew he would need to slap some mud on it before he left. It looked like something that the infant Moses might have been launched in, and was identical to model reed boats he had seen in the Antiquities Museum in Cairo. Yet again the ancient world had caught up with him, like a hiccup from the past, unpredictable, unnerving. He stepped on the plank, swaying precariously for a moment as it decided whether to keep him on land or tip him towards the river, and then he slid down it as it slapped into the mud, caught his balance, and turned round.

Charrière reached over and handed him the paddle. "I'll be waiting for you."

Mayne nodded. "Before dawn. I'll be back."

Charrière turned and was gone. Mayne stepped towards the boat, then leaned forward and grasped it like a canoe, his left hand holding the paddle and one side of the boat, his right hand the other. He pushed off and brought his legs in, kneeling down and wobbling the boat to test its stability, then laid the paddle in front of him and reached down to splash mud over the reeds, darkening them to make the boat less visible, taking care to make as little noise as possible. After a few moments he straightened up and began paddling silently out of the creek, aiming for a window that had just lit up on the upper floor of the building on the opposite shore.

Now would begin the greatest test of his life.

CHAPTER 21

MAYNE LET THE BOAT GLIDE SILENTLY towards the mud bank below the palace as he crouched low and trailed the paddle with the blade held vertically to act as a rudder. For the last stretch of the river he had let the sluggish current take the boat by the stern so that he was crossing diagonally, minimising his profile both to Madhist sharpshooters who might be scanning the river from Tutti Island behind him and to Gordon's Sudanese guards watching from the palace ahead. He had seen the guards on the balustrade, openly patrolling now that it was dark and they were invisible from the island. And he thought he had caught his first glimpse of the man himself, at the upper-floor window that had lit up when he had set out from the opposite shore; the shutters had opened and a figure had stepped out onto the balcony, where he was sharply silhouetted in the light from the room behind. It seemed cavalier in the extreme, the act of a man with a death wish, but then Mayne had seen the Sudanese soldiers below stopping and watching him, and had imagined the dervishes too treated to this spectacle night after night, coming to believe in the man's invincibility.

For now, Mayne's concern was his own vulnerability to fire from the Sudanese guards; had they spotted him, they would have seen him as an Arab in tribal dress crossing from the dervish-held shore and would have shot him down immediately. But he had just passed under the line of sight from the balustrade, and he felt marginally safer. Once he landed, he would need to make his way along the foreshore and into the streets, where he could meld in with the locals and approach the palace gate inconspicuously.

The boat bumped into the bank and drove forward into the mud until the stem was about three feet from the end of the duckboards. It was a place that should have been swarming with rats, but then he remembered that they had long ago been chased down and eaten by the starving people in the city. He knelt as far forward on the reed matting as he could, then jammed the paddle handle-first into the mud and used it to pull himself forward, rocking the boat until it could go no farther. He listened for a moment and looked up at the balustrade; seeing nothing, he launched himself onto the duckboards, feeling his holster slap against his thigh as he did so, and catching his robe so it stayed free from the mud and then quickly regaining his balance. The duckboards were well built, solidly anchored into the foreshore, and the boat would remain firm until he returned.

He stood upright and suddenly gagged, overwhelmed by a stench even greater than the fetid smell of the riverbank. He looked to his right, at the poles like tree trunks that he had assumed were for mooring, and immediately saw the source of the stench. What he had taken to be a clump of rags hanging from the nearest pole was the corpse of a man, so putrefied that it looked as if it had been excavated from a wet grave. The right hand and left foot were missing, and it was held up by a rope around the neck. He looked at the other two poles, spaced a few yards apart with duckboards beneath them, and saw that they too held corpses. It was like a ghastly vision of the crucifixion ground at Calvary, on the mud banks of the Nile. The corpse nearest to him had a placard round its neck, and he could see that the others did too, with Arabic script he could not make out. They had clearly been placed there to be seen from the dervish shore. It could have been days ago or more recently; he remembered the wretched people he had seen through his telescope in the city, already halfway to this state.

The corpse nearest to him was dripping single drops of dark liquid that plopped into the mud, forming a small pool that had attracted a swarm of sand hoppers and cockroaches. Suddenly needing to be away from the place, he made his way swiftly up the duckboards until he had reached a point some twenty yards beyond the stone steps leading up to the palace. He stopped and sniffed, taken aback. Somehow, through the stench, he thought he had caught a familiar waft, of cherry tobacco. He had a sudden image of Burnaby, not the hideously wounded man in the desert but the languid man in the tent beside Wolseley, watching the smoke rings from his cigarette rise up into the ceiling. He shook away the image; the smell was probably a trick of the senses brought on by this place, and Burnaby a raw memory of Abu Klea. He quickly veered left, ducking beneath the level of the balustrade and making his way along the riverbank. He could see where the wall of the compound that normally abutted the river now led to a gap on the foreshore where the mud had cracked and dried. He made his way down and around it, and climbed up the bank on the other side. He straightened his headdress and robe, knowing that the dirt of two weeks' desert travel and a bloody battle would not look out of place here, then quickly strode up the dusty street ahead.

Seconds later he was at the wrought-iron gates of the palace among a throng of people trying to get in: emaciated, shrunken bodies with hollow eyes, little different from the corpses on the poles. The women wore the tattered remnants of rainbow-coloured garments, the men filthy rags that had once been white *jalabiya* robes, any colour their clothing still had deadened in the wan moonlight, making them look like ghosts. Some wore

only loincloths, some no clothes at all. The women had
shrivelled breasts that could not have nursed for weeks;
one carried a partly swaddled baby that had clearly been
dead for days. They were like supplicants at the gate of
a great church, beyond begging for food or alms but
wanting divine intervention, to catch sight of the man
whose touch they believed could elevate them from this
horror and save them from the fate that was overtaking
them as they stood there. Mayne had no choice but to
push among them, pressing against their bones, moving
with them as they heaved ever forward against the barrier, for a moment feeling as if his own fate were to be
here forever amongst them, like the helpless supplicants
in purgatory in Corporal Jones's medieval paintings.
Then he was at the bars of the gate and saw the Sudanese guards on the other side, three men wearing tarboosh hats and carrying Remingtons. He fumbled with
the belt under his robe and pulled out his Royal Engineers cap badge, thrusting it through the bars, then
ripped off his headdress and opened his robe at the neck
to reveal his khaki tunic. "English," he exclaimed. "I am
a British officer. I need to see General Gordon. I need to
see *Gordon*."

At the sound of that name, the people around him
suddenly hushed, turning from the gate towards him,
staring up at him with the eyes of those who had been
rescued from certain death, yearningly grateful. "Gordon," said the nearest man, clutching him. "Gordon
Pasha." Others took up the chant. *Gordon Pasha. Gordon Pasha.* Mayne realised to his horror that these people had never seen the man, or were too far gone to tell
the difference, and that he was about to become their
messiah, the saviour who would heal their illnesses and
bring their dead children back to life and pour forth
grain in abundance from his outstretched hands. For a
split second he felt rage towards Gordon for bringing
this on him, for not being where he was now. He began
to struggle as the people tried to pull him away; he
dropped the badge and clung to the gate with all his

strength, feeling himself pulled back and lifted off the ground. "English," he bellowed at the guards. "I need to see General Gordon, now. *Gordon Pasha.*"

His shouting drove the people to an even greater frenzy, the women ululating and the men chanting, those at the back reaching over to touch him, others from the streets around running up to join in. He felt his strength falter, and his hand began to slip. The shortest of the three Sudanese, with a corporal's stripe on his sleeve, sauntered over and picked up the badge, turning it over and staring at it sceptically. Mayne remembered something else; he scrabbled frantically with his free hand at his belt and produced a handful of gold sovereigns, spilling some and throwing the rest through the bars, then holding on with both hands. "There is more," he yelled. "More gold!"

The corporal perked up, quickly collecting the coins and weighing them in his hands, then signalled the other two guards to come alongside. Just as Mayne was about to let go, the gates opened; he was dragged in and they were shut again, the soldiers beating the people back savagely with their rifle butts. The ululations turned to a low moan that increased in a crescendo and then dropped again, like a terrible sigh. The two soldiers used the flat of their rifles to push Mayne roughly between them, and then one of them pulled at his belt so that the remaining coins spilled out. They quickly picked them up while the corporal stood in front of him, turning the badge over and over in his fingers. "I will take this to Gordon Pasha. If he will not see you, I will throw you back to the dogs, *Turk.*"

He spat out the last word, and Mayne was taken aback momentarily; it was a term the dervishes used for all foreigners, yet this man knew he was English. The corporal marched off towards the palace, past two more guards and up a staircase. Mayne had to contend with the other two men now, both evidently convinced he was concealing more gold. They pushed him more roughly between them, trying to pull off his robe, and

one of them cocked his rifle. Mayne made a tactical decision. He could not allow himself to die for nothing so
close to his objective. He whipped out his revolver and
aimed it at the head of the nearer man, holding the grip
with two hands and thumbing back the hammer. "Drop
your rifle," he snarled. "*Now.*" The man did as he was
told; the second one followed suit, and they both backed
off uncertainly, glancing up to the balcony. Mayne kept
the pistol trained with one hand and shook off his robe
with the other. He had no need of a disguise anymore,
and if he was going to die here, he would rather die
dressed as a British officer, albeit in sandals and the dirty
cotton shorts he had worn under his robe. He straightened his crumpled tunic and Sam Browne belt and
waited.

A minute or so later, the corporal came back down the
stairs and across the gravel forecourt towards him. "You
can put that away," he said, pointing at the revolver.
"Gordon Pasha will see you."

Mayne remained where he was, revolver trained. He
was taking no chances. Then he saw that a figure had
come out onto the balcony, too far off to be identifiable
but unmistakably European and wearing a uniform. He
paused for a moment longer, then lowered the revolver
and holstered it. The two soldiers picked up their rifles
and came up to him, but the corporal waved them off
towards the gate. Then he grabbed Mayne's tunic and
pulled him close. "There is nothing for you in there,
Turk. He has nothing left to give." He jerked his head
towards the corpses hanging from the poles, visible beyond the balustrade. "Those men were Mahdi spies.
The Mahdi is coming at dawn. The jihad will sweep all
before it, and men like you had better join it or run.
Otherwise you too will end up feeding the vultures and
the crocodiles."

"*Insha'Allah,*" murmured Mayne.

The man stared at him, his eyes dark, unfathomable,
then pulled him close, so close that Mayne could smell
his breath, and whispered harshly in his ear. "Forty

thousand angels will join us. We will descend on the city like raptors. Join us, Englishman, and you too will rise to heaven, and the light of God will shine on you for what you do here today. Now go. *Insha'Allah.*"

He released Mayne's tunic, turned him around, and pushed him towards the stairs. Mayne reeled. Gordon's gateman had gone over to the Mahdi and would surely open the gates to the angels of death when they came swooping in. He knew he had no time to lose. He tripped over the edge of a flagstone, stumbled forward, and then regained his balance. Over the river and around the palace he saw only blackness. Ahead of him at the top of the stairs was a blinding orange light. He remembered what the guard had said about the coming of the Mahdi. He knew he had to be back across the river and in position before dawn. He reached the steps and began to mount them, his heart pounding. Everything hung on what happened next.

CHAPTER 22

MINUTES LATER, MAYNE WAS USHERED BY A Sudanese guard along the upper-floor corridor of the palace and into the room he had seen lit up from outside. It extended to the back wall of the palace, but the open door and corridor beyond led to a balcony overlooking the river, visible from where he stood now. Beside the door was a Remington rifle on an elaborate wooden shooting stand, aimed in the direction of Tutti Island; the action was open and Mayne could see that it had been carefully cleaned and oiled. He took a few more steps inside. The room was large, the size of an English country-house drawing room, and was lit at each corner by glass-topped oil lamps on stands, the walls and ceiling above them smudged with smoke. The centrepiece was a large Ottoman-style desk set close to the back wall, its surface covered with papers and note-books and maps, a brimming ashtray on one side giving off wisps of smoke. The room smelled strongly of cherry tobacco, and he realised that this was the source of the smell that had wafted over the riverbank earlier. But the most striking feature was the mass of artefacts laid out carefully on the floor, enough to fill a small museum: elaborate tribal clothing, including a patched jibba of the Mahdists; an extensive collection of weaponry, from leaf-bladed dervish spears and curved swords to kurbash whips and ornate flintlock long guns; beautiful handmade pottery, wood carving, and beadwork; and an array of ancient Egyptian artefacts, including small statues in blue-green faience and fragments of masonry with carvings on them.

A voice came from the door. "The Mahdi keeps sending me gifts." Mayne turned and saw Gordon. He remembered him vividly from the lectures he had attended in London several years before, but close-to he was shorter, more compact. He was wearing the evening uniform of an officer of the Royal Engineers, as if he were going to dinner in the mess, complete with the insignia of the Order of the Bath and his campaign medals for China and the Crimean War almost thirty years before. He looked pale, gaunt, his curly grey hair thinning on top, but his eyes were a brilliant porcelain blue, staring intently. He reached over and picked up an Egyptian *shafti* statuette with hieroglyphics on the front. "Do you know that for the followers of Muhammad, it is not the meaning of the word but the shape of the symbols that has significance, as well as magical powers?"

Mayne nodded. "I had a Dongolese guide who gave me a *hejab* with the prayer wrapped around an ancient Egyptian scarab. I do not believe he ever knew the name in the hieroglyphics on the scarab, though I recognised the cartouche of Akhenaten."

"Akhenaten," Gordon repeated, pausing. "Are you a student of the ancient Egyptians?"

"I have a passing acquaintance with hieroglyphics."

"What do you think of my collection?"

"Fascinating, sir. I've seen your material from China in the Museum of the Royal United Services Institute." Mayne pointed to a fragment of wall carving showing the distinctive crown and snake symbol of a pharaoh. "I'm particularly interested in ancient Egyptian antiquities in the Sudan, as they are something of a rarity, I find. I've been tracing them from the Egyptian border along the Nile. I believe that the pharaoh Akhenaten mounted some kind of expedition into the desert. At Semna we found a temple with a depiction of him in front of the Aten symbol of the sun."

Gordon looked at him piercingly. "At Semna, you say? Below the third cataract?"

"A temple to the crocodile god, Sobek."

Gordon glanced at his desk. "I must check my notes," he murmured. "My recollection is that Kitchener mentioned nothing unusual at Semna other than the remains of pharaonic fortifications on either side of the river."

"Kitchener was intrigued when I told him, and intended to visit for himself."

"You've seen Kitchener? How is he?"

"Champing at the bit. He wished it had been he who had been sent to make contact with you, but his face is too well known among the tribesmen, and he would have been at risk. He was with the desert column but was sent back from the wells at Jakdul."

"Kitchener is a first-rate surveyor and archaeologist, and a most loyal supporter of mine," Gordon said. "Though I own he would be a handful for any general to manage, and I feel some sympathy for Wolseley on that front."

Mayne paused, waiting, then offered his hand. "Major Edward Mayne, sir. You know from my badge that I'm a fellow sapper. Attached to the river column of the relief expedition."

"A relief expedition that has given me no relief at all," Gordon said with a tired smile. He shook Mayne's hand strongly and peered at his mud-spattered clothes. "You look as if you've been through the wars."

"A fair description, sir."

Gordon put a hand on his own immaculate red tunic. "I apologise if you feel discomfited, but I dress to keep up appearances. I am sensible to the fact that I am still governor general of the Sudan, even though the territory over which I exert jurisdiction has shrunk from an area the size of France to these city walls, like Constantinople at the end of the Byzantine Empire. At any rate, I still dress for dinner, though I dine alone, and apart from lime juice to fend off the scurvy and some carefully rationed bully beef, I eat the same as those poor people for whom I am responsible, that is to say biscuit and unleavened bread and water from the one remaining well in the city that has not become tainted." He paused, then picked up a decanter from a side table. "But I do have my small indulgences. They keep my mind from the hunger. Can I offer you a drink? I have brandy, Greek I'm afraid, so like firewater, though perfectly palatable after one's throat has become numbed to it."

"No thanks."

Gordon poured himself half a glass, then put it on the table. He peered at Mayne closely. "I know the name, but we haven't met, have we?"

"No, sir. My speciality is survey, and I'm in the field much of the time. But I took a refresher course at the School of Military Engineering while you were posted at Chatham, and I attended your lectures on the Sudan."

"Have you been out here long?"

"Since July. With General Earle's staff."

"Dragging whaleboats up the Nile? A scheme that would make Sisyphus in Hades glad of his own torment. And before that?"

"I first came to Egypt in 1882, after our invasion."

"Correction," said Gordon, picking up a cigarette from a box on his desk and lighting it, sucking in deep and blowing out smoke. "Not invasion, but *intervention*. An intervention to prop up the Ottoman regime in Cairo, against the wishes of the Egyptian army and the Egyptian people, in order to secure our controlling interest in the Suez Canal and keep the investors happy." He tapped his cigarette. "Have you much desert experience?"

"I carried out forward reconnaissance for the river column."

"Ah. You mean you are an intelligence officer. To whom do you answer?"

"Lord Wolseley, sir."

"Not Baring, in Cairo? Or Colonel Sir Charles Wilson?"

Mayne was taken aback momentarily, too tired to keep up his guard. "They both have an interest, inasmuch as they have read my reports."

"Wilson is an old friend, though I have found him distant in recent years, but Burnaby works for him and keeps me abreast of affairs." He looked at Mayne shrewdly. "Apparently there's a secret complex of rooms under Whitehall. There are operations afoot that even Burnaby is not privy to, and that Wilson reports only to the highest authority. But doubtless you know that."

Mayne had recovered his poise. "Colonel Wilson at this moment is with the steamers that are heading up-river from Metemma towards Khartoum. My mission is to persuade you to leave so that they may take you off to safety when they arrive."

Gordon leaned his head back, exhaled a deep lung full of smoke towards the ceiling, and then looked back at Mayne, a smile on his face. "Correction. Your mission is to provide me with agreeable companionship on this night. I have my Sudanese soldiers, whom I love dearly, but there is little conversation to be had. Ever since Colonel Stewart left, I have been starved of friendship. I still weep at the thought of his vile murder when the steamer *Abbas* was wrecked, for which I hold myself responsible. I have missed his counsel dreadfully."

"Kitchener has seen you since then."

"Only once, when he came in disguise like you. But he had little time, and our conversation had a very particular course, as I shall tell you shortly."

"You know he holds you in the highest regard."

"Too high, in my opinion. His desire for revenge may lead him to murderous courses of action that will muddy the waters even further."

"Or lead him to glory. There is talk of him as a future sirdar of the Egyptian army, as the one who may lead a force big enough to crush the Mahdi."

Gordon exhaled again. "Glory is nine tenths twaddle, wouldn't you say?"

Mayne remembered Burnaby's final moments. "For those who seek it, sir, yes. For those upon whom it falls, perhaps it constitutes that remaining one tenth and is a worthy thing."

"I believe, then, that Gordon of Khartoum is nine tenths twaddle and one tenth glory."

Gordon grinned, then took a deep draw on his cigarette, holding the smoke in and exhaling it out the window. He looked at his cigarette. "I do apologise. I've spent too much time alone and have forgotten how to be civil. I should have offered you one of these. I smoke them to overcome the terrible smell of decay from outside." He offered Mayne the box from the table. "And they help further to suppress my appetite—that is, what taste is left after ingesting the stench outside. Would you care for one?"

Mayne declined, and Gordon put the box back on the table. "Perhaps you don't enjoy the peculiar smell. It's cherry tobacco, from Morocco. They were given to me as a birthday present by Burnaby, and I've become addicted."

"I fear I have some bad news for you, sir. The worst. A week ago, near the wells of Abu Klea, there was a fight between the dervishes and the desert column."

"I know of it. My Sudanese spies were there. A *hell* of a fight, by all accounts." Gordon paused, suddenly looking crestfallen. "They talk of a great bear of a man, fighting with the strength of twenty, finally being brought down by a dervish spear." He sat down dejectedly, letting his cigarette burn between his fingers. "Fred Burnaby?"

"Your account tallies, sir. I saw him myself. He died as a soldier."

"You mean he died in great pain, with fearful wounds. I've been around glorious deaths in battle all my life. I know what it's like."

"Before we left Korti, he passed on his best wishes to you. As did General Buller. They all did."

"Burnaby's I accept, with sad pleasure. The others' are hollow words. How many more men must die in this futile campaign? It is a campaign for the satisfaction of those who are running it, not for the purpose of relieving Khartoum. That is the sad lesson of war, one that we learn through bitter experience. The game of war has become as self-perpetuating for us as it has become for the army of the jihad, fuelled by the bloodlust of the warrior, where the fight and the holy crusade becomes an end in itself."

"Have you felt it, sir? That attraction?"

"I am *not* a crusader, Mayne. I am not here to fight Islam. The Mahdi may not convey me to his cause, but I find little in Islam that would dissuade me from it, were I of a doctrinaire bent, and much to commend it. Yet I am regarded as a Christian warrior, and the evangelists hang on my every word." He picked up a thin volume from the table. "*Reflections in Palestine,* by Major General Charles Gordon," he said, and tossed it contemptuously back. "I went to Jerusalem three years ago with the perfectly sound intention of following up Wilson's work there to identify the site of the crucifixion. My aim was to debunk all those who have let their faith carry them forward into making spurious claims, and cloud their reason. And then my erstwhile friends go and publish a book without my sanction made up from the musings about religion I happened to have written in my notebooks while I was there. It reads like the worst sort of mysticism."

"I do not believe it tarnishes your reputation, sir."

"Speaking of my reputation, there is something I would like you to do." Gordon went over and sat down at his desk, then opened a folder and took out a sheet of paper. He quickly read it through and then glanced up at Mayne. With his pale face and watery eyes, he looked feverish, but he spoke clearly, with controlled passion. "There were many who believed that my cause in the

Sudan was the abolition of slavery, and many who were dismayed when I allowed it to continue under my jurisdiction. Some thought that was the beginning of my decline, that I had become seduced by the trappings of despotism, removing myself from the decencies of British behaviour. Some even clamoured for my rescue in order to pluck me from the moral vacuum that I supposedly inhabited. My *decline,* Major Mayne, I can assure you, has been brought on by constant anxiety over the arrival of relief, and I am worn to a shadow by the food question."

He put one hand to his brow, shutting his eyes for a moment, and then lifted the lid on a small brass ink pot and dipped a quill pen into it, raised it, and touched it lightly to the side of the ink pot to let the excess ink drain out. "Anyone who knows this country should be perfectly aware that such a law could not be enacted definitively without so radically altering the way of life here that it would require us to occupy the Sudan as a province, to control every aspect of it and to create a new society and new economy. It is only now, on the eve of an extinction brought about by lack of British resolve, when all institutions in the Sudan have ceased to exist, that I can sign a law mandating the destruction of slavery. It is too late for the people of Khartoum, but I can only hope that those slaves who have been put in the front ranks of the Mahdi's army will come to know of it, and will hereafter cease to obey their masters, whom they will have seen slinking in the background, cowards both as fighters and as arbiters of human justice."

He took the pen and held it poised to write. "The eighteenth of December was the anniversary of one of the most momentous events of our time, the proclaiming in 1862 by President Abraham Lincoln of the abolition of slavery in the United States. I drafted this document on that day, and it has been languishing since then as I have waited for a witness whom those who judge me will find credible. Will you be such a witness?"

Mayne stared at the document, then at Gordon. He remembered his mission, and Charrière waiting on the opposite shore. What Gordon was asking him to do now seemed unreal, impossible to digest. He swallowed hard and nodded. "Of course, sir."

"I will tell you this. If Abraham Lincoln had been in my position today, or Lord Palmerston, who abolished slavery in the British Empire, they would not have left Khartoum or this life without proclaiming the emancipation of the slaves of the Sudan. As God is my witness, and Major Edward Mayne, a commissioned officer of Her Majesty's Army in the Corps of Royal Engineers, I hereby bring this statute into law." He scratched his name on the paper and passed the pen to Mayne, who turned the paper to face him, leaned over, and signed. Gordon blotted the signatures with his handkerchief, blew on the paper, and held it to dry for a few moments, then folded it into a small square and passed it to Mayne. "Everything left in this room will be destroyed when the dervishes arrive. Have this, so that some may know of my final act."

Mayne took the paper, holding it for a moment hesitantly. He had already entered a netherworld where the execution of his mission would prevent him from openly contacting Wolseley ever again, and a document like this would not be believed unless it were passed on by authoritative hands. He put the thought from his mind and slipped the paper inside his tunic pocket. Gordon stood up, came round to the front of the desk, and put a hand on his shoulder, guiding him towards the open doorway with a view over the balcony. It was the dead of night, a heavy, overwhelming darkness that blocked out all the stars, allowing only a hint of moonlight to penetrate. Dawn was at least eight hours away, but the same thought was on both their minds. Gordon gestured towards the river. "When it is time, I will tell my Sudanese guards to escort you to the steps leading down to the landing stage so that you do not have to go out through the gates."

Mayne suddenly remembered something. "The corporal at the gate. I believe he has gone over to the Mahdi."

"Indeed. But he has served a purpose, as the other guards tell me what he preaches. Doubtless you have heard that forty thousand angels will descend upon this place tomorrow."

"I believe those were his words."

"It's from him that I ascertained with certainty that the Mahdi is attacking tomorrow. The man's treachery is of little consequence now, but I have ordered my bodyguard to do away with him during the night. It means that when they fight to the death tomorrow, as they surely shall, they'll know that they have a unity of purpose. They will fight and die as a band of brothers."

Mayne could just make out his reed boat pulled up on the shore beside the three posts with their macabre festoonings that looked so much like an image of the crosses bearing the three thieves on the hill of Calvary. He thought of asking, and then stopped himself. There was nothing untoward about executing miscreants in a place like this; it was part of Gordon's job, and the Mahdi doubtless did the same on the opposite bank to those who had dissatisfied him.

Gordon followed Mayne's gaze and then turned to him, his face spectral in the reflection from the river. "I would say this to the world. I stay here because I believe Jesus of Nazareth would have done as I do and not forsaken these people. But I am no messiah. I fear death as would any other man; even when it stares you in the face as it has done me for so long now, let me tell you, it is not something you welcome gladly. I do not want to die a lingering death with the Mahdi's men goading me as the Romans did Christ with their spears. I want to die as a soldier, not like a martyr, and like all soldiers I would say that when it comes, I would like it to be clean and quick. Can you see to that for me?"

Mayne did not know what to say. Gordon walked across to the rifle on the stand by the window, leaning down and peering over the sights. "I've amused myself by taking potshots at the dervishes on Tutti Island. But our batch of ammunition is faulty; some of the cartridges have been overloaded with powder. The excess gas blowing back from the breech nearly blinded me a few weeks ago. It's the reason I took to sleeping during the day. Even the hazy daylight in this place makes my eyes water uncontrollably."

"General Wolseley and his staff think you deliberately stand on your balcony at night in order to taunt the dervishes, and also to impress your own soldiers with your inviolability. The press have got hold of the notion, and there is even an illustration in a publication of the evangelical movement showing you on the balcony with your arms raised, illuminated by the sun, the people of Khartoum below eating the food that has poured from your hands, the bullets and shells of the Mahdi whizzing by you harmlessly."

Gordon went to the open window and stared out over the river, lighting another cigarette and inhaling deeply. "I keep a telescope on the roof, in full view of the dervishes, I own you that. I used it to look out for the relief force, but I gave up on that long ago." He snorted. "But as for the proposition that I have become immortal, what tosh. What *utter* tosh. What kind of man do they think I am?"

"Some think you are a saint, sir, and others that you have become unhinged."

"A *saint*. Well, those poor wretches outside the gate believe I have *barak*, the life force, as some too believe of the Mahdi. But it's just that we are both providers, and whether you offer food to the starving or a cause to the directionless, from their position at your feet you can appear very much larger than you really are. As for *unhinged*." Gordon paused and took another drag. "Enraged, frustrated, enfeebled, exhausted, yes, but *unhinged*? I ask any of them to take my place and survive a siege of three hundred and thirty days, days of false promises, of a relief force that was never going to arrive. All they had to do was send a hundred soldiers and two steamers; that would have been enough to take off all my staff and their families. I told Wolseley as much; I sent endless messages. In their absurd concoction of my character, they decided that I did not want to be rescued. And since then the Mahdi's army has increased many-fold, making those hundred men of my plea an absurd proposition."

He picked up a sheet from a pile on the desk. "There are forty thousand people in this city. Forty thousand starving wretches, most of them slaves for whom the only day of liberation in their lives is this one. They may see me as their saviour, yes, but it is because I give them food. That is what I spend my time doing here. I calculate the figures, and I work out how much is left; I give them just enough to stay alive. I keep the hospital running so that the few Arab doctors may relieve the sufferings of those diseased people who are not bound to perish. I own that what I am doing is merely giving sustenance to a dying man. The Mahdi *will* arrive, and these people *will* be slaughtered. I can do nothing about that, but I cannot leave them while I am still able to give them food. I *cannot* leave. If that is unhinged, then so be it."

Gordon dropped the sheet, letting it flutter to the floor, and put his hands up to his face, covering his eyes. Then he ran them through his hair and let them drop to his sides. He looked pale, almost luminous, and suddenly fragile, and Mayne realised for the first time how emaciated he was. This was a man who chain-smoked to keep his appetite down, who had made it his task to distribute scant supplies of biscuit among forty thousand starving people to make them last as long as possible. Mayne thought of the tedious hours they had spent in the School of Military Engineering learning about the economics of garrison management. This was hardly what the instructors would have had in mind, but Gordon was doing the job as he had been trained to do it.

Mayne pointed to the carefully laid out jibba on the

floor. "There are some who believe you have been influenced to convert to the cause of the Mahdi."

Gordon passed his hand over his face and then replied with an edge to his voice, as if trying to restrain himself. "It is true that I have a considerable correspondence with my friend Muhammad Ahmad. He is from a family of boatbuilders, you know, and he and I have a considerable shared interest in the technology of Nile watercraft." He gave a wry smile and then went over to the desk and picked up another sheaf of papers, taking one and reading from it. " 'In the name of God the merciful and compassionate, the Destroyer of him who is obstinate against his religion, blessings and peace be upon our Lord Mahomed and his successors, who have established the foundations and solid pillars of our faith.' " He put the letter down. "It goes on in the same vein. My Sudanese clerk translates them for me. They invariably end with the Mahdi offering me sanctuary and an exalted place beside him if I see his particular version of the light. He cites the case of my friend and his prisoner von Slatin, pretending to believe that von Slatin's conversion to Islam was not just an act of desperation to encourage his Sudanese troops before their final battle and an act of expediency to save his life when he was captured. And he mentions our mutual interest in the prophet Isaiah, as if I would believe that Isaiah from on high would be instructing me to join a holy war and destroy all those who are obstinate against my religion."

He pointed to the jibba. "As for the clothing of the Ansar, I studiously collect everything that comes my way, and let it be known that I want more, as I did during my time in China. Apart from my collection, there will be few other mementoes from this war, and none from Khartoum; the relief force will not arrive before the Mahdi occupies the city, and there will be no souvenir-hunting by our troops. But if Wolseley and his cronies so fervently believe in my imminent apostasy, then I have a mind to start wearing the jibba. It would be more comfortable in the heat."

Mayne turned back to the rifle on the stand. "The Martini is a better rifle, sir, but I have seen dervish sharp-shooters over the Nile use Remingtons to some effect."

"Are you a sharpshooter, Major Mayne? I had imagined so." Gordon looked at him, his blue eyes piercing. "What is your preferred rifle?"

Mayne paused. Had Gordon guessed? "A Sharps, sir. Model 1862, in .45-90 calibre. A thirty-four-inch octagonal barrel, made especially heavy."

"Ah, yes," said Gordon, rubbing his chin thoughtfully. "An American buffalo rifle. Aperture sights?"

"They are the best, sir. I first used them at the Creedmore range near New York when I went there with a team from the Royal Military Academy."

"Stiff competition, I should think."

"I won, sir."

Gordon looked out into the darkness towards the island, where the cooking fires of the dervishes could just be seen. "I believe an American soldier holds the distance record with a Sharps, during the Indian wars."

"One thousand four hundred and twenty-one yards over rough ground in the state of Montana in the summer of 1874. His name was Private Ephraim Jones, sir. I competed against him at Creedmore."

"And you won."

"Sir."

Gordon gestured outside. "Then I could do with such a rifle here, and such a sharpshooter. The first thing I did when I returned to Khartoum last year knowing it would come under siege was to make accurate measurements of the distances from the city to the far shore of the river, to allow my riflemen to find their range. It was a most interesting geometrical exercise. I had my Sudanese row a measured line across the river, and then took right angles from it to create a trigonometric survey of all the main points of the shore. Do you understand my reasoning?"

Mayne nodded. "Using triangulation you could thus

calculate distances from any points of fire along the river shore."

"The Mahdi holds the island and all the shoreline to the west, but the fort and the adjoining riverbank to the east is dead ground, of no value to him because it's too far away for his riflemen to shoot accurately, and his artillery is concentrated to the west and south where it can do greater damage to the entrances into the city. That fort provides good cover, though, and that's where you've left your companion, isn't it? I assume you have one. A spotter, perhaps. You've come here without your rifle and you would not leave that unattended."

Mayne saw no reason to deny it. "Sir."

"What is your estimation of the distance to that fort?"

Mayne remembered Kitchener's map. "Six hundred and fifty metres, give or take twenty."

"Six hundred and sixty-five metres. Bravo. You *are* good. Even at that range, with a cartridge that powerful, a body shot could be a clean kill. Am I right?"

"I've hunted deer with my Sharps at a thousand yards and dropped them stone dead."

"Have you ever hunted men, Major Mayne?"

Mayne swallowed, suddenly discomfited. "I'm a soldier, sir. Like you."

Gordon stared at him, then smiled and slapped his shoulder. "Indeed we are. Soldier first, engineer second, dilettante fossicker down the byways of archaeology and geography and natural history third. That's what they taught us. Isn't that right?"

"Sir."

"I know why you've come. And you know that I won't leave with you. There's nothing more I can do for the people here, but if the world knows the truth of why Gordon of Khartoum stayed to the end, then perhaps it will not be a pointless sacrifice. The Mahdi is coming at dawn. I will be on the balcony when they break through the gates. I will be in this full dress uniform, with a red tunic. You will not mistake me. I believe the sun will shine tomorrow for the first time in days; I can sense it.

You must choose your time well. For a few moments at dawn a sliver of light from the eastern horizon lights up the balcony and the mosque behind, but then as the sun rises it reflects off the Nile and obscures this place. I have seen it myself from the fort on the opposite shore. And watch your back. There will be others with their eyes on you. Mark my words."

Mayne did not know what to say. "Sir."

"Have I done my best for these people? For my country?"

Mayne looked into his eyes and suddenly felt a flood of compassion, and a flash of anger towards those who had orchestrated all this. "For Queen and country, sir."

Gordon put a hand on his shoulder and then picked up a leather-bound volume from his desk. "Good. Now, before you go, I trust that you will allow a condemned man one final request. It is of the *utmost* importance."

CHAPTER 23

GORDON LED MAYNE TO HIS DESK, POINTED him to a chair, and sat down himself behind the writing pad. He opened up the book he had been holding, and Mayne could see that it was a journal, filled almost to the last page with closely lined writing. Gordon gave him a penetrating look. "When I despatched Colonel Stewart to safety on the steamer *Abbas*, little knowing the fate that awaited him downriver, I sent with him the largest part of my archaeological collection as well as the latest volumes of my journal. All of that was lost when the *Abbas* was sunk and Stewart murdered."

"Kitchener mentioned your collection," Mayne said. "He told me you had an ancient stone slab packed beneath the boiler."

Gordon nodded. "That was the day that Kitchener was here. Our discussion was almost exclusively concerned with archaeology. And the loss of that slab would have been an *utter* tragedy had I not sketched the carvings on it."

He opened the back page of the journal and passed it to Mayne. An inked drawing filled the page, neat, precise, the work of a trained draughtsman. But the image was bizarre, different from any other ancient depiction Mayne had seen in the Sudan, almost like something occult. He looked at it with a sapper's eye. "It's a map, a plan," he murmured. "Rectilinear interlocking lines of communication, perhaps trenches or tunnels. They all seem to originate from one opening at the bottom, like a maze, a labyrinth."

"And the Egyptian symbols?"

Mayne peered closely. The central part of the drawing was blank, in a rough square shape, presumably representing a missing part of the sculpture, but radiating from it over the rectilinear channels were long thin lines ending in shapes like closed hands. "That must be the Aten symbol, the rays of the sun," he said. "And the hieroglyphic cartouche to the right clinches it: that's Akhenaten."

"And the other ones?"

Mayne stared at the individual hieroglyphs that appeared in several places on the image. "The crocodile beside Akhenaten's name means sovereign, pharaoh. The other one's a symbol of a rolled-up papyrus and is most curious," he said. "It means wisdom, or knowledge."

Gordon placed the book back on his desk with the page open. "I am going to tell you a little story. There was once a boy living beside the Nile north of Khartoum who was testing his first boat, a reed boat like the one you paddled over the river this evening. He had built it himself, cutting and collecting the reeds and bundling them together, and in the process had come to know all the creeks and byways of the Nile shore intimately. One day he came across something extraordinary: an ancient temple half inundated by the river, its upper surface revealed in a storm where it had lain buried in sand for thousands of years. He managed to squeeze inside, and discovered an ancient wall carving of remarkable form, not a depiction of battle or pharaohs but a cluster of rectilinear shapes that he did not recognise, that looked nothing like hieroglyphics or the Arabic script he had been taught by the Sufis. Do you remember when you arrived I showed you the lettering on that little *shafti*

statue, and I said how in Islamic tradition the shape sig-
nifies more than the meaning? Well, the boy saw the
shape and was terrified, thinking it was some ancient
incantation, and quickly left. After the next Nile flood,
the shoreline was banked over with sand and the temple
once again buried. The boy continued to excel as a boatbuilder, but he had another gift, an ability to see visions
that drew people to him, and he became a student of the
Sufis. His family despaired of him, the last of generations of boatbuilders who had plied their trade on the
Nile since time immemorial, but he was set on a different course. His name was Muhammad Ahmad'Abdallah."

Mayne stared at him, astonished. "The Mahdi?"

Gordon nodded. "Ten years ago, when I first came to
the Sudan, his fame was already spreading, but he was
no more than a Sufi mystic living on an island in the
Nile. I travelled extensively along the river, and he came
to know of me after I visited his family's boatyard and
drew sketches of their watercraft, showing them images
of ancient boat models I had seen in Egypt and telling them of my interest in the antiquities of the Sudan.
He had not forgotten his discovery as a boy and he invited me to his island. I recognised the hieroglyphs of
Akhenaten from his description, and it was then that
we discovered our shared passion for the Old Testament prophets, for Isaiah and also for Moses. We both
believed that the pharaoh of the Book of Exodus at
the time of Moses was Akhenaten himself, and that
Akhenaten and Moses shared the same vision of one
God, a vision that Muhammad Ahmad believed had
come to them during an expedition to the southern desert. I became gripped by the idea, and spent much of my
time on the search for proof, anything that might allow
us to trace the expedition and find the place where we
believed he had experienced his revelation. I persuaded
my friend Heinrich Schliemann to take time off from
Troy and join me in the desert, and I brought a few others into my confidence: Rudolf von Slatin; an American
officer on my staff named Charles Chaillé-Long; Colo-

nel Sir Charles Wilson; and Herbert Kitchener. Wilson
and Kitchener I knew I could count on because of their
deep involvement with the archaeology of the Holy
Land. And finally, you may be surprised to know, Prime
Minister William Ewart Gladstone."

"*Gladstone?*" Mayne exclaimed, remembering what
Kitchener had told him. "But you have surely been at
loggerheads with him over your insistence on remaining
in Khartoum."

"His involvement has been kept in the strictest secrecy, because he has not wanted his name to be associated with a quest that some might see as mystical. But he
has in truth been my staunchest supporter. He tried his
damnedest to dissuade me from returning here, and
his irritation with me has a genuine basis to it. He tried
to persuade me that what I had sought could wait until
the Mahdist revolt had dissipated and we could return
to the Sudan peaceably, but I told him the revolt was
never likely to end within our lifetimes, and the quest
would be lost. I felt that if I could make a discovery that
drew together one who was regarded as a Christian soldier and another an Islamist visionary, then there was
hope for some unity of vision that might emphasise the
singularity of our beliefs, not their differences, and make
war less of a certainty."

"So you came out here for that purpose? For the archaeology?"

"My purpose in coming out here was in truth as I
have told you: to arrange for the safe passage of my staff
and their families from Khartoum, and to do all I could
for the people of this city. But my archaeological quest
was not disassociated from my aim to lift the veil of
conflict from this place, and to stem the jihad."

"Did you find the temple?"

"Muhammad Ahmad showed me the place, and I set
my people to work. The temple was deeply buried, and
it took months of effort. By the time the inner chamber
was revealed, Muhammad Ahmad was no longer part of
the picture; he had become the Mahdi and the centre

of the whirlwind that envelops us now. It was only after I had discovered the wall carvings and brought them to the light of day, when his spies among my workmen reported back to him, that he understood what he had seen as a boy for what it was. It was not early writing or some ancient spell. It was a map."

"Did you show it to him?"

Gordon shook his head. "By then we were enemies. But he sent his followers after me to try to take the carvings. I kept them here in the storerooms of the palace, hidden away, and eventually put them on the *Abbas*. To enthuse them, he let his followers believe that he was after gold, that I had found clues to some ancient El Dorado of the desert. Indeed, that is what the first pharaohs who came here thought too, seeking to extend the borders of Egypt beyond the desert but also hunting the oases and wells for evidence of an ancient civilisation, just as we do today. If they truly found their El Dorado we shall never know, for they were repelled by the warriors they called the guardians of the desert, savage fighters like the Ansar of the Mahdi today. In two places where Akhenaten went, I have found depictions of battle against Egyptians in which these enemies are victorious, almost as if Akhenaten were leaving the images as a warning for others from Egypt not to follow him."

Mayne thought for a moment. "The crocodile temple where I saw the image of Akhenaten. It had just such a depiction of carnage in battle."

Gordon leaned forward, his voice intense. "It was the hunt for ancient gold, treasure they believed I had hidden away for secret despatch to Egypt, that led the Mahdi's men to ransack the *Abbas*, diving repeatedly on the wreck to search for it. But little did they know that there was a far greater treasure concealed there, a treasure that the Mahdi had sent his emirs to discover when they waylaid and murdered Stewart and his men."

Mayne looked at the crocodile symbol on the drawing and suddenly remembered the channel that Lieutenant Tanner had discovered at the cataract, from the Nile to the crocodile temple. He studied the drawing again, seeing the interconnectedness of the lines, their origin at one source. "Do you remember at Chatham studying hydraulic engineering, looking at Venice and the island cities of northern India? This isn't a labyrinth. It's a complex of canals, some of them rising over the others. That entrance must lead from a water source, a river. I think the reason why this has never been found is that it's underground."

Gordon nodded. "Agreed. And I think the water source had to be a river, to keep enough volume flowing into a complex like this and to keep it from stagnating."

"In this part of the world, that can only mean the Nile."

"Agreed."

"Amarna, Akhenaten's capital city?"

"Schliemann and Chaillé-Long explored the site exhaustively and found no evidence. They even employed divers using compressed air cylinders to inspect the edges of the river underwater, but they found no indication of a channel."

Mayne was at a loss. "Somewhere out here in the desert?"

Gordon put his finger on the blank square in the centre of the drawing where the Aten sun disk should have been. "Until we find that piece of the puzzle, we are floundering in the dark. I believe that there may have been something there, a depiction, a symbol, a hieroglyphic inscription, that might have given some indication. That's what I've been out here searching for, scouring any site we find in the desert with connections to Akhenaten. That's why Kitchener was so excited by your report of the crocodile temple. We believe there may have been clues in other depictions that Akhenaten had carved in these places. If this was his dream, then he would have wanted to indicate it somehow, his singular achievement."

Mayne stared hard at the depiction. "But what was it, this place?"

Gordon's eyes blazed. "A great city. An underground city."

Mayne stared at the arms of the Aten. "A city of light."

Gordon put his finger on the papyrus-scroll hieroglyph. "A city of *knowledge*. Schliemann and I spoke about it before he departed for Troy. He had a most remarkable suggestion. He posited that by doing away with the old priesthood, Akhenaten would have been liberating knowledge kept for countless generations in the temples of Egypt, written down on scrolls and passed on by word of mouth through the temple clerks, knowledge that the priests controlled and kept secret, knowledge that they could use sparingly when needed to enhance their prestige, to impress on the people the favour given by the gods to the priesthood. Schliemann is a student not only of Troy and Homer and the age of heroes but also of the very distant past, of the very beginnings of humanity before the first cities and the first priests. He believes that much knowledge of medicinal cures from those early times when humans lived close with nature had been lost by the time of the pharaohs, but not all of it. He thinks that Akhenaten may have wished to do away with the old temples and to create one place that would be the *only* temple, one place to worship one God. And in it he would put all that accumulated knowledge, a great compendium of it collected from the beginning of time."

"So not a city of knowledge," Mayne murmured. "A *temple* of knowledge."

"Do you see, Mayne? *That* is what I have been seeking. Here, in this city of the walking dead, whom I shall soon join."

"What would you have me do?"

"Take my journal for the last days of Khartoum. It ends today; when I saw that you had arrived, I retrieved it from my bedroom and quickly finished it. See that it reaches Captain John Howard at the School of Military Engineering. Do you know him?"

Mayne nodded. "Kitchener told me he is to have charge of all the artefacts you send back."

Gordon swept his hand round the room. "Sadly not including any of these. Everything here will be looted and destroyed. And the original carved panels are lost beneath the sands of the Nile."

"There may be hope one day," Mayne said. "When this land is free of the jihad, it may be possible to bring compressor divers to the spot."

Gordon lit another cigarette and exhaled forcefully. "This land might one day fall again under our jurisdiction, but it will never be free of those who believe in jihad. And for those whom the Mahdi has appointed as his successors, those of his closest circle who know the true wealth of our El Dorado, the quest for the temple of light will be all-consuming and never-ending, becoming in their minds like the light that shines through from the east as they pray. It is a discovery that we must hope does not become the domain of those who would use it to gather more supporters bent on destruction and jihad. Whosoever among my people are able to continue this quest must know that they are not the only ones."

"Kitchener will surely take up the mantle."

"Perhaps. But he will be driven towards his own destiny. Schliemann cannot hope to finish Troy in his lifetime. Von Slatin is a prisoner of the Mahdi and may never be free. And Chaillé-Long I no longer trust. His theories of the location of this complex do not seem remotely credible, some as far-fetched as Atlantis. He has gone back to America and may not be heard from again."

"Then it is for archaeologists of the future."

Gordon wrapped the journal in waxed brown paper and tied it up with string from his desk. He passed it to Mayne, who reached into his tunic pocket and took out the folded paper containing Gordon's edict abolishing slavery, and then slipped it under the wrapper and into the journal. Gordon took another drag on his cigarette and tapped the package. "Have no fear: I've learned my lesson from *Reflections in Palestine*. This book contains no mystical ramblings, no musings about God. It's the journal of a commanding Royal Engineer, full of facts and figures. But that's what it's been about, Mayne, when all is said and done. It is facts and figures that would have kept Khartoum alive, yet it is facts and figures, minutely calculated by Wolseley—daily average distances up the Nile, ideal tonnages of whaleboats—that have inhibited our rescue and will lead to the city's destruction."

"I will see to it that it reaches Howard."

"One last request." He pointed to Mayne's holster. "I wonder whether I might have a look at your revolver."

"Certainly." Mayne unholstered his pistol and passed it to him. "Webley Government model, .455 calibre. The latest improvements, bought this year. The best revolver yet available for campaign service, in my opinion."

Gordon inspected it appreciatively, spinning the cylinder and breaking it open, careful not to eject the cartridges. "My problem is this." He took out his own revolver and placed it on the table. "Webley-Pryse, in .450 calibre. Perfectly serviceable but lacks punch. I don't think it would put down a dervish coming at me with forty thousand angels egging him on. If I'd had time to visit my agent in Piccadilly before coming out here, I'd have bought one of yours."

Mayne took out the box of cartridges from his belt, handed them to Gordon, and picked up the Webley-Pryse. "A straight swap. Your need is greater than mine. I just wish I could help you with a sword."

"I'm most grateful, Mayne. And not to worry." Gordon reached behind the desk and pulled out a Pattern 1856 Royal Engineers officer's sword. He unsheathed it halfway, revealing the blade, immaculately polished and oiled. "When I was a cadet at the Royal Military Academy, a fearsome old quartermaster sergeant taught us swordplay, a man by the name of Cannings. Probably long gone by the time you were there."

"Quartermaster Sergeant *Major* Cannings, sir. Probably still there now. We all thought he was old enough to have been at Waterloo."

"*Gentlemen,*" he would say. "*These 'ere swords is not for display.*"

"And then he'd proceed to split a melon in half with it."

Gordon suddenly gave Mayne a steely look, all humour gone. "Well, I intend to do Cannings proud. Only this time it won't be melons. There will be people out there among my staff shooting themselves rather than be caught by the dervishes, and there will be others who will go over to the Mahdi. But if I get half a chance, I'm going down fighting. Soldier first, engineer second. You remember?"

"Impossible to forget, sir."

"Will you see to that, Mayne? Will you give me that half-chance?"

Before Mayne could think of a reply, Gordon had walked over to the sideboard to pick up his brandy glass and take another cigarette from the box. He lit it and took a deep lung full, and then downed the glass in one gulp, exhaling with satisfaction and pouring himself another. He took it and stood in front of Mayne, the pallor in his cheeks tinged with colour, then raised the glass and the cigarette. "And you need have no final qualms that I might go over to the Mahdi. He has banned alcohol and tobacco. I still need my creature comforts." Mayne thought he detected a twinkle in those brilliant blue eyes, a brief spark in a face haunted by what he had been obliged to oversee during the past weeks and months, and by what lay ahead.

Mayne held out a hand. "I must go. It will be light in a few hours."

"Of course. And thank you for coming. It has been *most* agreeable. I fear I've rambled, but I am a man not used to company, especially that of a fellow sapper with such congenial shared interests." They shook hands, and Gordon led him to the door. "And look after that diary. If there's anything to be salvaged from this sorry mess, it's in there."

Mayne began to walk down the corridor. There was a chill in the air; the warmth of early evening had gone. He felt like a priest walking away from a condemned man's cell for the last time, but it was worse than that; he was more like an executioner having sized up his victim. He felt nauseous, but perhaps because of lack of food and the terrible stench, and he was suddenly light-headed, and blinked hard. His mind was reeling from what he had heard. He had to keep up his strength for what was to come next.

Gordon had remained at the door, watching him; now he spoke again. "And Edward?"

Mayne stopped and turned around. "Sir?"

"Godspeed, Edward."

Mayne heard the words, and then he heard his own voice, disembodied and wavering, as if he were watching himself on a distant stage.

"Godspeed to you too, sir."

CHAPTER 24

MAYNE SLID THE REED BOAT INTO THE WATER and pushed it towards the bank of the creek, feeling his feet sink into the ooze as he clung to the stern. The water was cool and dark, and he tried not to think of the horrors he had seen floating in it off Khartoum or of what might lurk in its depths. The level of the Nile had fallen at least two feet since he had left the creek the evening before, and the plank he had laid on the bank of the far shore was now just out of reach even though he propelled the boat as far as he could onto the mud. With a final effort he hauled the boat out of the water and used it as a support, holding on to it as he struggled up the muddy bank toward the plank. He stopped for a moment, panting hard, and wondered what it would be like to fall backwards into the water, to kick off from the bank and let the river take him, whether he would be mired in the horror of this place or whether the current would find him and take him past Khartoum and the cataracts and out into the sparkling clarity of the sea, away from here forever. He felt himself sinking, and snapped back to reality. He heaved his legs up one after the other, then squelched and sucked through the mud until he reached the plank and pulled himself up onto it. He was dripping with ooze, but he no longer cared. All that mattered to him now was to get back to Charrière and set up his rifle before the break of dawn.

He remembered his conversation with Gordon, and patted the journal in his upper tunic pocket. Something had been nagging at him, and then he remembered: it was the empty square in the centre of the drawing Gordon had shown him, where the ancient sculpture had been missing a piece. Gordon had said that he and his companions had searched everywhere for clues to its appearance, in ruins from the time of Akhenaten across the desert. And then Mayne remembered the slab he had taken from the wall in the crocodile temple, the one that he had given Tanner to pass on to Corporal Jones for safekeeping. It had lines radiating from the edge where it had formed part of the Aten symbol, but it also had shapes on one corner, obscured under slime. He cursed himself for remembering too late to tell Gordon: it might even have persuaded him that there was a shred of reason left for staying alive, for coming across the river with him. But there was nothing to be done about it now. It was too late.

A few minutes later he was back at the edge of the mud-brick enclosure surrounding the fort. There was still enough moonlight to see a reflection off the fetid pool inside, its surface stilled by the cold. Charrière had been busy; the embrasures and crumbled openings in the wall had been filled with clumps of thorny mimosa bush, concealing the interior from prying eyes. Mayne whistled quietly, knowing that Charrière would have seen his wake as he paddled across the river. He peered over the wall, pushed aside a branch of mimosa, and made his way inside. Charrière lay awake beside the embrasure overlooking the river, wrapped up in his grey army blanket, his face swathed in his Arab headdress. Beside him Mayne could see the khaki wrap containing his rifle. He crawled alongside, slipping down the edge of the muddy crater that led to the pool, seeing Charrière watching him. Mayne knew he did not need to say anything. He had come alone, without Gordon.

He took his telescope from on top of the bag, rolled in front of the embrasure, and trained the telescope on the palace. Gordon's light was still on, and he looked up to the roof where Gordon had positioned his own telescope. For a split second he saw movement, a flash as the distant lens caught a hint of moonlight on the surface of the river, and then it was gone. But it was enough to show that Gordon had been watching him, following his progress past Tutti Island and the dervish sentries, seeing that he had made it back to the fort. Both men now knew that the die was cast.

Mayne lowered his telescope and looked at the island, sensing movement there too, and could just make out the palm trees swaying on the shore. He felt a prickle of wind on his neck, and then he saw another gust. It was barely perceptible, but it was as if there were some great beast slumbering under the river and building up its strength for dawn. Somewhere out there were a quarter of a million men of the Mahdi's army, on the island, along the far shore of the White Nile. The thought of it made him feel light-headed, as if all those men were sucking the oxygen from the air. Oxygen seemed in short supply here, like water in the desert, essentials of life that had been cut off from Khartoum weeks ago and were now dwindling by the hour.

The brush of wind made him think of his rifle, of the effect on a bullet flying across the river. He wiped his muddy hands on Charrière's blanket, knelt up, and unwrapped the bag, revealing the teakwood case inside. He unbolted the lid and opened it up. Everything looked pristine, unaffected by the jostling it had undergone over the past two weeks. Seeing the rifle quickened his pulse, excited him; he stroked his finger along the octagonal flats of the barrel and touched the forestock, smelling the gun oil. He used a small screwdriver to loosen the clamps that held the components rigidly in place, took out the barrel and receiver and then the removable buttstock and assembled them along with the breechblock. When he had finished, he tested the action,

lowering the loading lever to drop the block and reveal
the breech, drawing back the hammer, pulling the rear
set-trigger and feathering his finger over the main trigger, knowing that the slightest pressure at full cock
would bring the hammer down on the firing pin. He
eased the hammer back to the half-cock safe position,
opened the ammunition box in the case, and took out
one of the long brass cartridges; each contained ninety
grains of the finest powder, hand-loaded for him by his
gunsmith in London, enough to propel the .50 calibre
bullet out of the muzzle at over eighteen hundred feet
per second. He carefully inspected it, then dropped the
loading lever to open the breech, pushed the cartridge
inside, and closed the lever again, causing the block to
rise into place behind the breech and the action to lock.

He lay forward and pushed the barrel of the rifle out
of the embrasure in the wall, careful to avoid any mud
or debris getting near the muzzle. He eased the butt into
his right shoulder, flipped up the rear sight, and then
looked through it, shutting his left eye as he always did
when aiming, seeing the crosshairs of the front sight
through the eyepiece aperture. He checked the elevation
on the rear sight, six hundred and fifty metres, the nearest the setting would allow to the estimate he had made
from the map measurements provided by Kitchener and
the distance that Gordon himself had calculated, with a
minute upwards adjustment that Mayne had made when
he test-fired the rifle over a measured distance near the
Nile south of Korti. He looked up from the sights,
wetted the forefinger of his left hand, and held it in the
air. He sensed nothing; the wind had gone. He eased the
butt from his shoulder and propped it on his bag, leaving the rifle balanced on the embrasure. He was ready.

He lay on his back, looking around. The air seemed
preternaturally still, unnervingly so. Somewhere in the
distance he heard the cry of a tropical bird, a harsh,
grating sound, perhaps what counted in this place as
the dawn chorus; but the sky was still dark. He realised
that the brickworks to the left had gone quiet, the place

where the wounded cow had blindly circled round
and round, groaning and wheezing. He saw that Charrière was cleaning his hunting knife, wiping congealed
blood off the blade and leaving streaks of darkness on
his blanket. Mayne gestured towards the brickworks.
"You've been busy."

Charrière said nothing, but he finished cleaning his
knife and laid it down on the edge of the blanket, its
blade gleaming dully. It was a knife that Mayne himself
had used years before to butcher deer, and one that
Charrière's ancestors had blooded through generations
of hunting and war; its worn bone handle and the point
of the blade, shaped through countless resharpenings
and honings, seemed so perfectly fitted to Charrière that
it had become an extension of himself, just as Mayne
felt with his rifle. Charrière stared intently for a few
moments at the rear of the fort, as if scanning for something, then turned to Mayne, his eyes unfathomable
in the gloom. "The cow dropped dead. Something big
came up and dragged it down into the river."

"A crocodile?"

"I saw only marks on the ground. I was not here."

Mayne looked at the knife and thought again. "Our
pursuers?"

"I found three of them asleep in the desert."

Mayne stared at him. "Identity?"

"They were Sudanese, but each with different tattoos,
from different tribes. They had English tobacco and
Martini-Henry rifles. I did not linger."

Mayne thought hard, wondering who they might be.
"Did you travel far?"

"I took your rifle case on my back. I crossed the river
at the point north of Khartoum where the White Nile
joins the Blue Nile. I went far down the river, for several
miles. I saw the steamers."

"You *saw* them?" Mayne exclaimed, alarmed. "You're
sure they're the ones? They shouldn't be that close to us
yet."

"I saw the turrets with gun emplacements, and the

armour plating the sailors have built around the edges. They were anchored but getting up steam. The soldiers had been ashore foraging for wood, chopping up water-lifting devices for fuel. The Nile is falling at a rate of three feet a day. They must have seen the mudflats and decided to press on."

"That means they could be here very soon."

"They could be here shortly after dawn."

Mayne thought hard, his mind racing. It was essential that he complete his mission before the steamers hove into view. He must be gone before any of the British soldiers or sailors saw him. He turned again to Charrière. "Did you see anything else?"

"I walked through the Mahdi's camp. I passed thousands of them asleep on the desert floor. They have their spears beside them, polished and sharpened. Less than an hour from now this place will light up in more ways than one. The artillery is positioned to blast at the main gates of the city. The main force will come over the river from the west, and others will attack the landward defences to the east. Khartoum will be overrun within minutes. The Ansar will be at the gates of the palace at dawn."

Mayne thought for a moment. "Our pursuers. You said you found three in the desert. There were four when we saw them behind us at Abu Klea."

"He's here."

"What do you mean, *here*?"

"Don't look." Charrière lowered his voice. "He followed us here yesterday evening. He's an Ababda tribesman; he was their tracker and he's good. He returned to their camp in the night and saw his companions with their throats cut, and now he's come back here. He will make his move soon."

"Where is he?" Mayne whispered.

"I've been watching him while you've been loading your rifle. He's been making his way around the wall to the entrance where you came in. When I laid those mimosa branches in the gaps after you left last night, I made it so that I can see out through them, but he will not be able to see in without looking over them. Don't move. He's there now."

In a single lightning movement Charrière tossed off his blanket, picked up his knife, and threw it past Mayne, the blade swishing through the air so fast he could barely see it. There was a shriek from behind the wall, and Charrière bounded forward, followed by Mayne. Charrière pushed through the branches and reached the man, pulling the knife out of his chest and preparing to lunge again. Mayne grabbed his arm and stopped him. "Let me question him first."

The man had a grey robe but no headdress, and a wickedly curved knife lay by his side. He had the three slashed marks of the Ababda tribe on his cheeks. He was a warrior, but his eyes were full of fear, and the red stain from his chest was spreading over his robe, the blood pooling on the ground below. Mayne knelt down close to his head. "Who sent you?" he snarled.

The man gargled, spitting out blood and foaming at the mouth, his eyes wide, his skin turning grey. He gave a death rattle, and his head slumped backwards. He had said something, two words, but Mayne had heard only the second clearly: *Pasha,* the Ottoman word for general. It could be any number of Arab leaders who sported that title; the Ottomans and their minions were masters of intrigue, and any of them could have spies and secret missions in the desert. But how could these men have known to follow Mayne and Charrière from Korti? Who else could have wanted them dead before they reached Gordon?

And then he remembered. The Sudanese used *Pasha* for the British too; he had even done it himself in Khartoum for Gordon. It was how the doomed General Hicks had been known to his Egyptian troops. And there was someone else, someone who had been called that by his fanatical bodyguard.

His heart pounded.

Kitchener Pasha.

He looked up at Charrière. "It was Kitchener. I'm sure of it. He was suspicious of me and must have guessed my role. He idolised Gordon and couldn't bear to think of what I might be planning to do." He rocked back for a moment, feeling overwhelming relief. For days now he had been nagged by uncertainty, wondering whether Colonel Wilson might have had him followed, or even Wolseley. But Kitchener would have acted alone; in the desert he followed no orders. Mayne remembered Burnaby's dying warning: *don't trust anyone*. Burnaby had been watching and listening during the Korti conference and would have sensed the depth of Kitchener's loyalty to Gordon. Mayne shut his eyes for a moment. He felt in control again, and a sudden need to be behind the sights of his rifle, focusing on what he did best.

A huge explosion rent the air, and a shower of light crackled and cascaded down on Khartoum. It was followed by another, and then a distant drumming of gunfire that came through the still dawn air as if it were right next to them, the reports echoing down the river. Mayne saw the city lit up by the explosions, its shattered whitewashed buildings collapsing into the ground like the carapace of some long-dead river monster, and then he turned around and for the first time saw a sliver of dawn above the eastern horizon. He looked at Charrière. It had begun.

They both moved quickly back through the wall and lay down at the embrasure. The distant gunfire had become a continuous crackle to the northeast, somewhere near the junction of the two Niles, and was joined by a distinctive thudding of artillery that sounded like British nine-pounders, the guns that had been mounted on the steamers. They must be coming up through a gauntlet of fire from the Mahdi's forces on either side of the river. Mayne looked at the pastel orange light that was now spreading over the city and being diffused by the smoke of the explosions. If the steamers survived the barrage, they would be rounding the corner of Tutti Island in less than half an hour.

They suddenly heard an extraordinary sound, a noise that Mayne realised must be the stomping of feet, the sound they had heard at Abu Klea but magnified here a hundred times, accompanied by thousands of tom-toms and a quarter of a million men shrieking and chanting, screaming death to the unbelievers. A cloud of dust rose over the landward end of the city, and he saw thousands of dervishes spilling over the defensive ditch and into the streets. It was like a tidal wave smashing through a coastal town, drowning the streets and tossing everything aside as it surged forward. It was all happening astonishingly quickly; twenty minutes earlier the city had been dead quiet. He whipped up his telescope and watched the dervishes run screaming towards the palace, in a matter of seconds reaching the residential quarter where the officials lived. He saw a man in a tarboosh and robe hurriedly lead a woman and five children out to the riverbank; he shot them all in the head with a revolver, six rounds, then flung the empty gun at the advancing dervishes, one of whom cleaved his head with a sword, sending the top half spinning off in a spray of blood and brain into the Nile. Seconds later the first dervishes reached the gates of the palace, pressing against them as Mayne had done a mere eight hours before.

He panned the telescope to a point just above the palace that he had spotted when he had lain here looking at the city the afternoon before. He had needed to find a feature he could see with his naked eye, a point of reference he could aim at before dropping the sights to the balcony; it would help to give structure to a scene whose details might be less easily visible this morning but which he had memorised, that he could see as clearly in his mind's eye as if it were a photograph. He found it now: the conical roof of a mosque that rose behind the palace just above and to the left of the balcony. He put down the telescope and tried sighting the rifle, placing the crosshairs on the roof and then dropping them infinitesimally below and to the right, where Gordon had

said he would be when the Mahdi's army arrived at the
gate.

He looked at the palace gate again, at the horde of
dervishes who must by now number in the thousands,
filling the streets and alleyways, with more of them
pressing in every second. And then he saw Gordon on
the balcony above the compound, exactly where he had
said he would be. Mayne had expected it, but it still sent
a shudder through him. Gordon was wearing his dress
uniform with a red tunic, his sword in one hand and
Mayne's revolver in the other. Mayne felt a sudden surge
of something like pride: an officer of the Royal Engineers was not going to go down without a fight. He fervently hoped that Gordon would have the chance to
dish out some death before he was taken down. Then
the gates collapsed in a crescendo of noise, and the dervishes stormed over the soldiers who had been in the
courtyard, reaching the bottom of the stairs and beginning to clamber up them. The soldiers in the upper-floor
windows were firing as fast as they could reload, more
steadfast than Mayne had expected given the certainty
of death. And then he saw Gordon in action too, laying
about him with his sword, firing the revolver point-
blank at dervishes coming up the stairs, kicking them
back into the mass below, shouting orders to his Sudanese riflemen shooting from the windows beside him.

Mayne whispered under his breath: *please God finish
him now*. A single bullet, a single spear; there were
enough of them flying around. But still Gordon was
there, untouched, standing with his feet planted apart
facing across the river, facing Mayne. The dervishes had
fallen back in a wide arc below the stairs in front of him,
their spears raised, standing their ground even while
the remaining Sudanese soldiers still fired into them,
until they too went silent, their ammunition presumably
expended. Then Mayne saw why the dervishes had
stopped: two emirs on horseback had ridden through
the throng and stopped below the balcony. They seemed
to be reading something to Gordon, talking to him.

Mayne felt himself stop breathing. They were trying to take him alive.

He was going to have to do it.

He put down the telescope and raised the rifle, cocking it and setting the trigger. He peered down the sights, finding the mosque, dropping infinitesimally below and to the right until he found his mark. He could no longer see detail, but he was aiming at what he knew was there, a tiny splash of red, drawing his mind towards it as if he were looking through the telescope.

His throat was dry and his stomach felt cavernous. He realised that he was shivering, that he had not registered the cold. But it was more than that. He had suddenly lost focus. *This had never happened to him before*. He knew that it was Gordon, that he should never have gone to see him, should never have allowed himself to know his target as a human being. And they had got it all wrong: Gordon was no messiah, or a martyr in waiting. He was a man who had come back to Khartoum to find something and who would not leave until he had discovered it. The Gordon he had been sent to kill was a fantasy in the minds of others. When he returned he would tell them, and that false Gordon would be extinguished, and his mission would be done.

Charrière had picked up the telescope. "He's in full view," he said urgently. "The steamers are coming. Take the shot now."

Mayne felt himself tighten up again. They were hunters, and he had the deer in his sights, just like the first time as boys when Charrière had talked him through it, settled his nerves. He closed his eyes for a split second, sending himself back to that day beside the lake in the forest, then opened them, seeing nothing but the tunnel of the sights and the target beyond. And then in his mind's eye he saw Gordon as he should be, Gordon as he might be right now, never allowing himself to be taken prisoner, lifting his revolver and firing his last round at the emir, then charging down the stairs with his sword raised, hacking and stabbing until he was cut down.

He touched the trigger. The rifle jumped; there was a crack, and the report echoed down the Nile. He dropped the weapon and pushed away from the wall, sitting up on his knees and shutting his eyes. He slowly exhaled, feeling as if he would never need to breathe again. He felt the thirst he had first felt in the desert with Shaytan, the thirst that felt like dust in the throat, only this time he did not want to quench it; he wanted the desert to be part of him. He began to breathe again, shallow breaths, barely perceptible, and he opened his eyes. On the horizon over Omdurman to the west, he saw the strip of orange widen, wavering and shimmering between sand and sky. Gordon had been right: the sun would shine today. The noise that he had somehow blocked out since aiming the rifle suddenly came back in full force, a din of shrieking and musketry and claps of artillery fire. The city was heaving with dervishes, and he could no longer see the steps of the palace. He looked down the Nile; the steamers had not yet appeared. He and Charrière would be able to leave before Colonel Wilson arrived, before anyone on the boats saw him and his rifle. It had all gone according to plan.

Suddenly the wind was knocked out of him and he was held in a vicelike grip from behind, his neck pinned back and his right arm pushed up in a half nelson. He struggled, kicking his legs, but his arm was pushed up farther. He felt the breath against his neck, and then saw that the forearm around his neck was brawny and scarred and wearing a braided bracelet. He relaxed and let himself fall back against the man holding him: it was Charrière. "Do you remember how we used to wrestle as boys?" he said. "You always won."

"That was when you were my adopted brother, Kahniekahake."

"And now?"

"You have earned that name again today, Eagle Eye.

And now you will join our ancestors. Your spirit will fly like a swift arrow towards the sun."

The grip tightened. His arm was pushed up farther and pinned hard against Charrière's chest, allowing him to release his right arm. Mayne heard the sound of a blade being drawn, and he felt a hard flatness against his own chest. He felt numb, too exhausted for games. "What are you doing?"

"My job."

Mayne tried to struggle. "What do you mean?"

"*Nobody must know*. The final words Wilson spoke to me."

"That's what he told *me*. And nobody will know. Especially if we leave now, before the steamers arrive."

"They are two days downstream. I didn't see them last night. The gunfire we heard was a small Sudanese garrison in the fort of Omdurman under siege."

Mayne shut his eyes: this was real. He should have expected it. Wilson would arrive too late. Gordon would be dead, killed by the forces of the Mahdi. Wolseley would withdraw honourably, British prestige saved. People would forever remember the glorious battle of Abu Klea; Gordon would become a saint.

And nobody would ever know the truth.

He swallowed hard. "And why not you? If you know, how can you live too?"

"Nobody believes an Indian. Especially one living the rest of his life alone on a lake in a forest."

"Why?" Mayne said, suddenly too tired for it all. "Why do it?"

"General Wolseley was always good to my people. And Wilson came to me after my wife and child had died."

"Wolseley? Was he in on this?"

"It was he who presented the plan to Wilson. You were the right man for the job. But even you they could not trust to talk one day."

Mayne shut his eyes. He realised how little he knew, and how this theatre of war was in reality a play of personalities, twisting and encircling one another like weeds in a current, using history as their stage just as the pharaohs had once used the Nile. There were a few good men: Fred Burnaby was one; General Charles Gordon was another. And there were some who once drawn in would never be allowed to leave, whose price for believing that their cause amounted to something greater was to be left forever as detritus of war.

What he would not tell Charrière was that he had been given the same mission. It was why he had tried to persuade Wolseley to let Charrière go home with the other voyageurs. His revolver, the one he had exchanged with Gordon, was meant to be used against Charrière: it was to be at a time of his choosing, at someplace on the return journey where Charrière had ceased to be of use to him. Neither of them was meant to come out of the desert alive.

He could not see Charrière, would never see him now. But he remembered the cold dark eyes, the eyes of a hunter, like his own. He should have known it would end this way. *It could end only this way.*

"The bowstring has been released, Kahniekahake. The arrow that will take your spirit is already flying. Soon it will pass between us and you will see the sun."

He felt himself lifted bodily, felt his gorge rise, a tightness below his chest. He gasped, and then remembered something. "My tunic pocket," he said, his breathing short. "Gordon's diary, his drawings. Captain John Howard, School of Military Engineering. Will you send it to him?" He felt the feeling go from his limbs and his voice weaken. "My servant, Corporal Jones . . . 8th Railway Company. Tell Howard to find him. He's got something of mine. An artefact. Will you do that for me?"

"I will do that for you."

"And Charrière my blood brother . . ."

"What is it?"

Mayne could barely whisper it. "When you get to our

lake in the forest, watch out for strangers coming on the water. They will try to silence you too. Trust nobody."

Charrière held him tightly. He suddenly felt terribly cold. He would need to drink and to eat to shake off the chill. He would go to the wells of Jakdul. An oasis in the desert. Nobody would find him there.

He convulsed and coughed blood. He saw his blood pool on the sand, become the desert. Then all he could see was an enclosing constriction, a narrowing tunnel. He relaxed, knowing what it was. He was looking down the sights of his rifle, excluding all else, seeing only his target, utterly focused. It had always felt good.

Then he saw it: a flash of light, burning like the sun, searing down the walls of the tunnel like outstretched arms, reaching out to envelop him.

He knew what Gordon had seen.

Then nothing.

CHAPTER 25

CORNWALL, ENGLAND, PRESENT DAY

JACK SAT IN HIS STUDY IN THE OLD FAMILY house at the IMU campus in Cornwall and stared at the portraits of his ancestors on the walls, feeling as listless as at anytime in the forty-eight hours since he and Costas had been forcibly evicted from Sudan. A few hours ago he had received more bad news, that Hiebermeyer and his team had been escorted across the border into Egypt from their site at Semna, apparently also under orders from al'Ahmed. The only consolation was that the finds from the site, including the golden scepter, had been taken secretly by Aysha's cousin to the Khartoum museum, where they had been placed in the vault. One day it might be possible to return to the Sudan, but for the time being it was a closed shop. Jack looked at the two old envelopes he had taken from *Seaquest II*, the one from Lieutenant Tanner and the other from Corporal Jones, and wondered where the contents had gone. He had taken a jolt, but he was not going to give up on this trail. He needed time, maybe a few days away. He knew he should pick up the phone and call Maria. And he knew he needed sleep.

Rebecca knocked and came into the room, bringing him a cup of coffee. "You should drink this. And you need to get away for a day or two. Then you'll see everything in perspective. As Uncle Costas says, everyone takes a few knocks down the road, and what's a risk without bombing out from time to time. It's all part of life's rich tapestry. Anyway, everyone knows that working in the Sudan is a game of chance, with this kind of thing likely to happen whatever you do. And you did nothing wrong. You went to the site in good faith believing you had a permit, and you were trashed by one of the trickiest customers in the Middle East."

"I let Maurice and Aysha down. They should never have had to leave the site at Semna the way they did. It was virtually a one-hour evacuation."

Rebecca shook her head. "Maurice called me because you're not picking up when he calls. They'd already made the decision to leave. They'd had bandits show up at night, and Aysha's cousin, the guy acting as their guard, had become really afraid. Aysha said that as soon as she realized that, she knew she had to get out. There was no way they were going to stay there with the baby. And anyway, the Egyptians are topping up Lake Nasser again, so the whole site's going to be inundated in a couple of months."

Jack picked up a small object from his desk, the green-stone scarab he had found inside the crocodile temple, and stared at the cartouche on the base. He wondered who had lost it there, and when. It had been with him since he had borrowed it from the Sudan, and now he felt he wanted to return it, not to a museum but back to the shimmering sand inside the temple where it could then spend another eternity.

"You know that the Muslim tribesmen of the Sudan pick up old scarabs and use them as good-luck charms," Rebecca said. "They wrap prayers around them and put them in little bags around their necks. That thing seems so close to Akhenaten, a scarab of his wife Nefertiti, but it might have been lost in there a lot more recently and have a completely different significance. It's what you told me about artifacts that survive between different eras and cultures taking on new meanings."

Jack put down the scarab and stared at it. "I also told you I didn't believe in good-luck charms."

"You said you believed in yourself."

Jack took a deep breath. "Okay. I'll talk to Maurice. But I still feel I have to make it up to him somehow. Something big in Egypt."

"Dad, you found him a pharaoh's golden scepter. And not just any pharaoh, but his favorite, Akhenatan. That takes some beating."

"Maybe I can do something to help at the pyramid of Menkaure. After this I might take a rest from diving for a while. I could do some work on land."

"Dad, you didn't say that. Get over it."

"That sounds like Costas talking. He doesn't have to face the board of directors tomorrow."

"Actually, he does. He volunteered to go along to make sure the record was straight. Anyway, let's face it, you run this place. You created the board of directors."

"When I created the board, I relinquished my control over IMU to them so that I would be just another employee. I'd seen too many institutions run like tin-pot dictatorships."

"They're hardly going to fire you, Dad. Come on. Anyway, I'm going back up to your great-great-grandad's archive in the attic. One of those boxes is going to have that letter from Lieutenant Tanner, I'm sure of it. It might just give us the clue we need to whatever was in that other envelope. We don't have to go back to Sudan to tie up that story. And get on the phone to Maurice, Dad. You're his best friend. You owe it to him."

Rebecca marched out, and Jack put his feet up on the corner of his desk, staring again at the portraits on the wall: the first Jack Howard, an Elizabethan sea dog who had made his fortune as a privateer plundering Spanish treasure ships, and then fought the Armada under Drake and Raleigh; beside him Captain Matthias Howard, who had traded in tobacco from his estates in Maryland and Virginia before turning his attentions to the east, where he had put his money into an East Indiaman and doubled the family fortune, allowing him to build the present house; and on the opposite side of the door Colonel John Howard, Royal Engineers, Jack's great-great-grandfather, who had served with distinction in India before disappearing on a quest into Afghanistan, one that Jack and Costas had finally brought to resolution almost a hundred years later. They were all there in Jack's mind, not just those three but the many men and women in between who had given him his sense of identity, had made him feel that he was part of the tradition of exploration and adventure and risk-taking that was in his blood.

He knew he did not have to live up to any of them, only to the ideal he had set himself. And since Rebecca had arrived in his life, it had not just been about him but about her too, about how he could help her to feel that same urge that had always driven him forward, a relishing of the voyage of discovery as much as a yearning for the destination, for the prize that sometimes remained elusive. If there was anything he had learned from being an archaeologist, it was this: that too often the treasure at the end of the quest was an illusion, an ever-receding mirage, and the real discoveries were the ones made along the way, revelations of ancient and present lives, voyages of self-discovery and friendship.

Perhaps chasing Akhenaten's quest had been like that. They had made fabulous discoveries. A whole chapter of Victorian history in the desert had opened up in a way that Jack had never anticipated. And he now understood better what made men tick who had gone off by themselves in search of revelation, men like Gordon, men like himself. He had a hunch that somewhere within those months in 1884 and 1885 was a man who still could not be found, a void at the center of the story, yet who was somehow inextricably tied up with the fate of Gordon; it was a void that Jack had found himself trying to occupy as he struggled to imagine what had really gone on. He stared at the portrait of Colonel Howard in his uniform, wishing yet again that he had

been able to talk to him but feeling closer now to understanding what it was that had motivated the explorers
and archaeologists of that generation. For Jack these
were discoveries of significance. Perhaps the story of
Akhenaten's quest, of his fabled lost city of light, could
now be finished, a book to be shut.

He thought about what Rebecca had said, and about
those things that had so excited him about his ancestors: exploration and adventure and risk-taking. He had
taken a risk in going to the site of the *Abbas*, and it
had not worked out. Risk-taking was all about accept-
ing the possibility of failure. Perhaps he had been too
lucky during his career and needed to learn humility.
Rebecca was about the future, and that was where he
needed to put his mind now. He took a deep breath and
exhaled slowly. Sitting in the middle of his desk was the
press release from Sofia about the *Beatrice*, waiting to
be read. He might not be able to tie up all the loose ends
in the Sudan, but the discovery of the *Beatrice* was a
fantastic result, and he would do everything in his power
to make sure that the project put IMU in the best possible light. He pushed back his chair, put his feet down,
and picked up the report, feeling better already. He
remembered what Sofia had called their submersible,
Nina, after Columbus's ship, and how she had wanted
IMU to go to the Americas: maybe she was right. It had
been almost eight years since he had taken an IMU team
to Canada and then to Mexico on the trail of crusader
gold. For several years now, while there was so much
going on elsewhere, he had resisted pleas from their U.S.
representative to start a new project in America. That
was where he would go next. He needed a fresh start,
new horizons, like Columbus. He would talk about it
tomorrow morning when he had the meeting with the
IMU board of governors to explain the *Abbas* incident
so that he could end the grilling on a positive note. And
he would get Hiebermeyer to call in to outline his plans
for returning the sarcophagus of Menkaure to its right-
ful place inside the pyramid at Giza.

He thought of that word: *pyramid*. It triggered something, a very distant memory. He put down the report and picked up the brown envelope that Corporal Jones had sent to his great-great-grandfather, the envelope that he thought had contained some kind of artifact. He looked at it again, tracing his fingers over the careful handwriting of the address, and then glanced at the portrait of Colonel Howard. *That was it*. He remembered now. His pulse quickened and he sat upright, thinking back forty years. It had been in this very room; he and his grandfather had been standing in front of that very portrait. His grandfather had been telling him how as a young boy he had been allowed once a week to go upstairs into the attic where his own grandfather had lived, to see his stamp collection. It had been during the few years of Colonel Howard's retirement before his final quest into Afghanistan, and he had lived not here but in a cruck-framed half-timbered cottage in a remote village in Herefordshire, a secluded place where he could get on with his writing projects without distraction. His daughter and grandchildren had lived downstairs. But it was not the stamp collection that had so intrigued the little boy. It was an ancient artifact, a square stone with carvings all over it, sitting in a niche in the old timbers of the wall. His grandfather had remembered it so clearly all those years later because the big timbers of the cruck frame came together to form an inverted V shape in the attic, just like a pyramid. And that was what he had seen on the ancient stone: a pyramid. Colonel Howard had told the boy that he had been sent it from Egypt, and that it had once been in an ancient temple.

Jack was suddenly coursing with excitement. *Could it still be there?* The cruck-framed house was still in the possession of the Howard estate, lived in by one of Jack's elderly aunts. He pulled out his phone, scrolled through the address list, and made a call. There was no reply, and he left a message. He drummed his fingers against the desk. He could make it up there today and return in time for the meeting tomorrow morning. It would be a long drive, but he could do with it. And if there was a result, it would be something else he could throw in front of the board of directors.

Rebecca came bounding through the door holding a small brown parcel that looked about the same vintage as the envelope Jack had been looking at, though hers evidently still held its contents. Jack knew there would be numerous interesting items among Colonel Howard's papers, and this package was too big to be Lieutenant Tanner's letter. She was flushed with excitement, but Jack held up his hand. "Before we get distracted by anything, I may have made a breakthrough. I remembered something your great-grandfather told me years ago about an ancient Egyptian artifact shown to him by *his* grandfather, Colonel Howard. It's *just* possible that it's the artifact that was once in the envelope that Corporal Jones sent him. And I think I know where it might be. We might have to drop everything and go on a long drive."

"Hold it right there, Dad. First, this." She took a single sheet of old letter paper out of the package she was carrying, cleared her throat, and stood upright. She sniffed, and Jack realized that she had been crying. "What's wrong? Are you all right?" he asked.

"It's just this," she said, holding up the letter. "I'll be fine." She cleared her throat again. "This is the final page of the letter from Lieutenant Tanner at Semna to Howard. It's very affectionate; they seem to have been great friends. Tanner was in love with Howard's sister-in-law and was planning to marry her when he returned from Egypt. I think the letter was written somewhere dusty, not at a desk. He'd been doing something grim, burying some comrades, and the tone of the letter is as if he's making the best of a bad situation, taking his mind away from it."

Jack leaned forward, suddenly riveted. "That would be the sangar, and the grim business would be the burial of the two soldiers killed there by the Mahdist sniper.

Incredible. This really gives the story behind Maurice and Aysha's discoveries."

"He mentions the crocodile mummies," Rebecca said. "As an archaeology enthusiast he must have recognized them for what they were, as the soldiers were digging through them to make the graves."

"Read the entire page, Rebecca."

She took a deep breath, and began:

> As well as the extraordinary crocodile mummies, there is another remarkable archaeological discovery here that I'd love to tell you about but it will have to be another time, when I can sit down undistracted and do it justice—suffice to say that Edward Mayne was here with us, and went with the major of the Canadian contingent and myself into the underground temple, through the barest of cracks at the top of the door—that really gives the game away to you, doesn't it, but it's not fair to keep you on tenterhooks until I write next time; at any rate Mayne took a small stone slab with carving that he instructed me to give to his servant, Corporal Jones, who you will remember from the Rampa expedition when he was a sergeant, and I instructed Jones to send it on to you if Mayne should be killed. It may be merely of passing interest to you, I fancy, but as I believe you have been appointed curator of Gordon's antiquities—for which my congratulations—it would make sense for you to be its recipient. Corporal Jones, incidentally, is for the Railway Company, to keep him out of mischief and away from any fights, though I fear we may all be in line for that in due course, with the Mahdi's army growing daily. Mayne is for headquarters at Korti and some secret mission, I know not what. He has being doing reconnaissance out here. (You will remember that he instructed us in sharpshooting when we were juniors at Chatham; he has his rifle out here, I believe it is a Sharps, tho' he keeps it concealed. It was he

who used one of our rifles to pot the Mahdist sharp-shooter who killed our two poor soldiers.)

My dear John, I am fed up with war already and would wish nothing better than to take up an appointment like that held by Kitchener in Palestine and carry out archaeological survey, or perhaps back in India. Egypt is now crying out for archaeologists as will the Sudan if we can finish this infernal war and get Gordon out alive. But if I were to be an archaeologist in Egypt, then your sister-in-law, darling Maria, would have to live in Cairo, and I would wish that on no English woman on account of the cholera, certainly no English woman wishing to bear children. I would not wish my wife to endure the sufferings of your own dear wife Georgina when your poor boy Edward died in Bangalore. Perhaps if there is no survey post I will find a position at the School of Military Engineering and we can communicate not by letter but daily and in person. I should like that above all things.

I am called by General Earle to the river. More anon.

YOUR MOST AFFECTIONATE FRIEND
AND FELLOW ARCHAEOLOGIST,
P. Tanner, Lieutenant, Royal Engineers, at Semna,
November 24th, 1884

Rebecca looked up and put the letter on Jack's desk. "I was sad because you said he was killed only a few weeks later. It seems such a waste. I almost think of him as still being there, at that date, waiting for a life ahead that would never be fulfilled. You can say what you like about Gordon, but this was the cost."

Jack took the letter and looked at it. Now he knew the name of the sniper: Mayne. He quickly walked over to the cased book collection that he had inherited from his grandfather and pulled out several volumes of the Army List for the 1870s and 1880s. "Here it is," he murmured. "Edward Mayne, commissioned into the Royal Engineers in 1868, captain 1878, major 1884. Served in the Red River expedition in Canada in 1871. Always a survey officer, or on secondment. This is interesting. He disappears completely from the list after 1885. Missing, whereabouts unknown."

"Killed in the desert campaign?"

"If so, not on official operations, otherwise it would have been recorded. But it wasn't unknown for men to ride out and disappear without trace in the desert."

"And did you notice? Tanner mentions the plaque."

"Yes," Jack said excitedly. "I'm sure it's the square slab that was missing from the carving on the wall in the temple. It might, just *might*, contain some clues as to the meaning of the image in the carving. Even if I can't go back to Sudan, we might at least be able to wrap that one up." His phone flashed and he picked it up, reading the message. "*Yes,*" he exclaimed. "Your great-aunt Margaret is back at home. Told me off for leaving an answerphone message instead of sending a text. That's a modern eighty-year-old for you. That's where we're going. She'll be delighted to see us this afternoon. We'd better be on our way."

"Not before you see what else I've found. We can read it in the car."

"Okay. Let's be quick about it. Fire away."

She held the brown parcel in front of her. "This was at the bottom of the first box of Howard's papers. It was sent to him at the School of Military Engineering in Chatham from a remote location in Ontario through the Canadian Department of Indian Affairs. It seems to have taken a long time getting out of Canada, as no postage was put on it. You can see that on one part of the envelope it's marked 'Veteran,' and the Canadian Department of Veteran Affairs seems to have decided to cover the costs. Beside 'Veteran' it says 'Nile, 1884–5.' But the postmark from Ottawa is the twenty-fifth of January 1925."

"That's almost fifteen years after Colonel Howard died."

"It was unopened. It must have been forwarded by the

School to his last known address, and someone stashed it with his stuff."

"Do we know who the sender was?"

"His name was Henri Charrière. I remember you talking about Canadian Mohawk Indians on the Nile, and I looked him up in a book you recently ordered for the library on the subject. He's in it, though there are few details. He served in the Red River expedition, like Mayne. The two men must have known each other, because Charrière was with the voyageur contingent on the Nile on that day in 1884 when Tanner wrote his letter. Unlike the other Indians, there's no record of when he went back to Canada, and he didn't return to live in their communities. There's a note saying that a man with his name with a veteran's pension was living in 1922 in a cabin beside Lake Traverse in Algonquin Park, a wilderness area in Ontario. He must have been at least eighty years old by then. How he ended up with what's in this package, and why he sat on it for so long before deciding to send it to someone in authority, is a mystery."

"Show it to me while we walk out."

"You might want to stay sitting just for this bit. I opened it to see the cover, but I thought you might want to be the first one to open the actual book."

Jack took the package from her, glancing at the grubby envelope covered with stamps and nearly illegible writing, and he admired Rebecca's tenacity in deciphering it. He slipped the volume out and weighed it in his hands. It was a ruled notebook, a diary or a journal. He realized that he was looking at the back cover upside down, and he flipped it over. There was a handwritten title on the cover. He read it, and then read it again, barely taking it in. He coughed and read it out loud: " 'The Journal of Major General Charles Gordon, CB, Garrison Commander at Khartoum, 14 December 1884 to 25 January 1885.' "

He sat back, stunned. It was the lost final volume of General Gordon's diary. He could scarcely bring himself to open it. This would surely at last reveal the truth of those last days in Khartoum. He pressed the journal against his chest and then put it carefully back into the envelope and handed it to Rebecca. "Yours for safekeeping. That may be the most extraordinary treasure of this whole quest. You can begin reading it to me in the car."

Four and a half hours later, Jack pulled off the main road and drove down the narrow lane into the village where his great-great-grandfather had lived. It seemed a world away from the desert of Sudan and the war against the Mahdi, but these villages were the idealized image of England that many of the soldiers dreamed of while they were on campaign, and today they were often the places where the last residues of undiscovered papers and artifacts from those years were to be found. He had not been here for a long time, but he remembered the route through the picturesque village square and up the side lane to the row of half-timbered cottages, the rolling summits of the Brecon Beacons looming a few miles behind. He stopped outside the front gate, switched off the engine, and enjoyed the silence after the drive, letting Rebecca sleep for a few minutes longer.

It had been an extraordinary few hours of revelation as she had picked her way through the diary. Gordon's last entry on the morning of the day he died was a neatly written statement that Jack could remember now from memory: *Major Mayne of the Royal Engineers has arrived, with a companion. He is to have this journal for safekeeping so that it may be published and known to the world. Now I know I am to die. I have stayed with the people of Khartoum to the last.*

Everything about it was astonishing. Now Jack knew where Major Mayne had gone. He and Rebecca were certain that the companion had been Charrière, as that would explain how he came to have the diary. Why it had taken him so long to return it, beyond the lifetimes of most of the players in those events, remained perplexing. Mayne himself must have died for Charrière to have ended up with the diary, perhaps during that final apocalyptic day when the Mahdist forces overran the city. What Mayne was doing visiting Gordon in his final hours was a mystery. There was no other mention in the historical records of a British officer reaching Gordon so late in the day. It must have been a covert mission, top secret. The phrase that repeated over and over in Jack's mind was Gordon's final sign-off: *now I know I am to die*. Had he simply become resigned to the inevitable, to the inescapable outcome of the Mahdi's attack? Or had he known something else? Jack had remembered Lieutenant Tanner's letter mentioning Mayne's rifle, and he had begun to think the unthinkable. Had a British officer been sent in secret in a last-ditch attempt to persuade Gordon to leave, to ensure that he was not captured by the Mahdi and paraded in front of the world? Had that officer been chosen because he was also one of the army's most skilled marksmen, with instructions to deploy that skill should Gordon refuse to leave? He had remembered the iconic image of the death of Gordon, standing fully exposed on the balcony of the palace; using satellite imagery, Rebecca had determined that he would have been within range of a sharpshooter with a high-powered Sharps rifle on the opposite side of the river, shooting to ensure that he was killed yet leaving no evidence that his death was anything other than that of a soldier fighting to the last against an overwhelming enemy.

And then on the last page of the diary they had seen a diagram of an archaeological discovery that Gordon had made somewhere along the Nile, a stone plaque that he had sent away in the *Abbas,* and Jack had realized that it must have been the one that he and Costas had so nearly recovered and must now be in the hands of al'Ahmed and his family. It was a precise illustration of parallel and intersecting lines that Jack recognized from the carving that they had found inside the sarcophagus of Menkaure. Gordon had labelled it with the same term that Captain Wichelo of the *Beatrice* had used to describe the plaque in the coffin: the City of Light.

The pieces were suddenly falling together. Listening to Rebecca read the journal, Jack had realized that the archaeology from thousands of years ago and the history from little more than a century ago were inextricably intertwined; had it not been for the archaeology, he would not have embarked on the quest to find out more about Gordon in his family papers, and Rebecca would never have made the discovery. The journal had allowed him to see Gordon as if he himself had opened the door to that room in the palace at Khartoum in 1885, just as Major Mayne must have done; and he had seen neither a mystic nor a messiah but a man to whom the desert had given a clarity of vision that made compassion for his fellow human beings the guiding force in his life, for those in Khartoum who had come to rely on him for daily survival. He wondered whether Akhenaten too had been misunderstood by history, whether it was not the location of his revelation in the desert that was the discovery they should be seeking but rather the place he had turned to next, where the clarity of vision that he too had experienced might have led him to create something tangible, something of benefit to humankind, not in the desert to the south but in the heartland of the civilization along the Nile from which he had sprung.

And now there was one final piece of the puzzle to find, a piece that might provide the detail needed to bring those images of Akhenaten's city from abstraction to reality, to a place that might at last be within the possibility of archaeological discovery that had eluded Gordon and others on this trail for so long.

Rebecca woke and rubbed her eyes, looking blearily at the cottage. "We're here. Look, there's Great-Aunt Margaret." She opened the door and got out, and the neatly dressed old lady who had come down the path welcomed her with open arms. Jack followed, giving her a hug too. "It's lovely to see Rebecca doing so well," she said. "She's more amazing than all your adventures put together, you know."

"Well, she's part of them now."

Aunt Margaret led them through the beautifully tended garden towards the front door; Jack had to stoop to enter the cottage. At the bottom of the stairs she turned around and faced them. "Now, before we have tea and Rebecca tells me all her news, I know you'll want to see what I found after you told me what to look for, Jack."

"You didn't have to, Great-Aunt Margaret," Rebecca said. "We don't want you hurting yourself."

"Oh, there's a bit of the adventurer in me too you know, Rebecca. I don't know how much your dad has told you about me, but I'm not called Howard for nothing. When you told me you thought it might have been plastered or painted over, I took my basket of garden tools up there and set to. I haven't had so much fun since I broke into the fifth High Llama of Llora's tomb in the Karakorum Desert and got away with his sacred prayer roll, almost."

Rebecca coughed politely. "You did what?"

Jack coughed a bit more loudly. "Aunt Margaret has, um, a certain history. She worked for MI6. She's classified up to the hilt."

"Oh," Rebecca said. "You mean like Miss Moneypenny?"

"No, I mean like 'M,'" Jack said. "She's actually Dame Margaret Howard, though she never calls herself that."

"Such a silly title," Aunt Margaret said. "Use it outside Britain and they think it means you run a brothel." She hesitated at the foot of the stairs and looked at Jack. "Before we go up, lest I forget, your friend Costas has been on the phone."

"Really? What about?"

"Do you remember when he and I first met more than ten years ago? It was at the inauguration of IMU."

Jack paused. "I remember the two of you talking at

great length about poetry, about the Arthurian legends.
You'd just retired, and you were going to return to your
undergraduate passion from Oxford days and write a
book about the Holy Grail, about how the legend influenced generations of explorers on their own quests."

Aunt Margaret reached over to a small table beside
the front door and picked up a brown paper parcel tied
with string. "When Costas called me this morning, he
said that the desert had made him think of T. S. Eliot's
The Waste Land, and then of the Holy Grail quest that
was the inspiration behind the poem. He said that the
place beside the Nile where you found the crocodile
temple reminded him of the Fisher King, the wounded
warrior who guarded the Grail, yet whose kingdom was
turned to waste as he did so. And then when you were
forced to leave the Sudan, he thought of the fragmenta-
tion of the Grail quest, about how it had become an
aimless journey with no beginning and no end, like the
march to nowhere of the characters in Samuel Beckett's
play *Waiting for Godot.* And then he remembered how
there was one who through it all was destined to achieve
the Grail and heal the wasteland."

"We studied the legend in school," Rebecca said.
"You mean Sir Galahad."

Aunt Margaret handed her the package. "Will you see
that Costas gets this? It's a Victorian edition of Malory's
Morte d'Arthur, rather tatty I'm afraid. It was owned by
Colonel Howard; he loved this kind of stuff and apparently used to spend his evenings by the fire here reading
Sir Walter Scott's Waverley novels and Tennyson and
anything in Old English and Norse literature on quests
and adventure."

"Maybe it was an escape from the fear of those years
in the lead-up to the First World War," Rebecca said,
holding the book tight.

"Perhaps," she said. "But I think many like him at
that time saw their lives in those terms, and for them the
lesson of the Grail story was that the quest was as important as the destination, a treasure that might remain

always out of reach. Colonel Howard had one last quest to fulfil, one that had begun in his early years with a discovery in the jungle of southern India, and perhaps reading this fired him up to resume the journey that gave his life excitement and meaning."

Jack cocked an eye at her. "This story is really for me, isn't it?"

Aunt Margaret smiled. "I don't need to be telling you it, do I?" She jerked her head up the stairs. "I told Costas he really didn't need to worry. You've made it here. You're back on the quest again."

Jack glanced at Rebecca. "With a little help from my daughter."

Aunt Margaret gave him a steely look. "Oh no. You made it here because *you* wanted to. Jack Howard is not designed to wander about in the wasteland. You're here because it's in your genes. It's in mine too, so I know it."

Jack grinned. "All right. Point taken."

"Come on then," she said. "Chop-chop. Tea's getting cold. We can't be talking all day."

She led them up the creaking stairs past the first floor and into the attic. Jack stooped low through the entrance and followed her past boxes and crates to the massive cruck timbers that gave the cottage its name. "This is where Great-Grandfather used to work," she said. "When I arrived here after retiring, his desk was still there, but I've moved it down to my own study. It's a little dusty up here." She pointed up to the apex of the crux, where fragments of plaster and chips of paint had come off the wall and fallen onto the jutting timber frame below. "There you go. It looks a bit like the image on the Khedive's Star, don't you think? Those pyramids. I've got the Star awarded to Great-Grandfather for service in Egypt."

Jack stared. In the hole was a square stone block about fifteen centimeters across and covered with incised carving. He knew without hesitation that it was the missing piece from the wall carving of Akhenaten in the crocodile temple. It had the arrangement of lines that he recognized, including several from the sun symbol of the Aten in the top corner of the chamber wall that terminated just beyond the block. He also recognized the arrangement from the diagram in Gordon's journal, the image of the labyrinth complex that Gordon had retrieved from the riverside temple.

That had been expected. He had been as close to certain as he could be that the block came from the wall. What he had not expected was the image in the center.

It was not one pyramid but three, an image known the world over, one of the iconic views of archaeology: the three pyramids at Giza. The smallest of them, the pyramid of Menkaure, where Vyse had found the sarcophagus and the plaque, had a line drawn from the center of it down into the complex of lines below, as if it were somehow joined to them, like a portal.

Jack reeled with excitement. Now he knew where Akhenaten's City of Light had been. Not in the depths of the Nubian Desert, not in the place where Akhenaten had experienced his revelation, but in the very heart of ancient Egypt, in the oldest and most sacred place possible, where Akhenaten could have envisaged himself ruling Egypt for all eternity.

And he knew that others might know of it as well, al'Ahmed and his followers, whose ancestors had known of Gordon's quest and who might by now have seen the plaque from the wreck of the *Abbas* and could be on the same trail. Suddenly time was of the essence.

Jack looked at Rebecca. "Do you know where Costas is?"

"With Sofia," she said. "Showing her the engineering department."

He pulled out his phone, clicked the number, and waited. After another attempt, Costas replied. "Jack. I've been meaning to call." Jack could hear the rumble of machinery in the background. "I guess this is about the board of directors' meeting tomorrow. We need to get our story straight."

"The board of directors can wait. I need you to be on

a flight with me this evening, with all of our dive gear prepped."

"Just give me a moment to square it with Sofia."

"That's a new one," Rebecca whispered.

Aunt Margaret nudged him. "Go for it, Jack. I don't know where you're going and what you're doing, but give 'em hell."

Costas was back on the phone. "Jack."

"What's your status?"

"Where to?"

"Egypt. We're going to a pyramid. We're going to *dive* inside a pyramid. This is as big as it gets. You good with that?"

"You bet. Good to go."

CHAPTER 26

ON THE GIZA PLATEAU, EGYPT

TWO DAYS LATER, JACK STOOD BY HIMSELF on the Giza plateau outside Cairo, dwarfed by the huge mass of the pyramid of Khufru to his right. Twenty minutes earlier he had used the special pass supplied by Aysha to make his way through the heavy police cordon that had blocked off the plateau for weeks now, part of an unprecedented program to improve security and allow essential safety and conservation work to be carried out. For Hiebermeyer and his team, it had been a godsend, a unique opportunity for sustained exploration inside the pyramids. On this occasion Aysha was not the permit-issuing authority; control of the site had been taken over by the Egyptian Ministry of Defense. The temporary one-day permit she had engineered the week before to send a robot into the pyramid of Menkaure had been extended for a week. Jack had called Maurice from England to tell them of their extraordinary find of the pyramid depiction on the stone slab, and had been on the plane the next day to join *Seaquest II* on her way back from Spain and organize the airlift by helicopter to Alexandria of the equipment that he and Costas would need for today's excursion. It still seemed an extraordinary plan, but it was exactly what Jack needed. After long days of soul-searching after their eviction from the Sudan, he was thrilled to be in the field again.

It was still only early afternoon, but the sun already had a reddish hue to it, the light filtering through the dust and low clouds that obscured the desert horizon to the west.

Jack checked a quick text message from Rebecca, who had flown back for her final term at school in New York, and then looked up at the pyramid beside him, shading his eyes against the glare of the sun. He remembered once asking Rebecca to imagine that the pyramids had never been built, and then trying to persuade people that structures of that scale had existed in antiquity; it would be met with flat disbelief. Looking at them today, he recalled the pyramid-shaped basalt outcrops he had seen in the Nubian Desert from Semna, and he found himself wondering whether the idea for these extraordinary structures had been imported from the natural landscape of the desert homeland of the ancestors of the ancient Egyptians. He made a mental note to try it out on Maurice and then trudged forward beside the massive blocks at the base. It was curiously unsettling being here at a place normally visited by thousands every day, in a landscape whose features were entirely man-made and yet seemed so implausible that the mind rebelled against the idea. He tried to see them instead as natural extrusions of the limestone substrate jutting out of the desert floor. It made the human presence seem oddly ephemeral, the same feeling he had experienced in the Sudan thinking about the Gordon relief expedition, as if the imprint of all those people could be swept away by a breeze across the sand like the tide of the sea cleansing a foreshore.

After another ten minutes of brisk walking to the southwest, he had passed the second pyramid and was within sight of the pyramid of Menkaure, only one tenth the mass of the great pyramid but at sixty-five meters still a huge monument, the height of the dome of St. Paul's in London. In front of the entrance he could see a pair of Toyota four-wheel-drive vehicles and a tent and several people busily carrying boxes and gear. As he approached, he spotted the distinctive form of Hiebermeyer in his shorts and battered cowboy hat, and beside him the even more distinctive form of Jacob Lanowski, inscrutably wearing a lab coat in the desert. Lanowski was hooked up to a contraption that looked like an early one-man rocket platform and was walking it forward like a Zimmer frame. Aysha and Sofia were photographing something among the tumbled masonry fragments in front of the pyramid, and Costas was nowhere to be seen.

Hiebermeyer spotted Jack and bounded up, his face wet with perspiration despite the cool November air. "Good to see you, Jack." He shook hands vigorously. "We haven't got any time to lose. Your equipment is due in half an hour. Who knows when they might revoke our permit."

Jack watched Lanowski. "I won't ask."

"Geophysics. Some kind of sonar contraption. Says it can detect water as well. I haven't seen any result from it yet, but the other stuff he's brought has been pretty good."

As they reached the vehicles, there was a familiar honking and snorting sound behind them, and then a very large tongue wrapped itself around Hiebermeyer's face, making him splutter and push it away. Jack looked around and saw a camel looming between them. Costas was on top, in full Lawrence of Arabia gear but with aviator sunglasses. He peered down at Hiebermeyer. "You know, camels really do seem to like you."

Hiebermeyer wiped his face, grumbling. "Aysha says I'm like a salt lick."

Jack looked up at Costas. "You seem to have overcome your aversion to camels."

"Just needed time to get my desert legs," Costas replied, jumping off and patting the animal affectionately on the neck. "Just as long as you stay away from its rear, everything is all right." The camel emitted a strange blubbery noise, and an indescribable smell filled the air. "Well, almost all right."

They moved away to give the camel some space, and Jack gestured over at the two women. "Here they come now." Lanowski had also spotted them and was struggling out of his contraption. Hiebermeyer waved them towards the pyramid. "Come on. I'll talk as we walk."

"Akhenaten," Costas said, struggling to keep up. "Why we're here."

"Right," Hiebermeyer replied. "First we find that Akhenaten inscription at Troy about the frontier defenses, mentioning Semna. Then you and Jack finally decide to find the sarcophagus of Menkaure. High time, if you ask me. On the back of that, I decide it's time to have a look at this pyramid again. Meanwhile Aysha begins excavating at Semna, and we start to find evidence of Akhenaten's expeditions into the Nubian Desert. I *never* thought there would be any connection between Akhenaten and the pyramids. But I should have known better. He was a consolidator, not an expander. He wanted not to export his vision like the jihadists but to bring it back to the Egyptian people. And not to the Egyptian royal capital where he had grown up—Thebes, a place he had left in disgust, with its priests and falsehoods—but to an older, purer place where the Aten could be seen every day shining through the forms that had been created by his ancestors, that would take on a new meaning under his control. To the pyramids at Giza."

Costas was almost running alongside him to keep up. "But before Jack found that plaque from the Akhenaten depiction with the pyramids on it, what gave you the connection with this place?"

"It's what I *always* tell my students. It's what I told Aysha when she first came to me. Always go back to the original texts. And I don't mean the ancient texts. I mean the books and manuscripts of the first European explorers in Egypt since the eighteenth century. A huge amount has been lost since then: wall paintings destroyed after tombs were opened and exposed to the elements, inscriptions hacked away and looted. The journals of the first archaeologists are a unique resource, often recorded in meticulous detail."

Jack peered at him. "Colonel Vyse?"

Hiebermeyer beamed, stopped, took three worn volumes out of the satchel he was carrying, and laid them side by side on the sand. *"Operations Carried on at the Pyramids of Gizeh in 1837."*

"The book that contained the clue to the sarcophagus of Menkaure," Costas said.

Hiebermeyer nodded enthusiastically. "Jack and I dreamed of discovering that sarcophagus when we were at boarding school. It was something we could both be passionate about, me as a budding Egyptologist, Jack as a diver. And then our Cambridge tutor Professor Dillen gave me this first edition of Vyse's work as a graduation present. I pored over every word of it but then set it aside and returned to it only earlier this year when Jack told me about that tantalizing note about the wreck of the *Beatrice* slipped into the edition of the book he had been shown in England. I knew that something about those books had been niggling at me since I'd started to think about Akhenaten again at Troy, and as soon as I opened them I realized what it was. Vyse hadn't just investigated the pyramids at Giza. He'd travelled extensively up the Nile as far as the great temples at Abu Simbel, and much of the first volume is taken up with an account of his discoveries. What I'd completely forgotten was that he went to Amarna."

"Akhenaten's new capital," Costas murmured.

Hiebermeyer opened one of the volumes to a bookmarked page. "At that date Amarna was scarcely known. After Napoleon had invaded Egypt, his Corps de Savants visited the site in 1799, and Sir John Gardner Wilkinson first surveyed it in 1824. But Vyse gives us a unique record of tomb inscriptions he found there several years later. That was what had been niggling at me. When I read it again, I could barely contain my excitement."

"Spill it, Maurice," Costas said.

Hiebermeyer pushed his glasses up his nose and cleared his throat. "Vyse tells us that the interior consisted of three small apartments and appeared to have been covered with paintings, by then almost entirely defaced." He put a finger on a section of text and read it. "'Processions of prisoners of a red complexion, but with the features of Negroes, were amongst the figures that could be made out; also a solar disk with rays, like that over the entrance, and beneath it the figures of a king, and of a queen dressed in high caps, the whole being surrounded with various hieroglyphic inscriptions.'"

"That sounds very like the imagery in the crocodile temple," Jack said.

"Wait for what comes next," Hiebermeyer said. "'Over the door of this tomb, a solar disk was inscribed, from which rays with hands at their extremities extended as from a common center; two figures, one of them apparently that of a king, were represented as worshippers in a kneeling position; and on each side hieroglyphics and circles, or disks, were introduced.'" He pointed to a small drawing that Vyse had included in the text, showing the image he had just described. "Take a look at this. The lower part of that depiction, below the kneeling worshippers, forms a truncated pyramid, like a large altar. But if you extend the sides upwards, they reach the Aten symbol and you have a complete pyramid. Seeing that, I worked through all the known pyramids of Egypt. By Akhenaten's day, many of the lesser pyramids would already have been crumbling and were a long way from the main administrative centers. So it had to be one of the Giza pyramids; it would have been entirely consistent for Akhenaten to choose one of them to celebrate his new god, in the center of the most sacred ancient site in Egypt. And I doubted whether it would have been one of the two larger ones, which were still associated with the cult of Khufru and his son and would have been far more difficult to modify to

Akhenaten's purpose. So it had to be the pyramid of Menkaure."

"And that was confirmed for you when we found that slab packed inside the sarcophagus showing Akhenaten," Jack said. "Something that Vyse may well have taken from inside the burial chamber too, from a wall sculpture that has since disappeared."

"Yes, but that wasn't my only clue." Hiebermeyer bounded to the edge of the pyramid and put a hand on one of the huge slabs of stone cladding the lower courses of the structure. "You see these?" he said. "Granite, brought all the way from Aswan near the border with Sudan. Each slab weighs at least thirty tons. An incredible feat of transport, bringing them all the way downriver and then dragging them across the desert to this place more than four and a half thousand years ago."

"But the cladding was left incomplete," Costas said.

"The standard view is that the cladding was abandoned at Menkaure's death, but the exterior was then completed in mud brick before the pyramid was dedicated to his father."

Jack peered at Hiebermeyer. "I know that look. You have another theory?"

Hiebermeyer stared at him. "Where else is there granite in this pyramid?"

Jack paused. "If I remember correctly, the core of the pyramid is built of local limestone quarried here on the plateau, except for the cladding and some stone around the burial chamber, which is also Aswan granite."

Hiebermeyer slapped his leg in excitement. "Exactly. And that's where I made my great discovery. While you two and Sofia were in your submersible finding the sarcophagus that once lay inside the pyramid, I was taking Little Joey for a sniff around the antechamber. You'll be astonished at what I found, Jack. *Astonished.*" He turned to Lanowski. "Jacob, can we see the 3-D isometric view?"

Lanowski pulled an iPad from his bag, tapped it, and handed it to Hiebermeyer, who pointed at the image on the screen as they crowded around. "Here you see the entire known complex inside the pyramid—known, that is, until today," he said with a glint in his eye. "Up here in the entrance shaft you can see the triple portcullis, the three massive granite slabs placed there as deterrents to tomb robbers at the time when the chamber was sealed up with Menkaure's mummy inside. Now look at this." He tapped an icon and another image appeared, a close-up photograph of a slab of stone. "Do you recognize this?"

Costas peered closely. "Well, it's granite. Red granite from southern Egypt. And it's got hieroglyphs on it. That's the crocodile, isn't it? We've seen that before. It means pharaoh."

"Good. We'll make an Egyptologist of you yet. And the others?"

Jack stared at them. "That's the cartouche of Akhenaten."

Hiebermeyer beamed at him. "And guess where Little Joey found that? She extended her miniature camera into a crack behind one of the portcullis slabs."

"Good God," murmured Jack. "That cartouche is a standard royal quarry mark, isn't it? That means this was quarried at the time of Akhenaten."

"It means that the granite slabs around the interior of the chamber don't all date to the time of Menkaure after all. It means that over twelve hundred years later, the pharaoh Akhenaten ordered those chambers to be sealed like Fort Knox, using the hardest stone available in Egypt and building a portcullis that would have taken a team of masons months to chisel their way through."

"Do you think this pyramid was reused, that it was Akhenaten's tomb?" Jack said incredulously. "I thought they'd pinned that down to the Valley of the Kings."

"That's only ever been guesswork," Hiebermeyer said. "And I think this was more than just a tomb. Jacob, your results?"

Lanowski cleared his throat. "I brought our deep-penetration radar here, the one we used to find your crocodile temple in the Sudan. The Giza plateau has been crisscrossed numerous times by geophysics teams, but nobody's used equipment with the penetration depth of ours. A run over the desert immediately to the east of the pyramid, in the direction of the Nile, revealed the usual mass of tombs and quarries in the bedrock beneath the sand. But underneath all that was the faint shadow of something else, at about the level of the river. It looked like large rectilinear structures, rock-cut channels or canals."

Hiebermeyer glanced at Jack. "Colonel Vyse noted that in many places the ground seemed hollow. And all he did was bang it with a metal rod. See what I mean? The clues were there in his book, in the first accounts of this place. But Lanowski's data were incredible. Our IT people at the Institute at Alexandria are refining it now to make the image clearer. It looked like a ghostly outline of part of the image we've already seen several times, the one that Akhenaten is shown inspecting in the slab from the sarcophagus you saw underwater, and the maze-like image drawn in Gordon's diary from the slab in the wreck of the *Abbas*."

"A mortuary complex?" Jack said. "A city of the dead?"

"That's what I'd have guessed," Hiebermeyer said. "The ultimate preparation for the afterlife, like King Tut's tomb but on a grand scale, a labyrinth of chambers under the pyramids. But I think it was more than that. I think Akhenaten envisaged the site of the pyramids as the main temple to the Aten. I think this underground place wasn't shrouded in darkness like a lost tomb. I don't think this was a city of the dead. I think this was a city of the living. A city of light."

"How do we get to it?" Costas asked.

"Do you remember the image of the smaller of the three pyramids on Corporal Jones's plaque? It showed a line descending from the center of the pyramid into the ground. As soon as Jack sent me that image from his aunt's house, I was back here like a shot. I realized what something else I'd discovered while I was looking at those granite cartouches was all about. Or rather something else that Little Joey discovered." He pointed to the tent set up beside the parked vehicles. "Follow me." He led them over, glanced at his watch, and then scanned the plateau in the direction of Cairo to the east. Jack knew that he was looking for the telltale pall of dust from an approaching vehicle; they needed it to be their IMU equipment arriving from Alexandria and not a security convoy from the Egyptian authorities.

Hiebermeyer ducked inside the tent and Jack followed, the others coming behind. He gestured towards a laptop open on a table surrounded by a jumble of wiring and control panels. The screen showed a frozen image of an interior space with a dark cylindrical shape in the background and a metallic articulated arm in front. Costas leaned forward, staring. "That's Little Joey!" he exclaimed.

Lanowski beamed at Costas. "I stripped her down so that she could get into the really narrow spaces. The way you'd configured her, she wasn't going anywhere we wanted."

Costas turned his head slowly and stared at him. "You did *what*?"

Lanowski beamed at him again. "This is a previously unknown passageway. I found it using the echo-sounder, and then we unblocked it and sent in the robot."

"It's a shaft that lets sunlight into the antechamber," Hiebermeyer added, his voice tinged with excitement. "It was when I saw the intensity of the beam and its direction that I realized we were onto something new. It shone down onto a slab of granite on the floor, one that Vyse seems to have left undisturbed, distracted perhaps by the discovery of the sarcophagus chamber. Little Joey triggered something and the slab slid aside. It's like a well, with perfectly smooth sides, and the beam of light reflected off a polished surface and then far down into the depths. At the bottom is water, Jack. *Water*. That's why you're here. I believe that whatever lies below us was not only lit up by the light of the Aten, the beam of the sun streaming through the temple, but was also a place of underground canals linked to the Nile and therefore to the Nile's source, the place in the desert far to the south that Akhenaten saw as the birthplace of the sun god."

"We'll need climbing gear for that shaft," Costas murmured.

"We've set up a wooden frame with a fixed belay rope to allow a descent. If you can get down there with diving equipment, we can see what lies at the bottom."

Jack stared at the screen, his mind racing. "What about Little Joey? She can operate underwater, can't she?"

Hiebermeyer coughed. "We've had a slight hitch."

Costas reached over and wiggled the control handle. The image on the screen remained frozen. He narrowed his eyes at Lanowski. "You've got her stuck, haven't you?"

Lanowski opened his arms. "If I hadn't streamlined her, she'd never have gotten into that passageway and we wouldn't be here."

"And she'd never have gotten jammed." Costas stared at the jumble of cable around the computer. "I knew I should never have trusted anyone else with my toys. It's going to take me a while to sort this out. The first thing is to get inside and try to free her physically."

"No time for that now," Hiebermeyer said. "I'm expecting a visit from the Egyptian security chief at any time. As far as they're concerned, we're just doing a visual evaluation of the new passageway. I need to get you and Jack into that pyramid with your equipment before they arrive."

"How did you get the security people to keep their distance until now?" Jack asked.

"I told them that Little Joey found a keg of gunpowder rammed into a crack above the entrance to the antechamber."

"Gunpowder?" Costas said incredulously. He pointed

at the cylindrical shape visible on the screen. "Is that what that is?"

"It's covered in black dust, the exuviae of insects and bats," Hiebermeyer said: "But the wood of the barrel's perfectly preserved."

"Standard early-nineteenth-century excavation technique," Jack said. "That's how Vyse explored the interior of the pyramids. He blew his way through them."

Costas gestured at the vertical gash up the north side of the pyramid, and then at the fragmentary remains of blocks tumbled below on the desert floor. "Looks like someone had a good go at it there."

Hiebermeyer nodded. "You're right, but not using gunpowder. That was the sultan Saladin's son in the twelfth century, at the time of the crusades. He ordered the pyramids to be destroyed, but this was as far as they got before giving up."

"Why destroy the pyramids?" Costas asked.

"Same reason the Taliban ordered the destruction of the Bamiyan Buddhas in Afghanistan," Hiebermeyer replied. "Saladin's son decided that the pyramids were against Islam. There's been a threat from extremist groups in Egypt to carry on where he left off. The Egyptian government is taking it seriously."

Costas looked skeptically at the pyramid. "That would take a small thermonuclear bomb. One for each pyramid."

Hiebermeyer nodded. "It's a well-known fact that extremist groups by now have collected enough fissile materials from the former Soviet Union to make several devices big enough to do this kind of damage. It may seem like an extravagant waste of resources, when they could bomb London or New York, but the analysts I've spoken to think otherwise. Destroy the pyramids and you destroy Egypt's tourist economy. The radioactive fallout over the suburbs of Cairo wouldn't necessarily turn the Egyptian people against the extremists, but with the right rhetoric it might make them feel that they had suffered the wrath of Allah for not having bowed to the cause before now. Egypt is already tottering towards becoming an Islamist state, and this could make it a fundamentalist one. With Egypt gone, the next in line would be Sudan and Somalia, and then Libya and Tunisia and Algeria. There would be a nuclear war in the Middle East, and Israel would be obliterated. The extremists would therefore gain far more for the cause of jihad by blowing up the pyramids than by setting off their bombs in a Western capital."

"Got you," Costas said. "So that explains the new perimeter fence being built around the plateau."

"It also explains why this is the last chance we're ever likely to get for a look inside the pyramid. The whole of the Giza plateau is coming under the jurisdiction of the Department of Defense rather than the Antiquities Authority. From now on, it'll take an act of God to allow anyone to ferret around in places where a bomb might be concealed."

"What about our friend al'Ahmed from the Sudan?" Costas asked. "He seemed to be after the same thing that we are. Jack read me a passage from General Gordon's final journal volume about how the Mahdi as a young man found a temple by the Nile with that plaque of Akhenaten inside, the one that Gordon took and we located in the wreck of the *Abbas*. If al'Ahmed's knowledge of the plaque goes back to the Mahdi, and if his divers manage to get it out of the wreck, he may by now have seen a depiction of the pyramid similar to the one that brought us here."

Jack pursed his lips. "I think the depiction in the crocodile temple and the one in the Nile temple found by the Mahdi were identical. The clue for us was the missing slab from the crocodile temple that showed the pyramid, whereas the other temple depiction may have been intact. If that also showed the clear image of the three temples at Giza, then al'Ahmed would be hot on this trail as well."

Aysha looked at Jack. "Ibrahim flew out from Wadi Halfa this morning to help get your gear together on

Seaquest II for today's dive. You wanted to get him out
of the Sudan, and we did it in the nick of time. The IMU
Lynx did a covert pickup near the border and was chased
by Sudanese police helicopters. I managed to collar him
at Alexandria before I drove here, and he said that as of
yesterday there still had been no diving on the *Abbas*
but a team was being assembled. They needed to find
Sudanese navy divers who were competent with the
IMU equipment they confiscated from you. So I don't
think al'Ahmed is on our trail yet, though it might be
only a matter of time. His family business is based in
Egypt and he can pull strings here as well. It's another
reason why we wanted you and Costas here as quickly
as possible, before someone in the Egyptian government
whom al'Ahmed can bribe decides to pull the rug from
under us."

"But he's not a fundamentalist," Costas said. "He's
not going to want to destroy this place."

"He's an Islamist and would ally himself with extremist groups if it furthers his interests," Aysha said.
"But his focus is the same as ours. He wants to find
Akhenaten's City of Light. And we want to get there
before he does. There may be something there just as
potent for the future of world order as the fate of the
pyramids, and we want to make sure it stays out of his
control. We need to see what lies underneath the pyramid now."

"One question," Costas said. "What about that keg
of gunpowder?"

"I managed to uncoil the fuse, which is hanging down
into the antechamber. You can still smell the sulphur
on it."

"Ah," said Lanowski, and poked around in his lab
coat pocket, producing a cheap orange lighter. He tested
it and threw it to Costas. "I bought this off a little boy
at the entrance to the site. I felt sorry for him. I *knew* it
would have a use."

Costas lit it and stared at the flame. "What exactly are
you suggesting, Jacob?"

"Well, Colonel Vyse did pretty well with it, didn't he? Found a lot of stuff. Maybe he was onto something in that passageway."

Costas took his thumb off the lighter, thought for a moment, and slowly nodded. "I'd have to get Little Joey out first, of course. What do you think, Jack?"

Jack glanced at Sofia. "I don't expect anyone's mentioned it to you. Put Costas anywhere within sniffing distance of explosives and he's gone."

Sofia marched up to Costas, took the lighter, and tossed it back to Lanowski. "I have a better idea," she said. "Why don't you use this to light the barbecue we're going to have on the beach when this is all over. The party that Jack always promises Costas."

"The party that never happens," Costas said glumly. "Because there's always some other fabulous treasure to discover."

Two Range Rovers came barrelling down the track towards them in a cloud of dust and pulled to a halt at the end of the walkway into the pyramid. Jack saw Ibrahim get out of the first vehicle and an IMU helicopter crewman he recognized from *Seaquest II* exit the other. He put his hands on his hips and turned to the others, a steely look in his eyes. "Okay," he said. "The gear's arrived. Let's get this show on the road."

Chapter 27

"Jack! Hold tight!"

A huge thud resounded through the burial chamber of the pyramid, shaking the condensation off the stone walls of the shaft where Jack was suspended precariously on a rope. He spun crazily around, kicking off the walls to stop himself from crashing into them, holding on to the rope that tethered him to the wooden frame they had set up over the top of the shaft. He raised the visor of his helmet and looked up, tasting the moisture in the air and seeing the wavering beam of Costas's headlamp almost twenty meters above him. "What the hell was that?" he yelled, his voice booming up the shaft.

"It was in the entrance tunnel," Costas called down. "A giant stone slab dropped into it about five meters up from the burial chamber. It was deliberate, an ancient booby trap. One of those devices to deter tomb robbers. You must have triggered something on the way down."

Jack tried to slow his swinging as he looked at the curious arrangement of stone slabs about five meters above him that stuck out of the sides of the shaft like the spokes of a wheel, leaving an aperture in the center just big enough for him to drop through. He remembered feeling a slight give in the stones as he stood on them. He had studied the elaborate traps that the pyramid builders had set around the burial chambers; it was conceivable that those stones had triggered an alignment in the masonry that caused the slab to drop. But this trap was not simply to deter tomb robbers. He stared down, his headlamp beam reflecting off the smooth walls that dropped to a shimmering pool of water some ten meters below. It was to protect access to something infinitely more valuable, to a treasure that made the adrenaline course through Jack as it did when he knew he was on the brink of a great discovery.

He stared back up. "So we're trapped?" he yelled.

"You got it. That slab must weigh ten tons. And the light shaft above the chamber isn't even wide enough to let in a pigeon."

"At least nobody can follow us inside."

"That's great, Jack. Really reassuring. Makes spending the rest of eternity entombed like a mummified pharaoh really worthwhile."

"Keep focused," Jack shouted back. "We're doing what we came here to do. This shaft must lead to some other access point."

He looked down again, searching for the glow from the chemical light stick he had dropped into the water at the bottom of the shaft, but it was gone. He pulled another out of the thigh pocket on his e-suit, cracked it, and dropped it, watching the green glow tumble down and then splash into the water, revealing the shimmering sides of the shaft and then also disappearing to somewhere far deeper. He looked at the electronic display inside his helmet, checking that the air supply in the streamlined console on his back was still full, and monitoring the temperature inside his suit. He had told Costas to focus, but he was the one who needed to focus more, and Costas knew it. The intercom had failed to work inside the shaft, and when he had shut his visor he had been sealed off completely. He realized how much he had come to rely on Costas beside him, his companion for more than twenty years on countless dives into caves and mine shafts and other enclosed spaces. But this time Jack would have to confront his greatest fear on his own, his fear of being closed in, of finding no way out.

He felt his heart pound and his breathing quicken, and he stared down again into the water. There was nothing visible yet, nothing to confirm his hunch. All he had to go on was instinct born of years of luck and intuition. He had to summon all his determination and keep going down the shaft until he knew the truth. He concentrated on that objective as he looked down, feeling the belay clamp on his harness, jigging his body up and down to test his weight against the rope. As his beam played on the surface of the water, he saw something bubble up like a ghostly exhalation from three thousand years before, a waft that made his nostrils tingle. It was a familiar odor, a recent one, but he could not pin it down.

Costas shouted from above. "You smell that?"

"It's come up through the water," Jack yelled back. "Must be some kind of natural gas, methane maybe. We should use our breathing gear."

"It smells just like the Nile," Costas yelled back.

Jack remembered. *Of course.* It was the distinctive smell of the Nile through Cairo, a river whose manmade canals had once lapped the pyramids but was now almost three kilometers distant. He suddenly remembered the story of the wild man who had appeared out of nowhere in the streets of Cairo in the 1890s, with hair and a beard down to his chest like a holy man, showing everyone who would listen to him a Royal Engineers cap badge and a corporal's chevrons, claiming that he had been a British soldier captured by the Mahdi; he said that he had escaped and come to Cairo with knowledge of an ancient underground city beneath the modern streets but had become trapped there and survived for years eating scraps of ancient mummies and rats and fish from the river. Could it be true? Jack thought hard: *fish from the river*. Could the water below be an ancient channel from the Nile? If so, it was their way out. And it was the way to a discovery that would astonish the world.

He shouted up the shaft. "Oh, by the way. My aunt Margaret has a book for you. A copy of Malory's *Morte d'Arthur*."

"I know," Costas bellowed down. "Rebecca gave it to me."

"You didn't need to be worried, you know. About me, I mean. But I appreciate it."

"It's what friends are for."

Jack looked down, dazzled by the glare. "I'm not so sure now, though."

"What do you mean?"

"I mean about the quest. This looks like it might be a one-way ticket."

"Come on, Jack. It can't be as bad as that crocodile pool. That was the entrance to the underworld. This is the City of Light. And you're about to go diving again. You love it."

Jack looked down, feeling his heart race with excitement. It was true. He loved it. He looked up at Costas. "Okay. I'm going in. Open the slab to let the light in."

"Close your visor," Costas boomed back. "It could be dazzling. Good to go?"

"Good to go. See you on the other side."

"You better."

Jack pulled down his visor and locked it shut and then activated the polarizing filter to reduce the brightness. On the way down he had seen a series of highly polished obsidian slabs built into the wall at alternating heights, and Costas had realized that one of the narrow sunlight shafts built into the side of the pyramid was angled into the burial chamber such that the light would strike the upper panel and reflect down to the pool below. A stone cover over the first panel pivoted back to expose it, but they had decided not to experiment in case the light dazzled Jack on his way down. But now, with only a few meters to go, it was time.

Jack heard the scraping of the stone cover being

moved. Then it was as if he were staring into the flash of a camera, shocked and dazzled. The light from the sun was magnified by the panels and seemed to burn like fire at each stage down the shaft until it hit the water. The pool acted like a lens, focusing the light down on another mirror far underwater that reflected off into the unknown, in the direction of the Nile.

Jack suddenly realized what had happened. He was seeing what Akhenaten had seen, the light of the Aten; he was bathed in it, as Akhenaten had been. He remembered all the images that had brought him here, the clues in the carvings, the extraordinary image of the pharaoh and the labyrinth of channels and tunnels, the arms of the Aten spreading over it all. Akhenaten had not just built a new capital city at Amarna beside the Nile; he had come here, to the heart of Egypt, to the pyramids of Giza, to a place that all his energy and the light from the Aten would illuminate, a place where the wisdom of the ages and the knowledge of the world would be under his aegis, where he would reign forever as one with the Aten, as king of kings.

There was a sudden jolt. The radiating slabs of rock above had snapped together, cutting Jack off from Costas and severing the rope. He fell, splayed out and spinning, managing to right himself so that he was falling feet first, and then he hit the water and fell far under, deep into another world, his eyes shut.

When he opened them again, he knew that he was about to make the greatest discovery of his career, one that could change the course of history.

He had found Akhenaten's City of Light.

Author's Note

MENKAURE AND AKHENATEN

The Gordon relief expedition has always fascinated me because of my own family connection with the story, outlined below, but I also have a long-standing interest in the archaeological backdrop to this novel. I first became intrigued by the story of the brig *Beatrice* while researching Greek and Roman antiquities lost during shipment to Britain in the eighteenth and early nineteenth centuries, when the risk of wreck for sailing ships was high. One artifact that never made it was the sarcophagus of the fourth dynasty pharaoh Menkaure, taken in 1837 from his pyramid by British colonel Howard Vyse and loaded on board the *Beatrice* at Alexandria, never to be seen again. Apart from the fictional marginal note in Hiebermeyer's copy of Vyse's *Operations Carried on at the Pyramids of Gizeh in 1837* (London, 1840), the evidence for the *Beatrice* discussed in Chapter 1 is genuine, including her previous use in trade to Canada as revealed in Lloyd's *Register*. An unpublished watercolor of her in Smyrna Harbor, Turkey, painted in 1832 by Raffaele Corsini, appears on my website. The wreck and the sarcophagus remain undiscovered, though there are indications that she may have foundered close to the location off Spain of the fictional excavation in Chapter 1.

* * *

It is not known whether Colonel Vyse had the sarcophagus of Menkaure packed full of other artifacts, and the plaque of Akhenaten discovered by Jack and Costas is fictional. Akhenaten for me is the most intriguing of all the pharaohs of Egypt for having "broken the mold"— albeit only for his lifetime—in a culture that resisted change and intellectual development for so long. His conversion to the one God, the Aten, and his likely identification as the pharaoh of the Moses story in the Old Testament, have made him the subject of extensive speculation and controversy, not least by Sigmund Freud in *Moses and Monotheism* (London, 1939). The unusual physiognomy suggested in Akhenaten's images may have set him apart as a child and caused him to be derided, just as the future emperor Claudius was to be in Rome; it is intriguing to speculate whether this was a factor behind his rejection of the world of his upbringing. The relief carvings of him with his beautiful wife Nefertiti and their children are among the most human of all pharaonic portraits, suggesting that his revelation of the Aten swept away not only the old gods and priests but the unhappiness that he might have experienced in his youth.

Very little is known about the early life of Akhenaten, and the idea that he made a secret expedition to the Nubian Desert to seek revelation is fictional. However, this idea is appealing on several counts: in the desert he would have been able to leave behind the gods and priests of the old religion whose existence clearly troubled him, and he may also have been visiting a place he saw as his ancestral homeland. At Buhen and Amada, two forts established in Upper Nubia centuries earlier during the Middle Kingdom, inscriptions show that in year 12 of Akhenaten's reign an expedition was sent south into Nubia for an unknown purpose (Amada Stela CG 41806). What is certain is that two temple towns were constructed beside the Nile in Upper Nubia during his reign, at Kawa and Sesebi. Both were focused on temples to the Aten, and both contained tantalizing hints of the significance to Akhenaten of the southern desert: at Sesebi the finds include a unique depiction of the Aten as "Lord of Nubia," and the ancient name for Kawa, Gem(pa)-aten, means "the Aten is discovered."

The possibility that the year 12 expedition may have been sent to find gold is highlighted by the discovery of evidence for gold processing at Sesebi, the basis for Hiebermeyer's fictional discovery near Semna in Chapter 6. The Middle Kingdom forts at Semna are among the best-known Egyptian remains in Sudan, not least for their dramatic location above the Great Gate of the second cataract, now submerged as a result of the rise in the level of the Nile caused by the Aswan Dam. A vivid firsthand account of Semna as it once appeared is provided by Colonel William Francis Yates in *Campaign of the Cataracts: Being a Personal Narrative of the Great Nile Expedition of 1884 to 1885* (London, 1887): it was a "wild and lonely spot," where "from the ruin-crowned cliff on the east bank . . . one sees only the serrated ridges and calcined peaks of a savage solitude." Yates describes the archaeological remains: on the "windswept summits of steep impending cliffs . . . lie two ruined temples [*sic*]; the massive but crumbling walls of a fortress crowns the whole crest of the cliff on the east side." My depiction of the geology and river topography is derived from fieldwork carried out in 1902 by Dr. John Ball (*Quarterly Journal of the Geological Society* 59:1, 1903), as well as during excavations at Semna carried out from the 1920s to the final project in the 1960s before the sites were inundated.

In my novel I have imagined a lowering of the level of the dammed water that has allowed some of the upper-plateau ruins to be revealed. The excavations to the 1960s showed that Semna had been the hub of a complex of river forts built in the nineteenth and eighteenth centuries BC, when the pharaoh Semnosret I and his successors attempted to expand into Nubia; the finds complemented the "Semna Despatches," an archive found in Thebes in 1896, to which the papyrus dispatch in Chapter 6 is a fictional addition. The cult of Sobek, the crocodile god, is particularly associated with the pharaohs of those dynasties, and large crocodiles may have been more prevalent in the south where there had been less hunting—some perhaps even the size of the behemoth in *A Frightful Incident*, a print from an account of David Livingstone's explorations that can be seen on my website. A good deal is known of the cult from the temples at Arsinoe—known to the Greeks as Crocodilopolis—and Kom Ombo, as well as from crocodile mummies, several of which have recently been subjected to CT scans at the Stanford School of Medicine in California. The submerged temple to Sobek in this novel is fictional but is in a plausible location; Semna was a perilous point in the river where the risk of crocodile attack might have been high, so it would have been a suitable place for acts of propitiation, even sacrifice. My idea of a submerged temple was inspired by the project in the 1960s to raise the Abu Simbel temple facade to its present location beside Lake Nasser, leaving the inner chambers deeply submerged within the cliff face where only divers can access them today.

THE GORDON RELIEF EXPEDITION

In the autumn of 1884, the world was gripped by one of the high dramas of the Victorian age, the plight of General Gordon in Khartoum and the progress of the expedition sent by the British to rescue him. Each week the *Illustrated London News* published beautifully detailed prints based on sketches sent by correspondents in the field, allowing readers to follow the expedition mile by mile as it struggled south through Sudan against the flow of the Nile. As a boy, I was given a bound annual volume of the *Illustrated London News* for that year by my grandfather, and I loved poring over those pictures: they seemed to show the ultimate imperial adventure. Readers saw the empire at its best: soldiers and sailors, Canadian voyageurs and West African boatmen, all banded together in harmonious resolve, for a cause that could not be more noble. And when the action shifted from the Nile to the desert, the illustrations showed thrilling scenes of battle, of bayonet against spear, of British resolve in the face of desperate savagery. By the time the stalwart few dispatched in the river steamers had fought their way up to Khartoum, the fact that they were too late was almost secondary. In that peculiarly British way, the failure itself became heroic, the more so after Gordon was elevated to saintly status for which martyrdom was almost a necessity. Generations of future soldiers could dream of fighting against the odds to rescue their own Gordons yet worship the image of a man who had chosen to die honorably, revolver and sword in hand, grimly intent on taking as many of the enemy with him as he could, rather than make an easy escape and abandon the women and children he had sworn to protect.

This picture, of course, is only one take on these extraordinary events, and there is another, darker version, full of ambiguity and apparent contradiction. As I moved beyond my boyhood fascination and went on to study classical antiquity, I was much influenced by the "big man" theory, in which domineering personalities provide the main driving force in history. Applying this prism to the events of 1884–1885, against a backdrop of world events that would seem to have their own momentum—the resurgence of Islamic jihad, and the crystallisation of power politics in Europe that would eventually lead to the First World War—it is the extraordinary personalities that stand out, some with motivations far removed from the heroic ideal. The Victorian military, especially the more cerebral branches such as the Royal Engineers, could attract men of ambition, intellect, and idiosyncrasy who were often given free rein in the field. The personalities in this story could not have been greater: Gordon himself, inscrutable and fascinating, with a messianic charisma that gripped the world during those months; Muhammad Ahmad, the self-styled Mahdi (Chosen One), a former boatbuilder and Sufi, who held more men under his sway than any European ruler; Lord Wolseley, the outstanding British general of his day, a fastidious stickler for detail and control; and men of lesser rank but expansive personality, including the flamboyant Colonel Fred Burnaby, arguably the greatest adventurer of the late Victorian age, and Major Herbert Kitchener of the Royal Engineers, future nemesis of the Mahdist revolt and commander in chief who would lead the British army into the bloodbath of the First World War.

Whether Gordon himself in the end really wanted to be rescued and whether those who were sent to rescue him ever really intended to do so are questions not easily answered. Looming in the background are the figures of Queen Victoria, ardent supporter of Gordon and spokeswoman for the vox populi, and Prime Minister William Ewart Gladstone, a man who professed not to be able to abide Gordon, despite their shared fascination with the ancient history of Palestine and the lands of the Bible. Gladstone has appeared elsewhere in my fiction, in *The Mask of Troy*, where he sees the fall of Troy as a dark portent of modern times yet where his aversion to war is tinged by realism. Once it had become clear that Gordon could not, or would not, be rescued, Gladstone may have been obliged to exercise a directive of appalling necessity in order to ensure that he was not captured; the image of Gordon in chains would have enraged public opinion and severely damaged British prestige at a time when international brinksmanship was the order of the day. Any sign of weakness might have led Russia to order the invasion of British India, as could have happened when the Russians clashed with the Afghans in the "Panjdeh incident" of March 1885, a mere matter of weeks after the fall of Khartoum. Gordon the martyr was perhaps a weight that Gladstone could more easily have borne than Gordon the pitiful captive—or, worse still, Gordon the convert to Islam, driven to shocking apostasy by government indifference to the plight of his beloved Sudanese, standing alongside the Mahdi. If these were indeed Gladstone's calculations, then events were to bear him out, conflict with Russia being avoided and British prestige left intact, though the great European war he most feared was forestalled by only a few decades, and the final destruction of the Mahdist revolt by Kitchener at Omdurman in 1898 did little to extinguish the flame of jihad kindled in the desert in the 1880s that has become such a dominating threat to world peace today.

The basis for the account in this novel of the Gordon relief expedition includes unpublished material related to my great-great-grandfather, Colonel Walter Andrew Gale, Royal Engineers (RE), who was a personal friend of Lord Kitchener and in charge of the Gordon Relics Committee while he was secretary of the RE Institute from 1889 to 1894. His *Report of the Gordon Relics Committee* (1894) is in the RE Library at Chatham, where the museum contains a fascinating collection of Gordon memorabilia that provided much initial inspiration for this story. Among published sources, I have relied where possible on firsthand accounts, notably Colonel Sir Charles Wilson's *From Korti to Khartoum* (1885), Colonel William Francis Butler's *The Campaign of the Cataracts* (1887), and Lieutenant Colonel E. W. C. Sandes's *The Royal Engineers in Egypt and the Sudan* (1937), the last incorporating eyewitness records of RE officers present during the campaign.

Many contemporary accounts of Gordon are overtly hagiographical, extolling both his heroic attributes and his religious zeal; the same applies to many biographies of Lord Kitchener. I have sought to understand both men by reading their own writings and correspondence, in the case of Kitchener his contributions to the multi-volume *Survey of Western Palestine,* published in 1881–1885 when he was in his early thirties, as well as accounts from 1884–1885 that reveal a man of extraordinary energy and presence, a fearless adventurer quite distinct from the later image of the First World War field marshal so fixed in popular memory.

The essential source for Gordon is the compendious diary he wrote while besieged at Khartoum—unfortunately not including anything he might have written in his final days—published in 1885 as *The Journals of Major-General C. G. Gordon, CB, at Kartoum, printed from the original mss;* something of his religious vision is also revealed in the account of his time in Jerusalem, *Reflections in Palestine, 1883,* published after Gordon was already in Khartoum and possibly never seen by him.

Ironically, given the mystique that was built up around the man, his journals allow a more intimate, detailed picture of Gordon than is possible for any other of the main characters in this story. The tenor is overwhelmingly practical, not mystical; his daily concerns included the food supply, the likely arrival of the relief expedition, and the other professional checklists of a besieged garrison commander, including ammunition expended, a tally of incoming fire from the Mahdist forces, and lists of wounded and killed. His emphatic instructions to edit out extraneous material suggest that he would have been appalled by the notes that his admirers had seen fit to include in *Reflections in Palestine.* Several of the incidents he recounts in the fictional encounter with Mayne come from his journal, including the faulty ammunition in a Remington rifle that nearly blinded him (December 12) and his reflection on Abraham Lincoln and slavery (23 November) when he incorrectly identified18 December as the date in 1862 of Lincoln's proclamation. In creating dialogue, I have used words and phrases from the journal to represent his use of language, including his reference to the Mahdist forces as "Arabs," as was the case for most of the British officer accounts of the campaign, including that of Colonel Butler.

Gordon's last journal entry, quoted at the front of this novel, has an air of finality about it, like Scott's final entry from the Antarctic. Yet it was written on December 14 when he still had more than five weeks to live, and the assumption has to be that he continued to keep a journal to the end. Whether or not he would have chosen to reflect on his archaeological and ethnographic collections is unknown. However, he had shown much interest in these matters years earlier when he had even invited Heinrich Schliemann to join him; and several of his appointees to administrative and army positions in the Sudan, including the American adventurer Charles Chaillé-Long, had something of the treasure hunter about them. It may never be possible truly to know what Prime Minister Gladstone thought of Gordon, but it is conceivable that their shared fascination with biblical history and archaeology would in private have transcended the gulf that had appeared between them publicly, one that widened after Gordon's death when Gladstone was vilified for failing to order a rescue expedition in time.

Another pivotal character in this story is Sir Charles Wilson, who was blamed by Wolseley for failing to reach Gordon in time after Wilson was obliged to take over the desert column when its commander, Brigadier General Herbert Stewart, was mortally wounded in the battle that followed Abu Klea. Wilson's own published book, noted above, rebutting the criticisms of Wolseley, is the best eyewitness account of the final stages of the campaign; much personal correspondence and writing related to his wider career is found in Colonel Sir Charles Watson's *The Life of Major-General Sir Charles Wilson*, published by the Royal Engineers in 1909. The breadth of Wilson's activities, as a mapmaker, geographer, and intelligence officer, from North America to Asia Minor and the Sudan, make him one of the great unsung achievers of the Victorian age, and it is fascinating to speculate that his role as founder of the War Office Intelligence Department—the antecedent of the modern Secret Intelligence Service—might have included the sanctioning of a "mandate to kill" that has become such an ingrained part of our view of covert intelligence activities since the novels of Ian Fleming were first published.

Colonel William Francis Butler describes a long-range "rifle duel" between his men and the Arabs near Kirbekan, the basis for my fictional action between Major Mayne and the Mahdist sharpshooter in Chapter 8. His description of the cataracts is invaluable because much of the atmosphere of the place was lost after the Aswan Dam was constructed, and today it requires some imagination to see the place as it would have been in pharaonic times or during the days in 1884 when the Gordon relief expedition struggled against the Nile towards Khartoum. A fascinating recent project to study the length of the railway built by the Royal Engineers to supply that expedition shows how much detritus remains in the desert, much of it in a remarkable state of preservation: spent ammunition casings, tins and tobacco packaging, the remains of camps and supply dumps, and places where burials undoubtedly exist, swept over and lost beneath the shifting sands of the desert. These investigations are a new kind of archaeology, giving a vivid basis for understanding the challenges of ancient campaigns into the desert as well as a fresh perspective on precisely what went on during those fateful months leading up to the fall of Khartoum in January 1885.

The description of the battle of Abu Klea in Chapter 11 is inspired by eyewitness accounts, including that of Colonel Sir Charles Wilson. Some 1,400 British troops

confronted at least 11,000 dervishes; in ten minutes of
ferocious fighting more than a thousand dervishes were
killed, at a cost of 81 British killed and 121 wounded.
The battle became one of the most famous in military
history, the last time the British fought in a square, in a
conflict immortalized by Rudyard Kipling in his 1890
poem "Fuzzy-Wuzzy":

> So 'ere's to you, Fuzzy-Wuzzy, at your 'ome in the
>   Soudan;
> You're a pore benighted 'eathen but a first-class
>   fightin' man . . .
> We sloshed you with Martinis, an' it wasn't 'ardly
>   fair;
> But for all the odds agin' you, Fuzzy-Wuz, you
>   broke the square.

(Along with "dervish," the British soldiers commonly
referred to their Sudanese enemy as "Fuzzy-Wuzzy," a
term originally coined for the wild-haired Beja of the
Red Sea coast who were the first of the Sudanese the
British fought in pitched battles, in early 1884, when
they did actually break a square.)

One of the casualties at Abu Klea was Colonel Fred
Burnaby, who was discovered by an officer lying against
a rock surrounded by dead dervishes, a spear having
"inflicted a terrible wound on the side of his neck and
throat," and his skull "cleft by a blow from a two-
handed sword." The expression that I have Burnaby
using, that he was "bowled over a terrible crumpler,"
comes from an eyewitness of that day, Count Albert
Gleichen, a Grenadiers officer serving with the Camel
Corps, who used it to describe the death of a dervish
(Gleichen, A., *With the Camel Corps on the Nile*, London 1889, p. 135). The young soldier who had first seen
Burnaby and called the officer over wondered why "the
bravest man in England" should be dying without suc-
cor; his last words as the boy propped him up were supposedly "look after yourself." Burnaby had ridden out

of the square to help bring skirmishers back in, an act of near-suicidal courage that cost him his life; it was the type of act for which the Victoria Cross was invented, and perhaps he would have been awarded it had his commanding officer, Brigadier General Stewart, and not himself been fatally wounded two days later, before having the time to write dispatches and make recommendations for the fight at Abu Klea. Burnaby died as he had lived, larger than life, yet he should be remembered as much for his achievements as an intelligence officer and adventurer, revealed in his marvellous book *On Horseback through Asia Minor* (1878), still in print and widely read today.

There is no single authoritative eyewitness account of the death of Gordon. One of the best known of many fanciful images, *General Gordon's Last Stand*, by George William Joy (1893), showing Gordon waiting coolly at the top of the stairs, revolver in hand, as the dervish spearmen approach him from below, probably contains elements of the truth; an account by Gordon's servant Orfali suggests that Gordon and his Sudanese bodyguards fought to the end, and Gordon personally accounted for several of the enemy. What does seem certain is that he was decapitated and his head taken to the Mahdi, where it was seen by his captive, the Austrian officer Rudolf von Slatin, a friend of Gordon and future inspector general of the Sudan, whose box of Gordon relics resides in the Royal Engineers Museum. "A brave soldier, who fell at his post. Happy is he to have fallen. His sufferings are over," von Slatin famously told his captors. It was von Slatin's account of the treatment of Gordon's body that hardened Kitchener's resolve to wreak the terrible vengeance he eventually inflicted on the dervish army at Omdurman thirteen years later, including the desecration of the Mahdi's tomb.

Sir Charles Wilson's operative, Major Edward Mayne, is fictional, though he bears the surname of an Anglo-Irish family who figured in the Army List—another Mayne appears in the Second World War in my novel *The Mask of Troy*—and I have based his career and interests closely on Royal Engineers officers of the period. The same is true for his subordinate at the cataract, the fictional Lieutenant Tanner, who is killed along with General Earle in the battle that the river column was eventually forced to fight at Kirbekan, when more than two thousand dervishes were killed for the loss of some eighty British soldiers. In my fiction, Mayne's servant, Corporal Jones, missed the battle because he had been reassigned to the 8th Railway Company, RE, building the line south of Korti; he also appears in my novel *The Tiger Warrior* in the 1879 Rampa Rebellion in India as Sergeant Jones (having subsequently been reduced in rank for misdemeanor) and is inspired in part by a real-life soldier from that railway company, 17818 Sapper M. Knight, whose Khedive's Star and Egypt medal with the clasp "The Nile 1884–85" are illustrated on my website.

Colonel William Francis Butler writes of his astonishment and pleasure at seeing a Canadian birch-bark canoe on the Nile above the second cataract; it was paddled by William Prince, "Chief of the Swampy Indians," whom Butler had last met fourteen years before during the Red River expedition in Canada, a man "grown more massive of frame . . . but still keen of eye and steady of hand as when I last saw him standing bowman in a bark canoe among the whirling waters whose echoes were lost in the endless pine woods of the great Lone Land."

One of the most extraordinary aspects of the relief expedition was the employment of Mohawk Indians from Canada to help navigate the whaleboats that were supposed to take British troops on to Khartoum. As well as West African "Kroomen"—boatmen from the Kroo (Kru) tribe, admired by Wolseley when he led his campaign against the Ashanti in 1873—the expedition included 400 Canadian voyageurs, drawn from the community of backwoodsmen and fur traders who had helped Wolseley's Red River expedition in Canada in 1870. The elite among them were some sixty Mohawk men from the Ottawa valley, Iroquoian speakers, many with French blood, who were descendants of the feared Iroquois allies of the British in the wars against America. By the mid-nineteenth century they specialized in guiding rafts of logs down the Ottawa River and would have been familiar to the British army engineers and their families based in Ottawa to build and maintain the Rideau Canal, part of a communication and supply network designed to impede American attack. In my novel, Major Ormerod, second in command of the contingent, as well as Mayne's companion Charrière, are both fictional but are inspired by real-life characters; several of the Mohawks on the Nile were veterans of the Red River expedition, and at least one had also served in the Union Army in the American Civil War. The voyageur contingent was a civilian force and suffered no battle casualties—of the sixteen deaths, six were drownings in the Nile, the rest from illness—though it provided a precedent for the dispatch of Canadian volunteers to the Boer War and the First World War, when soldiers of Iroquois and other aboriginal descent had a high reputation as scouts and snipers and many were killed in action.

As an archaeologist, I have always been fascinated by the reverence given to relics of Gordon after his death, when he was promoted in popular imagination to something akin to sainthood—a transformation ironically possible only through his death but that was undoubtedly encouraged by those who wished to deflect public attention from their failure to rescue him. His elevation had begun while he was still alive and burgeoned once he was in Khartoum. His *Reflections in Palestine*, compiled from his notes "with anxious care by more than one of the writer's friends," shows an almost mystical reverence towards his every word, with every inchoate thought they could find put into print; Gordon the saint might have looked upon their efforts with indulgence, but it is hard to believe that Gordon the Royal Engineer would have approved. Afterwards his admirers hunted everywhere for relics, some of them of dubious authenticity. The Royal Engineers Museum contains a fragment of the wooden staircase where he was thought to have died, said to have been removed from the palace at Khartoum when it was demolished in 1898; any doubts about its authenticity would be dispelled in the mind of the believer by the silver case topped with a cross that holds it, just like a medieval reliquary. More bizarrely, the museum houses a box said to have come from Rudolf von Slatin, containing among other things one of Gordon's teeth, his last match and pencil, and the corpse of a fly said to have walked on his nose!

The Gordon Relics Committee was concerned not with these kinds of relics but with the important collection of ethnographic, historic, and archaeological artifacts that Gordon amassed during his various postings, including much material from the Sudan. A remarkable display of this material in the Royal Engineers Museum at Chatham was one of the inspirations for this novel. Gordon had a considerable interest in archaeology, in common with many of his fellow engineer officers— men who by vocation were concerned with structures and artifacts—and like many of them he was a devout though idiosyncratic Christian, fascinated by the Holy Land and the discoveries being made there and in surrounding lands touched on by the Bible. Two of the engineers on the Gordon relief expedition, Kitchener and Wilson, were among the foremost field archaeologists of the nineteenth century, responsible for surveys in Palestine that remain the basis for archaeological knowledge of the Holy Land today. They were also close friends of Gordon's, and as the senior intelligence officers of the relief expedition were deeply implicated in everything that went on. All three men would have shared a fascination with the archaeology of Egypt and the desert to the south because of its biblical connections; it is possible to imagine them joining together on the kind of collective endeavor envisaged in this novel, with Gordon's search for artifacts allied to his own yearning for the personal revelation in the desert that he might have imagined inspiring Akhenaten as well as the Mahdi.

The events of 1884–85 had a dramatic impact on archaeology in Egypt. The war with the Mahdi and the rise of jihad in the Sudan in the 1880s have much modern resonance, but the fascination with this period today stems not only from the grip that the Gordon relief expedition held over the nation—indeed, the world—at that time but also from the fact that many in Britain today have ancestors who served in Egypt and the Sudan or visited during the early years of British rule. My own maternal great-grandfather went to Egypt with the 6th Dragoon Guards in 1882, arriving shortly after the battle of Tel el-Kebir; my daughter's maternal great-great-grandfather was a civil engineer who worked on the first Aswan Dam in the 1890s, when he lived with his family in Cairo. Aside from those who were stationed in Egypt, the opening in 1867 of the Suez Canal, the "Gateway to India" and the primary motivation for British interest in Egypt, meant that the thousands travelling to and from India who had previously gone via the Cape of Good Hope now went past Egypt, and a stopover in Cairo to see the pyramids, and Luxor became as obligatory as the sites of Greece and Rome had been to the "Grand Tourists" of a century before. The fascination today with ancient Egypt stems from the accessibility of its monuments after the British takeover, not only to wealthy travellers but also to soldiers and their families going to and from India. From that perspective, the war with the Mahdi and his successors—drawing the British ever further into involvement with Egypt and the Sudan—is closely interlinked with the rise of Egyptology as a discipline and the development of archaeological investigations that eventually led to fabulous discoveries such as Tutankhamen's tomb.

In the 1880s, the more adventurous tourists could travel by boat on the Nile to Akhenaten's capital at Amarna and the temple at Abu Simbel, its original site now submerged deep beneath the waters of Lake Nasser just north of the border with Sudan. Few ventured farther south into the Nubian Desert, where the Aswan Dam has greatly changed the appearance of the Nile today, inundating the cataracts that proved such an obstacle to Wolseley's expedition in 1884. The surrounding desert remains much as it was then; at the battlefield of Abu Klea, the British zariba can still be traced, and it is possible to find the odd Martini-Henry cartridge, but it is a place like others of much greater antiquity in the desert, from the time of the pharaohs and even earlier, where the wind and the scorching sun seem to have reduced evidence of human endeavor to the same dusty footprint.

Muhammad Ahmad, the Mahdi, died in the same fateful year as Gordon, whether by illness or by poison is uncertain. The possibility that his assassination was ordered by the British cannot be ruled out; Kitchener's intelligence network and loyal Ababda followers could have found a way to infiltrate his camp. Kitchener had sworn to avenge Gordon, to take a dervish life for every hair on Gordon's head, a promise amply fulfilled in 1898 when he led his army against the Mahdi's successor at the battle of Omdurman, just outside Khartoum; but his desecration of the Mahdi's tomb earned the opprobrium of Queen Victoria herself and helped to fuel a new generation of jihadists.

Today at Khartoum there is little left that was visible in 1885, with the palace being a more recent structure and the changing course of the Nile having altered the appearance of the foreshore and Tutti Island. However, the palace was built on the site of the original, and it is possible to look out on it from the far shore of the Blue Nile, as my character Mayne does, from the site where an abandoned fort is marked on contemporary maps. The disposition of the Mahdi's forces and the appearance of Khartoum in its final days are documented by eyewitness accounts, including that of Colonel Wilson, who came within sight of the palace in the steamer *Bordein* the day after Gordon died.

Outside the city at Omdurman, the tomb of the Mahdi has been restored; Omdurman is also the site of one of the few surviving relics in Sudan of the 1884–1885 campaign: the hull of the *Bordein,* saved from scrapping in 2010 and now on display. The site where the *Abbas* was wrecked, the basis for the dive in this novel, has never been investigated underwater, though the account of guns and equipment being thrown overboard suggests that artifacts must still exist on the bed of the Nile; the site was visited by Colonel William Francis Butler several months after the wrecking, when he saw much material strewn about. My inspiration for its appearance comes from a wreck of similar size, date, and depth that I have dived on frequently in Canada, in a freshwater environment that would have preserved timber and metal in a way similar to the Nile. You can see a film of me diving at night on that wreck, and another of me shooting a Martini-Henry rifle, as well as images of medals, contemporary illustrations of the Nile campaign, and portraits of the main historical characters involved, on my website www.davidgibbins.com.

The quotes at the front of the book, and the quote on the Leviathan in Chapter 6, are derived from an 1885 edition of the King James version of the Bible; at the front of the book and in Chapters 14 and 21 (the letter from the Mahdi) from *The Journals of Major-General*

C. G. Gordon, CB, *at Kartoum, printed from the original mss* (cited above); in the Prologue (the hymn to Sobek) from *Papyrus Ramesseum 6* (EA10759:1), translated in the British Museum online Research Catalogue; in Chapter 3 (the Semna dispatch) from *Semna Despatches* 80–1 (BM10752), also in the British Museum online catalogue; in Chapter 4 (War Office report on Semna) from Lieutenant Colonel H. E. Colvile, *History of the Sudan Campaign, compiled in the Intelligence Division of the War Office* (1889); in Chapter 9 (on crocodiles) from Plutarch, *Moralia 75*; and in the Author's Note from William Francis Butler, *The Campaign of the Cataracts* (cited above), and Rudyard Kipling, *Barrack-Room Ballads* (1892).

ACKNOWLEDGMENTS

I AM MOST GRATEFUL TO MY AGENT, LUIGI Bonomi, and to my editors, Tracy Devine in New York and Sherise Hobbs in London, to my previous editors, Martin Fletcher and Caitlin Alexander; to Barbara Feller-Roth in the U.S. and Jane Selley in the UK for their excellent copyediting; to the team at Bantam Dell, including Gina Wachtel, Sarah Murphy, Crystal Velasquez, Carlos Beltran, Kristin Fassler, Susan Corcoran, Steven Boriack, Ashley Woodfolk, Erin Korenko, and Caron Harris; to Alison Bonomi, Amanda Preston, and ajda Vucicevic at Luigi Bonomi Associates, and to Nicky Kennedy, Sam Edenborough, Mary Esdaile, Julia Mannfolk, Jenny Robson, and Katherine West at the Intercontinental Literary Agency; and to Gaia Banks and Virginia Ascione at Sheil Land Associates.

I am grateful to my mother, Ann Verrinder Gibbins, for her critical reading of all my work, to my brother Alan for diving with me and for his photography and video work for my website www.davidgibbins.com, and to Angie Hobbs for her support. Much of the inspiration for this novel came during periods of travel and exploration funded in part by grants from the Palestine Exploration Fund, the British School of Archaeology in Jerusalem, and the Winston Churchill Memorial Trust. For unpublished material and help during research, I am grateful to the staff of the British Museum, the Ashmolean Museum, the Oriental Collections of the British Library, the National Army Museum, and the Royal Engineers Museum and Library at Chatham in Kent; I am also grateful to John Denner, Fred Van Sickle, and Paul Clare for assisting in my "experimental archaeology" with Martini-Henry and Remington rifles of 1884–1885 vintage.

This novel is dedicated to my daughter Molly, with much love.